Sweet SEAS

SCARLETT FINN

Also by Scarlett Finn

NOTHING TO...
NOTHING TO HIDE
NOTHING TO LOSE
NOTHING IN BETWEEN: ONE
NOTHING TO DECLARE
NOTHING TO US
NOTHING IN BETWEEN: TWO
NOTHING TO SAY
NOTHING TO GAIN
NOTHING IN BETWEEN: THREE
NOTHING TO YOU
NOTHING TO THIS PREQUEL: ONE WILD NIGHT
NOTHING TO THIS
NOTHING IN BETWEEN: FOUR
NOTHING TO DO
NOTHING TO FEAR
NOTHING IN BETWEEN: FIVE
NOTHING TO DENY

GO NOVELS
GO WITH IT
GO IT ALONE
GO ALL OUT
GO ALL IN
GO FULL CIRCLE

KINDRED SERIES
RAVEN
SWALLOW
CUCKOO
SWIFT
FALCON
FINCH

EXILE
HIDE & SEEK
KISS CHASE

THE EXPLICIT SERIES
EXPLICIT INSTRUCTION
EXPLICIT DETAIL
EXPLICIT MEMORY

THE FORBIDDEN NOVELS
FORBIDDEN DESIRE
FORBIDDEN WANT
FORBIDDEN WISH
FORBIDDEN NEED
FORBIDDEN BOND

WRECK & RUIN
RUIN ME
RUIN HIM

MISTAKE DUET
MISTAKE ME NOT
SLEIGHT MISTAKE

THE BRANDED SERIES
BRANDED
SCARRED
MARKED

TO DIE FOR...
TO DIE FOR TRUTH
TO DIE FOR HONOR
TO DIE FOR VIRTUE
TO DIE FOR DUTY
TO DIE FOR LOVE

RISQUÉ & HARROW INTERTWINED
TAKE A RISK
FIGHTING FATE
RISK IT ALL
FIGHTING BACK
GAME OF RISK

FORBIDDEN PREQUEL DUET
ALL. ONLY.
ONLY YOURS

LOVE AGAINST THE ODDS STANDALONE COLLECTION
SWEET SEAS
HEIR'S AFFAIR
RESCUED
MAESTRO'S MUSE
GETTING TRICKY
THIRTEEN
REMEMBER WHEN...
RELUCTANT SUSPICION
XY FACTOR

LOST & FOUND
LOST
FOUND

ONE

DARIO CORREA TIGHTENED his grip on her upper arm. "You're hurting me," Sassi Robins winced, trying to twist her arm free. But he was too strong.

Coming to this abandoned dockside warehouse for the meet was supposed to resolve her issue with the thug. Instead, she seemed only to have inflamed his want for reprisal. There was a fire in him, a determination that she'd underestimated.

Tugging her closer, Dario leaned in to loom over the top of her. "I'll give you four weeks, Sexy Sassi. Four weeks to come up with the money your papi owed me or you belong to me."

Gritting her teeth, she didn't break eye contact because she wouldn't give the asshole the satisfaction of seeing her uncomfortable or in pain. "Not a chance!"

Grabbing her other arm, he hauled her to him and forced his mouth onto hers. Sassi spat him away.

He let out a hiss of frustration. "You've always thought you were better than me, better than everyone. But, look at you now, here, begging for mercy," he sneered, taking a vast amount of pleasure in her predicament. She hadn't begged, but resented the fact that it may come to that. "You're so sure you can come up with thirty grand? I'll give you a chance to scurry around and do it, if you're so sure you can. You get me my money or you give yourself to me."

He disgusted her. "Thirty grand or sex? Really, Dario? Are you that hard up?"

His lip curled with perverse pleasure. "I don't want a night. I'll own you forever. You'll say 'I do' and raise the next generation of Correas and you'll love every second."

Not a chance. Sassi hadn't wanted Dario to touch her in high school and she didn't want him touching her now. It didn't matter that most other women would think he was attractive and his money didn't hurt how attractive he was, to others anyway. Nothing could move her to wanting him.

But her father's debt was giving Dario a chance to do what he'd failed to do at school over a decade ago. Damn her father for dying and leaving her to deal with his gambling debts. She damned her brother too, for leaving town before Dario caught up with them again.

With her brother, Stuart, at her side, Sassi had been dumb enough to think that she could face the trouble. Stuart had been hiding them for a month and the whole time she'd argued the case for reasoning with Dario.

Eventually, she'd taken matters into her own hands and arranged this meeting. Except as soon as she'd told Stuart, he'd scarpered. Sassi was alone. She had to fix this alone.

"I'll get you your money. I'll bring it here in six weeks," she said, every extra day she could buy was vital. "And, yeah, I'm confident. There's no way I'll let you lay your hands on me."

Leaning back, he leered at her body. "I'll cut my fiancée some slack, I'll give you the six weeks. You be here at midnight, six weeks from today, with my money or I'll track you down. I'll track down your brother, and every other person you ever loved, and I'll make all of 'em suffer for a long time before I put them out of their misery… and I'll still make you marry me."

Thrusting her away, he scanned her body again and his mouth slanted like he anticipated getting what he wanted. The idea of being with Dario made her sick, and his demand seemed petty and vindictive. But he was a man who could do a lot of damage. He knew people, and delighted in torturing others. Sassi wouldn't let that happen to anyone she cared about.

Nodding at his men, they cleared out and Dario disappeared in their wake. As soon as the door on the warehouse slammed, she sighed.

Shit. What was she going to do? Thirty grand was no small order.

The only asset anyone in her family ever had was her grandmother's house. Sassi had believed it was paid for when her dad inherited it fifteen years ago. But it wasn't. No, that was wrong, it had been paid off before her grandmother died. Since then, without telling anyone, her father had taken out two mortgages on the property so he could indulge his love of gambling.

The mortgages might not have been a problem, if her dad had bothered to pay them. But the house had been foreclosed on while her dad was dying in the hospital. Sassi had been kicked out and lost most of her possessions in the process. Her father's medical bills were still outstanding and her brother had been evicted from his apartment for failure to pay rent. The locks would be changed before the end of the week. Not that it mattered, they couldn't stay there while they were hiding out from Dario anyway. But whatever was left of their possessions were still in there and Sassi had nowhere to move them to.

Losing the apartment wasn't all Stuart's fault. He'd been trying to cover bills and expenses and there just wasn't enough money to go around, which was probably another reason he'd chosen to disappear. Her brother had no apartment and, as far as he was concerned, a sister with a doomed plan.

Being on her own, Sassi was gaining a better appreciation of her brother's pessimism. She had no job, no home, and no family support. Yet, she was supposed to find thirty thousand dollars and get Dario off their backs?

Her cellphone rang. That would be disconnected soon too, she hadn't paid the bill for weeks. Not having a phone was the least of her troubles, but she'd embrace it while she still could.

That's what she thought until she saw Karen's name flashing on the screen. Karen was her brother's ex-girlfriend. Sassi didn't want to be the one to explain that Stuart had vanished and they had no way to contact him.

But she couldn't ignore the woman who was the closest thing she had to an ally. So Sassi answered the call. "Karen?"

"Listen, this might be insane," Karen said, nerves rattling her.

Intrigued, Sassi was also suspicious. "What?"

There was no immediate response. The last thing that Sassi needed was Karen hesitating for so long that the phone got disconnected while she was on it.

But she did eventually speak. "I just got a call from a guy desperate for a cook."

Karen worked at a temp agency connecting employers to employees. Trusted with several of her own accounts, she'd offered to give the siblings dibs on jobs that would help them raise cash fast. Sassi would guess that Karen had tried to call Stuart first, but she wouldn't have gotten through. Stuart was ducking calls, or maybe his phone had already been disconnected.

"I'm a pastry chef," Sassi said.

She'd started her career as a baker during weekends and summers in high school. After graduation, she'd gone on to get official qualifications and started her own small business doing orders for coffee houses, bars, and restaurants, as well as taking on contracts making cakes for weddings and other events.

Or she had.

While her dad had been dying in hospital, she'd given up most of her clients. It would take time to build up her clientele again; time she didn't have. Not that she'd ever made close to thirty grand in six weeks before even if she had a full schedule.

"But you can scramble eggs and make meatballs or something, right?"

Karen's voice brought her back to the present. Sassi wasn't that great at haute cuisine, but she could do comfort food. "Yeah, but restaurants don't want—"

"This isn't a restaurant," Karen said. "It's only a four-week job. I know the mess you're in and… he said he'd pay fifteen hundred a week and pay a one-off ten-grand stipend to anyone who could be ready to cast off before dawn without complaint or delay."

"Cast off?"

"It's on a boat, a salvage vessel, and… I don't know how serious he was, but he said there was a bonus at the end of the job… he said it could be up to a hundred grand."

Gasping, Sassi felt hope for the first time. The figures were so good that even without the bonus, they'd get her over halfway to her goal. Even just a fraction of that hundred-grand promise could save her from a future of sexual servitude.

Grabbing a pen from her long strap hobo bag, Sassi tucked the phone on her shoulder under her ear and prepared to write on her hand. "Give me the details and don't send anyone else. Tell him I'll do it, say whatever it takes to get me the gig."

"I can text you—"

"No," she said. Karen was one of the few people who knew the situation, so Sassi could be honest with her. "I don't know how long this phone will last. Tell me now. And will you clear out Stuart's apartment as soon as you can? Store everything at your place, I'll make it right when I get my bonus."

Karen had a key. She and Stuart had been together for years, though her brother had always been wishy-washy about making the final commitment. In her opinion, Karen was a keeper and her brother was a dumbass.

"Where… Where is Stu?" Karen asked without disguising her trepidation.

So Sassi had been right in her assumption that her stupid brother hadn't been decent enough to tell the woman who loved him where he was going. Somehow, she took no comfort in that triumph.

"He split," Sassi said, believing that someone should tell Karen the truth, especially given that her pseudo-sister-in-law might just have saved her hide. "He'll come back when this is all straightened out. I know he will."

Truth was, she didn't know anything for sure, but Karen was a good catch and she had a kind heart. Stuart would be a fool to let her go for good. They'd only broken up last week when Dario had turned up the heat and started threatening to hurt those they cared about.

Sassi and her brother had agreed that they should endanger as few people as possible. Anyone they cared about could be hurt to punish them, and Karen would be top of that list since Sassi had no romantic interest for Dario to target.

Karen's groan was one of disapproval. "You shouldn't be dealing with this alone, Sassi, honey. Oh, it's so typical of him to run off like a coward."

Her resentment toward the man who'd just recently broken her heart was understandable. Instead of offering excuses for his behavior, Sassi gave her brother an out. "This job could be our way out and Stuart can't even boil water, so he's no cook. This is on me," Sassi said. "Give me the details."

Karen gave in and told Sassi what she needed to know. Writing the specifics on her hand, she began to make plans. She'd pick up her kit from Stuart's and while she was there, she'd whip up something delicious to tempt her new boss and colleagues.

It never failed.

She wasn't hearty to look at, but any doubts they had would be erased by some cheesecake muffins or homemade bear claws. She'd cook up a storm and pack some ingredients and tools, as well as a few jars of her homemade jelly.

Sassi didn't know what supplies she'd have to work with. Though Karen had said the ship would be stocked, Sassi guessed that was for meals. If she wanted to maximize her bonus, she'd have to pamper and spoil the boss's stomach and she only knew one way she could do that: dessert.

TWO

IF THERE WAS ONE thing that didn't bother a baker, it was getting up early.

So when Sassi was told to be on the docks at five AM sharp, she didn't blink.

The sun wouldn't rise for another two hours, but Karen had mentioned nautical twilight or some term like that. Sassi knew nothing about boats or about sailing, but she assumed that didn't really matter; she'd been hired for her cooking skills.

Because she was worried about meeting the tough standard expected of the meals, Sassi had gone overboard bringing her own supplies. That meant she was traipsing along the dock pulling two suitcases, wearing a huge backpack on her back, and a small one on her front, as well as wearing her usual oversized hobo bag.

She'd never looked more like a hobo in her life, and figured she should've grabbed a shopping cart and collected some cans on her way to complete the look.

After begging her way through the security gate

to get onto the docks, one thing became clear in a hurry: this was no high-class operation.

Sassi didn't really know what she'd been expecting. But when she thought about sailing, she thought of sleek yachts and cruise liners. She thought of uniforms and table manners. Her assumptions were nowhere near the mark.

Instead, what she found were a lot of noisy, dirty boats with chipped paint and stained ropes. Grubby sailors jeered her on her walk along the docks from their boats. It was sort of impressive that in near darkness, while she struggled with her luggage, these Neanderthals were still cat calling even though she'd probably never looked less attractive.

At the security gate, she'd told the guy hanging against the fence that she was Eros' new cook because that's what Karen had told her to say. He'd looked down to her feet and back up to her face again before laughing and punching in a code to unlock the gate. Why had he laughed?

Sassi had been preoccupied with the gate guy's amusement until the first sailor shouted out to her. Maybe there weren't many women down on the docks at this time in the morning; that could be why she was drawing so much attention. But she'd been taught well and was street smart enough to know not to respond when the predators outnumbered her.

It wasn't easy for Sassi to hold onto her sass, not until she saw how huge most of these guys were. After that, she was okay with just keeping her eyes front and striding forward.

Feelings of dread joined her as she kept on going, looking for the boat that she'd been told she wouldn't be able to miss. If this had been any other job, she'd probably have turned and headed back inland by now. But, if she did that, she was admitting defeat.

The plain truth was, she needed this job. She needed the money.

How bad could it be?

This was a legitimate job. The captain... what was he called again? Carson Swain... Yes, Captain Carson Swain. He was the one who had called a temp agency looking for a cook. That was legitimate, right? If he wanted a sex slave, or just someone to beat on, he wouldn't identify himself to a reputable company, would he?

Unless he'd used a false name... but then he would have to give the ship a false name and—

Eros.

There it was. The name was written in thick dark letters that stood out on a red hull. They could be black, could be navy, could be a lot of things... But it didn't matter, that was the moniker she was looking for.

Shit. The boat was huge and not what she was expecting at all. There was a tall white tower of decks nearer the front of the boat. The back was long and flat with a huge crane towering over it. She couldn't see any people or many details because of the dark and the proximity of the boat to the dock. But she hadn't expected all those antennae to be sticking out the top. With all those masts and spinning things adding to the height of the white block, it was taller than a building.

"You lost?"

Whipping around, she inhaled when she registered the height and width of the man striding toward her with a thick length of wound rope around his shoulder. "I..." Uncurling her fingers from the handle of her suitcase, she tried to be subtle about sliding her hand into her hobo bag to seek out her pepper spray. "I'm not lost, I'm looking for Eros."

Gruff and impatient, there was nothing welcoming about the stranger. "You found it, but I don't want to hear about what Swing did to you. Call a cop or a priest, I don't give a shit."

Wasn't that nice. All her ideas of good ole chivalry and naval decorum went out the window as she absorbed his features. He had thick, dark hair that looked as black as ink and as unkempt as the beard covering his jaw. He got closer and she found no civility in his eyes, in fact they narrowed to disgust when he reached her.

"You're a dainty one; there ain't an ounce of fucking fight in you. You've wandered out of your comfort zone. I'm surprised you made it this far with the Swag Wagon in port."

If that was a threat, she'd take it. As long as he was talking, he wasn't acting. Her finger moved over the trigger on the can of pepper spray. If this guy even thought about touching her with so much as a fingertip, she'd unload the whole damn can in his face.

The smell of the sea didn't completely overtake the scent of musky man and musty rope, but that rope was the only thing preventing her from pulling the can out. It looked heavy, really heavy. It was looped round and round, each length had to be four inches in diameter, but he was holding it there on his shoulder like it weighed no more than her purse. Still, while the coiled rope was there, he would be at a disadvantage if he tried to take her down.

"You'd be surprised how far my comfort zone stretches," she said, holding her ground. "Tell me where to find Captain Swain or move the hell out of my way."

The flare of surprise on his face told her that he wasn't used to people speaking back to him. But Sassi wasn't going to be intimidated just because he was built of solid muscle, a foot taller than her, and probably twice as wide.

As fast as the surprise had appeared, it vanished. He narrowed his eyes to a grumpy growl again, blazing more disgust before he spoke. "What do you want with Swain?"

"He's my boss, and I don't think he'd like you loitering out here trying so hard to intimidate his new cook."

Sassi didn't know a thing about the man she was going to be working under, but she hoped there was at least some chance that he was a decent guy given that she'd be stuck on a boat with him and his people for the next month.

"Aw, shit," he exhaled and bent his knees to toss the rope off his shoulder, letting it drop to the ground. Planting one foot, she slid the other back, setting her stance wide while pulling her pepper spray closer to the top of her purse. If this was when he was going to make his move to attack, she'd be ready. "What the fuck am I supposed to do with a twig like you? You're a fucking waif."

His tone was offensive enough, his words were a smack in the face. "You don't do a damn thing," she said, forcing herself not to call him an asshole. Then she started to put pieces together… and… oh… uh oh… he meant… "Oh no."

"Yeah, sweetheart. Captain Carson Swain, at your service," he said, though she didn't believe he'd do a thing for her even with a gun to his head. There was nothing warm or happy about his introduction.

"You're the captain?" she asked.

Swallowing hard, Sassi realized this was grimmer than she could ever have thought. This guy wasn't as bad as the Neanderthals she'd seen on her way here, he was worse.

His physical size pretty much guaranteed there wasn't a thing on this earth he couldn't take by force if the notion took him. Who would stand up to a guy as mean and rough looking as him? There would be zero chance of anyone else ever triumphing in a fight against him.

His black gaze trailed down to her feet. "I'm the cap'n, and you ain't no cook."

She had no idea how he could tell that from looking at her, especially since most of her was covered up, still laden with luggage. Proving her skills was not going to be hard; it would actually be fun. Taking him down a peg would be her pleasure.

Smiling, she unzipped the bag on her chest, so she could get to the plastic tub of cookies she'd put on top. "I bet you're a cookie man," she said, switching off the sass in favor of her best attempt at charm.

Sassi did have a tub of muffins too, but he didn't seem the soft and sweet type. He was tougher and chewier. His head tilted forward; she'd surprised him. Good. Sassi had never been accused of being predictable.

"What the fuck?"

Opening the tub, she reached inside to break off a piece of cookie. "Open your mouth, Captain."

She could do seductive if she had to, but Sassi tried to be selective about who she turned it on for and she didn't want to give him the wrong idea. "Not a chance, sweetheart."

Pushing out her lower lip, she wished she had the advantage of her cleavage, but it was covered up.

Dumping the cookie back in the tub, she licked her fingertips and re-zipped the bag. "Okay, then turn me away," she said. "You and your crew can do with cold cereal instead of bacon and pancakes every morning." Sassi made a show of looking left then right. "'Cause I don't see any one else asking permission to come aboard your dingy."

His jaw ticked before he clenched it tight. "It's a ship, not a dingy, and insulting Eros guarantees you won't set one fucking toe aboard."

Damn, she'd insulted him. The only way to ingratiate herself now would be to appeal to his ego. She hated doing that, especially with a guy so clearly arrogant enough that he needed no encouragement to believe he was the best.

"I'm sorry, Captain," she said, licking her lower lip to draw it in between her teeth. "I didn't mean to insult your friend. Eros is beautiful; intimidating, so large and powerful." Picking up the end of her hair, she coiled it around her index finger as she let a fingertip from her other hand touch a snap on the front of his coveralls. "A silly little girl like me would never—"

"You a lush?" he asked, pushing her finger away from his sternum with the back of his rough hand.

"A lush?" she asked, unable to hide her offence. "You think I'm a drunk? Screw you, asshole! I flirt with you, you're rude. I accidently say something that hurts your precious feelings and you sulk. Then, I try to make you feel better by praising the hunk of junk you worship and you insult me. You know what, asshole, shove your fucking job up your ass! I don't need you any more than I need the other shit I've got going on in my life. I've had about as much of fucking men as I can take! Fuck you."

Spinning around, she was ready to march away, but his arm came under hers and he grabbed her wrist to whirl her around to face him again. "That's the attitude you bring on my ship, Waif. You say you can cook? It's not like I've got a lot of options. So if you work hard, don't complain, and quit the innocent babygirl thing, we won't have a problem."

Was he trying to provoke her into showing her spunk or was he just an asshole who'd accidently stumbled on it?

Snatching her wrist back, Sassi withdrew a step. "What makes you think I want your stupid job now?"

"'Cause what kind of fucking woman comes

down the docks at five AM unless she needs it? My crew members need to have backbone, you've proved you've got that, now get your fucking ass on board, Waif."

Tipping up her chin, she opened her arms to grab the handle of each of her suitcases at her flanks. "Stop calling me waif."

"I'll call you whatever I want; everyone's got a nickname on the sea," he said and nodded sideways. "Leave the dunnage." He must have read her blank expression. "Your baggage. Shake a leg. Flank speed… When the captain says move, you move. Can you follow orders, Waif?"

Something about the question, abrupt and gruff though it was, made her want to flirt again. Wait. What was that buzz in her belly? He took half a step toward her and she inhaled. The nearer he got, the more intense that vibration in her skin grew.

But he was a dirty, smelly oaf. A lunkhead. A brute.

Hmm, why did her belly feel so light?

Twisting away, she chose to ignore her mutinous body, and spoke to him over her shoulder. "Maybe if you can ask nicely," she said and flounced toward the gangplank.

She heard her cases move and the captain cursed under his breath. "You trying to sink us before we cast off?" he asked. "What the fuck you got in here?"

Everything she valued in life, but she didn't say that. Steadying herself with a hand on each side of the gangplank, Sassi took one careful step and then another. The captain crowded up behind her, trying to move her forward faster, using his bulk against her.

He was so solid and strong that she had to hurry to try to put space between them, except his long legs ate up the gangplank and she couldn't go fast enough to maintain any distance. Sassi felt flustered and didn't like to be harassed.

In an attempt to turn the tables, when she got to the top of the gangplank, she stopped dead, right before stepping onto the deck.

"What's the problem?" he griped.

Turning her chin to her shoulder, she steeled herself. "Are you always in such a hurry, Captain Swain?"

"You want your stipend? Get your tush on board, Waif, and I told you to cut out the flirting."

Without hiding her smile from herself, she moved forward. The boat rose on the swell of the water to meet her and she stumbled, catching herself on the cold painted wall opposite the end of the gangplank.

Sassi didn't appreciate the snicker she heard behind her. But when he grabbed her elbow and pulled her down the deck, she re-thought how she'd goaded him and remembered what she'd thought about how he could take what he wanted from anyone by force.

"Where are you taking me?" she asked.

"Your luxury cabin. Buckle up, sweetheart, Eros is gonna take you for a ride."

A ride. An adventure. Maybe this was the Voyage of the Damned. But if she stayed ashore she'd be damned for sure; there was no way to make the money for Correa without this job. The captain was a brute, but she could deal with whatever he threw at her providing he paid her.

The money, that's what this was about. As long as she kept that in sight, Sassi could handle anything.

THREE

THE SWEET-SMELLING, petite wench hadn't been happy when he'd shown her to her single berth cabin, which was on the same deck as the mess. She should be fucking glad the cook got a private cabin. Sure, it was fucking small, but this wasn't the Hilton.

Eros was a working ship, everyone had a role, and she was here to do a job. Swain might have neglected to tell her that she'd be the only female on board, thinking that if she knew, she might have second thoughts about joining the crew.

To his chagrin, she'd been right when she pointed out that he didn't have a lot of options. They had to get underway, he couldn't waste time at port looking for another cook. But he wasn't a complete jerk, he planned to talk to Jockey, his first-mate, to make sure all the boys kept their hands to themselves.

Sassi Robins.

On the phone, the temp agency chick had told him the name of his new cook. It hadn't occurred to him to ask for her measurements because he hadn't cared about who she was as long as she could cook.

Except, after seeing the slightness of her delicate facial features, he was thinking it might have been smart to be explicit about needing someone hardy. This lass seemed too dainty. He didn't have time to pander to someone who might expect special treatment.

It was his own fault that he hadn't probed further. After being assured by the temp agency woman that this Sassi could cook and she'd have no problems following orders, Swain had accepted her as a done deal. His to-do list was long and he hadn't had the time to think twice. There were too many other things to arrange before they shoved off; he hadn't cared much about who cooked his bacon in the mornings.

For him and his crew, this job was a real coup. He'd made a bid for it and missed out to the Swag Wagon. But they'd pulled out at the last minute. Swain was happy to step in and save the day, even if it meant scrambling to get everything organized.

His cause hadn't been helped when he learned that Eros' usual cook, Raise, had been arrested for drunk and disorderly just as Swain was signing on the dotted line to accept the job. There was an outstanding warrant meaning that Raise wouldn't be joining them on this trip and possibly the next one.

The rest of the crew was easier to corral. Swain and his first-mate, Jockey, lived on Eros full-time, so they were always around. Foist, his engineer, had no wife or commitments to keep him in one place. He'd been happy to sign on last minute, just like Swain's deckhand, Swing, and their apprentice Fidget.

Pulling together a couple of divers wasn't too hard, Swain had enough ships in his fleet and contacts in the industry that he could do what needed to be done. The two divers would double as night-watch relief after Eros picked them up in Miami.

A cook was always more difficult to come by. Anyone could throw eggs in a pan, but decent cooks were like gold dust, so they were snapped up quickly and often signed their articles far ahead of time.

Raise had really dropped him in it this time. The bastard.

Being out on the water for weeks at a time, working hard and long, the only thing his crew had to look forward to on a daily basis was chow. If he didn't secure someone with skills enough to satisfy his crew's appetite, he could face a mutiny.

But now they had a woman aboard.

And not just any woman; a woman who smelled like candy and smiled like she was thinking of tempting men to sin. Swain was glad she'd been trussed up like a cart horse when they met. If he'd been able to look too close at her figure, he might have refused to take her on board. As it was, he could imagine her as a school matron and forget that he'd noticed her slender arms and delicate wrist.

Good thing he had no time for women like her.

Swain liked his women willing and his affairs simple. But if the new cook tried any of that flirtatious crap with his crew, God help her. A man could only be pushed so far before he'd lose his patience.

There had been no alternative, he'd had no choice except to accept the woman. In addition to asking Jockey to keep the men in line, Swain would have to watch her to ensure she didn't cause trouble. If he caught her playing with his men, he'd put her in her place.

But she was onboard now. An official member of his crew.

Her cabin was in the same passageway as the mess. He'd pointed it out up ahead on the other side of the deck, so she could make her way there after she was settled in. The last thing he wanted to do was waste time with handholding. He had preparations to make; there was no time to give her a guided fucking tour. His crew was on their way, and he wanted to get underway as soon as possible.

Swain had dumped her cases in her room and then decided to forget about her.

Though he was still a little distracted. He'd never known anyone to come onboard with so much luggage. But as long as she kept it in her room and passed inspection later, he'd let her keep it.

If things went their way on this job, Eros would have to get used to being laden with plenty of cargo. She could hold up to the extra weight.

***

SASSI HAD STILL been scanning the small bedroom the captain had led her to when he came back and dropped her cases behind her without saying a word.

The narrow space was depressing. The metal walls were painted gray; the floor and ceiling were a darker shade of the same dull color. Her basic shower room was just big enough to stand up in. It didn't even have a window.

There was a window in the bedroom, but it was tiny. A little glazed circle on the far wall, just above the skinny metal bunk with its thin mattress and woolly blanket. But the bleak décor and the limp pillow weren't enough to discourage her. She had everything she needed, a roof, a bed, and two spaces to stow her things: a dresser that was bolted to the wall and a box beneath the bed.

For now, at least, she was safe.

Karen had said that Sassi would have uniforms provided. So she guessed that's what the black polo-shirts in the bottom drawer were meant to be. They were way too big and cut for a male stature, but they were embroidered with the words "Swain Salvage" in small letters on the breast.

Fine by her.

Sassi worked fast to unpack her things because she wanted to get to the kitchen. Most of what she'd brought were supplies for the kitchen. Until she knew what they had in storage and what equipment she had to work with, she couldn't begin to build a menu.

She had no idea how to begin planning for entrees; Sassi was used to working up dessert menus. But she had a feeling that her specialty, comfort food, was going to be well-received around here.

Thank goodness for that.

FOUR

SASSI MADE A GOOD dent in getting the kitchen cleaned up. A sudden grumbling roar almost knocked her off her feet. For a good minute, she stood there braced with a hand on the counters wondering if the ground was about to give-way beneath her feet.

"We got a stowaway?"

Spinning around, her wide eyes landed on the scruffy older man just inside the doorway. "I, uh… I'm the new cook," she said, and the rumble increased. "What is that noise? Why is the whole kitchen vibrating?"

"Galley," he said, tossing a pile of newspapers onto the table that was just to the left of the door.

It was a long skinny table with seating around three sides, shoulder-high backrests along the wall and at the head of the table, with an open back bench on the other long side.

Beyond the top of the table were three metal stairs that descended to a large open space. It seemed to be some kind of recreation room. Fixed couches lined the back wall and there were bolted-down tables in each corner. All the furniture she'd come across so far was bolted down. A wall separated the kitchen from the rec room. On the recreation side of it was a TV cabinet, and even the TV was screwed down.

Sassi hadn't had a lot of time to explore, but she was impressed that there was a TV at all, though she doubted it would work when they got out to sea.

"Ga… galley?" she asked when he started toward her.

The corner of his wry mouth twitched and the wrinkles around his eyes deepened like he was amused. "It's not a kitchen, it's a galley. You've gotta learn a whole new language out here. I'm guessing you ain't spent a lot of time at sea?" She shook her head as he offered his hand. "Jockey, I'm the first-mate."

At least he was polite enough to be introducing himself up front. "Sassi," she said, shaking his spindly fingers that were stronger than they looked. Jockey had bulk about him too, not like the captain did, but she wouldn't bet against this guy either. "Sassi Robins… Are all of the crew so… raw?"

Jockey outright grinned at her and when his head went back in a laugh, his dark gray hair fell from his temple to reveal a scar that ran all the way down to his ear. Gulping, her stomach flipped, and she started to fear what she'd gotten herself involved in.

"Hey, now, I think that's a mighty nice compliment," he said. "I'm guessing you met the cap'n… he ain't as bad as he seems. This job landed on us last minute. He likes to be prepared, and this one caught us off-guard. We were meant to be holed up in port for six months for maintenance… Not that none of us are complaining about being at sea."

They might not be, but the reality of what she'd signed on for was becoming all too apparent. She was going to be offshore, far offshore, without escape, surrounded by these… raw men.

But her ability to protect her virtue became secondary when the implication of what Jockey had just implied filtered through. "Maintenance?" she asked, wondering how scared she should be. "Is this boat safe?"

"Oh, Eros is sea worthy all right," he said, peeking past her. "What you cooking up?"

"Breakfast," she said and folded her arms. "The captain called this the mess. Why are you calling it a galley?"

"The mess is where we eat," he said, nodding backwards. "The kitchen is the galley."

To her it was all one big room, even though it was split level and had a dividing wall between the galley and recreation space. All she could see from the galley was the dining table and door.

"And here I thought we spoke English in America."

"We're still in dock, so we're still in America, sure," he said. "But you're on sovereign Swain land now. His are the only rules that matter." Opening the fridge at his side, he sought out a soda, and she wondered how he could down the syrupy liquid this early in the day. "Cap'n banned smoking in here, you smoke?" Sassi shook her head, she never had. "You follow orders. You take 'em like gospel, hear? Discipline's my responsibility and you don't want me letting the cat out the bag." She had no idea what secret he was referring to, but she'd already appeared to be idiot enough that she didn't want to ask. "You make coffee?"

He had to be able to smell it, but she guessed the question was better than a command. "Uh, yeah," she said and opened an overhead cabinet to be faced with a bunch of insulated mugs.

As soon as she closed the cabinet, he reached

over her and opened it again. "You must've noticed everything around here is bolted to the floor. That's 'cause on a ship, shit tends to move around. Spillage can cause all kinds of problems, so we use these."

Made sense. Jockey unscrewed the lid and took the coffee carafe from the machine to fill his mug. "What happened to your last cook?" she asked.

Finding out why she'd been needed in such a hurry just made sense. Whoever had been in her position before her had left the kitchen—oops, galley—all higgledy-piggledy. She'd have to reorganize it when she got a spare minute.

"Cap'n made him walk the plank."

Although she was startled, it didn't take long for her to squint with suspicion. "He did not."

"Sure," Jockey said. Nodding, he tossed an arm around her shoulders to lower his face near to hers. "Didn't you know? Our captain is a real, life pirate."

"Yeah, right," she said, easing his arm away. "You think 'cause I have breasts that I'm going to be fooled by your sea yarns? I'm green, I'm not gullible."

But he crossed his heart. "Swear to Poseidon, let him strike me down."

Sassi didn't want to get a reputation for being easy to con, but he did look dead serious. If she asked him any questions, and the claim was false, he'd laugh in her face. If it was true, she wasn't sure that she wanted to know the details.

An impulse to flee struck her. But she swallowed her anxiety about working for a pirate and changed the subject. "Would you like a cookie?"

Scurrying deeper into the galley, Sassi pulled her cookie tub from another cabinet and went back to offer him a treat.

Now it was his turn to look surprised. "You make cookies?" He selected one and bit into the sweetness. His expression loosened to amazed delight; relief made her grin. "Raise never made nothing like this."

"Raise?"

"Our last cook," he said. "His food was all about clogging our arteries." Jockey was actually happy about that, nostalgic almost, while she had to dampen the roiling in her stomach. "If it don't drip with grease, we don't want it."

Her stomach revolted again. "I don't know about that but I'll do my best."

She'd been sure that the captain was all muscle. If his diet was that bad, maybe there was no fitness behind the facade.

Shouting outside the door made her peer around Jockey who must have heard it too because he turned around. Two men stumbled in. The larger of the two had the scrawnier one in a headlock, he dragged him into the room, guffawing as the little guy complained.

"Oh my God," she exclaimed and started to move forward intending to help the victim.

Jockey put an arm out to block her. "Don't pay them no mind, they're our resident gofers."

"Jockey!" the large guy said, letting the smaller one loose at the same time he noticed her. "Fuck me, the cap'n finally got a wench to take the edge off these long trips… Come o'er here, honeypie. Come sit on Swing's lap."

Her mouth opened. If the captain thought she was going to whore herself to any bastard on his order, she'd smack him down hard.

"Hey, now you know the cap'n's rules about fornication on board," Jockey said. Sassi became aware of how the first-mate still had his body angled in front of hers. Was he hiding her body from these guys or protecting it? "This here's our new cook, Sassi."

Grabbing the cookies from her, Jockey tossed the box to the guy in front.

The pimple faced boy beside him peeked inside when the big guy took the lid off. "Cookies!" the young one exclaimed and grabbed two.

"Just like momma used to make," Jockey said. As the guys dug into the cookies, the first-mate stepped back to put an arm around her. "That big one there, he's Swing. He's a gorilla, slow, but he's got a good heart, doesn't always think before he talks. Don't you worry, cap'n let's his crew fix problems the traditional way. And you being a female, you can pick any guy on crew to fight for you. Word to the wise, pick the cap'n, he never loses a fight and won't see a woman disrespected."

Her jaw loosened. "Fight for me?"

"Sure! You don't want to take Swing on; he ain't smart enough to know when to stop swinging." Maybe that was where he got the nickname. "We call the little 'un Fidget 'cause he doesn't know how to sit still. Boy's eyes are working if his hands ain't. Cap'n's got his work cut out keeping that boy busy. Only time he doesn't look like he's about to piss his pants is when he's eating, and without Swing, forget it; the boy's a danger to himself out there. Captain knows his momma, she about begged him to keep Fidget outta trouble."

So the captain had taken the youngster on as a favor to the mother? Was there a relationship there? Fidget looked young, but not that young. He was still a man, maybe around twenty. But maybe the captain had a thing for older women… or the woman wasn't older. It could be that she'd been a young teenager when she had Fidget.

"How old is the captain?" she heard herself ask.

Jockey looked down at her, curiosity or astonishment on his face. "Fidget ain't his, Captain ain't like that. If he'd got Margo in trouble, he'd have married her. Don't you forget our captain's an old-fashioned guy."

Old-fashioned. She didn't really know what she was supposed to take from that. But Jockey was looking deep into her like she should get it. "I don't—"

"Yo! You pricks!"

Jockey turned at the same time she noticed a guy with floppy dirty-blonde hair hanging in the door, wearing a frown and looking unhappy. "Foist, where you been?" Swing called out.

"That's Foist, our engineer," Jockey said to her in an aside.

"Me and Swain are out here doing all the work. Get your fucking asses on deck now, we're casting off." His severe eyes popped to her. "That means we want chow soon."

Though there had been no proper introduction, Foist clearly knew who she was. She had to be easily identifiable. That made Sassi curious about how many women were onboard, she hadn't seen another one yet.

"I'm on it," she said.

"All hands on deck!" Foist shouted.

Jockey smiled. Swing and Fidget jumped to it and ran out after Foist. "Uh, can I ask about supplies?" she asked before the first-mate could go after the others. "I'll be fine with what's here for a few days, but there has to be more in—"

"Cargo holds are below decks," he said. "I'll show you when we're underway. Do inventory fast, we used Raise's old chits to stock the ship. But if there's anything else you need, the captain can email an order to our guy in Miami."

"Miami?" she asked. It wouldn't take four weeks to get to Miami and back. "That's where we're going?"

"We'll land there by nightfall, spend the night, and get underway tomorrow." Underway where? But she didn't have time to ask because Jockey was already on his way to the door. "Guys will be hungry in an hour; Captain and me will be down in two. Anyone's hands go wandering, hit the intercom on the wall."

So that was what the little box with the speakers and the buttons was. "Don't worry about me," she said as he stepped out. "Hands I can handle."

Alone in the galley, Sassi took a deep breath. This was a kitchen, just like any other, even if it did have a different name. Breakfast. The crew wanted breakfast. She could do breakfast, it wasn't hard. Especially when, after meeting the crew, she'd learned that their standards were pretty low.

Noise outside took her to the circle window above the kitchen sink. Out on the pointy front of the boat, she saw Swain on the deck twisting some kind of crank. The thick muscles in his tanned arm worked beneath the bold ink that circled his flesh. She couldn't see from here what the tattoos were, but it was clear he had a few of them.

The sun would be up soon; the sky was already beginning to gray and color. A new day meant a new beginning. She had to make this work or these first weeks of her new life at sea may also be the last of her life.

FIVE

"I'D RATHER ARRIVE in Miami early and spend an hour offshore waiting to dock than arrive late," Swain said to Jockey as they entered the narrow internal passageway flanked by rooms that included his new cook's cabin.

Swain knew she shouldn't be his first thought. But, of their own volition, his eyes sought her door. The scents emanating from further down the ship distracted his thoughts from what might be going on behind that door during this voyage.

"Smells like she's doing good," Jockey said, giving Swain a shove to hurry him up.

Jockey had been his second in command since he started out. Swain owed a lot to the old man; he was more of a mentor and a father-figure than a colleague. But his first-mate always followed orders without complaint. Sure, he might tell him he was talking out his ass in private, but Jockey never undermined him in front of the crew.

Ever since he was a kid, Swain had known Jockey as the smartest man he ever met, and he'd never seen him excited like this over the prospect of food.

After going past the cook's cabin, which he guessed was empty if she was in the galley doing her job like she should be, they heard the music and the laughter coming from the mess.

Why were his men raucous at this time in the morning? Usually they were complaining for the first few days about his schedule and his crew was always grumpy before breakfast. Even though they should've eaten by now, he'd never known breakfast to turn into a party.

But his first-mate wasn't discouraged; he seemed eager to follow the smell of their first meal of the day. It was mixed scents of bacon, coffee, and something sweet.

Swain didn't want to jump to any conclusions about her abilities. Holding his reserve and maintaining suspicion had always served him well. He'd give new people a chance, but they had to prove themselves before he'd trust their capabilities.

The cook was no different and she wouldn't be cut any slack just because she was a female. She'd be expected to sweat as much as any of the men and better be capable of handling the pressure.

When he and Jockey rounded into the mess, all thoughts of her capabilities fled. The only thing he could focus on was the sweet little ass in tight skinny jeans on the other side of the room. Bent over the furthest galley counter, it was pert, perfect, and out of place in this grubby, masculine space. From the silence that had fallen on the room, he'd bet he wasn't the only one checking out the female form.

The crackly music they'd heard in the passageway was still playing. From her position, he'd guess she was fiddling with the FM radio that hung beneath the porthole over there. It was only supposed to be used in port; the signal wouldn't last when they were constantly moving. But he wasn't going to tell her that while he had this view. In fact, he found himself hoping it would take her a while to find the station she was seeking.

Fuck, what an asshole.

Forcing himself to look left to the table, he saw Fidget, Foist, and Swing salivating over the new cook.

Heat in his chest became rage in his belly and his attention snapped around to that ass, which was now moving in time to the music, tormenting his men more.

Whistling, Swain marched toward her. If he'd got to her faster, he'd probably have smacked her hard. "Waif!" he called out.

Then it happened.

She straightened up and spun around to look at him. The moment she did, he came to a dead stop. Her eyes were a deeper blue than the thick ocean that he loved so much. Her chestnut hair was tangled in a messy knot on the top of her head, and she'd used a folded bandana tied just behind her hairline to try to tame those wild locks. Her skin, clear, sun-kissed and smooth, looked like it would taste sweeter than the scents oozing from the stove.

Her full soft lips turned up and he wondered if she was wearing makeup or if their deep red hue was natural. Never in his life had Swain hankered after a member of his crew and he'd sure never noticed their mouths.

"Captain!" she said and swanned forward a step.

She moved like she was on castors. The sleeve of her black Swain polo shirt slipped off her shoulder, revealing a taut triangle of unblemished flesh over a skinny collarbone obvious beneath the skin.

The buttons of the top were undone. He'd guess from the way the hem clung to her waist that she had it tied at her lower back, probably to keep it off the stove. It didn't matter that she'd just had her back to him, he'd been too preoccupied by the sight of her ass to notice what she'd done with her top.

Her bare hips were on show too between the waistband of her low-riding jeans and the angles of what he'd always considered a conservative uniform. Only she could make a man's polo shirt look salacious.

More anger burned in him when he noticed the length of her lashes and the curve of her neck down to the ball of that feminine shoulder. What the hell was he doing noticing her figure?

"How do you take your coffee, Captain?" she asked, unhooking an apron from beside the commercial fridge. When she put it on, he read his name emblazoned across her breasts. Pride, and something like possession began to seep around the anger in his belly… he didn't like it. Didn't like any of this.

Smudges on the fabric suggested that she'd already worn the apron that day. Damn, she was a hard worker… he respected hard workers. But respecting her wasn't going to alleviate any of the tension around his contorted insides.

The apron was too big for her too. The neck strap was tied at the back of her neck to shorten it and when she wound the ties around her waist it almost doubled like a skirt, which he figured was good because it should cover up her distracting ass. But her alterations to the garment also told him that she was resourceful… he admired resourceful people who didn't see problems or defeat, only challenges and the chances for victory.

She backed up to reach for the coffee pot in the machine on the counter beside the fridge.

Pouring him a cup, she handed it over, wearing a smile. "I'll bet you like it strong," she said, coming over to hold up an insulated cup with its lid screwed on; the guys had taught her well already. "Would you like something to eat, sir?"

Did she know about that sexy lilt to her voice

that made everything she said sound like a come on? He didn't like it. It made him edgy and the hairs on the back of his forearm stood up.

"Cap'n, she's hot! Fucking amazing! You did good. You should check this out!"

Swing had never sounded so excited. Swain turned his back on Sassi to scan the table that he hadn't noticed was filled with food. Bacon, eggs, pancakes dominated the middle; there were biscuits and condiments and pitchers of juice.

"We ain't never had a spread like this," Jockey said, sliding onto the bench beside Foist. "'Specially not on the first day."

"Watching all the work you boys did to get us underway inspired me," Sassi said, going over to the table with the coffee pot to offer everyone refills.

Once all their lids were screwed back on, she put the pot back in the machine. Swain realized he'd been standing there stuck to the spot watching her glide back and forth across the room like she belonged there already. Jockey was filling a plate and Swain couldn't refuse when his first-mate held it up to him.

Going over to the table, he sat at the end of the bench with his back to the galley, which was almost the complete opposite of where he was supposed to sit at the head of the table. But he figured that if he didn't look at the wench, he could get rid of the anger that was making him tetchy. Slumping down, Swain glared at the food he'd been given as Jockey filled a fresh plate for himself.

The steaming meal did smell great. Swain wasn't easily impressed, but if this tasted as good as it looked, he might have found a permanent replacement for Raise. Though, he'd have to have a conversation with her about how she wore her uniform before making her any offers of future employment.

The first bite of bacon made his mouth water. He

almost cursed when he tasted her scrambled eggs and there was an edge to her light, fluffy pancakes that made him crave more before he'd even cleaned his plate.

"Now you boys remember to save space for the pie," Sassi called out from the galley.

With his mouth full, Swain raised his eyes to his crewmates to see that they were as shocked and enraptured as he was.

Swallowing the delicious food he had in his mouth, he looked up when she came to the foot of the table to add fresh pancakes to the stack. "You brought pie?" he asked.

Sassi laughed. "I'll forgive you that slight, Captain. I made pie. From scratch, with my own bare hands," she said. "Apple pie. And if you boys like donuts I'll make those for after breakfast tomorrow."

"You can make donuts?" Jockey asked. "Like fresh?"

Swain didn't blame his first-mate for sounding so amazed. They'd never had such a talented cook onboard before.

"Sure," she said, like it was no big deal. With a shrug, she put a hand on his shoulder to lean on him as she spoke.

His own mess had never felt more like a dockside diner. The good kind. Except, Sassi was nothing like any waitress he'd ever known. Who would make apple pie and donuts and charm this group of bastards without proper introductions? Maybe she didn't need him looking out for her after all.

"Marry me," Swing said.

Fidget laughed, but Swain wasn't sure his deckhand had been joking. He had to admit that even he was guilty of trying to formulate ways that he might sign her onto permanent staff, and she'd only been working for him for a few hours.

Though, he soon began to shrug off the idea. He couldn't have a woman like her onboard too often. It would only be a matter of time before one of his crew pushed too far, and then she'd be running in fear.

Sure, she was happy and smiling now, but what would happen during poker or on fight night when the testosterone was high and the group got rowdy?

"You're a sweetheart, Swing," Sassi said. Swain almost choked, no one had ever called Swing a sweetheart before. "But you can't marry a girl just 'cause she knows how to make waffles and donuts and apple pie."

Swing looked genuinely baffled. "Can't think of no better reason. You sound perfect. Unless… you frigid?"

"Hey!" Swain said before he thought to speak. "She's crew, show respect."

"Are you suggesting that you boys never talk about sex, Captain?" Lifting his attention to the feisty brunette who was still leaning on him, he saw her crook a brow. "I bet you boys get really explicit around here, plenty of dirty talk turning the air blue." When Swing whooped, she turned her smile on the deckhand. "Calm down, honey. It's a little early to be getting that excited."

"I can get excited any time of day," Swing said and her smile got wider.

Was she flirting with his deckhand, the dirtiest, least respectful guy on his crew? Sassi hadn't seemed like the type to like her guys simple, maybe he'd been wrong.

"I'm more of a night time gal," she said. "Anything goes before sunrise long as my guy asks nicely."

This time all the guys at the table whooped, even Jockey. Swain was too stunned by the man opposite him to even think about joining in. "Jock," he chastised.

His first-mate shrugged and shoveled more food

into his mouth. "The girl says she can handle herself."

Sassi, pleased with herself, turned to disappear back into the galley, leaving the guys to their food.

"Yeah, but will she let any of us handle her," Foist said from the corner of his mouth.

Seeing the intention in his engineer's eyes that were focused behind him, obviously checking out the cook, Swain knew the time to set the boundaries had come already.

"No," Swain said, eyeing them all. "She's off-limits, to everyone, hear me? No one touches another member of the crew until I see a marriage certificate."

He'd had female cooks before, but never like Sassi. They were usually older and more homely, so he'd had no worries about any of his men screwing around with them. He'd expected Swing to make advances and Fidget to do a lot of staring, but Foist?

His usually reserved engineer never bothered with the ship drama. Foist kept to himself and spent his time with him and Jockey rather than the idiots subordinate to them. It wasn't like Foist to get involved in their drooling. But Sassi was hot and with a mouth like that, she wasn't doing herself any favors.

"That's a bit extreme, Cap'n," Jockey said.

"Foist, wheelhouse," Swain barked at the engineer.

Jockey let Foist out of the booth, but before Swain could respond to what his first-mate had said, Swing began to hum in delight and a sweet scent wafted over, hitting him, hard.

Sassi appeared beside him; Swain didn't know if the smell was coming from her or the steaming tray in her hand.

Sliding the tray onto the table, she opened her hands at the warm golden crust of the pie she'd just put down beside him. "Voila," she said and held up a knife before sinking it into the pastry to cut a slice. As she moved the slice onto a small plate, she pushed the rest of the pie toward Jockey and crouched at Swain's side, peeking up at him through her thick lashes. "Do you like hot pie, Captain, or would you prefer to build some suspense and let it cool?"

Circling her lips, she began to blow on the hot fruit seeping from between the layers of pastry. Moist heat pricked his forearm that was laid on the table beyond the new plate. Fuck... Was that...

He'd never hit a hard-on for any member of his crew before, but there it was in his pants beneath the table.

Goddamnit.

Her fingers hooked onto the edge of the table and she leaned even closer.

He could touch her, could take that tiny wrist and guide her hand under the table, onto his thigh, up to—

"Pass me a fork, please," she said, and opened her hand to Jockey, who obliged.

To Swain's horror, she rose a fraction and used the side of the fork to cut the front triangle of pie. Taking it to her own mouth, she touched the fruit to her top lip. He'd thought she was going to eat it, but instead, she blew on the fruit and touched it to her lip again before smiling and licking off the smudge of filling.

"What are you doing?" Swain asked, fixated on her.

Raising the fork toward him, she smiled. "I wouldn't want to burn the captain on my first day, would I? Will you open your mouth for me now?"

The guys at the table were loving this, but his eyes were locked onto hers. He'd told her to cut out the cutesy babygirl act, except this was... different. She wasn't acting innocent; that glint in her gaze betrayed that she knew exactly what she was doing.

Grabbing her wrist, he yanked the fork away and tossed it down the table.

Fuck this.

He was the captain and he didn't let anyone mock him, especially not a flake of a girl, her first day on the job. He didn't even care that the guys started to cheer as he dragged her out of the mess and down the passageway.

Throwing open her cabin door, he jerked her forward and hoisted her over the frame into the room to thrust her forward.

When he was inside, he slammed the door so hard that the whole ship probably lurched, but he was too incensed to notice.

Before he opened his mouth, she shifted to widen her stance and set her eyes on fierce. "You lay one finger on me and I'll scream rape so loud they'll hear me in Aruba."

It took him a second to register how quickly she'd changed from innocent imp to this ferocious fighter. "Maybe you should've fucking thought about that before you started the sex talk!"

Her eyes narrowed. "If one of your men says the word sex, do you drag him to his room and attack him?"

"None of my men get on their knees and try to spoon feed me!"

Her shoulders went back as her chin rose. "Guess Jockey was wrong about you."

Now his hackles rose for a different reason 'cause his first-mate knew him better than anyone else and she had no right to pass judgment on their friendship. "Oh yeah, wrong about what?"

"He said you'd never disrespect a lady, and I feel disrespected right about now."

"You ain't no lady, you're crew," he said, trying his best to keep a thick black line of differentiation between the two because until now the two had resided in different areas of his brain.

"I'm both," she said. Showing spunk in her defiance, she reached behind her to untie her apron. When it was loose, she whipped it aside, hooking it on her elbow. "Want me to prove it?"

She actually undid the snap on her jeans and his mouth opened to say yes, but he managed to dam the word at the last moment. Driving a hand through his hair, Swain took a breath instead of saying something he'd regret.

"Goddamnit," he grumbled to himself.

"Jockey said he's responsible for discipline on this boat. If I did something wrong, shouldn't he be the one shouting at me?"

Shouting at her, what the fuck was he doing shouting at her? He didn't raise his voice to his crew, he'd never had to. A growled threat or a glare was enough to put any guy in his place. And women? Women never pushed him like this, none dared.

Bowing lower, he hissed at her. "You're the first crewman who's made me wish they hadn't outlawed flogging."

The way her body loosened told him she'd descended her high horse and the gentle slope of her lips was almost a smile. "I didn't think you'd be this sensitive about me standing behind you… I promise not to do it again."

"Standing… behind me? What?"

She scrunched her nose like maybe she was laughing at him without actually laughing. "There would be something sort of sexy about it if you weren't such a grouch… and if you learned how to shave."

Swain's hand moved over his jaw. It had been about a week since he'd put a blade to his face, maybe more. "It's been a crazy week," he said and then wondered why it sounded like he was apologizing.

Ha, she better get used to hairy men, sweaty men, men with disgusting habits and no decorum. The longer they were at sea, the less that most of the guys cared about manners and hygiene.

She came a step closer. "Look, you're the captain, your approval means something around here. You don't like what I do, I get cut, right?"

It made no sense to him that she'd be worried for her job. "We're out on the fucking ocean, Waif, where the fuck am I gonna put you?"

"Are you diabetic or something?"

This woman had a way of throwing a wrench into his thoughts at every turn. "What the fuck?"

"Do you have something against sugar, or is it something against eating what I bake? Do you think I'm trying to poison you?"

It didn't take her long to relax after she figured out he hadn't brought her here to force himself on her. The distance of the small room between them was enough to give her courage, but she didn't seem to notice that he was still blocking the door. She wasn't going anywhere unless he gave her permission.

"I ate the breakfast, bacon and pancakes."

She exhaled and folded her arms, which reminded her she was still wearing the apron, so she proceeded to unhook it from her neck to toss it on the bed. "Everyone ate those."

Shit, her polo shirt had sunk lower and the swell of her breast came into view along with a neat triangle at the top of her bra cup where it joined the strap. The damn woman needed to keep her shit together.

"What the fuck is this?" he asked, his hand leaping from his side toward her chest.

Luckily, he pulled it back before he made contact. It wasn't until he clenched his fist that he realized he'd actually been about to grab her.

Her eyes dropped for a second, she blinked them back to him, her expression blank. "It's a bra," she said. "I guess the bear-face thing doesn't get you much action with the ladies." Reaching to the side, she pulled open the top drawer of her dresser and pulled something out. It wasn't until she tossed it for him to catch that he realized it was a sheer black bra. Sheer like completely transparent and for some reason that made his attention return to her chest as he considered how she'd fill it out. Shit. "Figure it out on your own time, Cap'n, can I go back to work now?"

"You wear your fucking uniform like the rest of us," he said, pissed off that she'd crept under his skin and got him mad again.

"Uh," she said, picking up the shoulders to show how broad it was. "Then you better get me some shoulder pads. You're seriously pissed that I'm not built like a quarterback? I do what I can with what God gave me."

Biting his tongue hard, he squeezed his lips together so tight that they probably disappeared. But, fuck, he couldn't argue with that. God had been generous to her, and generous to those who got to stand this close. But she wasn't built like any previous member of his crew.

"You keep staring and I'll think you want a show."

Snapping himself from his daze, Swain got even more pissed off when he registered her unimpressed expression. It wasn't like he was ogling her. Swain was not one of those guys, never had been, he'd never needed to be.

"Don't flatter yourself, Waif," he sneered. "I get plenty of action on shore leave, I don't need to fuck around with my crew."

"Swing will be disappointed," she said and this time succeeded in folding her arms. "I have cookies to make before lunch… is there anything else you'd like from my underwear drawer, Captain?"

He'd never considered putting his hands on a woman in anger before, but this female managed to push his buttons. How the fuck did he become the sleaze in this when she'd been the one all over him in the mess?

But he had nothing; no quick quip or command to bark. Sassi must have known it too because she sashayed forward and slunk around him to slip out of the room. So much for her not going anywhere unless he moved, she was small enough to squeeze right past him.

Crushing the fabric of her bra in both hands, Swain yanked it so hard that the two cups came apart. He pitched the scraps across the room.

If she wanted to play, he'd let her play, but he'd take great pleasure in saying 'I told you so' when one of his guys asked her to prove her salt. He'd bet every boat in his fleet she'd retreat before she'd ever let one of his men claim her.

And, damn it, he better be right because if he had to watch any other man enjoying that infuriating wench, he might bring back flogging after all.

SIX

IT TOOK THE better part of the day for Swain to get her out of his head.

After lunch, he and Jockey were in the wheelhouse briefing the other guys on their course. From Miami, it would take nine or ten days to get down to the site depending on conditions.

Swain leaned over the map to talk about the plan but noted that no one was asking questions or commenting like they usually would. Lifting his head to check out why his men weren't engaging, he was surprised to find them all staring toward the bow. Expecting to see an obstacle in the water, he couldn't understand why no one had warned him they'd need to take evasive action.

But when Swain turned to follow their line of vision, he was struck by the same spell that had seized his men and lost the power of speech for a good half minute.

There on the forecastle of his fucking pride and joy was his dainty cook. Wearing nothing more than a white string bikini and a pair of oversized sunglasses, her hair was scooped onto her head again, but several strands had escaped their bounds and were being whipped around in the sea breeze. She had nothing on her feet and was propped on her tiptoes, teetering left and right, making her way forward.

"She doesn't have her sea legs yet," Foist said. Swain had never heard a smile like that in his engineer's voice. "If she goes over, I volunteer to go in after her."

The woman stopped to gaze out over the water before she spread a towel flat on the deck.

"I don't think I've ever said I love you before Captain," Swing said, sounding kind of like he'd swallowed his own tongue when Sassi bent over to smooth out the towel before she kneeled down on it. "But I do. She's the best thing you ever bought for Eros."

There was that rage again. Damn it. If this woman stayed aboard his ship Swain was going to have a heart attack. His blood pressure had never been high, but he didn't need a doctor to tell him that the wench was threatening his health… and his sanity.

Jockey came around the table. "I'll go talk to her."

Thank fuck someone else understood that the cook's actions were inappropriate. As his first-mate began to pass, Swain slapped a hand to his chest, his focus locked on the beauty lounging near the bow.

"No," he muttered. "I'll do it."

Swain had never moved from the wheelhouse to the bow so fast and he'd traversed this ship in storms surrounded by thirty foot waves that demanded he flee for his life.

When he stomped over to Sassi, she was lying on her back, soaking up the afternoon rays with a once-white kitchen timer on the deck beside her. Stopping, he cast a shadow over her, but she didn't acknowledge him. He couldn't tell if her eyes were open or closed because she was wearing sunglasses, but there was no way she hadn't heard him marching up.

"Madam like a mojito?" he asked.

The wench smiled. "Was that a joke, Captain?"

Not one that was meant to make her laugh.

Gritting his teeth, he told himself not to yell at her again. Once in a day was enough. At least, it should be enough, maybe she wanted more.

"Get up," he hissed.

"I don't see—"

"Get on your fucking feet, Sassi."

Inhaling through his nose, Swain breathed out while she shifted onto her knees. Was it just him or was she spending longer than she had to kneeling in front of him?

Bending down, he grabbed her arm to haul her onto her feet. She tried to tug away and objected with a sound of offense, but he dragged her up all the same.

Shit, he shouldn't be manhandling a woman. Except, she was crew, and he had the right to discipline his crew any way that he had to…

Why did that thought immediately make him picture pinning her to the bulwark to press himself against her?

"Geez," she said. "I guess even the up-close view of the tits doesn't prove I'm a woman. Do I need to get naked to get some respect?"

She might think her objection was putting him in his place, but this time he bit his tongue so hard that he tasted blood. Naked sounded about fucking right to his dick.

It took all of his effort to remember why he'd come storming down in the first place. "What do you think you're doing? This isn't a fucking pleasure cruise!"

"What is your problem?" she shouted and worked hard to wrench her arm free. "Goddamnit, I made your meals. Your dinner is in the oven, I have my timer…"

She spun around and bent over, giving him a more intimate view of that ass he'd admired this morning. Instead of jeans this time it was adorned with a skimpy white bikini brief held in place with two little strings on each of her hips that would take him seconds to loosen. There wasn't a knot he couldn't identify and tackle; she shouldn't challenge a sailor with that kind of test.

When she whipped around, it took him a second to notice that she was holding a timer an inch from his face. Right, the timer, shit. She wasn't presenting her ass, she'd been retrieving her timer.

"Nothing will burn, you and your men will be fed, I promise. I have the rest of the afternoon! What's wrong with me taking a little break? I did inventory after breakfast and made three batches of cookies before lunch. I made more cookies this afternoon, and dessert, and I made cherry pie for supper. I've prepped the donut dough for the morning so I can fry them for you fresh! What more do you want from me, Captain? You want baklava? Soufflé? Baumkuchen from a spit? What?"

Okay, he didn't know what that last one was, but she'd proven that she wasn't shy about hard work. There was nothing wrong with her taking a break. As he started to feel guilty about his attitude, the ship shifted and she stumbled sideways out of his shadow.

The sun caught the shimmer of her skin and it made her glow. This woman was like silk, smooth and beautiful, but stronger than steel.

His body reacted to her figure and he cursed himself for responding to a member of his crew like maybe they were an option for intimacy. Crew, shit, his men were still in the wheelhouse enjoying the view.

Regaining his bluster, Swain sidestepped to block their view because that lurch wasn't only caused by the water; someone was at the wheel playing games. They knew he wouldn't move against the sway of the ship, but she wasn't as steady on her feet.

"We take breaks fully clothed around here," he said and that made her look at her breasts.

"I'm dressed," she said, gasping in mock offense. "All the important parts are covered. Don't tell me you and your crew are squeamish, or are you offended that I'm not covered in tattoos and scars?" When her hands went to her hair, she started to finger her scalp like she was searching for something. "The only scar I've got was a gift from my ex-boyfriend."

That's what she was searching for in her hair? One word came to mind. "Headboard?"

"Vodka bottle," she said. The volcano of fury that burst in his chest made him consider diving into the drink just to get back to shore to pay the fucker a visit. "In his defense, he was aiming for my brother who'd just hit him with a chair."

She said it like it was nothing.

Everything she said intrigued him. What the hell kind of men did she date? And why was her brother hitting guys with chairs?

This girl was an enigma unlike any other.

Grabbing her wrists, he pulled her hands out of her hair, he didn't need to see a scar. "Bar room brawl?" he asked, trying to figure it out.

"Cock fight," she said, lifting a shoulder. "My dad was unconscious… it's a long story."

Now her dad was involved too? What the hell kind of family did she come from? If Swain hadn't known it wasn't a good idea for him and the guys to keep their hands off her before, he knew it for sure now.

The dithering dad, violent brother, and boyfriend with a bad aim would be enough to discourage any guy.

With that thought, he quickly let go of her wrists.

Her smile got so wide that she showed her straight, white teeth. Bowing toward him, she lifted her chin. "Don't worry about those guys, Captain. I can handle them… the ones who are still alive anyway."

Shit. The brawl ended in murder? This woman lived a dark life. No one would know it by looking at her. But it made sense. What better way to run from the law than to escape to the sea? Many had done the same thing for centuries.

"You killed one of them?"

"Broke his heart," she said, gazing over the water. "Some would say."

That he could believe. "The boyfriend?"

Taking a breath, she brought her attention back to him. "This is getting deep for a first date, wouldn't you say?" she asked. "You came down here to yell at me for getting my hoo-has out, stay focused, Captain."

He wouldn't let any of the other guys talk to him that way, but part of him was grateful for the reminder. "Right," he said. "Stay in uniform, that's an order."

The breath she took was so deep that her shoulders rose and fell. "You yelled at me this morning for not wearing it right and now I'm supposed to sleep in it?"

Yeah, okay, maybe he was being unfair.

When they got to the salvage site he and his crew would be stripping down and changing on deck regularly. Board shorts were part of the Swain uniform when they were in and out of the water and their dive suits all day. At that time, it would be a double-standard to tell her she couldn't wear a bathing suit.

But, that body, fuck, it was going to get someone on the crew into trouble. The woman was a master of sugar and baked treats, but from the look of her figure she rarely indulged herself. Either that or she worked out a lot. Slender and toned, she had the perfect form for a man to play with.

Noticing her breasts again, he took his time looking down the curve of her waist to the flare of her hips. The line of her bikini briefs was held straight between her hip bones leaving a narrow gap between fabric and skin, perfect for his hand to just… shit. He had to stop letting his mind make these sexual leaps.

This woman was his cook and he was being a cock; a sleazy fucking asshole who shouldn't be building sexual fantasies that involved his subordinate.

"Flirting with the guys and walking around in skimpy bikinis is going to get you into trouble," he said.

"Are you telling me you hire rapists?"

The boat lurched again, just the tiniest bit, but it was enough to make her stumble against him. The squash of her breasts on his torso made his dick salute in an instant.

No. No. This wasn't good.

Usually he'd take the time to find himself a woman before they left shore. But he'd been in such a rush to get everything ready that he hadn't had the time to think about drinking and seduction. He hadn't enjoyed a woman for a while and that was his excuse for his juvenile reaction to this one.

If he'd known his cook was going to be a sexy nymph sent to test them all, he'd have found a way to make the fucking time to take the edge off.

Wrapping his fingers over her shoulders, he eased her back, wishing that he didn't have to touch her because she was softer than sun-melted butter.

"I'm saying I don't want either of us to find out," he said.

The sunglasses still covered her eyes, but he

could feel her gaze rise to his. "No man has ever violated me before," she said with a vehemence in her tone that made him curious. "I can't say none have tried."

He wanted to know what that meant, wanted to know what kind of bastard would try to force himself on a woman, and he wanted to know what she'd done to protect herself.

"While you work under me, you're my responsibility, wholly my responsibility. I take that duty seriously. A captain's value is set by his crew."

"Your crew value you. They respect you," she said. "Highly. All of them… they were talking at lunch. The loyalty around here is humbling."

"You're a part of our crew now," he said, feeling like it was important to let her share a piece of that security though he couldn't figure out why because this woman was impenetrable.

Instead of being gratified, she smiled. "Then it shouldn't matter what I wear because no crewman would violate another, right?"

Stepping away from him, she moved into the sunlight and stretched her arm above her head to wave at the wheelhouse. The woman knew exactly who was watching; she knew exactly what she was doing. When the horn blasted, he whipped around, ready to curse his crew. But when she opened her mouth in a rapturous laugh, Swain's knees were taken from under him.

She didn't just talk like she was naked in a man's bed, she laughed like he'd just tickled her most intimate spot.

Fuck.

Swain was getting mad again. The horn blasted once more. He glared at the wheelhouse and signaled for them to cut it out.

"You need to lighten up, Captain," she said.

She rested a hand on his forearm, but he

wrenched it away and forced her backward when he bowed to swipe up her towel. "Get your fucking clothes on, Waif," he demanded, throwing the towel at her. "Break's over."

Storming away, he was going to give his crew a good dressing down for being so frivolous with their safety system, but she called out.

"Jockey said you'd let me write an order for supplies that we could pick up in Miami."

He stopped.

Damn it, he couldn't ignore legitimate business.

Glaring over his shoulder, he nodded for her to follow and marched on. He'd set her up with what she needed and then he'd get back to his crew and away from her.

SEVEN

SASSI DIDN'T FIND it easy to keep up with the long-legged captain when he marched back inside and along the corridor past her bedroom and the mess to the end. Turning right, he ran up a flight of stairs to a square landing before turning ninety-degrees right and running up another half dozen.

Crowding in at his back because there wasn't much space on this top landing, she heard him grumble before he unlocked a door and moved forward.

Reminding herself to step over the frame at the bottom of the door, she expected to go into another cold metal room.

This was anything but.

The first thing she noticed was the warm wood flooring and the paneling that went all the way to the ceiling. To the left were three circle windows with a messy desk facing into the room beneath. A file cabinet stood behind the desk, against the wall underneath the furthest away circle window. On top of that was a printer-scanner.

Her casual eye moved right, past the dressers, and came to a stop on a huge bed in the back right corner.

"Is this your bedroom?" she asked, assuming only the captain could have such a sumptuous room.

"It's my cabin," he said, doing something with his keys.

Dashing past him, Sassi crawled up on his bed and lay down in the middle to exhale. Oh, it was so soft, way softer than hers, though she'd only laid on her bed for a minute this morning to test it.

Spreading herself out, she smelled nothing but fresh linen like the sheets had just been changed that day.

"What do you think you're doing?" he snapped.

Sassi was getting used to his brusque mood and wasn't intimidated by it. Clambering off the end of the bed, she ran through the door just beside it to find the bathroom with full bath and separate shower.

"You have a bathtub! Can I use it?"

"No!" he barked like she'd just made the most ridiculous request.

Peeking into it, she noted how clean it was and wondered if it had ever been used. "Doesn't look like you use it much."

"The captain doesn't have time for laying around."

Swinging around the door frame, she ran a fingertip across a rung of the ladder attached to the wall by the built-in closet doors.

"Someone thought you did or they wouldn't have put a tub in the bathroom."

"It's called the head," he said, watching her scamper around the room. "You're not gonna have time for soaking in there either."

Leaning on the door they'd entered by, Sassi folded her hands behind her. "I have an hour this afternoon and you'd probably have preferred me in there than out on deck."

His interest slithered down her. Given the bikini, and the show she'd put on outside, Sassi couldn't blame him for looking.

Waving to the wheelhouse had been a bit of fun. Before she went outside, she hadn't really thought about where the other men would be, just that she needed a break. Jockey had told her that Swain would be spending the day in the wheelhouse, but she hadn't considered that she'd be putting on a performance for anyone.

All she'd figured was that so long as the captain was on over watch, she could be confident that the other guys wouldn't be able to hurt her. Not that she was afraid of anyone on the crew, not really. She'd actually begun to warm to them. Despite their rough exteriors, she didn't think any of them would harm her.

Sunbathing was Sassi's way of enjoying what might be her last days of freedom. If she didn't come up with the money, she'd have to marry Dario or else she'd watch Stuart and Karen suffer. But Sassi feared she'd take her own life rather than give herself to that snake.

"I told you to keep your clothes on," he grumbled.

"No one would see me in the tub," she said, but the corner of her mouth curled. "Unless that's your way of telling me you want to watch." His attention snapped up like she'd just pinched him. "Hope you treat me better than you treat my underwear."

At first, she'd been pissed off to find her ripped bra in her cabin. It didn't take long for that tension to sink lower into a part of her anatomy that she hadn't thought about for a long time. Her breasts had tingled at the idea that they might have been liberated by his vicious, arousing, act.

Okay, so her chest hadn't been in the bra when

it had been ripped. There was nothing sexual about what he'd done. He'd probably just been leaving her a message that he wasn't happy with her and she got that.

But a fantasy played out in her mind, one involving an overbearing Captain with a bad attitude and a cook who couldn't stop goading him even though she knew it wasn't the best idea to tease him.

"I shouldn't have done that," he said and retreated to behind the desk. "I'll replace it."

Pushing away from the door, Sassi started toward him. "You'll buy me underwear? How do you plan to do that out here?"

He unlocked the file cabinet and tugged a catalog from it. Tossing it onto the desk, he grumbled. "Order anything you want."

Intrigued, she picked up the booklet to flick through the hundred or so pages. "Clothes... Uniforms."

"He can put our branding on anything. I'll have Jockey add a note and ask him to rush the order. He'll deliver it to the ship," he said and cleared his throat. "There's a printed order form in the back. Fill it out with whatever you want, your... sizes."

There was something incredibly sweet about the gesture, or maybe it was the shift in his stance showing that he was uncomfortable that endeared her. "I'd appreciate that, Captain."

Probably because he was comfortable, he frowned and got stern again. "You're going to be with us for a month and we can't have a repeat of this morning."

"Sure," she said, hugging the catalogue to her chest.

"Fill it in and leave it on the desk." He tugged a blank sheet of paper from the printer. "Write down whatever you need for chow on this. When you're done, call through the intercom in the galley, and Jockey will send it all."

The first-mate would know their contacts, how the machine worked, and what to write in the extra notes to make sure their orders were ready to be delivered before they left Miami.

When he figured there was nothing left to say, Swain nodded once and came around the bed to head for the door again. Sassi turned on the spot to watch him go, amazed that he was leaving her alone in the bedroom.

"Captain," she said when he opened the door. He turned to look at her. "You have a great bed."

Even though his beard was thick, she saw his jaw move forward and his frustration made her smile. "Berth, it's my berth," he said.

"Then you have a great berth."

"Wench," she heard him mutter as he went out leaving her to her fun.

And as she scampered over to the desk and sat to open up the catalogue, fun was on her mind. Sassi could follow the spirit of his words without disobeying orders. If she was ordered to walk the plank for being mischievous, she'd do it.

Out here there was no debt, no Dario, no abandonment, no grief. Something about the ocean made her feel free. Sassi had been out there less than a day and already she was dreading the day she'd have to go back to shore.

EIGHT

YEAH, SASSI FELT like a bit of an idiot.

How many times did she have to hear that they were going to be in port that night before she realized the men wouldn't need fed?

It was still light when they docked. The men were quick to get to their plans of fun and debauchery on shore and disappeared the moment they were given permission.

Of course, everyone was planning to eat in the city. It made sense. The crew was going to be stuck out at sea where there were no bars, and no willing women, for weeks. They had to take this final opportunity while they had it.

The food that Sassi had prepared could be packed and stored, so there was no harm done. She'd got a head start on meals for the following day; that was the way she chose to look at it. But it was a little embarrassing. She'd been so preoccupied with her own concerns that what was being repeated around her hadn't filtered through.

Hours after they'd arrived in port, Sassi was in the kitchen boxing up the cookies and desserts as the casserole cooled. She was considering making some mac and cheese to serve as a midnight snack, in case the men came back to the boat hungry, when Swain walked into the mess with Jockey.

Except, it was a wonder she even saw Jockey. The sight of the clean-shaven captain took her breath away. Oh no. She'd known Swain was broad and attractive in a brute force kind of way. But when she saw the strength of his features, the squareness of his jaw and the intensity of his eyes that had somehow been dampened by the overwhelming facial hair, she was sure something smacked her in the chest. Her breath was sucked from her lungs so abruptly that she gasped.

The men stopped talking to look at her.

"What are you still doing here?" Swain asked.

Sassi heard his voice, its usual deep vibration wormed its way into her ears, making her heart pound in her chest. But as she opened her mouth, little sound came out.

"You okay, lass?" Jockey asked.

Though it was nice of the first-mate to sound worried, she couldn't acknowledge him. Her jaw was still moving like she wanted to talk, except her voice box had gone on strike.

"Waif, speak," Swain demanded, and his single stride brought him near enough that she got claustrophobic. She stumbled back. "What did I tell you about orders? Speak."

His brow was drawn down in a harsh frown, but there was even an edge of worry in his voice too. "Do you want pie?" she asked in a rush of breath then cringed at herself. What kind of stupid question was that?

"Pie?" Swain asked, looking at her like she'd just sprouted fins.

"No, lass, we're going out to eat," Jockey said, coming around Swain. The movement luckily broke her fixation on the captain. She hadn't blinked for so long that her eyes had been starting to sting. "Come with us."

"Oh no, I'll stay here," she said, grabbing for the galley like it was her anchor.

"Alone?" Swain said from behind Jockey. "No, you won't. I'm locking up. Do you think I'd leave you here to defend Eros alone?"

"So lock me in," she said. "I'm not getting off the boat... What if you leave without me?"

That was a ridiculous suggestion and not one she thought was true, but it was better to sound stupid than confess the real reason for her hesitation.

"A lot of trouble to go to," Swain said.

"We're addicted to your cookies anyway," Jockey said. "Not sure we're ever gonna let you leave."

Swain still hadn't even tried her cookies as far as she knew; he wasn't as kind as Jockey. "If I wanted to ditch you, Waif," the captain said, "I'd have tossed you in the drink."

"Miami and me don't get along," she said.

"You've been here before?" Jockey asked and she nodded.

There was a large Cuban community in Miami; a lot of people around here knew Dario Correa. It was unlikely that he'd have put word out to track her down yet. She'd only been gone a day. But if she was spotted by one of his minions who knew the story and reported back, Dario might think she was trying to flee.

If her being this far from home caused enough alarm, Dario might start looking for Stuart. There was a good chance Dario was already attempting to track her brother, but she didn't want to give the asshole more cause. Stuart was resourceful, but he could be sloppy if he got lazy... or high. With her out on the ocean, she'd be safe; her brother would be a prime target.

"Then come on," Swain said, showing little patience.

"I… I don't have any money," she said. Another lame excuse, but a true one. She'd used her last cent for supplies for this trip.

"I'll take your cut from your pay," he said. "Move your ass, Waif."

She couldn't tell them the truth and though she tried to search for another excuse, she couldn't find one. "Damn it," she hissed, dropping her fist to the counter. "Okay, but you have to let me get changed…" She started toward them, but paused by Swain. "And if someone gets hit with a chair, don't blame me."

"Your brother lives down here?" Swain asked.

"Her brother?" Jockey asked.

The captain had remembered her story, she liked that he paid attention. "No. Not exactly."

Though in truth, Sassi had no idea where her brother was. Miami would be one of the dumbest places for him to hide out. If he wanted to disappear and get off Correa's radar, heading north would've been a better option… or west… or east over the ocean, anywhere except south.

"We can handle ourselves in a fight, Waif," Swain said, giving her shoulder a shove. "Hurry up and change. We're leaving in five minutes, and if I have to toss you over my shoulder to drag you out, I will." Sassi wasn't sure she was averse to that and was thinking about it as she sauntered toward the door. Swain clapped, startling her. "What's your flank speed? Shake a leg, Waif."

Wearing a smile, she turned to walk backward, but didn't go any faster. "I don't know what that means, Captain. But some might say it's rude to talk about a lady's flanks."

She'd never noticed his smile before, maybe

because of the beard. Seeing it made her stop and match his amusement, he leaned toward her. "How many times I gotta tell you, Waif? You ain't no lady."

"No, I'm crew," she said, holding one of her wrists at the small of her back. "Under you."

"Under me," he said, his voice dropping an octave.

Oh, boy, there was something mesmerizing about his gaze. She'd never seen it this close before; he'd never bent this low to get in her eye line. Though there was a foot of distance between them, she felt a lightness seep through her. Starting in her thighs, the sensation ascended until it warmed her intimate core. This was more intense than the flip she'd felt in her gut on the dock first thing, and far more intriguing.

The reminder of their meeting, early that morning, suddenly made her worry. Her touching his face made surprise flicker across his expression, but he didn't move away.

"Will you be okay, Captain? You've been working hard all day and you were up most of last night. Maybe you should get some rest and—"

"This is our last shot at shore leave for a while," he said, "don't get much rope yarn time."

She laughed. The captain was a lot different when they were docked, ahead of schedule, and when his crew wasn't around. "I don't know what that means either."

"Come about, full steam ahead, and I'll tell you when we disembark," he said.

Sailor talk was part of his regular vocabulary, though she had a feeling he was playing with her, at least a little.

But Sassi wasn't averse to playing. "Aye, aye, Captain," she said and saluted.

"Now you're getting it."

Sassi wouldn't slow him down by taking an age to change her clothes. She'd had boyfriends tell her that other women took a long time getting ready or causing delays. But Sassi had been taught by her grandmother how rude it was to be late or keep someone waiting.

So she hurried to her room and pulled a dress from her drawer. Running a brush through her hair, she put on some lip-gloss, then slipped the tube into her cleavage before swiping on a little mascara. There wasn't need for anything else. Any sleek style she tried to tease her hair into would only frizz with the humidity anyway, so she let it curl in its natural way and ran her fingers through it.

Sliding on a pair of sandals, Sassi figured the shoes would be a nightmare to walk down the dock in, but they'd be fine once they got onto the street.

Running out of her cabin, she found Swain and Jockey waiting out on deck. Swain took his weight from a post and Jockey drew a smoke away from his lips. "Well, lass, don't you scrub up nice."

"Do I?" she asked. Looking down, the first thing she saw was her tube of lip-gloss sticking out of her cleavage and she laughed. "Oops."

"You don't need that shit," Swain said and reached over to pluck the tube from between her breasts.

With her hands outstretched, Sassi started forward to try to reclaim it, but it was too late, he'd already tossed it over his shoulder. The tube disappeared, either into the water or onto the dock. Shit. Didn't he know that stuff was expensive and she was broke?

Apparently not because his huge hands sank around her jaw and he used his thumbs to wipe the gloss away from her lips. They moved one after the other at least half a dozen times ensuring it was all gone.

"You put some crap on your eyelashes too," Swain grumbled.

How did he know that? After knowing her a day, how did he know her face so well? The rough skin of his thumbs rasped her lips, softer this time, but they were already swollen and probably red, like they would be if he'd used his lips instead of his thumbs to make his point.

Internally gawping at her shocking thought, Sassi didn't know why she'd made the leap from his hands to his mouth. But there she was, drifting in his gaze again, struggling to make sense of the flurry impeding her heartbeat.

"Do you want me to wash my face, Captain?" she asked, her voice soft.

The question was an admission that she'd follow any of his orders, even those that went beyond her duties.

"No time for that. Come on, time to eat," Jockey said, tossing his smoke away and nudging the captain. "Let's get going."

To her dismay, Jockey turned and leaped from the boat to the dock through the gap in the edge of the hull that had housed the gangplank earlier, except the boarding aid wasn't there this time.

"I can't do that," she said, grabbing Swain's corded forearm before he could jump too. "I'm wearing heels."

"What's the hold up?" Jockey called to them.

Swain looked down when she lifted her shoe to show him. "Take 'em off."

She squirmed. "I still can't jump all that way, what if I fall in?"

"You think I'd let you?" he asked. "I'm the one who'd have to fish you out. I've only got one good shirt. I'm not getting it wet."

He did look good in the button down. It was black, like the polo shirt he'd worn that day and the coveralls he'd worn that morning. Somehow though, it matched his eyes. "I like it."

She liked the shirt and the face; both made him more real, though no less intimidating. "It's not a jump, it's a step," he said, pointing ashore.

His frustration wasn't going to hurry her up. It didn't matter how exasperated the captain got, she was still hesitant. "A step for you with your long legs, I'll have to lift my skirt and—"

"Holy hell, woman," he said and bent over to push his shoulder into her stomach.

Screaming when he hoisted her off her feet, Sassi pounded at his back. But just like he'd said, it only took him a single step to reach the dock. There, he bent over again and put her back on her feet. Sassi was caught off-guard, and didn't have her balance, so she had to grab the arm of each of the men to steady herself.

"Can't wait 'til you have to do that drunk," Jockey said.

Oh no, she'd have to get back on the boat! How would she do that if the men weren't with her or if the men were drunk? Sassi didn't know the protocol if the captain hooked up and she had to come back to the ship alone.

But, apparently, the boat was locked anyway. Jockey must have taken care of that because she hadn't seen Swain do it and she'd been watching him closely, probably too closely. No boss had ever made her feel so feeble and so protected both at the same time.

Still not trusting her feet, she walked between the men and took each of their arms. If they were going to get lucky, she would be a hindrance and might cramp their style. But down here on the dark dock, she didn't think there were many women to hit on, least not the ones that came for free.

She didn't say anything as they traversed the

dock. Swain and Jockey mentioned a few of the boats, commented on their crews, and on the equipment they could see. All of it went over her head. They knew where they were going and when they stepped into the Dockside Bar and Grill, she guessed the duo had been here before.

It was a decent sized space, all wooden floors and walls with an open half-floor above held up by pillars that flanked the bar. It was dirty and loud, and the only women she saw were in uniforms, but it seemed like exactly the kind of place Eros' crew would fit in.

The guys pointed out a booth on the other side of the room. They went over and Swain slid in at one side. Jockey directed her in opposite the captain and then sat beside her. They'd barely sat down when a plump waitress in a bright red shirt came over, her bosom threatening to pop every button on the garment.

But the width of her smile made Sassi smile too. "Howdy, y'all, what can I get you?" the waitress asked.

"You eat steak, Sassi?" Jockey asked her.

"I sure do," she said. "Medium for me, and beer is fine."

When the waitress noticed her smiling, she widened her grin. "You're a lucky gal out with a couple of catches like these two."

Sassi laughed. "I sure am. But I'm trying to offload them. Do you know any gal willing to take pity on a couple of lonely sailors for the night?"

The waitress eyed Jockey then Swain, really taking her time over the captain. "Both of 'em? At once?"

That hadn't been quite what she meant, but was happy to go with it. "Sure," Sassi said. "They're real respectful."

The waitress tapped her pen on her pad for a moment, then her laugh blasted out of her. "Oh, honey,

I like you, girl," she said. "I'll see what I can do for ya, bet you need a night off."

"I've got four weeks ahead of me, alone with this pair, and a few of their friends."

The waitress circled her lips in a wince. "Some might consider that heaven."

"The nights I don't mind," Sassi said and side-nodded at her captain. "This one gets grumpy during the day."

The waitress laughed again. "Then we should get him fed and in a better mood, huh? Steak and beer all round?"

"Make theirs bloody, you know, how blue their steak is links to their masculinity. You can just bring out the cow and they'll tear it apart themselves."

The waitress was laughing again as she retreated from the table. Both Jockey and Swain pinned glares on her.

Sassi did her best to shrug with innocence. "What? I didn't get it wrong. Foist told me today steak on ship should always be blue. We talked for a while about dietary requirements… Foist's a real open guy."

Swain's bad mood was definitely his default, but he did it so well that she couldn't blame him for using the skill, kind of like her and her sass. "And the sex stuff?" the captain asked.

"Uh, I didn't say that word at all. You heard that in your own head." She angled her chin to examine him. "You seem to think about sex a lot, cap'n."

"And, on that, I'm going to the head," Jockey said and swung out the booth.

Music came on the jukebox in the corner. Sassi took the time to look around. They were slightly elevated because the booths were a step up from the lower part of the floor that was mostly filled with smaller circular tables. Beyond those was a small dancefloor, though there were only a few people on it. None of them were dancing, they were just drinking and gathering in small groups.

"You think you'll meet your ex in here?" The waitress brought their beer before Sassi could answer the captain. Swain tipped the server twenty bucks, which was generous of him. Sassi figured maybe he was trying to buy her silence. "So your ex…?"

"In here?" she said and glanced around again, taking the beer to her lips. "Which ex?"

Jockey appeared at the end of the booth, but instead of sitting down, he reached over to give her shoulder a squeeze. "Sorry to ditch you, but Locke's heading up to the Ment, I gotta go."

Backing off, Jockey shared a look with the glaring captain who was half out his seat. Then the first-mate melted away, leaving Sassi all alone with her captain.

NINE

SWAIN SANK BACK down into his seat and curled his fist around the neck of his beer bottle, clenching so hard, it was a wonder he didn't break the glass. Sassi was sure he was cursing when he bowed his head to glare at the tabletop.

"If you want to go with him, I can head back to the boat alone," she said.

"It's a ship," he hissed, his voice guttural, darker and more ominous than she'd heard it.

Seemed like a ridiculous distinction, but what he valued wasn't her call. "Okay, then I can go back to the ship," she said and started to shimmy along the bench. "I'll cancel our food order and—"

Lunging over the table, he caught her wrist. "You can't get off the ship by yourself, how you gonna get back on it? And I told you, you're not staying there alone."

"Okay," she said, yanking her arm away to tuck it beneath the table. "Then I'll find somewhere else to sleep."

His chin stayed close to his chest as he pinned

her with a vicious sneer. "Seen someone you like?"

Offense just made her angry. "Yeah, that's what I meant, I'll whore myself for a pillow to sleep on," she snapped. "Give me a break. I don't need you, your pity, or your boat. If you want to go get drunk with your buddies in the Ment, whatever the hell that is, you go, Captain. Do you think I can't take care of myself? You have no idea."

Again, when she tried to leave the booth, he grabbed her. This time he pulled her hard, dragging her to the center of the bench again.

"Tell me," he said, taking her aback. "I want to know. Give me an idea."

No chance. She shook her head. "I don't know anything about you."

"Anything about me?" he asked. "You know everything about me. The sea is my life; Eros my mistress. That's it, my whole life."

His life was the sea, she could buy that, but while she had him alone, Sassi took the opportunity to ask. "Is it true you're a pirate?"

Rolling his eyes up, he slumped into his seat. "Fucking Foist… no I'm not a fucking pirate."

"It wasn't Foist, Jockey told me."

"He's dicking you around."

But there was something about the way Swain was getting defensive that made her worry less about being taken for a fool. If it had been a flat-out lie, he'd have laughed in her face and accused her of being gullible.

She gasped in delight. "It's true, isn't it?"

"No, it's not true," he said, leaning to the side, probably seeking their food.

His avoidance made her grin. "You're a pirate!"

Reaching for her again, his grip was softer this time, but no less deliberate. "Would you be careful screaming that out?" Wow, she was in the presence of a real live pirate. He must have seen how it excited and amused her because he exhaled. "You know that means I'm a felon, right? You're grinning that you're on a date with a criminal. Pirates are criminals."

"Well, yeah, but not really," she said.

Their food was brought over and they both settled back in the booth. Swain ordered more beer though Jockey's was still sitting there untouched. Sassi pushed the first-mate's bottle toward the captain.

"What do you know about the job you took with Eros?" he asked, eating a dozen fries in one mouthful.

Sassi was still chewing on one when she realized she had no idea what they were going to do. "Are we going to steal something? Hold someone to ransom?"

There was almost a crooked smile on his flat lips when he began to cut into his steak. "Could be. You never know with us pirates. Are you ready to go to prison for me, Waif?"

He could be making fun of her. Sassi ate another fry, then picked one up to point it at him. "No, I don't think so. You wouldn't have called Karen if you were going to do something illegal. Who calls a temp agency to fill jobs on their pirate gang? There must be some corner of the dark web that caters to that."

"Dark web?" he asked, poking the condiments at the end of the table. "What do you know about the fucking dark web?"

She lifted a shoulder. "My brother sold weed on it for a while."

"Helluva criminal background you have," he said. "You lie to the agency about your criminal record? I asked for someone without one."

"Double standard, don't you think?" she asked, trying her steak. "If you have a criminal background, should you judge others who have one?"

"Do you have a record?"

"No," she said. "And I don't think I know anyone who could match being a pirate… You should advertise that, you'd get so many women…"

"I do fine," he said, with a lump of steak in his cheek. "Advertising it is not great for my legit business."

"Tell me what happened."

The steak was good, tender and juicy. People might judge a non-descript place like this from the outside. They'd walk right by thinking it was lowbrow. But it didn't matter to Sassi that there were no tablecloths or that there were spider webs in the corners and dirt on the floor. The food was good, it was warm, and right now at least, no one was causing trouble.

"I don't like talking about it," he said. He'd already finished his steak and stabbed into Jockey's to move it from the first-mate's plate to his own. "You want some of this?"

She shook her head. "No, I want to know how you became a pirate."

"And I said I'm not talking about it."

Inhaling, Sassi sat up straight. "Oh, come on, everyone wants to meet a pirate!" She deliberately raised her voice on that last vital word. "Meeting a pirate is hot! And a pirate would—"

"Okay," he said. "Pipe down. Fuck… you know how to get what you want, don't you, Waif?"

She grinned and leaned over the table. "So come on then, tell me what happened."

"I was a dumb kid, a stupid teenager. My dad was old navy. He was discharged not long after I was born, so I kicked around the docks all my life as he tried to find work. Felt like I was always on some boat going somewhere. My buddies and me were on this fucking cheesy cruise boat, going from A to B. We talked our way on. Stowed away. We'd missed the tramp 'cause my mate was hooked on a girl. Anyway, we got drunk thought it would be smart to dip the purse and hijack a lifeboat."

Her mouth fell open, this was a better story than she could've imagined. "No way."

Sassi wasn't really sure what the purse was, the purser maybe? They robbed something anyway.

"Plan worked great, 'cept we somehow forgot we only had oars and the coastguard had engines, two of 'em… I got two years."

This time when her mouth opened wide it was in a grin and she couldn't contain her laugh. "I love that story! Is it true?" He nodded. "You did two years in jail? Like real jail?"

"Juvenile."

Okay, so the jail part of the story wasn't so great for him, but wow, what cojones it had taken for a kid to do that. "How old were you?"

"Fifteen," he said. "I pled guilty, there was no denying it. I was charged with theft on the high seas, mayhem and piracy… So yes, technically, and only very technically, I am a pirate."

Dropping her flatware to her plate, she relaxed, her hands curling around the bench on either side of her thighs as she admired him. "That's hot… what did your dad say?"

He was still eating, but frowned. "How'd you go from 'that's hot' to my dad?"

"Boys are all about trying to get their father's approval in their teens," she said, picking up a fry, then pushing her half-empty plate away. When Swain pointed at it with his fork, she nodded and he switched his empty plate up for hers. "They usually do that by rebelling and pretending not to give a fuck what their father's think."

The captain tucked into her leftovers. "You think so?"

"I have a brother, remember? He and my dad

were always butting heads back then, and as the only girl in the house, it was a nightmare."

"Your dad raised you?"

"My grandmother did. She tried her best to raise me as a proper lady… didn't work out so great," she said. "We had a perfectly respectable life while she was around holding everything together. But she died when Stuart was sixteen, I'd just turned fourteen. I was stuck in a house with two grieving males, both of who insisted they weren't upset about losing her, and who turned their grief into acting like I needed some sort of Secret Service detail."

"You were overprotected?"

Her rebellious phase had started young and hadn't gone away in a hurry. "They tried their damndest, but I always had an answer or an excuse. My dad said my desperate need for independence and freedom would kill him one day."

"Where is he now?"

"Dead." That was a surprising enough truth that the captain stopped mid-chew. "Just over a month ago. His was the heart I broke."

"What happened to your mom?"

Her mom was the only light in her life, when she showed up. "She's out there, somewhere," she said, picking at the corner of the label on her bottle. "My mom's a free spirit. My name's the only thing she ever gave me. She and my grandmother despised each other with a real venom. Well, I guess my grandmother hated my mom, I'm not sure my mom has any kind of negative emotion in her. She and my dad made a go of things for a while, but she split when I was four, she drifted in and out after that. We lived with my grandmother and she did the raising."

"Did you get along with her? Your grandmother."

"Oh, I rebelled to the max, even back then," Sassi said, recalling some of the crazy things she'd done as a little person, really believing that she was making a statement. "I missed my mom and blamed my grandmother for sending her away… It was years before I found out the truth of what happened."

"What truth?"

"That my mom wanted an excuse to split… sticking around in one place wasn't her style."

"She should've tried a life at sea."

Somehow she'd forgotten where she was and who she was talking to. His mention of the ocean reminded her of reality.

Sassi's eyes darted up, then down. She sat up, drawing in a breath. "Shit, I'm sorry, Captain, I don't usually talk so much… I don't usually drink." But the beer couldn't be to blame for her loose tongue because she'd drank less than half the bottle.

"Talk all you want, I like to sail with people I can trust," he said. "We never know when our lives are going to be in each other's hands."

She wasn't making life and death decisions, and doubted she'd ever be in such a position of responsibility. "I'm the cook."

"So my life's in your hands every day. I should have Fidget start tasting my food," he said and the curl at the corner of his lips made her relax more.

When there was silence filling the space between their stare, they found themselves in a moment they might never get again.

Sassi had to take advantage of it. "I want to say thank you."

"Thank me? For what?"

"You didn't have to take me on, you could've let me walk away. You knew nothing about me and I know nothing about sailing…"

Picking up his bottle by the base, his smile seemed more knowing when he turned his attention to the room. "Yeah, I figured that out pretty fast," he said. "You and your agent should get closer together. She told me you'd served in the Navy."

Okay, so that was an outrageous lie and could've got her in serious trouble. Yet, she laughed. "Oh, God, did she? I did tell her to say whatever she had to, but my phone was disconnected before I could call her back and then… there was just no time… I'm sorry she lied… but it wasn't her fault, you shouldn't let it influence your decision to use her agency in the future… Karen is a good person and I'm sure she's done good work for you in the past and—"

"I've never used an agency before, and hers was just the first in the Yellow Pages…"

"Oh," she said, a little deflated. Sassi took another drink.

"But if you're the kind of person she has on her books, I'll be calling her again if I need crew in the future."

There was that eye contact again.

The captain changed into a different person on shore, or maybe it was the night that did it, because he'd been relaxed on the boat—oh, sorry, ship—before they came out. But he clung onto his ability to switch on the bad mood at any second because he'd gotten mad fast after Jockey cut out on them.

"She'll never lie to you again, I promise I'll talk to her when we get back."

Why did it seem he was so fascinated with her? "You got a connection with the temp agent? She your ex too?"

"No," Sassi said, exhaling a laugh. "My brother's."

"Ah," he said. "And where is your brother?"

Instead of telling the truth, or even a lie, she went with a joke. "He can't cook," she said. "And he gets sick on a pedal boat, so he'd have been no use to you."

His smile warmed a fraction though it didn't really get wider. "And he hits people with chairs... and deals weed."

"I'm not giving you the best impression of my family, am I?"

"Can't be any worse than mine," he said. "I never knew my mom. My dad was a strict drunk who I spent most of my life trying to get away from or fighting. Jockey was more of a father to me. I used to go hide under his billet. For a long time, wherever he was going, I was going too... I got him in trouble more times than I can count. I never really got the point of stowing away quietly when I could be working for a crust."

"Must have been a hard life," she said.

"I had everything I needed," he said. "My dad tried his best to make sure I got an education. When I did go to school they were always the best. I tried to stick it for a while, but I was always happier on the water... and there's a lot to learn out there."

Sassi had only spent a day on the water and she was getting that impression already. "I can't wait to find out."

Scooping both hands around his bottle, he pushed all the plates to the edge of the table, and when the waitress came to clear them, he ordered more beer, though Sassi was still nursing her first. "You've really never been out on the water before?" She shook her head. "Did you feel sick today?" Again, she shook her head. "It's good that you don't get seasick."

"Yeah, 'cause then how could I feed you?"

"That and it dehydrates you, so you can get really sick."

That didn't sound like fun. "I lost my balance a

few times."

"Don't worry about that, you'll get your sea-legs in time. We're not in hurricane season, the weather should be just fine. I'll try to keep her as steady for you as I can."

"Hurricanes, oh God…"

"It's ten days, sailing through the Caribbean and down the South American coast, some of the most beautiful waters there are… you'll be okay. Me and the crew will keep you safe… If you want to jump ship, now's the time to—"

"No," she said. "No, I'm looking forward to this. What happens at the end of the ten days?"

"We'll spend about the same amount of time diving the wreck, surveying whatever's left down there, and building an inventory, then we sail back the way we came."

Karen had said that Swain ran a salvage company. "Diving the wreck? You're going to salvage something?"

"We'll pick up a few things to bring back for the client, just as proof we found the wreck. But we have to figure out what's down there. We'll take pictures, map the site, do all the recce work, then we come back and negotiate a price for salvage. The client wants his cargo back, but we want our cut. Until we know what's down there, we won't settle on a fee."

It was more complicated than she'd thought, but made sense. "And after you agree on a price?"

"We sail back down and do the job."

"How long does that take?"

"Depends what's down there… and the weather, tides, currents, the exact location, lots of factors. They affect the price too, but we could be looking at a big payout. The client is eager to get the salvage underway."

"There's so much to think about."

"There sure is," he said. "Now you know about what I do, tell me how you got so good in the galley."

TEN

SASSI DIDN'T NOTICE the number of people in the bar increasing as the hours passed; she didn't notice the music getting louder. She did learn more than she'd ever thought she'd need to know about running a salvage operation and diving wrecks in all kinds of different conditions.

She also revealed more about her business and her trade than she'd ever discussed with anyone else. The captain hadn't been pissed off that she was a pastry chef. In fact, he seemed impressed that she'd run her own business so successfully for so long.

Captain Swain said it explained a lot, but that as long as she could cook regular chow, he had no problem with her making sweet treats for the crew.

When he explained how meal times were often the highlight of the crew's life, she felt better about her ability to treat them with things that they might not have expected to get.

The captain's arm swept over the table and he caught her hand in a gesture that seemed almost accidental. "I've got to hit the head, you okay here a minute?" She nodded. They had drunk a lot of beer. He'd had twice as much as she had, or more, but he didn't seem drunk at all. "Anyone comes near, you scream for Aruba, and I'll be here, okay?"

Her lips twisted, he was referring to what she'd said to him in her cabin. "Aye, aye, Captain."

"You love saying that," he muttered to himself and actually took her knuckles to his lips for a brief second as he stood to stride off to the bathroom.

What a surprise! The captain could hold a conversation, more than that, he was interesting to talk to and a good listener. The man's first impulse had been to scare her off when they met, but now, he was listening as she spoke. Learning about her. Sharing.

"Cozy over here."

The accented masculine voice startled her. Pello, one of Dario's men, sank onto the bench at her side. "Go away, Pello," she said, sliding away.

He advanced on her, pinning her in with one hand on the back of the bench and the other on the tabletop. Pushing closer, he moved down the bench toward her, forcing her to pin herself against the wall. "You're Dario's puta."

"I'm Dario's nothing," she said, forgetting for a minute to shrink, she shoved his shoulders. "And you tell him to keep his hounds off my ass. What the fuck are you doing following me?" And how had he managed it when she'd come by sea?

"I'm looking for your dog of a brother," Pello said, sneering at her with disgust all over his face. "I come here to this dirty hole looking for him and I find you."

There was nothing she could do to escape. He'd blocked her in, and was squashing her to the wall. She couldn't scream, couldn't get away, couldn't—

Pello's disgust cleared to surprise when he was hauled away and thrown against the post at the end of the bench. Sassi was still sort of dazed by the sudden move too, but got with it when she saw that a furious Swain was the one who'd got hold of Pello.

She pounced onto her feet on the seat and darted down to lunge over Pello, literally catching Swain's fist before he could land a punch.

"No!" she screamed. "Don't hit him, Captain!"

"Capitan," Pello said, the weedy guy was probably in fear for his life, but if Swain hurt a man so close to Dario, he'd be put on a list no one wanted to be on. "What is it that you captain?"

"Nothing," she said, leaping off the bench to squeeze herself between the men. "He captain's nothing, it's just a nickname. He's nothing. Please, Pello… you don't want to do this."

The last time she'd felt fear this strong was when her father's hand had grown limp in hers. It was the moment she'd known her daddy was gone. Her hands were shaking and she swallowed hard, but it made no difference to the lump in her throat.

Pello's disgust returned. "You're lucky you're not my mission, puta."

"Right," she said, clinging to that and nodding her head. "I'm not."

"If you come to him with this captain's child in your belly, he'll beat it from you," Pello said and when he dared touch a fingertip to her temple, it was Swain's arm that came around her to swipe it away. "In six weeks, you'll belong to us."

Swain's presence gave Sassi courage. Pello was a coward, even if he was good at faking otherwise. Steeling herself, Sassi gathered her disgust for this man's boss. "There's a chance that in six weeks you'll be taking your orders from me." Because if she was Dario's wife, she'd be thrust into a position of power and influence she'd never craved. "You remember that… friend."

Grabbing for the captain's hand, she about-faced to see he was glaring over her at Pello, with a malice pure as the black night bleeding from him. She shivered having never seen malevolence so potent and focused on one subject.

"Can we get out of here?" she asked, hoping that the captain wouldn't make more of this. Pello would have reserves he could call on, probably right here in this room, they weren't as lucky.

Swain threw a heavy arm around her shoulders and pulled her away, keeping his hatred on Pello until the last possible second. He dragged her across the room, out the door and in the direction of Eros.

As soon as they were out of sight of the bar, Sassi pushed away from his arm and picked up her pace. "What the fuck was that about?" he called after her.

Sassi moved as fast as she could without actually breaking into a run. "We have to get out of here fast," she said, skipping forward a few steps. Without slowing down, she bent over to tug off her shoes, and looped their straps around her wrist. "He won't be alone and we can't let ourselves be followed." When she didn't hear any response, she turned to glance over her shoulder and was dismayed to find the captain had stopped dead. "What are you doing? Move!"

"You forget who gives the orders around here?" he asked. "If you've endangered me or my crew…"

Sassi stopped too. The bottom fell out her stomach. "Shit. You're right."

She'd been heading back to Eros, but she couldn't go there, she couldn't take the risk that they would be followed. If she didn't make the money to pay off Dario, he'd vowed to come after anyone she cared about. She couldn't let that include Eros' crew.

All of her possessions were on the ship, but material things didn't matter, and she didn't own anything of real value.

Rushing back to the captain, she had to throw herself on his mercy. "A day pro-rated is a couple of hundred bucks, but a hundred will do... do you have a hundred bucks?"

"You want me to give you a hundred dollars?"

"I'll settle for seventy-five," she said, clinging to the front of his shirt. "Fifty? Just enough for a bus ticket back home." Her shoulders fell as her fingers loosened against his abs. "Home." There was nothing back where she'd come from. She couldn't rely on Karen, who'd already done more than enough by finding this job that Sassi had been smart enough to wreck after a day. "Damn it, I knew I should've stayed on the ship."

Sassi wasn't even thinking when she sighed and let herself lean on her captain, not until he put his arms around her and she felt the weight of the world leave her shoulders. All he was doing was holding her, but for some reason, it made her feel better.

Tears pricked her eyes. Damn it. She hadn't cried when her father died. Hadn't cried when Dario caught up with them that first time after the funeral and almost put a blade through Stuart's eye...

Sassi had kept it together, because losing grip of her emotions wouldn't accomplish anything.

"Waif," Captain Swain said, his voice softer than she'd ever heard it. "Are you in trouble? Not criminal, cops kinda trouble... are you in serious trouble?"

Giving in to one truth, she let her head fall back so she could look at him. "Not for another six weeks."

"What happens in six weeks?" he asked, but that was a question she couldn't bring herself to answer. Somehow, he got the answer he needed in her gaze because his grew more intense until he slowly nodded.

"Okay, I got it… We better hustle."

With his arm around her again, he began to guide her on the route she'd been hurrying before. "Hustle?" she asked. "I can't come back to work. I can't. If Pello or his guys follow us—"

"What?" he asked, holding her against his side and moving faster than even she had before. "They can't get passed security on the dock. Even if they do and they board my ship without permission, they're trespassing… and they're on our turf."

Our turf, not his, but *theirs.* He'd told her that afternoon that she was a part of his crew, but she hadn't realized what he meant. Now she felt the loyalty.

One meal with the captain and she was in.

He trusted her. It made no sense to her why, maybe he was just arrogant enough to believe he could take on any fight. Yet, hadn't she been the one to think about how he'd always win in any fight he took on? But she didn't want him taking on her battles. If any of the Eros crew got hurt, it would be her fault.

He took her back to Eros, carried her onboard, and didn't put her down until she was in her cabin. Issuing her orders, the captain told her to lock her door and stay inside until it was time for her to make breakfast. Then he'd touched the tip of his finger to the end of her nose and his gaze had met hers. In that moment, Sassi had known that if it came to it within the next four weeks, he'd protect her life with his own.

ELEVEN

WHEN SASSI'S ALARM went off the following morning, it didn't take long for memories of the previous night to put her on her feet. But her fear was quickly dispelled when she heard the rumble of the engine. It was five AM, first breakfast should be at six thirty. But when she ran to what Foist had told her was actually called a porthole, at the back of her room, she saw the distinctive lights of Miami fading away.

Showering fast, like there was a timer on the water, she threw on her clothes without drying her hair and ran out into the corridor. The mess was dark, most of the lights were off, and she didn't want to start banging on doors. So she kept on looking.

Rushing to deck, she ascended until she darted into the wheelhouse. Captain Swain was there with two guys she didn't recognize. The captain turned around when the two strangers looked at her. She found that the captain's eyes were a familiar shade of black annoyance. Was it the daylight that pissed him off? The sun wasn't here yet, but it was nearing the horizon.

"Sassi, this is Tune and Hector, they're part of our dive team and will take watch… guys this is Sassi, our cook… she's something special in the kitchen… or so the crew say."

She forced a brief smile to the new crew members, then stepped toward Captain Swain. "We left early."

"Yep," he said. "Captain's prerogative. Don't worry, all hands and supplies are on board." His displeasure slid down her figure. "You'll want to get your new uniforms from the mess."

Because she would look a riot with her hair all pulled onto her head and her baggy uniform hanging off her shoulder again. "Aye, aye, Captain," she said, but he didn't show the same familiar amusement that he had last night.

Was he pissed at her? He should be; he was leaving six hours ahead of schedule or thereabouts. The divers had come on board early. He'd have had to chase up the supplies that were being brought on board for her and no one else. She'd created nothing but havoc and she'd only been on his crew for twenty-four hours.

"Something else, Robins?" he demanded of her when she didn't move.

"Can I have a minute?" she asked, ducking backward, trying to ignore the new guys' surprise.

The captain cursed and mumbled something to the guys before marching over to grab her arm so he could haul her out onto the deck at the top of the stairway. "What?" he snapped.

"You didn't sleep last night, did you?" she asked and reached for his stubble, but he stepped back and then grabbed her upper arms to urge her backward until her spine was on the railing furthest from the wheelhouse door.

"Anyone asks, last night didn't happen,

understand?"

She nodded. "We left early—"

"Because I decided to. It's my decision, no one else's. This is my damn ship, my damn crew. I don't have to justify my decisions to anyone."

The crew had expected to have the morning in Miami. Rounding them up wouldn't have been easy, especially if any of them had hooked up. It had probably been their plan to still be out drinking. Yet here they were, back onboard, underway already.

"You did this for me," she murmured.

It took him a minute, but he eventually offered something of an explanation. "You called Eros a ship. Last night, after we left the bar."

Had she? If she had, she didn't realize she'd done it. "And that's why you did this for me?"

He let her go. "Don't you have something to go cook? The guys will be hungover." But she couldn't stop looking at him, no one had ever done something so decisive for her. This wasn't in his interest or his crew's, it served her, and he'd done it without her even asking him to. "Turn to, Waif."

"Aye, aye, Captain," she said and this time, when they were alone, he let a faint glint of amusement touch his expression.

That was it! They were alone!

Jockey had been with them last night, but Swain had explained his relationship with his first-mate, and she understood their closeness. Jockey had probably seen Swain in every state, happy, sad, angry, elated. Captain Swain didn't have to be so guarded around the first-mate and for some reason, he'd decided he didn't have to be guarded around her.

Except now he was more than her captain, already he was her friend, and he might never know it, but she owed him her life.

TWELVE

OVER THE NEXT four days, Sassi settled into her groove with the crew and with the captain. The schedule made it easy for her to please these men. All it took was a few made-to-order cookies; even the captain was a fan of her baking now.

He had less to say about her apparel too, given that her new uniform fit her. Having been given free rein to order what she wanted, her selection of Swain branded gear was more wide-ranging than the rest of the crew's. Sassi had polo shirts, tank tops, plain scoop neck tee-shirts, and lower cut V-necks too. She had pants and shorts, and even a couple of tennis skirts.

The crew had complained about her extensive choice in a good-hearted way. Swain had commented that that's what he got for handing a woman his credit card and telling her to shop.

It was a figure of speech. He hadn't really given her his credit card, she'd filled out the order form. After listing all the product codes on the sheet, she'd half expected Jockey to come back to her to say that she'd picked too many things. But he must have been feeling playful that day too because he'd emailed it to the vendor without question. She'd gotten everything she requested.

Sassi had felt bad when she saw the number of items, and had promised herself that she'd pay the captain back. Once she was gone, he'd probably have no use for any of the clothes. As time went on and she got to like her role and her crewmates more, Sassi thought about asking him if she could keep an item or two as mementos. But thinking of leaving the ship saddened her so much that she pushed thoughts like that away almost as soon as they popped into her mind.

Given that they were in some of the most beautiful waters in the world, and all the men were used to having her around, Sassi decided to take advantage of the free time she had that afternoon. The captain had reacted badly the last time she treated his ship like a cruise liner, but he didn't yell at her when she flirted anymore, so she guessed a lot of things had changed.

Donning her black bikini, Sassi grabbed her towel and made her way out to the bow. Once there, Sassi flattened her towel and lay down to relax in the sunshine, and ended up being there for so long that she yawned and thought about taking a nap.

Yep, she figured that the captain had to be okay with her chilling out. The wheelhouse had the perfect view of where she was. Tune and Hector were one watch team, while Jockey and Foist were the other. But the captain spent most of his time up there, working and regularly relieving the other men.

"Uh… Sassi…"

Fidget's uncertain voice made her tip back her head and lift her sunglasses. "What's wrong, honey?"

The youngster was working a short piece of rope in his hands and wanted to look anywhere except at her face. "Captain says you… you have to report to him in the wheelhouse, like… now."

Report to him? "Does he have a dinner request?" she asked. Fidget liked to look, and he laughed at her jokes, but he wasn't so great at the quips. Giving him a break, Sassi got up, taking her towel with her.

When she was on her feet, she cupped his cheek. "Thanks, honey."

While walking past Fidget, Sassi deliberately looked up at the wheelhouse and opened her arms in question. Swain couldn't respond, but he had to be on watch.

Sassi found she was right when she got up there. Putting a hand on either side of the doorframe, she leaned in to the wheelhouse without stepping in. The captain wasn't just there, he was alone up there.

The captain had other ideas. "Inside," Swain growled without taking his eyes from the sea ahead. "Close the door."

Stepping into the wheelhouse, Sassi closed the door for the first time ever. "Are you okay?"

Leaving his seat, he took his time to scrutinize her. "Why don't you tell me what fucking game you're playing so I can win it? Then you can move onto something else to keep you entertained."

She didn't like his cold attitude and didn't expect it either. Since Miami she'd felt like they were growing closer. They had trust and had shared some of their histories, she respected him and didn't know why he was acting like this when there was no one else around.

Confused, she didn't even sass him. "I don't know what I did. I'm not playing a game."

"On your first day aboard, weren't you ordered to stay in uniform?"

Maybe she'd misjudged how he'd react to her mischief, but she pushed one shoulder back to show him the Swain name embroidered on the material over her left breast. "I am in uniform," she said, and bit her bottom lip to hide her smile. "I've got your name on my ass too."

Turning around, she showed him the seat of the bathing suit. Sassi wasn't quick to turn back; she wasn't sure she wanted to see his reaction if it was going to be a negative one.

The last thing she expected to feel was the heat of his hard body moving against her spine, stealing her breath as he was so good at doing. His fingertips touched the balls of her shoulders. She bit her lip harder when they skimmed down her arms to her wrists.

Sassi wouldn't have expected such a brash man to have such a delicate touch. His fingers circled her wrists, their intention seemed so benign, at least it did until he clenched his fists hard around them and yanked her hands up to plant them flat on the door she'd just closed.

"You wanted my attention," he said, his mouth hovering just above her crown. "You've got it now… What are you gonna do with it, Waif?"

Did she want his attention? Sassi could argue that sunbathing on the deck many levels beneath the one he was on wasn't a way of getting his attention. She might say she had no idea he was up here, alone, in the isolated wheelhouse and in truth, she hadn't given it much thought. But, if she had, it wouldn't have taken much effort to figure out that he would see her.

Instead of insulting him with a denial, Sassi embraced the stirring arousal that was making her dizzy and dancing across her skin. She had his attention, oh God, he was admitting that she was on his mind. Sassi liked it. Damn her for it, but she did.

"I don't know," she whispered.

His palms opened on the back of her hands, pressing them harder. The power of his strength made her arch her hips, pushing her ass back into his thighs. He growled, resting his face in her hair, he bent his knees to line his groin up with her wriggling butt.

It was when she felt the thick, hard evidence of his reaction to her that she admitted to herself that his attention had been her goal. The bikini had been supposed to be a bit of a joke, she hadn't expected him to have this reaction to it. Maybe in her wildest fantasy he would've taken notice; he would've grabbed her and kissed her and made her submit to his carnal orders. But she could never have dreamed that this could be their reality.

Captain Swain always held it together. He always had his ship and his crew on his mind. Duty and responsibility were at the forefront of his actions. Sassi assumed that he'd found a way to block out his baser masculine needs; the ones that had preoccupied her dreams more frequently with every passing day.

But they'd been four days at sea, five if they counted the one before Miami, and he hadn't gotten any that night, she knew that for sure. Maybe this was when he started to feel the urge.

His control until now had been ironclad, and boy had she tried pushing his buttons. It was wrong to want him, to crave the touch of her superior. But, right then, as her ass rocked against his erection, she was pleased he was giving her what she needed.

His long fingers curled around her hips, gripping her so tight that she could feel his fingerprints imprinting themselves on her. He hadn't told her to move her hands, so she kept them flat on the door and she pushed back harder.

With her eyes closed and her lips parted to accommodate her shallow pant, Sassi stopped breathing completely when he tugged the string at her hip loose, leaving the lower part of her bathing suit teetering on a single hip bone.

One of his hands drifted over her hip, following the line where her bikini briefs should've been. It paused there, pressing flat to her lower abdomen beneath her belly button.

"The sun hasn't set," he whispered into the top of her head. It was a wonder such an abrupt man could make her laugh, but a whisper of one managed to escape her. "But if I say pretty please…"

"Yes," she exhaled, forgetting her laughter. All she felt now was urgent need. "Yes, Captain, please."

"If we're gonna be doing this stuff, it should probably be Swain." Her eyes opened and though he couldn't see her smile, it didn't matter, her happiness was for her. He'd never given her that permission before and she'd never called him that. "Unless… does the captain thing work for you?"

Making her own executive decision, she spun around, catching herself with her arms around his neck, holding him in a way she never had. "What if the pirate thing works?"

He sneered. "What if I tell you to swab the deck every day for the rest of the trip?"

Tightening the circle of her arms, she drew him lower. "I can think of something more productive to do on the deck."

His lips were just a whisper away from hers when the intercom squawked. "Cap'n?" Jockey's voice echoed through the room.

Talk about a mood killer.

Swain's eyes closed and he bared his teeth before smacking a palm on the door behind her.

"Fuck," he hissed.

"You there, cap'n?"

Letting her go, Swain stalked over to the intercom, casting an eye over the water as he did.

Nothing out there, nope, nothing for miles.

"What is it, Jockey?" he snapped, watching her retie the strings at her hip.

"You need relief up there?" Jockey asked.

With his elbows locked to straighten his arms and his hands flat on the counter under the intercom, Swain let his head fall as he muttered. "You have no idea." But he did glance at her for long enough to see her smile before he poked the button on the intercom again. "No, I've got another two hours up here."

"Just thought, maybe, you know, with Robins up there…"

She gasped and bounced forward a step. "Can they see us?" she whispered, looking around for any kind of spy cam.

"No, just Fidget can't keep his mouth shut."

So the youngster liked to gossip. He was the only one who knew they were in here… alone. He'd wasted no time in telling someone. Jockey probably thought he was doing them a favor, but she could see the abandon leave the captain's attention as it slid over her.

"Will you go below decks and put some clothes on for me, Waif?" he asked and she nodded, pushing her lips to one side. She hadn't meant to guilt him with her disappointment, but he pushed off his hands to straighten up and explain. "I'm in the wheelhouse, alone on watch…"

"I know," she said, nodding. "You don't owe me anything."

His teeth stayed together as his lips moved and his eyes devoured her. "Then why the hell do I feel like I do?"

Sashaying over to him, Sassi let her smile grow sultry. "That's probably your dick doing the feeling," she said, opening her palm over the shaft still thick and insistent in his pants. Pressing into him, she stroked his length once, then again, impressed by both his length and his girth. But he was big everywhere else, it would be a disappointment if his dick didn't follow the trend. She sighed. "Maybe some other time."

When she turned away, he snatched her wrist and hauled her back to him, taking Sassi so by surprise that she gasped.

"Standing behind me, when you flirt with the crew," he said. "You do that for protection, right?" She nodded. "That what this is?"

"For protection?"

Yes, she flirted with him more than anyone else, and tended to stick close to his physical presence when it was available. And she was more forward when he was around because she knew he'd always step in if anyone got the wrong idea of what she was saying or implying. But that didn't explain her instinctive urge to fantasize about submitting to him or her desire to feel his touch.

"Is it?" he asked.

"You'd protect me whether I was attracted to you or not... whether I have sex with you or not... wouldn't you? I don't need to share my body with you to be safe... In fact..." She paused before disclosing a revealing truth. "I have a feeling I'd be safer if I stayed the hell away from you..."

"You're probably right about that," he said, touching her nose. "Put on some clothes... The rest of the crew don't get to enjoy the Captain's girl, not ever... we clear?"

Suddenly, just like that, she was his girl, when they hadn't even kissed? Why in the hell was she nodding? Why did she feel that fizzing in her hips and across her breasts? Why were butterflies dancing and multiplying in her belly?

But that statement was his way of telling her they'd get there. He was letting her know that he was interested and that if she thought about dallying with any other member of the crew, there would be no chance of an intimate future for them. The captain's girl had to be held to a high standard, almost as high a standard as the one he held himself to.

This was complicated and insane. It could never be anything, and she'd be smart to stay celibate until she knew whether or not she had a future. But Sassi didn't want to disappoint him, and the fantasy of believing, even for a minute, that she could belong to him, was too powerful to resist.

THIRTEEN

THE FOLLOWING NIGHT, close to midnight, when the men were engrossed in their poker game in the mess and digging into their second cheesecake of the day, Sassi slipped out onto the deck.

One of her favorite spots in the night was standing against the rail outside her cabin's porthole that faced the back of the ship. She left the main passageway to get to the deck that swept around three sides of the superstructure. It was so quiet and calming that she felt like the only person on earth when she was there.

When she'd boarded Eros, she'd had no idea that after just six days on board, she would feel this intensely about the vessel or the voyage.

Standing there, contemplating her life, Sassi didn't hear the captain coming toward her. Even when she became aware of him when he propped a hip on the railing beside her, she didn't turn, but she did speak.

"I love that smell," she said. "I've lived by the ocean all my life, but it's different out here."

"There's nothing like it," Swain said and caught

a loose section of her hair that was flapping in the breeze. As soon as she felt the tension of him holding it, she reached up to take it from him to tuck it away with the rest on top of her head. "Are you ready to talk?"

Ready to talk? That wasn't what she assumed he'd sought her out to do. "Is that why you came looking for me? To talk?"

Glancing sideways at him, Sassi expected to see guilt, instead, his expression remained steadfast. "It's been five days since we left Miami. Your trouble didn't follow us. I thought you'd be pleased; that you'd relax the further away we got… but you seem more tense these last couple of days."

"It doesn't have to follow me," she said, wrapping her arms around herself. "It'll wait for me… I'm glad your crew is safe, and Eros too, but distance doesn't matter. We can put as many miles as you want between me and land. Time is what's against me. Every second that passes takes me one second closer to…"

"To what?" he asked, sidling closer. "What is it you're into?"

"It doesn't matter," she said and tried to turn away, but he caught her elbow to hold her in place.

"It matters if it's screwing with your head. I need you focused."

Getting defensive, Sassi didn't appreciate him implying that her work was sub-standard. "Have I slipped?" she asked, making eye contact. "Have there been complaints about the meals?"

"That's not why I need you focused."

Standing there in the dark night, staring into him, she wished she could regain that high she'd felt in the wheelhouse when she'd let herself believe the fantasy. "You don't know who I am, not really," she said. "I signed on for four weeks and four weeks is all you'll ever get from me, after that, I'm gone."

"Gone where?" he asked with a real sense of urgency like he was desperate to know, desperate for her to let him in. "Are you telling me someone wants to hurt you?"

That hadn't been what she was saying, but she could see how he took her statement that way. Sassi had meant that the captain wouldn't see her again. But he wasn't wrong to suspect there was potential danger in her future.

"He won't hurt me," she said, seeking the water, but it was just a black void at night. Only the scent of the spray and the beat of the waves on the hull betrayed that they were on the ocean at all. "I can't promise I won't hurt myself."

That, to her, was an inevitable truth. She doubted she'd last long as Dario's wife.

Swain didn't know the details of what they were talking about, so it was easy for him to be more optimistic. "Right," he said, lunging over to grab her other elbow to spin her around to face him. "I won't hear talk like that. You're my responsibility—"

"Not after we're back home," she said. "After that, it's every man for himself."

He shook her. "I want to help."

Her captain could be infuriating, but she held onto her patience. "You can't help."

"Don't be a martyr. Someone must be able to do something."

"My brother was the only other person capable of stopping this… but he's too much like my father."

"Where is he?"

"I don't know," she said. "That's just it, Captain, I don't have a clue."

Turning to the stern again, she hoped she hadn't signed her brother's death warrant by leaving the States. If Dario knew she was on this ship, that she wasn't on land any more, he might think that she was fleeing. That could lead to him assuming that catching up with Stuart was his only chance of receiving any repayment.

Sassi tried to reassure herself that Dario wouldn't kill his only chance of getting his money back. Stuart was resourceful; he could talk himself out of any mess. She had to believe that. Maybe he could offer to do work for Dario… Except, she didn't want her brother signing his future away.

All Stuart had to do was keep breathing until she got back, then she could fix everything. Dario would have his money and they'd walk away clean. Whatever they'd had to do to stay alive, they'd just never mention it again. It would be like the whole sorry affair never happened.

After that, she could build up her business again. Stuart could get back together with Karen. In short, they could return to the lives they'd had before their father screwed it all up.

Swain's fingers loosened for the briefest second before they tightened again. He pulled her forward, shaking her from her drifting thoughts. Blinking at him, she knew what he planned when he began to dip lower.

But she quickly dropped her chin and put a hand to his chest. "That stunt with the bikini, I'm sorry, it was… I didn't think it through, I shouldn't have played around like that. It was immature. I don't know what I was thinking."

"You were thinking you wanted my attention," he said. "You've had it since you stepped aboard, I was too stubborn to show you."

Something about being alone with him in the night air was screwing with her common sense. Lifting her chin, Sassi met his gaze. The softness in his eyes that he hid whenever he was on duty, whenever there were others around, was shining down on her. It wasn't softness like she might see in other men. But, by the gruff captain's standard, it was outright romantic that he'd grant her his complete focus like this.

And it was so nice, such a testament to his character, that he at least asked about helping her, even if the situation was hopeless without her bonus. Sassi couldn't, and wouldn't, ask him about that. Money was a dirty subject that just made her feel sick.

Her father spent his life going from one creditor to another, and she'd had no idea just how close he'd come to losing a kneecap or an eye so many times. Not until after he was gone. Though she hadn't put voice to it yet, Sassi had a sinking expectation that Dario wasn't the only one who'd be calling in outstanding debts. Soon they'd all be coming out of the woodwork.

Swain began to bow again, more slowly. Sassi knew she should be pushing the captain away, knew she should step back, should send out a firm signal that this would never happen between them, not ever.

But the fantasy began to play in her mind's eye again.

The fantasy of the gruff overbearing captain, who it turned out actually had a heart, taking control of her body, of her heart and her destiny.

At the same time his lips made contact with hers, Sassi exhaled and let her eyes close. A kiss. Something about the basic gesture of their two mouths coming together for the first time erased all kinds of trouble from her mind.

Contact with him had made her feel invincible like this before; his touch gave her security. Even as his lips parted and his entitled tongue advanced into her mouth, she didn't feel threatened. Sassi wanted to grab hold of him, to kiss him harder, to pull him to her, and to beg him to take her to his cabin.

It was just insane that she was letting this happen.

Stepping back, she touched her lips and rushed away to press her forehead against the cold metal wall under her porthole. "What are you doing, Sassi," she whispered to herself. "You don't kiss the captain."

"No," Swain said, his deep, certain voice approaching behind her. Grabbing her shoulder, he pulled her around and ducked down to her level. "But you let him kiss you."

Snatching her face in both his hands, he hauled her up to steal her mouth again. Pressing her hard against the wall, he made no apology for the fervor of his mouth that devoured hers in a deep kiss that grew more intense as he slanted to get closer.

This was exactly the kind of insanity that she shouldn't be getting involved with. This man was her boss. She'd be on this ship for little more than another three weeks and after that she'd never see him again.

He was so strong, so determined in his certainty. Swain knew where he belonged, knew where he was going and what he wanted from life and there was something alluring about that. Those attributes were almost as attractive as his determined arrogance. The stubbornness that bled from him betrayed how he'd never be swayed against his will.

Even the power of the ocean didn't set him off his feet. Sassi struggled to keep her balance on deck, but Swain never flinched.

Raucous noise around the corner made the captain break their kiss and just as he turned toward the sound to tuck her at his back, Swing came around the corner with Fidget in tow.

"Hey, Captain!" Swing declared. "We got another hand going!"

Cowering behind him was wrong. She'd used his protection before, and she wasn't sure he liked it when she did. Stepping out of the shelter of his body heat, away from his spine, Sassi put space between them. Swain reached back, seeking her out, but he didn't turn, which gave her the opportunity to avoid his grip.

"Deal me out," the captain said.

Sassi couldn't let this affair happen, she couldn't. Retreating from the men, she kept on going until she could sneak around the opposite corner and make her way to her cabin through the port entrance to the passageway.

She managed to get past the mess where Jockey and Foist were talking and into her room without facing anyone else.

"Shit," she said to herself and began to strip off so she could slip into a cold shower.

Screwing with any man when Dario had her in his sights was crazy. Swain might be capable, but Dario had manpower on his side and the element of surprise.

Stuart had broken Karen's heart because they couldn't risk her getting hurt. Sassi couldn't care about anyone, not now when their lives were in danger. She couldn't be responsible for the downfall of a giant like Swain.

Except as the water cascaded over her, she feared she already cared about him, and the Eros crew, enough that she'd already put them in danger.

FOURTEEN

ROLLING THE SPICE tin along the inside of her thumb and up the length of her index finger, Sassi stared out of the galley porthole toward the bow and the ocean beyond.

"Waif?" She kind of heard something, but was too lost in her daze to pull herself back to reality. "Sassi?"

Someone grabbed her shoulder and turned her around; she had to blink a few times to bring Swain into focus. She fixated on him for a couple of seconds before noticing Jockey seating himself in the mess.

Clearing her throat, she tried to remember what she'd been doing before drifting into her daze. Day eight on the water, lunch time, everyone had eaten except the captain and the first-mate.

"Oh," she said. "I was supposed to bring you lunch in the wheelhouse, what are you doing down here?"

"That was nearly an hour ago," Jockey called across the room.

Swain's palm on her cheek redirected her

attention to him. "What's on your mind?"

"Nothing," she said, shaking her head once, but her thoughts began to coast again when her eyes landed on his lips. "Only things that shouldn't be."

"Hmm," he said in such a gruff tone she snapped out of her musing again. "As long as that's all." To her surprise, he brushed his thumb across her lips before he began to retreat. "Feed us, Waif, we're hungry."

Jockey was unfolding one of the newspapers that he'd got from the wooden slot between the back of the bench he was sitting on and the wall. The papers were more than a week old, but they were all the guys had.

Swain sat at the head of the table, exactly where he was supposed to, and she went about making their food. Although Sassi knew better than to get distracted, she'd thought about little except her kiss with the captain the night before last.

Sassi had always been a fan of kissing, but Swain's kiss was unique; so forceful in its desire, so unapologetic and demanding. Somehow, he made her feel like the greatest treasure he could ever plunder. A smile curled her lips as she built the sandwiches and filled bowls with warm pasta. She'd never been kissed by a pirate, had never thought it was a possibility, and there she was about to serve lunch to one.

As amusing and titillating as that part of his past was, it wasn't the reason her thoughts kept floating back to him. Sassi didn't want Swain because he'd been bad once upon a time long ago; she wanted him for what he was now. Steadfast, committed, and loyal, he was the kind of decent guy who got his priorities straight and didn't waver from them.

"Foist says you charter other ships, Captain. He says you have a fleet," she said, taking them their pasta. "How many do you have?"

"Six," he said, digging into the pasta almost

before she'd put it down on the table.

She didn't know if she should feel guilty for delaying their meals or flattered that he was so eager to dig in.

"And he has his eye on a pair of beauties in New York too," Jockey said, winking when she gave him his food.

Swain tipped his chin up to catch some pasta sauce. "Nah, that's not gonna happen."

Jockey looked real disappointed. Sassi went to retrieve their sandwiches, then got Jockey his soda and Swain his coffee. "Why not?" she asked, resting a hand on the captain's shoulder as she poured java into his mug.

"My year's full, don't have time to go up there and do an eyes-on inspection," the captain said, curving his fingers around the back of her knee to hold her still.

With the table blocking the view of the captain's hand on her leg, the connection was hidden from Jockey. But the meeting of their eyes stuck for so long, there was no way that the first-mate could've missed it.

"He has to do his own full assessment before he'll commit," Jockey said with a curious edge to his tone.

"Smart," she said, still ensnared by the captain's intense gaze. "When you're parting with that amount of money, you should see what you're getting."

"Money has nothing to do with commitment," Swain said. "I'm loyal to my girls. I don't take 'em on unless I know I can give them everything they need. I stick by 'em through everything."

"Your girls?"

"All my girls," he said, telling her that he wasn't only talking about the ships anymore by the tapering of his eyes.

Jockey coughed. "You know, some of the crew been talking."

Digging into his food again, Swain managed to multi-task. "Bout what?" he asked, tightening his hold on her leg.

"The cap'n and the cook," Jockey said.

Surprised he'd been so blatant in bringing it up, Sassi was sure her face began to flame while the first-mate did his best to assess both of them, probably looking for clues of their guilt. Swain was no help. Completely unruffled, he just kept on eating like they were talking about the weather, but she squirmed.

"Jockey, I…"

But Sassi had no answers for him, even she and the captain hadn't talked about what they were to each other.

"Mind if I ask what's going on?"

Sassi was going to say there was nothing going on, but Swain shifted to widen his thighs. Hooking a strong arm around her waist, the captain hauled her down onto his lap and she had to think fast not to spill the coffee in her hand all over his lunch.

"I claim what I want, you know it," Swain said. "She's my girl, and you can let anyone who asks know it."

As if sitting on his lap wasn't shocking enough, his declaration that they were an item was way premature. "Captain," she said, trying her best to untangle herself from his arm, but it was pointless to struggle. He was strong enough to wrestle her like she was a gnat not a threat.

Jockey laughed and slapped a hand on the table, startling Sassi. She stopped fighting the captain to look over at the exuberant first-mate. "I knew it! I knew you were sweet on each other that first night in Miami."

"I was pissed off that you set us up," Swain said. "Guess I should thank you now."

Jockey laughed again. "Guess you should. It's

been going on since then?" The first-mate assumed that they'd been sleeping together since the first night she'd spent on the ship? Sassi expected the captain to correct him, he didn't. "That why we shoved off early? So she couldn't change her mind about screwing with the pirate and run off back to her family?"

"Yeah, and what the fuck, Jockey," Swain said. "Quit telling folk about that."

"Worked out for you, son. Worked out for you." Jockey had already finished his pasta and half his sandwich. He grabbed the other half and his soda, and shuffled out from the bench. "You've snuck around long enough. I'll let you enjoy your quality time, won't take news this good long to travel."

Jockey's laugh echoed through the corridor and until it quieted, Sassi stayed on the captain's lap, absorbing what had just happened.

It was the scrape of his fork on the bottom of his pasta bowl that woke her up. "What did you do that for?" she asked and squeezed her fingers under his on her torso. She thought he'd let her go, instead, he curled his fingers around hers to hold her hand. "Now the crew will think I'm a whore!"

"Who on the crew have you made out with?"

"Well…" she said and toyed with his collar, deliberately playing it coy to make him think twice about being presumptuous.

Dropping his fork into his bowl, Swain shoved it away so hard that it almost shot off the other end of the table. "Who? Was it Foist? That fucking cunt, I'll slit him bow to stern," he said and thrust up, forcing her onto her feet. "If Tune touched you, I'll toss him over and—"

"Ha," she said, blocking his way, driving both fists into his ribs. "See, you have the power to do all that stuff! When you piss me off, I can't do anything. You can do whatever the hell you like and I just have to take it! That is why I play with you! It's my way of evening the playing field."

Until she'd said it out loud, Sassi hadn't understood her own motivation. But it made so much sense. Swain had all the power, he was God on this ship, president, judge, overlord; she and everyone else onboard were subject to him.

Grabbing a handful of her hair, he yanked her head back to get down in her face. "I'll deal with you later, Waif."

The stinging in her scalp sped her heart and her thudding want for him. She inhaled, desperate for air that would fuel her desire.

Sassi didn't need sense, she needed satisfaction. "Deal with me now," she panted.

"Gimme their names," he hissed. "Who on the crew has kissed you?"

"You, Captain," she whispered, dragging her hands up and down his chest. "Only you."

Her breasts squashed into him and retreated as her chest moved with the need of her clamoring breath. "Keep it that way. That's an order."

The sexiest one he'd given her yet. She figured he must have sensed what his command did to her hormones, her attraction to him wasn't subtle. Coiling her arms around his neck, she held onto him when he scooped a rough hand over her cheek, through her hair to the back of her head. He gripped her hair tight in both hands to angle her head. Pulling it back, he planted his mouth over hers.

It was afternoon, still light outside, she had dinner in the slow cooker… she should be making dessert… Instead, Sassi was being rushed backwards into the galley and hoisted onto the counter, forced to accept the captain's hips between her thighs.

His mouth trailed down her neck. "Swain," she breathed out his name like it was a request.

The word inspired him to suck harder on her throat. Sassi yelped, filled with pleasure at the bruising force of his entitled mouth.

Getting a rush from the taste of her own creation on his tongue, she grabbed for the end of his shirt and pulled it up, trying to get access to his flesh. Her fingertips met the ridges of his abdomen and she lost her ability to be rational.

Her mind knew this was a stupid mistake. Her body and her heart didn't care. There. Two against one. Mind outnumbered.

"Miss Sassi, do—"

Fidget's voice stopped at the same time Swain tore his mouth from hers and spun on the youngster. "Out!" Swain roared.

Fidget's whole body shook in response to the captain's fury. Poor Fidget was trembling, stuck to the spot, wide-eyed and terrified.

"Wait, no," she said. "It's okay, Fidget, honey, he's sorry he shouted."

Swain turned his red-faced ferocity on her, he grabbed her thighs and yanked her to the edge of the counter. "No fucking way you're sneaking off this time, Waif."

Splaying her hands on his chest, her legs slid up and down the outside of his. Her eyes were round, her lips wet, and her need pounded in her ears. "Take me upstairs," she said, hoping he'd agree to take her in his private cabin above this public room.

His frown changed hue. Either he was surprised or it was taking him a minute to figure out that this was really happening. Snatching her hand, Swain hauled her off the counter and dragged her across the room, past the still frozen Fidget and out. He took her down to the end of the corridor and upstairs into his cabin.

When they were inside, he swung her around and immediately started to stalk forward, forcing her to retreat toward the bed. "For this job," she said, holding up her open hands. "I'm yours, any way you want me… But the minute we dock, that's it, we're strangers… You don't know me, you can't get involved. Don't ask questions. That's it. Over." Her calves hit the bed, but he kept on coming until he was pressed against her. "Those are my terms, Captain, tell me you accept because I really don't want to have to walk out of here."

Bending over, he hooked his hands behind her knees and lifted her to boost her onto the bed. "Like I'd fucking let you walk out," he said and grabbed his shirt at the back of his neck to pull it off before dropping down on top of her.

He must have known that his torso was her weakness. As soon as she got her hands on him, she thought of nothing else except the hot skin responding to her hands and the mouth consuming hers.

Stripping off her uniform with his capable hands, Swain seemed determined to get her naked. When she was in her underwear, he captured her hands to take them off his torso. He stretched them high over her head and locked them inside one of his fists. He tried to squeeze a hand around to her back to unhook her bra, but Sassi fought him, pushing herself down into the mattress.

His desire burned as hot as his fury and he growled at her, curling his lip to show his clenched teeth. He was actually holding back, he wanted to go faster, to take her harder. Her captain was restraining himself. But she didn't want that.

"Rip it," she said, her voice less than a whisper. "Tear it off."

This was the fantasy coming to life. No holding

back. He obliged. Grabbing the flimsy fabric and ripping it not only between the cups, but he tore off the straps too and flung the material over his head to descend and suck her nipple hard between her teeth.

Sassi yelped and writhed, screaming out his title and his name. She didn't want to be restrained, didn't want to think about consequences or right and wrong. This was Swain's territory and Sassi was desperate to be too. Why shouldn't she worship this man with the passion he wrung from her?

The need in her was so frenzied that the flick of his tongue sent her into orgasm. Her whole body tensed. "Swain," she panted and begged, but didn't really know what she wanted him to do. "Please, Captain, I... I can't... I'm done."

"No, you're fucking not," he said.

The sound of torn fabric again razed the air.

Parting her legs when his hips rose, Sassi expected to feel his dick, but his finger slid into her instead. It was thick, long, and skilled enough to torment her into another release.

She lost the rhythm of her breathing. One inhale was overtaken by the next, her eyes began to cross, and she thought she might pass out from endorphin overload. But just as she was sure she'd have to beg him for mercy, the weight of his body left hers.

As soon as he was gone, she wanted him back. "Swain," she said, pushing her hair up out of her blurred eyes.

"Don't fucking move, Waif."

Even if she tried, she couldn't. Sassi struggled just to roll her head to the side to watch him kicking off his boots and dropping his pants.

"Oh fuck," she muttered and might have heard the whisper of a satisfied laugh, but she couldn't take his eyes from his dick for long enough to check if it came from him or her masochistic subconscious.

Thick, solid, and ready for her, it was as intimidating as the man it was attached to. Sassi held her breath when the captain climbed back on top of her and kneed her thighs further apart.

Until now when they'd locked gazes there had been a curiosity that added to their intensity. Now it was all anticipation; their curiosity was about to be satisfied.

Sliding himself into her, Swain started slow, letting her adjust, to feel his length, to accommodate his girth, and probably to give himself a break too. Sassi had already come twice, the poor captain was falling behind. He'd be on the edge, she hoped he was on the edge, and didn't mind him taking the wheel. But she also didn't want him restraining himself for her sake.

Stroking his chest, up over his shoulders, she clasped the back of his neck and pulled him down for a kiss, then pulled him further, rubbing her cheek on his, letting her lips meet his ear. "Full speed ahead, cap'n," she whispered. Swain exhaled like he was grateful she'd given him the permission he needed. "You don't have to be gentle with me. I trust you."

When he slammed hard into her, she screamed at the unexpected impact of his hard body against her pelvis. Her hormones couldn't keep up, her belly squeezed around the delight and desire pumping through her, turning her sanity to soup that he could drink in at his will.

This wasn't like sex she'd had before. His primal need could only be sated by her. She knew it. He was using her body to satisfy himself, but she didn't feel used, Sassi was powerful. Fulfilling the desires of the man responsible for the lives of every person on board, and the very fabric of the vessel that kept them alive, was an intoxicating drug.

"Swain," she said, her voice getting higher. His

thrusts got faster and deeper; he pushed her into an orgasm that squeezed every muscle in her body tight. "Oh, fuck!"

Surging forward, he drove into her and cursed a string of obscenities that she'd never heard before, but she loved every one of them.

Her captain flipped over, landing on his back on the outside of the bed, leaving her by the wall. So they'd done it. Or rather, she'd done it. She'd had sex with the captain. With her boss. With a pirate. Except instead of feeling guilty or remorseful, she was invigorated and excited and overwhelmed with gratitude and hope.

Rolling toward him, Sassi kissed the black tattoo on the ball of his shoulder. "Do you have to get topside?"

"I have a minute," he said, lifting his arm from between them to put it around her.

Pulling her body against his, he squashed her breasts into his ribs. But he still hadn't looked into her eyes. Sassi had been the one to demand they put an expiration date on their relationship. Thinking about the way she'd done it, maybe the captain was thinking she'd been presumptuous. Maybe he hadn't wanted it to last beyond this encounter.

"Foist says we should arrive at our coordinates tomorrow night after dark," she said, spreading her hand on his stomach. "You think that's right?" He nodded. Hmm, usually if anything would get him talking, it was the job. "It's been a smooth trip."

"Got a chance of some weather on the way back," he said. "We might hang back an extra few days or we'll battle through it."

Extra few days. Curling her hand into a fist, her nails scratched his skin. Sassi was on a clock at the other end of the trip. She couldn't afford to waste any extra time on the ship, not when she still had funds to scrape together in the days she'd have on land before Dario's deadline. If she didn't get her bonus from this voyage, she'd still be fourteen thousand short. Dario might cut her some slack for a couple of thousand, but not almost half what he was owed.

Sitting up, Sassi drew up her knees and rubbed her face with both hands. The last thing she wanted to be thinking about when she was in bed with Swain was the possibility of walking down the aisle to Dario.

Swain stroked her back. "Don't worry about it, Waif. You'll be safe below decks."

Safety wasn't what was on her mind. "Will we get paid for extra days?" she asked, embarrassed that money had come up at all, let alone in bed after the first time they'd been intimate.

His hand stopped moving on her back. Sassi didn't want to, but she made herself peek over her shoulder. The scowl he wore made her heart drop. "Yeah. How much do you need?"

No, absolutely not. She was not going to take more money from him than she was owed for the work she did. That might not have been what he was implying, he was probably just curious about why she'd asked. Swain did have a history of trying to pry into her trouble.

Deciding there and then that she wouldn't let that part of her past or her future into this bubble with them, she threw her body on top of his and kissed him. "Are you hungry?" she asked, brushing her lips on his. "I've got cookies downstairs. Cake. Donuts... I can make melting cake... I made my own ice-cream yesterday, it should be set. You're not huge on chocolate... I can make bread and butter pudding or banana loaf..." An idea made her inhale. "Baked Alaska!"

But he grabbed her before she could leap up and sprint away. "You're staying right here."

"My baked Alaska is impressive," she said.

He combed his fingers through her hair and rolled her onto her back. "Impress me here."

"Is that sailor speak for a blow job?"

There was something of a smile on his lips as they danced over hers. He moved in like he was going to kiss her, but didn't. Swain, instead, tightened his grip on her body, and just slid his tongue along her lower lip. "Later. I'm not done with your pussy yet."

"You're not, huh?" she asked. His mouth skimmed down her neck and the heat of his breath prickled against the groove at the base of her throat. "Oh, Swain, my heart's ready to jump out my chest."

Sliding a hand up her body, he settled his fingers in her cleavage, resting his palm over her heart. "It's excited."

"'Cause of you," she said, "I never worried about surviving this voyage until the captain brought me to his bed."

"The cap'n followed the cook's orders," he said.

Accentuating her lower lip, she traced her fingertip down his hairline past his temple. "It was just a simple, little request, Captain. You were so generous to accommodate me."

Closing a hand around her breast, he enjoyed fondling her, squeezing and toying with the flesh he'd admired in her bikinis. "It's my job to look after my crew's needs."

"I'm so pleased I'm the only woman on your crew," she said and when his hand slid away from her chest, she pouted and grabbed it to put it back. "I like you doing that."

"Your tits are real responsive," he said, sucking in a breath then ducking down like he was about to dive beneath the water.

Kissing her nipple, he teased it with the tip of his tongue and sucked it against his tongue, making her laugh morph into a whimpering moan. "Oh, that's nice, baby," she purred, arching her back and running her hands into his black hair.

It was thick; soft between her fingers. Sassi liked how they disappeared into it, how her digits could sink into its sumptuous length that curled over his collar and around his ears. Sassi was so focused on what his mouth was doing that she didn't notice his hand sliding down between her thighs until he began to massage her clit with a fingertip.

"Mmm," she exhaled, her hips writhing against his torment. "Captain…"

"Captain."

She heard the word repeated and at first thought it came from her lips. But when she heard it again and realized the tone sounded masculine and that her own lips hadn't moved, she panicked and grabbed Swain's hair to pull him up.

"Swain, what is that?" she asked, her eyes darting around, trying to find the source of the voice.

"Intercom, baby. Stay put."

Vaulting up the bed, Swain stayed on his chest and stretched over to the box on the wall above the fixed nightstand. "I'm busy, Jock," he said after pressing the button.

"We picked up a pan-pan," Jockey said. "What you want to do?"

When Swain exhaled and muttered out a few curses, she stroked his upper arm. "What's a pan-pan?"

"Distress call," he said. "No imminent danger, but someone out there needs help." Reaching over again, he spoke into the intercom. "You make contact? Get any details?"

"Dead in the water," Jockey said.

She gasped and sat up. "Someone's dead?"

Twisting toward her, Swain smoothed her hair

that had fallen over her cheek. "The vessel, baby. Someone's not going anywhere fast. Either they're out of fuel or there's a mechanical issue."

Bringing her knees higher, she curled on her side facing him, and reached out to touch his chest. "And no one knows engines better than you," she said, scratching her nails in the hair on his chest. "Foist says your skills are unparalleled…" Curling her leg over his, she slid it up and down his thigh.

"Two minutes ago you were worried about being paid if we were out here too long, now you want to head off course?" he said, tensing up. It didn't take her man long to get crabby. "And the babygirl act doesn't work on me, I told you that the day we met."

Maybe not, though she wasn't convinced he wasn't swayed. Wriggling closer, she draped an arm around his neck and rose to brush her mouth on his. Pressing her chest into him, she whimpered and urged her mouth closer, opening his lips with her own and sinking her tongue into his mouth.

"Captain," she whispered and eased him onto his back so she could climb on top of him. "You wouldn't let anyone get hurt, would you? There's a captain out there with a crew in need. What if that was us?" She kissed him again and coiled her fingers around his erection. "I'd be mighty proud serving under a captain who cared so much… I'd sure want to impress him."

Slowly licking her lips, Sassi began to kiss her way down his body until she could close her lips around him.

As she sucked on him, learning how to please him, and how to make him feel good, she heard his voice again. "Change course and tell 'em we're on our way, Jock," he grumbled.

"You coming topside?" Jock asked.

Breathing in through her nose, she sucked her captain as far into her throat as she could and heard him groan. "Not for a million bucks," he mumbled.

"Cap'n?"

His body shifted, "Clear the channel, Jock. Fuck off. I'll be there in a minute."

When he relaxed again, his fingers combed through her hair on her crown. Still sucking and pleasuring him, Sassi reached up to tangle her fingers in his.

"Relax, Captain," she said, kissing his thigh and his groin, then the head of his dick. "Let me make you feel good."

FIFTEEN

SWAIN DID LET her finish. After she'd swallowed, Sassi crawled up his body and somehow ended up talking about the fantasies she'd had that starred him. But she'd only been talking for a few minutes when the deep rumble of his low snore made her look up to find he was asleep.

Sassi had trust in the other guys onboard to keep them on the right course and she guessed it would take time to rendezvous with this other vessel anyway. So it seemed right to give the captain a chance to rest. She used his shower to clean up, kissed him while he slept, and gathered up her clothes, though she had to sneak back to her own room to change her underwear.

After going to the galley, she buzzed Jockey in the wheelhouse to ask how long it would be until they met the boat in distress. He didn't seem surprised that she knew about it. Fidget must have told the others what he'd seen in the galley.

Jockey told her it would be a couple of hours; the boat in distress was far from the coast. A couple of hours was good and would give Swain some chance to catch up on the sleep he'd lost since starting this voyage. Sassi asked that the Captain not be bothered.

That request led to a gap of silence, which made her second guess making it. She didn't think anything of making the suggestion when it came out of her mouth. It wasn't supposed to be an order, she wasn't getting ideas of acting above her station.

As far as she was concerned, a man was asleep, and shouldn't be woken up because he wasn't needed. Sassi would never ask something that might endanger Eros. If Swain was required, she'd go jump on him herself… to wake him up, not for other fun reasons.

But the first-mate managed to calm her down just with the warmth of his voice when he'd agreed.

A little more than an hour after she'd had that conversation with Jockey, dinner was ready. Tune and Hector had eaten first and just gone up to the wheelhouse for their watch, though she didn't know how their usual routine would work out with them on their way to answer the distress call.

The table was set for the second seating when the rest of the posse piled in sans the captain. Sassi was just putting the bowl of mashed potato in the center when Jockey, Foist, Swing, and Fidget entered to take their places around the table. The group were rowdy, even for them, and were arguing about something.

"What's going on?" she asked, going toward the galley to start cleaning up.

"The boys here are having a little disagreement is all," Jockey said.

"About what?" she asked, pouring the excess gravy into a jug to let it cool.

At the midnight change over, there were usually men in the galley seeking a snack. It always helped to have things on hand anyway. Sometimes there would be a buzz on the intercom and those on watch would ask for something to be taken to them. Because she didn't have the best balance on deck, she was given a reprieve from carrying up laden trays if it was dark, especially when there was a swell and a breeze. Swing or Fidget would take care of serving duties for her on those occasions, but it was still up to her to provide the food.

"Folks who don't know what they're doing shouldn't be out on the water," Foist said. "We should leave 'em out there a while, teach 'em a lesson."

"We don't know how long they've been out there," Jockey said. "It's not fair to leave 'em."

"Maybe we rattle 'em a bit," Swing said.

Sassi wasn't sure how they'd go about that. "What do you know about the boat? The crew?" she asked.

Swain darkened the doorway, fixating his usual black scowl on her. Stepping inside, he stopped at the end of the table, staring at her like there was no one else in the room. Oh shit, was he mad? As her captain or as her… whatever they were.

"Captain!" Swing exclaimed.

Jockey reached out and gave his arm a nudge, but Swain kept staring.

Swallowing her nerves, she retrieved his plate from the oven and hurried to the table to put it in the top place-setting. "I laid your place for you," she said, curling her lips into her mouth, waiting for him to react.

The others had to have noticed his mood because a hush had descended over the crew. No one made a sound when Swain stomped the length of the table to take his seat at the top, still scanning the food.

"You okay, cap'n?" Jockey asked.

Swain was still examining the table. "Where's yours?" he asked and glared at her.

"I… I didn't—"

"You eat with me," he said. "Every meal, understand?" She nodded. "Grab a plate. Fidget move your fucking ass down closer to Foist. Robins sits at my side, every meal."

A chorus of, 'aye, sir' rippled down the table while she scurried off to get her plate. As soon as she put it on the table, he dragged it closer to his then snatched her wrist to pull her down. Seated at the end of the bench, there wasn't much room for her legs because Swain's were right there perpendicular to her. Instead of getting awkward, Sassi tucked her knee behind his, and coiled both legs around his strong calf.

Swain put his elbows on the table edge and locked his fingers to hold his arms in an arch. "Tell me what I need to know about the pan-pan. How far out are we?"

"Bout forty minutes," Jockey said and proceeded to fill him in on what had happened.

Because the captain's plate was still empty, she took the liberty of filling it from the bowls on the table, being generous with every spoonful. Putting it down in front of him, she licked her fingers clean and started to build a plate for herself.

Sassi didn't typically sit and eat with the others though she was usually in the galley beavering away, cleaning or baking while they chowed down.

"Before their radio went down, you didn't get details?" Swain asked, eating and focusing on his crew.

Returning to the table, Sassi sat and wrapped her legs around his calf again before she started to eat her own portion.

"Sounds like they don't have a fucking clue," Foist said. "They couldn't give us the spec or nothing."

"Complement?" Swain asked, but there was no answer. "Okay, we're not going to do a full assessment in the dark. If they don't have radio then they don't have electric; their generator and back-up must be shot… Did they take damage?" Again, there was no response. "Okay, we secure the vessel, triage injuries and we'll assign 'em cabins here." His focus moved onto her. "Soon as you're done eating, you pack your shit. The boys will move it to my cabin."

They'd had sex once and now they were going to live together? Sassi took a minute with her shock. "I… what? Why?"

"There could be a crew of forty rowdy drunk sailors on that vessel. Space is limited, everyone will have to double-up," he said, his brows moving closer together. "Horny drunk sailors."

"It could be a boat full of hookers or sorority girls… horny sorority girls," she said, but lost her own argument as she considered how she felt about young nubile bodies like that writhing all over her captain. It might not be a bad idea to stick close to him and maybe stake a claim. The rest of the crew cheered, but Sassi's face settled in a frown before she made eye contact with Swain again. "Okay, I'll move into your cabin."

The way one of his brows relaxed made her think he'd been in her mind reading her thoughts, but he wouldn't tease or show amusement while the rest of the crew was around. "I'll take watch tonight," he said and her hand fell to her plate.

It seemed she wasn't the only one shocked by that declaration. "You can't take watch after an hour's nap," Jockey said.

When Sassi stopped looking at the captain, she realized everyone's attention was on her. "Why are you all looking at me?"

"'Cause they assume now that I'm fucking you, I'll listen to your hissy fits," Swain said.

"Then they don't know you very well," she said. Sassi would never ever undermine or manipulate him in front of his crew. No way. They all relied on him and his authority had to be absolute, it ensured that they all stayed alive. "But if we're taking a vote, I agree with Jockey."

"You had a bunch of sleep to catch up on," Jockey said. "You never slept a full night through when we were in port… Tune and Hector are already set up for watch."

"It'll be a late one anyway," Foist said. "We'll have to take shifts watching the other crew."

Because they didn't trust strangers to wander Eros' passageways unchecked. A shiver went through her. "Do you think they'll rob us or hurt us?" she asked, thinking how little she wanted to meet a career pirate.

"You've got every bastard on this crew watching your butt, Waif. No cunt's touching you without my order."

On their crew or the other one, she didn't know what he meant, and thought it was unlikely that he'd order any other man to touch her. But that did lead to a kind of relationship/subordinate gray area, she was obliged to follow his orders, whatever they were.

Swing sucked in a breath. "Hey, cap'n, how come you say no forni… foric…"

"Fornication," Jockey said.

"Yeah, how come you said none of that with the cook without getting hitched and then you get to do her? Are you doing her?"

"I'm the captain," Swain said. Swing's mouth opened in silent confusion. "You never heard that captains can perform marriages? I take her to be my wedded wife. Waif, you take me?"

"I, uh…" All eyes at the table were expectant, eager for her response. "Sure, I guess."

"There," Swain said, scooping up so much food that his fork disappeared. "We are fucking married."

That was one way to get around the rules. Swing and Fidget cheered; the youngster beside her seemed really overjoyed. She was pleased to see the laughter dancing in Jockey's eyes too. The first-mate shared a look with Foist, who she couldn't see, before turning to the captain, who was still eating.

Good, okay, so she knew it wasn't really a legally binding marriage. Except, when she'd said the words a zip of emotion had shot through her. She couldn't spend too much time thinking about what that meant. She just couldn't.

Eating fast, Sassi finished her food after Swain and most of the other guys were on seconds and talking about some boxer or fighter, something she didn't know anything about.

Leaning toward Swain, she whispered, "I have to prep dessert."

He dropped his focus to her and kept his voice low to keep their conversation as private as it could be. "Go pack," he said. "It's in the fridge?" She nodded, hoping his question showed an anticipation of trying her sweet treat. He'd always been kind of indifferent about her desserts, but she liked the idea that he might actually enjoy what she prepared. "We'll figure it out."

Trying her best to be subtle, she grazed the side of her little finger against his forearm that was resting alongside his plate. "Do you really think there are forty horny guys on the ship we're going to help?"

"You didn't think of that before your little stunt earlier, did you?" he mumbled. "Captains consider lots of elements before making decisions. First and foremost, the safety of his own crew. I never should've ordered a course changed based on the skill of your mouth."

Smiling at him, Sassi knew she shouldn't show the rest of the crew he'd flattered her. That might betray to them that the captain had said something nice to her and he was busy trying to be grumpy in front of them.

Yes, he was right. She should've let him go to the wheelhouse to quiz the other boat and get all the information he could before they lost their radio. After that, he could've made an educated decision on if it was best for Eros to use their resources and possibly endanger themselves to make the rescue.

Instead, she'd kissed him, put him on his back, and persuaded him. And that was why she was flattered. Swain had, in his own way, just admitted that she did have the power to manipulate him; he probably would have listened to her hissy fit if she'd thrown one.

Sliding right to the end of the bench until her ass was teetering on the edge, Sassi tightened her legs around his to balance herself and tipped her lips up to his ear. Taking her hint, he lowered his head a fraction, it would be obvious he was listening to her, but everything else about his posture said professional salvage captain.

"If you're on watch all night, I'll have no one to share that big bed with," she murmured, stroking a hand over his thigh beneath the table. "Will you really be able to leave me in your bed all night? Untouched?"

She eased back just enough to find his eyes. "You didn't just say that," he said. Sassi held her breath, hoping he wasn't mad. "You fucking with my command?"

Panic tightened her chest until his gaze fell to her mouth. There was something in his tone, but it wasn't anger. He might want to be mad, but he wasn't. Letting her hand slide higher on his leg, she found out what it was. He was hard.

Oh fuck, that made her blood speed to a torrent. "I promise to fuck on your command," she said, doing her best to rub her cheek on his stubble to hide her words. "Is that what you mean?"

"On your feet, Waif," he snapped, pulling away from her. "Go get your shit together, you've got orders."

Getting too close at the dinner table with so many eyes around them was stupid. Swain couldn't be gentle in front of his people, he had to be abrupt. Her captain was right. She did have orders. If she wanted to use her influence with him in the times it mattered, then she had to show she was willing to defer to him as much as possible.

In the end, he was the captain. Whatever he decided was law. Sassi would never defy him. In private, she'd give her opinions; but when it came time to jump, she'd always comply with his commands without hesitation.

SIXTEEN

SASSI ASSUMED THAT the crew from the other ship would be hungry and it was her job as cook to feed all the hungry mouths on the ship.

The rest of the Eros crew had various important tasks to complete and she wanted to stay out from underfoot. While they worried about assigning cabins and stowing important cargo, she stayed in the kitchen baking pie and meal planning.

It hadn't taken long to pack the belongings in her cabin. Most of what Sassi had brought was in the galley, stores, or had been eaten already. But she packed what remained. Most of it was her uniform apparel and she hoped she wouldn't be expected to share that if there were females on the other crew.

If she had to, Sassi would share her personal clothes with them. But, for some reason, she was protective of her uniforms. Maybe it was wearing Swain's name—something she'd come to realize she found pretty damn hot—and she didn't want any other woman wearing it.

Swain popped his head through the mess door,

smacking his palm on the inside of the wall. "I need you, Waif."

"Now?" she asked, struggling to quickly untie her apron. "How do you have time for sex now? I thought you were securing the other ship.

"Not for sex," he said like she was trying his patience. "I need you on deck."

"For what?"

He took the final step into the room. "She asked less questions before I nailed her," he muttered to himself. "You remember what you were scared of? About the other crew?"

Sassi let her head move in a shallow nod. "That they would be a bunch of slobbering mangy dogs set on violating me," she said and paled. "Oh, God, how many are there? You're not going to lock me up for my own safety, are you?"

"No, but I might do it for my sanity," he said, storming over to her. "There's a woman over there. I need you to deal with her."

She didn't understand. "Why? You know what to do with women. You got me into bed, didn't you? Charm her."

His lips thinned for a second. "Aye, that sounds like me. She's refusing to come aboard."

"Just one woman?" she asked and he nodded. "How many men?"

"One."

Her whole body relaxed and she breathed out her relief. "A couple. Thank God for that."

"Why thank God?" he asked, wearing a scowl.

"If they're focused on each other, they're not going to get handsy with us, are they?"

"You want to see the guy before you think about trading me in?"

Whether he was teasing or serious, she didn't

care and wasn't impressed. "We're not swinging. We've been together a day, it's too early to switch it up like that."

"We won't ever be switching it up like that," he said and snatched her hand. "Get out here and tell her we're not fucking pirates."

Sassi licked her lips. "Well, I can't say that, can I? At least one of you is," she said. His glare told her he didn't appreciate her quip. But she wasn't deterred and grinned. "It's funny, I worried about how a new crew might scare me; I never worried that my crew might scare someone else."

His scowl faded. He loosened and moseyed closer, skimming a hand onto her hip. "That's the first time you've referred to us as your crew," he murmured, making it clear how he appreciated her identifying with them.

She considered it for a second. "Huh," she said and sighed. "I think of you all as my crew. I guess I just didn't want to…"

"What?"

Winding her arms around him, she relaxed against his body. "At first I didn't want to be presumptuous because you seemed so close and I was new. After I started to like all of you I guess I was worried about…"

"Getting too close."

He finished her sentence when she ran out of the nerve to do it herself. "I'd never thought about life at sea before this… I'm surprised by how much I like it."

"We can talk about your future at sea later. It's cold out there. We need to get them over here and into shelter."

"Okay," she said, pulling away from him to go deeper into the galley.

Retrieving a box of cookies, she held them up

and then hurried back to him.

He grabbed her hand to drag her along toward the passageway. "Do you ever go anywhere without cookies?"

"It's a great way to make new friends," she said. "You're the only one who ever refused my cookies."

"You're still smarting about that, huh?"

Trotting along behind him, she ran to keep up though he held her hand tight, forcing her to move. "I'm just saying, if you hadn't, maybe I'd have given it up a day or two earlier."

"I'll remember that next time I find a waif bearing treats," he mumbled before pushing down the dogs to open the door to urge her out onto the deck.

Foist, Swing, Fidget, and Jockey were all on the deck around the gangway. There was a smaller boat, a yacht tethered to the side of their boat with a bunch of buoy's between the two crafts. Eros' huge blazing flood lights drowned the smaller boat in light, illuminating a blonde woman on the deck. Wrapped in a blanket, shivering and crying, she had a man at her side. The man was trying his best to talk to and comfort his partner, but she kept pushing him away.

If they'd been stranded out here for a while, all good humor had probably long since dried up. Sassi wasn't surprised to see the woman sniping at the man who was trying to put an arm around her. "I'd probably be just as pissed at you," Sassi muttered to Swain who sank his hands into his pockets.

"If we were alone, dead in the water, I'd have sabotaged the vessel myself and I wouldn't put out a call for rescue."

"No?" she asked, rubbing her arms that were cooling in the breeze. "What would you do?"

Taking off his hoodie, he didn't ask before putting it over her head. Keeping her cookie tub tucked against her, Sassi slid her arms into the sleeves one after the other and rolled them up as best she could.

Swain leaned down to whisper in her ear. "Keep you prisoner for as long as you'd let me get away with it," he said, pulling up the hood of the sweater he'd just put on her. "You're with a pirate now, Waif."

While she absorbed the new fantasy he'd just planted in her mind, Swain put an arm around her to urge her over to the others who were gathered around the open space in the hull where they would usually disembark. Between the two vessels was a drop to the black water lapping between the two parallel hulls.

"Ahoy," she shouted and immediately felt like an idiot, especially when Foist laughed and she had to smack his chest to shut him up. Ignoring the engineer, she kept her focus on the other crew… such as they were. "Are you hurt? Is it just the two of you over there?"

Sassi figured she should've asked Swain some questions about what they knew already, rather than getting caught up in another nautical fantasy. "Look, Gumdrop, look see, there's a woman," the guy exclaimed, trying to get close to his shipmate again.

Him calling her Gumdrop suggested the pair were together. This must have been a romantic getaway, shame it ended this way.

The woman kept sniffling, but did look up, so Sassi opened her hand in a wave and kept her smile warm. "All woman here," she said, thinking that with Swain's oversized hoodie hanging low on her thighs, she didn't have much of a figure on show. "I know you're probably really scared. I understand that. But you don't have to worry about the intentions of these guys. My crew are capable. They're a rough looking bunch, but you'll never find a more skilled and good-hearted team. I promise you, none of them will hurt you."

The woman sniffed and wiped her nose on her

hand. "How do I know… how do I know they're not making you say that?"

This woman had seen a lot of movies, Sassi thought, but she was being smart. Turning around to seek out Swain, she needed direction. "How does she know that?" she asked her captain.

The woman shrieked. Figuring something terrible must have happened, Sassi spun around. Except no one had moved, nothing was different. "Are you the captain?" Gumdrop asked.

Sassi winced.

Oops, she had forgotten that all the men's uniforms had their roles emblazoned on the back. So the hoodie she was wearing declared her to be captain. It should've been obvious that the garment was way too big for her. Therefore, not hers. The flaw in that supposition was that her uniform hadn't fit when she first got onboard, so it wasn't outside the realm of possibility that all her clothes were this big.

"She's his wife!"

Gasping, Sassi turned to see Swing pointing at her and Fidget nodding. Sassi was so shocked that she almost missed the serious expressions Foist and Jockey shared with an equally stern Swain.

"His wife?" the woman called, Sassi was still examining her crew. "You're not wearing a ring."

Swain took her shoulders to ease her aside so he could move forward. "We don't wear 'em. They're too easily lost at sea."

Her jaw swung loose again. It was one thing to joke about it in the mess with the more innocent members of the crew. It was another thing to perpetuate a lie with strangers whose trust they were trying to gain.

"Prove it," the woman shouted.

"Prove it," Sassi muttered. "How are we supposed to—"

Throwing an arm around her, Swain yanked her back in a dip and forced his mouth to hers, wasting no time in thrusting his tongue between her lips. Sassi balled her fist and pulled it back as if she was going to punch out, but it didn't go anywhere.

In fact, after about three seconds, the cookie tub hit the deck and she twisted toward her captain to curve her hand around the back of his neck. Her fist loosened and drifted toward him. She smoothed her palm down his shirt until it could snake underneath and open on his abs.

When he tugged her away, Swain's arm around her shoulders was the only thing keeping her aboard. Intoxicated by the pleasure of that kiss, she felt dizzy and would probably have fallen right through the gangway if he wasn't there holding her up.

"Trust us now?" Foist called out.

Concentrating to unblur her focus, Sassi peeked around to see the couple were now huddled together talking to each other. There was some sniping, emotions were still running high, but it was progress.

"Damn convincing kiss," Jockey said, nudging her so hard that she stumbled into Swain whose attention was fixated over her head on the bickering couple.

"This is taking too long," Swain muttered.

Sassi hoped he wouldn't command them to sail away and abandon the couple. Their boat was in darkness and they had no way to communicate with anyone else.

Surveying the scene, she put herself in the woman's place and one thing came to mind. "We need a gangplank," she said. "This deck is too high."

"There's a door on the lower deck we—"

She scowled at Jockey. "You can't ask her to jump into a tiny doorway. She's about the same height as me and my legs wouldn't make it; that's like a gap of ten feet."

"It's three max," Foist said, coming into their group.

Noticing that Swing and Fidget had retrieved her cookie tub, Sassi was glad that there were more sweet treats in the galley. Those boys would polish off their sweet treasure hoard fast.

"You said yourself that they don't know what they're doing," she said to Foist. "And if they end up in the water, who has to get them out? If they go in the water, I'll be going in there too."

Swain's eyes darkened as they zoomed in on her. "Don't threaten me," he said.

"I'm not threatening you. I'm telling you that I'm a strong swimmer and I—"

"Strong swimmer, huh?" he asked and bent over to hoist her onto his shoulder. "Let's test that."

Carting her around the superstructure, toward the opposite side of the ship, he passed the spot where they'd shared their first kiss and carried on to the port side.

"Swain," she said, kicking her legs and punching his back. "Stop it! Put me down!" He bent forward a little and slid her body down his. Sassi braced to go right over the edge of the ship. Instead, he dumped her butt on the side. "Don't do that, you scared me."

Though technically the danger wasn't gone. She was sitting on the side, still teetering close to going overboard. With her ass over the edge of the ship and her legs around his torso, her captain was the only thing keeping her on board.

"You abandon ship when I tell you to," he said. "Someone hits the drink, you raise the alarm, you don't go in after 'em."

The hood had slid from her hair during their kiss and she felt the chill of the sea creeping around the back of her neck. "I can't see someone in trouble and ignore them."

His arms tightened around her. "You disobeying my command?"

"No," she said, shaking her head and looping her arms around his neck.

"Good. 'Cause as of today you're this ship's most precious cargo and we don't dump the most valuable goods if we can help it."

Grinning, she pulled herself even closer, urging him down until her chin touched his. "I'm valuable?"

"Sure, who'll make donuts and pie if you're not around?" Growling at him, she had actually been drawn in by his teasing. He was so damn good at leading her on a merry dance. But he became more sincere. "Waif," he soothed and kissed her.

"Did you hear? He calls her Gumdrop," she said, crossing her ankles over his hips, which actually made her lean back more because of the angle of her legs.

Swain didn't miss her show of trust. She was dangling over the edge of his ship and didn't have a single reservation about trusting him to keep her safe and dry.

"You like that? Want me to call you Gumdrop?"

Just the idea of him saying something so ridiculous made her laugh. "Waif is just fine," she said, and opened her mouth to pull him into another kiss.

They were still kissing when someone cleared their throat. Jockey was a few feet away, caught in the light reflecting from the back of the starboard floodlights. "Cap'n, the lady's requesting a gangplank."

Swain nodded. "Do it."

Jockey side-stepped then paused to smirk. "Your wife need a Mae West?"

"No, I've got her for now," Swain said.

"What's that?" she asked both of them. "A Mae West?"

"Life preserver," Jockey answered.

She smiled, expecting Swain to get defensive or grumpy because he wasn't really going to dump her overboard. That and they weren't really married.

"Haven't decided if I'll let her go yet," Swain said, and did actually release the tension in his arms enough that she dropped an inch, causing her to whoop and grab for him. "Not so funny now, is it, wife?"

He hadn't even looked at her, he was still focused on Jockey. Sassi didn't know how he knew she was smiling, but when she grabbed his tee-shirt in her fists, she squeezed them tight. "If I'm going in, you're coming with me," she said.

This time her captain did bring his attention around to her. "I know the quickest, easiest ways back onto the ship, do you?"

"Yes," she said. "I'll hold onto you. And don't you forget, husband, if we're married, there's no more girl in every port for you. I want a faithful husband. So if you ever want to empty your balls with a woman again, you better keep your wife happy… and onboard."

Jockey wandered off to leave them alone. Sassi was aware that she was keeping the captain from his duties but was enjoying him too much to let him go.

"I'm not worried. My wife promised to fuck on my command."

Laughing, she let her head fall back and that was when he pulled her forward, easing her onto her feet on the deck again. "I did! Damn, I didn't think that one through."

While she enjoyed their teasing, he held her close between him and the side of the ship. As the humor slid away, she noticed intensity in the way he looked into her. "You're fun, Waif," he said, using his index finger to tuck away a loose strand of her hair. "You care, but you don't take yourself too seriously…"

It was as if he was trying to say something to her,

but she couldn't quite decipher it. "What does that mean?"

"It means you were right," he said, the rough callouses on his fingers rasping down her jaw. "You'd have been safer staying the hell away from me… But it's too late for you now. You're in it."

In what? She didn't know what he meant. Swain took her hand to pull her back around to the others so they could return to work, and Sassi was left wondering just how she'd let herself be drawn into this. This was fast turning from what she'd thought was harmless fantasy into her reality… It wasn't a bad one to be in. But it wasn't one that could last.

SEVENTEEN

"SO YOU… YOU live here?"

"This is the only address I have," Sassi said to Whitney, also known as Gumdrop, the woman who'd been rescued from the yacht.

After the couple were on board Eros, the first thing that Whitney wanted was her luggage brought over too. Swain had point blank refused to let them bring their belongings onboard; he said they wouldn't be there that long. His attitude left poor Whitney in stunned silence.

So Sassi had put an arm around their female guest and guided her to the cabin that was meant to be occupied by the cook. Encouraging Whitney to shower and change into some borrowed clothes, Sassi tried to make their visitor comfortable.

Whitney was taller and less busty, but they were roughly the same size. After Whitney had freshened up, Sassi had taken her into the mess where they'd found Swing and Fidget keeping Clive, Whitney's shipmate, company.

Doing her best to play hostess, Sassi had

arranged it so the couple could sit together, putting Swing and Fidget on the bench with their backs to the galley and the guests opposite with their backs to the wall.

"You don't have any property on land?" Whitney said.

"Not a scrap," Sassi said, folding sugar into the meringue she'd whipped. "Everything I own is on this ship."

"So if you weren't here, you'd be…?"

"Sleeping on the beach," Sassi said, trying again to make the woman smile, but neither of their guests seemed to be in a smiley mood. Though she guessed that made sense after what they'd been through. "How long were you stranded out here?"

"Since last night," Whitney said, taking the time to sneer at the man beside her. "He told me he knew what he was doing. I can't believe you did this to me."

"Gumdrop," Clive said and tried to pick up her hand, but Whitney snatched it from his reach and slid down the bench, away from him.

"Don't you worry, the cap'n will get your boat mended," Swing said. "Him and Foist know everything about every engine."

Whitney turned her disgust on Clive again. "Nice to know there are still some real men in the world. What a shame he's already married…" She yanked the diamond from her ring finger and slapped it onto the table. "You can take that back, there's no way I'll marry you now."

Hiding her cringe, Sassi turned her back on the table and began to spread the meringue on the chocolate bread pudding mix she'd cooked earlier in the day. It always paid to have a dessert on the go because her boys would always hoover up whatever she made.

The gym was a level below this one. Foist said

he'd never done so much cardio on a voyage before. Sassi took that as a compliment, though he probably hadn't meant it that way.

It was sort of sad to witness the end of a relationship; Clive didn't look like a bad guy. He'd just wanted to treat his fiancée with a nice romantic sail. He probably hadn't meant to come this far into the ocean and he wouldn't have meant to breakdown.

Swain, Jockey, and Foist were assessing the other vessel to make sure there were no leakages or immediate threats of fire. The captain had said they'd do their full check and repair tomorrow. But he wanted to make sure there was no chance of the yacht exploding and taking them down too.

"Your captain is an abrupt man," Whitney said. "I don't know how you live with him. He could've let me pack a bag. I don't see why it was such a problem for me to bring a few essentials… No offence to you, but I would prefer to wear my own clothes."

Most women could identify with that. Sassi also wasn't ignorant to the fact that Whitney had removed silk and donned cotton. Her clothes didn't even come close to matching the designer labels this lady was accustomed to.

With her meringue in the oven, Sassi put the gloves on the counter and set the timer. "Let me see what I can do," she said, putting the timer on the counter by the fridge before going to the table. "Now, Swing, don't touch anything, but don't let the place go on fire, okay?"

Swing nodded. She touched his face to smile before skipping out of the mess. The top-tier trio of her crew was over on the other vessel. Whitney was right; she should be allowed her own possessions. Bringing her own toothbrush and sleepwear shouldn't be seen as a travesty given that the couple had been through a trauma.

When Sassi got out on deck, she looked from

Eros to the Dreamboat and didn't see anyone around. The gangplank was still rigged between the ships, at a sharp angle from their higher deck to the yacht's lower one. Without the handrails, the thing was little more than an extended, narrow ramp. Whitney had freaked and Sassi hadn't blamed her; she'd thought at the time that she was glad not to be the one crossing it.

Now, it appeared she had no choice. Either she went back into the mess without trying or she took a deep breath and just did it. Swain would do it and he valued people who did what needed to be done.

Marching over to the top of the gangplank, she wouldn't be beaten by such a small space. The gangplank was long because it had to reach between decks, but the water exposure was only a few feet, just like Foist had said. Jumping onto the end, she put her arms out and balanced herself before speeding the few steps down onto the yacht.

When she jumped onto their deck, she grinned and wanted to cheer for herself. But admitted that would be dumb. If the guys in Eros' wheelhouse were looking this way, they'd be able to see her, and she didn't want to make a fool of herself.

This was a nice boat.

Looking around the bow she was standing on, Sassi admired the shiny white panels and smoked glass that made up the wheelhouse… if that's what it was called on a boat like this. It didn't have a sail, it was the type of boat that had an engine, probably more than one. It was only a fraction of the size of Eros, but it was luxurious.

This could be what was classed as a sports yacht. It had a couple of decks and what looked like entertaining space that she noticed as she moved down the port side to try to find a way inside. Going down some stairs, she rounded through a set of doors and found herself inside a living space that had a kitchen beyond.

But she didn't get much of a look at the darkened galley because the trio of men talking in the middle of the living room turned to her.

Although she still gazed around in wonder, Swain came stalking toward her. "Is Eros on fire?" her captain demanded.

"What?" she asked, focusing on him. "No! Why?"

"Are you being chased?"

Smiling, she wondered if he was playing with her. "By who?" But he wasn't smiling, he was scowling. Sassi flattened her lips, trying to project deference and solemnity, though she didn't think she'd pulled it off because his scowl deepened. "No, sir, I'm not being chased."

"Then you have no fucking reason to be here," he said. Grabbing her arm tight, he hauled her in the direction of the door. "Never leave your post without the captain's permission."

"Ow, Swain," she said, putting up a fight as he pushed her, but he stopped when she shoved him back. "If manhandling me ends in orgasm, I'm all for it. But we don't hurt each other for the sake of it." He let her go and she rubbed her arm. "I can't ask your permission if you're not aboard. Whitney wants some things from her cabin. A toothbrush and a change of underwear isn't too much to ask."

He moved like he was going to grab her again, but stopped himself and paused. After contemplating it for a second, he twisted away to sweep his arm in a gesture for her to carry on. She did. Jockey and Foist moved aside for her to march between them and she kept on going to the end of the space where there was a set of stairs with a couple of doors at the bottom of it.

Swain was behind her all the way down, and reached around her to open the door to her right. Sassi went into the dark bedroom. It took a minute for her eyes to adjust to the lack of light and a flash behind her made her turn.

Her captain was aiming the beam of a flashlight on another door. "Head," he said then swung the light around to a dresser. "Clothes."

"Thanks," she said.

He held the light to help her grab what she thought Whitney might need from the bathroom. After closing the head door, Sassi went to open the dresser in the bedroom. Intimidated by the labels on the clothes and the quality of the underwear, she admired the softness of the lace of a bra. Her captain came up behind her. She thought he would comment on what she was doing, instead, he ducked to kiss the side of her neck.

"I'm sorry," he murmured and put the flashlight on the dresser to wrap her in his arms. "I'm sorry, Psyche."

Turning to face him, the name made her curious. "Psyche?"

"Eros' consort," he said. "A mortal woman turned into a goddess to be with her husband for eternity."

They were alone, he could relax and let himself be soft with her. Sassi wasn't sure she liked it when he let her in. If they started to care about each other… if they grew to care about each other more… this situation could end in heartbreak.

No, it would end in heartbreak, for him anyway. Sassi could protect herself. But her captain would be smarter to use her for physical relief and nothing else. She could never be anything else.

"We don't have eternity," she said, linking her fingers at the back of his neck. "How do you know so much about Greek god stuff?"

"All the ships are named after the gods and goddesses," he said. "The first boat I ever bought was called *Hestia*. I read a few books and I dunno, somehow it became tradition."

"Never had a Psyche?"

"Not until now," he said and ducked to kiss her. Being a goddess was quite something to live up to. When she was alone with this man, he made her feel worshiped. As much as she wanted to be admired like that, in the way no other man had ever revered her, she couldn't let this get away from her. "I'm sorry I hurt you."

Picking up her arm, he began to kiss the spot he'd gripped upstairs. She shivered. "Not your fault... I'm sensitive there," she said, because it was the same spot Dario had grabbed. It wasn't still physically sore. But, psychologically, she hadn't forgotten what he'd done to her. "I'm sorry I disobeyed orders."

"I have rules for a reason," he said, still brushing his mouth over her skin. "What if there had been a problem with one of the lines and we'd come away from Eros?"

"My captain's lines? Loose? Please," she said, tugging his mouth to hers. "But if I had to be stranded anywhere, it would be on the same vessel as you... I could've played out another fantasy."

"You and your fantasies," he muttered, but let her walk him backward toward the bed.

"Yes," she whispered, rising to her tiptoes to kiss him. Pulling his belt from its buckle, she kept distracting his mouth and urged him to sit on the bed so she could climb into his lap. "Me and my fantasies... Are you going to punish me for them, Captain?"

Grabbing her wrists, he flipped her onto her back and pinned her down with his weight and tight grip. "Depends," he said. "This is your fantasy... tell me what you want."

"I don't want you to ever apologize for being rough again," she said, pushing her shoulders into the bed to present her breasts, which he was happy to fondle after switching both her wrists into one of his adept hands. "And I want you to fuck me hard and fast right here."

Running both hands down her body, he scooped his long fingers around her hips. "The underwear turn you on?" he asked, licking her jaw and nipping her chin before kissing her.

"You turn me on," she said and then put pressure on his shoulders to push him up enough that she could look at him. "I'll never be like her… I'll never be expensive and refined."

Easing further back, his brows moved closer together. "Gumdrop we dragged off here?" he asked and she nodded, gnawing on her lip. "Would you trade Eros for this?"

"This dingy?" she asked and shook her head, struck by the barb of offense that impaled her. "How could you ask something like that? Eros is my home, she's special to me…" Eros was a masculine name, but the ship was a she. All ships were 'she' apparently. It sickened Sassi whenever she thought about walking away from the vessel that had cradled and cared for her; sometimes more than the idea of losing the crew. "I feel nauseous now you've said that."

But when she tried to move out from beneath him, Swain snagged her wrists and slammed them onto the bed above her head. "That's how I feel when you compare my wife to that prima donna… I would never touch a woman like her."

She shouldn't be jealous or insecure, but Sassi wanted to tell him he wasn't allowed to touch any woman other than her. On Eros his options were limited, and as soon as they were back on shore with civilization, he'd be a free man.

Rather than get deep, or address their lack of claim to each other, she made a joke. "I should've checked out their galley before I refused the switch. If they have a double oven up there…"

Tipping her head left to right, she pretended to be weighing options.

The corner of his mouth twitched and he dropped his head onto hers to stop it moving. "Eros is overdue for upgrades, maybe put in a requisition request and you never know…"

He was happy to make her sexual fantasies come true; now he was offering to make her culinary dreams a reality as well. Swallowing the truth that wouldn't escape from her consciousness, she again had to admit that she'd never set foot on Eros again once this voyage was over.

"You're a fantasy behind, Captain… You haven't satisfied my last request, so I can't make a new one."

Rolling onto his side just long enough to pull off her jeans, he was quick to return to his position above her, and began to finger her clit. "Aye, aye," he said, lowering his mouth onto hers.

Sassi had said that she was his for the duration of this job. Some part of her wanted to stay on the waves forever because if they never went back and were always on this job, she would never have to let her captain go.

EIGHTEEN

FIXING THE DREAMBOAT'S engine wasn't going to take much. The kicker was that there was still fuel in the tank; that bastard Clive just didn't know what the fuck he was doing. All the glitz and expense that surrounded the damn dingy, yet the fucker scrimped on basic maintenance. It wasn't the yacht's fault she hadn't been looked after.

Swain was ascending the gangplank between the vessels with Jockey just behind him. They'd been over there since lunch. All of his Eros' duties had been neglected in deference to getting the Dreamboat going. The longer they stayed at anchor, the more money he and his guys were losing.

"We get them underway at dawn," Jockey said behind him. Wiping engine grease from his hands, Swain stuffed the rag in his pocket when he was done. "If Gumdrop gets out of bed. Sas had to serve our guests a private breakfast they slept in so late. It's not fair on the lass to ask her to serve every meal three times."

Once to his shift, then to the second team, and

now to their guests. Going into his cabin last night to find a naked woman sleeping in his berth had been a strange experience. The vision she'd made had preoccupied him all day. Not that he'd let her stay asleep for long, but it was a good view while it lasted. He'd never had a girlfriend on board during a voyage before. Women caused a distraction. He'd always been particular about that, but he was fast learning he liked it.

From the corner of his eye, he noticed movement on his forecastle. Going to the handrail at the top of the stairs, he shaded his eyes from the sun and saw his woman bent over. Mm, that ass. He'd never get enough. Right now, she was wearing a little black tennis skirt that he knew she'd got with her uniform delivery, meaning it bore his name. She was bent over so far that he could see the curve of her backside. While it was his instinct to enjoy the view, he realized that Tune, who was in the wheelhouse with Swing, would be getting the same view.

"Hmm, if I was ten years younger…" Jockey said.

The first-mate was the only man who'd get away with saying something like that and he only got away with it because Swain knew he was no threat. Jockey was protective of Sassi in the same way he was of every crew member younger than him, which was all of them.

"You wish, Old Salt," Swain said, giving him a shove. "And try twenty-five years. You need to be fit to keep up with a wench like my Sassi."

Taking his fingers to his mouth, Swain whistled loud to get her attention. It worked, she straightened to turn around. That was when he saw his waif had been pouring something from the large clear pitcher in her hand into the cup that was propped in the dainty fingertips of their esteemed Gumdrop who was strewn across the fucking forecastle in a bikini with Clive laid out next to her.

"I'll wring her fucking neck," Swain hissed, gesturing for Sassi to come over.

"Don't you say nothing to upset Sassi. She's a good girl."

"Not the waif," he said, growling as he watched Sassi teeter on her tiptoes toward the stairs he was at the top of. "The fucking prima donna."

Sassi wasn't wearing her shades, like she usually did when she was out in the sun, and although she was smiling, he didn't like what he saw. "Captain," she said, holding up her pitcher as she ascended to them. "Would you like some fresh-squeezed orange juice?"

"Fresh-squeezed?" Jockey said. "What's wrong with the normal stuff?"

"Whitney doesn't like concentrate," she said and bit her lip, raising her shoulders like she was excited. "I'm going to make kiss-me cake."

"Kiss me, what?" Jockey asked and put a hand on her shoulder. "If you gotta make a cake to make him kiss you then you got a problem, lass."

Swain felt his irritation rise. "No, silly, with the orange rind… but it takes a while, so I better hustle," she said and started forward. "Oh, Whitney asked if I can get champagne from the Dreamboat. Can I go over there, Captain?"

"No," he snapped so abruptly that he startled both Sassi and Jockey. His girl's smile faded, but he couldn't shake his mood. "Where the fuck are your sunglasses? And where did she get a swimsuit?"

Squirming, she curled her free hand around the curve of the pitcher. "I know you don't like it, I'm sorry," she said. "She was going through my clothes and she found my white bikini. I tried to tell her it wasn't allowed, but—"

"I don't give a damn what she wears; she can lay

about there all day for all I fucking care."

Sassi leaned back, shifting her weight onto her back foot. Any discomfort or contrition left her when she angled her head to glare at him. "So you're happy to ogle her in a bikini, but the sight of me turned your stomach?"

Jockey hissed. "Oh, son, you've got trouble on the high seas now."

His first-mate slapped his back then took the pitcher from Sassi and scurried away up the stairs to the wheelhouse with the juice. "She's not crew."

"Right, so she's a lady," she said and exhaled. "I can't believe this. You're really going to go up there and leer with the other guys. You're going to jeer and drool… Well, Captain, don't you think for a second that you'll be getting yourself off in me thinking of her."

She tried to take a sure step past him, but he got in front of her and grabbed her arms. "You too long before the mast, Waif? I don't fucking drool over women. You've got your own rules. You cover up 'cause I don't want the dogs on our crew seeing what's mine. I don't give a fuck if they line up to jerk off over her naked tits. She's nothing. You and your body belong to me."

Thrusting her fists to her hips, she elevated her stubborn chin. "I wasn't yours that first day," she said. "The day you came down to shout at me on the forecastle. I wasn't yours then."

If they were going by when they'd had sex, she wasn't his the second time she'd tried sunbathing either; the day he'd sent Fidget down to retrieve her. But if they judged his ownership from the minute he knew he wanted her, it had started below decks at breakfast on day one.

Pulling her to him, he loved the way her breath rushed from her lungs when he was forceful. "The captain's wife does not serve like a maid."

"It's my duty to play hostess," she said.

After what she'd said last night when they were on the Dreamboat, he wasn't sure her motivation was as simple as that. "Listen here," he said, grabbing her chin to pull her face nearer to his. "She is not better than you. You are not her servant."

"I didn't say that—"

"She's wearing your clothes and I'll bet your shades too. You're squeezing oranges for her and asking me for champagne, are you kidding me? Waif…"

He didn't want to keep kicking her and waited for her to concede.

Eventually, she exhaled. "Okay, fine, but, what do you want me to do? She's not comfortable on Eros yet."

"She's comfortable. Soon as a woman's happy to get that naked around a bunch of mangy dogs like we are on this crew, she's comfortable."

Hopefully Sassi was thinking about the first time she'd stripped off in front of the crew. Peering over her head, he saw Gumdrop sitting up and turning toward them like she might be trying to seek out her slave.

If that woman needed to be reminded of her place on this ship, Swain was happy to oblige. Scooping his hand around the back of Sassi's head, he turned them to give Gumdrop a profile view of the full-on kiss he planted on his girl's mouth.

Their guest might think she had rights around here, but they only lasted as long as he let them.

When Sassi was suitably dazed, he grabbed her hand and pulled her toward the stairs. "Come on," he said.

"Where are we going?" Dumb question, the stairs only led to the wheelhouse, unless she planned to climb the mainmast. "Wait, no, I can't go in there."

She must have figured it out, but he wasn't

deterred. "You're on watch with me, Waif. That's an order."

"They'll think I'm jealous, that I want to keep an eye on you."

He stopped at the top of the stairs to face her. "Let one of them say that out loud," he said, pushing his fingers over her hair that was massed in a mess on top of her head. "I get annoyed when they're around because I don't like sharing you with other men." Her uncertainty vanished and her lips parted as they always did when she was surprised. "Even your time. I don't like them breathing the air you breathe… It does something to my skin, makes it crawl to think of any man anywhere even close to you."

Swain didn't wait for her to respond. He guided her forward to ease her into the wheelhouse in front of him. "You're relieved, Tune," he said. "Swing you go help Fidget with his duties."

There was no doubt in his mind that the men had been doing exactly what Sassi had said they would be doing: drooling over Gumdrop. Tune and Swing shuffled out.

Jockey's eyes darted between them, his brows lowered. "You relieving me too, Cap'n?"

"No, you stay," Swain said.

If he didn't have a chaperone, he might be tempted to take advantage of being alone with his girl, given that the ship wasn't actually in motion. They were in open water, which was why he insisted on someone being on watch at all times. But he wouldn't be much good at his job if he was distracted by his female.

Sassi bounded over to take hold of the wheel. "Will you let me drive?"

Swain was right behind her. "Sure," he said, putting a hand on top to make sure she didn't turn it. "Soon as you show me your license. What tonnage you qualified to handle?"

Though she scowled at him, he couldn't stop the corner of his lips from curling. "I don't know," she said, scratching his stomach with a fingernail. "How much do you weigh? I guess with the mass of your ego you must edge into the tons."

Jockey laughed. Swain swept his arms around her, trapping her between him and the wheel. The wench was still smiling like she was so proud of herself. He bared his teeth before kissing her and picking her up to carry her over the hatch that led to his cabin below.

In their cabin that morning, Sassi had asked about the ladder attached to the wall between the head and closet doors. She'd been intrigued when he told her it led up to the wheelhouse. If she ever wanted to climb up and visit him, he'd welcome the surprise.

"Sit up here," he said, sliding her onto the raised wheelhouse settee, a three-sided rectangular booth with a central table. "Stay there."

Nodding sideways to Jockey, he indicated he should join him at the long chart table behind the settee. "We're gonna lose two days to this," Jockey said to him. "Think we'll make it up?"

"What's the latest weather?" he asked, noticing that Sassi had her elbows hooked over the back of the settee. Her cheek rested on her arm and she was just gazing at him. "What, Waif?"

"Nothing," she sighed. Swain couldn't tell if she was mocking him with her dreamy stare or not. "Ignore me. Keep going."

Yeah, he hadn't managed to do that from the second she'd set foot aboard, even when they weren't on the same deck. "Wind," Swain said, drawing his eyes away from her to drag them to Jockey who was doing a bad job of hiding his grin.

"Behind us all the way unless there's a shift,"

Jockey said. "We've got a lot of planning to do for the dive."

Swain couldn't concentrate with the feel of Sassi's proximity making his skin prickle. Shoving away from the chart table, he went around to lift one of the settee seats to reveal a compartment beneath.

Pulling out a laminated sheet and a length of mousing line, he slammed both down in front of her. "Here, Waif, practice."

She picked up the sheet and actually lit up when she saw it was an instruction sheet for a bunch of knots. Grabbing the line, she crossed her legs and concentrated on the sheet.

Thank God for that.

If she was doing something with her hands, she wouldn't be gawping at him. Just like Fidget, she was easier to deal with if he gave her a task. "Right," he said, dropping his hands to the chart table opposite Jockey. "What were we talking about?" But his first-mate wouldn't stop smirking. "In the mood for some keelhauling?"

Laughing, Jockey, squeezed his lips together in a crappy attempt to calm himself. "Bout time, son. It's about time."

"Baby, I can't do this one," Sassi declared, her voice laced with concentration when she lifted the laminate over her head in one hand and the rope in the other.

He noted which one it was and grabbed the line to untangle it. "It's easier to practice this one with two lengths, Waif," he said. Within seconds he'd tied the knot and handed it back to her.

She examined it for a moment. "It's not two on the sheet."

Swain took it back from her and untied it. Tugging his pocket knife from his belt, he split the line and tied it again to show her. "You need one if you want to make a loop. But for practice, you can use two… Trust me, wife," he said, and handed over the line.

"Thank you," she said, grinning at him and going back to her practice.

The curve of her creamy neck distracted him. The loose strands and sections of her soft hair that had slipped from the knot on her head were creating lines and waves on her smooth skin that he wanted to go over and sweep aside. She tasted so sweet back there, and when he kissed that arc where her neck disappeared into her shoulder, she breathed out a little whimper that…

Clearing his throat, Swain closed his eyes, and shook his head, amazed that he'd lost himself to ideas of seducing his cook when he was supposed to be busy being captain in his wheelhouse.

"Can we get to work?" Swain asked Jockey who was still fixated on him and wearing that stupid smirk.

"You know what that knot's called, lass?" Jockey called out to her without answering his captain.

Swain hadn't thought about what he was doing when he was tying it, he'd just gone through the motions. But he knew where his first-mate was going before he'd explained it to the waif. It didn't matter that he glared, Jockey's amusement grew and he carried on regardless.

"No," she responded, examining the knot.

"That's a true lover's knot," Jockey said, enjoying this situation way too much.

"And Jock will be on emergency rations the rest of the trip," Swain said.

He didn't need a knot or his friend's mocking expression to tell him he was falling for the tenacious cook he'd hired at the last minute. Sassi made him want to protect and perform at his best.

Swain had never cared about what people thought about him or his masculinity. He'd never cared about machismo. But he'd seen the way she looked at him when he took control. She'd told him flat out that he made her feel safe, and for as long as he had her, he wouldn't let her down.

NINETEEN

"YOU ARE A difficult woman to get alone."

Sassi had been sitting on deck in her favorite spot for probably near half an hour, staring down at the knot that Swain had tied that day.

She didn't know exactly how long she'd been there. Her watch was lost somewhere up the sleeve of Swain's hoodie that she'd stolen from the back of his seat before coming outside.

If she was going to be interrupted by anyone, she'd have expected it to be her lover. But Swain wasn't the man approaching her. Clive was the one sauntering up to her, hands in his pockets, looking humble and yet proud both at once.

"Am I?" she asked.

He held her sunglasses toward her. "Yes, you are. Your crew stick close to you."

Taking the glasses, she tucked them up her sleeve with her knot. "You needed to get me alone to return my sunglasses to me?"

He smiled and turned his back to the stern to lean

on the handrail and look down at where she was sitting on a bollard that had rope around it.

"No, that was just the excuse I came up with to use if anyone caught us talking."

The hair on the back of her neck prickled. "Caught us? Why would you care about that? We're talking. That's it. That's all we're doing. All we're going to do."

Best to head off any presumptuousness at the pass. Hence her firm tone.

Clive just smiled like he'd got her message. "Yes, but I wanted the excuse in case anyone asked what we were talking about." He folded his arms and grew serious. "I want to offer you a job."

"A job?" Typical she should be desperate for one for so long and then two cropped up at once. "I have a job."

"Yes, but this is temporary, isn't it?" he said. As she got nervous, he got smug. "You're not really married to the captain. Tune filled us in. It's something you told the more gullible crew members to justify your affair. This isn't permanent security for you and I can offer that. I'll pay you a thousand dollars a week."

Smirking, she was pleased he made the decision so easy. "I make more than that here."

"Whatever you make, I'll double it." It would take just ten weeks to pay off Dario if she gave him every cent. She'd be out of the deadline, but maybe she could buy some extra weeks, or if she proved herself, she could ask Clive for an advance. "Money is no object. Whitney likes you and she's used to getting what she wants. Good help isn't easy to find."

"And that's what you want me to do? Help you?" she asked because it was always best to be explicit.

"Your desserts are exquisite. Entrees could use some work, but training someone with the basic skills is easier than training a novice. You could expand your role as you see fit. But it would offer you security. A permanent role. You could build up a nest egg."

Because one day Whitney would get bored with her and she'd be dumped like Clive had been last night. The couple must have forgotten about that at some point and made up because Gumdrop, as the crew had taken to calling her behind her back, was wearing her diamond again.

"I can't believe this," she said because she really hadn't seen it coming. "I can't believe you're offering me a job."

And such amazing pay, but she didn't say that part aloud.

"So you'll do it?" he asked, shifting in a display of optimism. "Whitney will be pleased. You can leave with us in the morning. Pack your things and—"

"No," she said, leaving her perch to stand up. "It's an incredibly generous offer and I appreciate you making it. But my place is here."

"I can straighten things out with your captain. He'll understand when he sees what a package I can offer you, stability, benefits."

Once upon a time, that would've been an offer too good to pass up. But Sassi wasn't even tempted to consider it. "There's more to life than stability and benefits," she said.

Stuart would think she was insane for rejecting the offer that could solve so many of their problems… and maybe she was.

"Like what? If you're playing hardball—"

"No," she said, sighing out a smile that betrayed how at peace she was with her decision, knowing it was the right one. "There's such a thing as loyalty… as devotion. It might not last forever, but I am loyal to my crew and I'm devoted to my captain." Her heart felt strong and in this anonymous moment, she could accept the truth, even just for a few seconds. "I am devoted to him. Eros feels like a home and to someone like me, who hasn't had one of those for so long, that means more than any amount of money. Thank you again, but there isn't any place else in the world I want to be."

His incredulous expression told her he didn't get it. "The offer will remain open, if you want to rethink, you can change your mind and decide to come with us any time. I'll see you in the morning before—"

"No, you won't. Dreamboat was loaded already. There are donuts, pancakes, fruit salad, juice, and yogurt in the galley ready for your breakfast in the morning. Captain Swain wanted you ready to get underway before sunrise to give you maximum time to get back to shore. I won't see you in the morning, he'll have you gone before I leave his bed."

"It's an insane decision to stay with a man like that just for sex," he said, blustering like he really didn't get it.

It was okay that he didn't, she didn't want him to. "I'm with him for more than sex and I don't have to justify my decision to you," she said and shook his hand. "Bon voyage."

Leaving Clive on the deck, even though he probably had more to say, she headed to the mess.

Down the stairs behind the dinner table in the rec area, there was a booth in the far corner and that was where her people were. Sassi loitered by the mess door, trying to get Swain's attention without making it obvious to the others. It didn't take long for him to notice her and make excuses.

As her captain approached, Sassi heard Clive's cabin door close in the passageway behind her. Good. She hoped he'd stay there all night and avoid possible confrontations with her crew. His superior attitude had rubbed them all the wrong way.

"Waif?" Swain asked and put a hand on her shoulder. "Something wrong?"

She made herself smile to allay his worries. "No, I just came to tell you that if anyone's hungry, there's food in the fridge and cookies in the cabinet. I'm going to bed."

His frown didn't lessen as he bobbed his head and examined her. "Want me to join you?"

"Yes," she said, grabbing for his tee-shirt. "But just whenever you're ready. Finish your game."

"Okay," he said and ducked to kiss her quick.

Clutching him tighter, she moved in against him before he could turn away. "Can I make a request?"

"I just said I'd come to bed and you said—"

"Not a sex request, I… I know you want the Dreamboat to get underway before dawn."

"Yeah."

"Can they leave before I have to make breakfast? Their galley is loaded, there's nothing else I need to do for them."

The blackness that grew in his eyes made them seem hollow. "What happened? I saw that fucker walk outta here. I figured he was going to bed. Did he make a pass at you? I'll cut his lines now, toss him in the drink and let him swim after his precious Dreamboat."

She had to cool Swain's jets before he overreacted. "He didn't make a pass at me. He…"

"He what?" Swain growled.

His voice was so deep and fierce that she worried it could hurt his throat, so she found herself stroking his Adam's apple. "He offered me a job."

Swain's fury became surprise. "He what?"

"I said no, but his attitude made me uncomfortable. I'd just rather not spend any more time with him."

Straightening his spine, he peered down his nose at her. "A job?" he asked. "More money?" She nodded in the interests of honesty, but hadn't really wanted to admit that to him. "If you want to take it—"

"Do you want me to take it?" she asked, having not expected him to chase her off Eros.

"How much more money?"

Was he trying to judge if he could match it or how much Clive wanted her? "Would you forget about the money?" she asked. "He tried to sell me on stability because it's a permanent position."

As if she'd just suggested they marry for real, he seemed taken aback, which wasn't like him. "You didn't tell me you wanted to talk permanent… My men work as and when I need them. I just put out word when I need to put a crew together. I call the usual suspects until I have all the positions filled. Doesn't usually take long. If you need work in future, I have six ships, someone always needs a cook."

So he'd hire her as long as he didn't have to sleep with her beyond the four week limit? She hadn't come to the mess expecting to get in a fight.

"Forget I said anything," she said and tried to walk away, but he grabbed her back.

"No, you want to talk about this, we'll talk. I didn't realize there was a chance of poaching this far out."

It didn't take much to put him in a bad mood under normal circumstances, but tonight he was on express speed. "I don't want to talk about it."

"You brought it up," he snapped.

That he was so snide made her think he was hurt or just disgusted that she might have thought about betraying him. "I brought it up to ask if you could get rid of them before I woke up, not to open negotiations. Full disclosure is the best policy, that's why I told you about the job offer 'cause, you know, in case you hadn't noticed, we're sleeping together."

"That mean you wouldn't have told me if we weren't having sex?"

It felt like he was trying to start a fight with her, but she wouldn't rise to it. "I'm going to bed, Captain. Do whatever pleases you with them, with me, with whoever you like. Goodnight."

Spinning around, she flounced from the room to head for the captain's cabin. This had been a weird few days. Sassi couldn't wait until their guests were gone and things could get back to normal around here.

TWENTY

THE DREAMBOAT WAS gone by the time Sassi woke up on her tenth day at sea. It took another two days for them to reach their destination. Thanking God for GPS, Sassi didn't know how anyone found anything at sea before its invention.

It was even more incredible that they got the right spot because they dropped anchor in the dark when she could barely see the water let alone guess where in the ocean they were. It amazed her how little her captain relied on his eyes and how much he trusted his gut.

Swain told her it was all about the way the wind made the hairs on his arm move and the sensation of the spray on his face. That off-hand statement might have made her swoon a little, even if he just frowned at her in response.

Though Swain told her they were less than fifty miles from the mainland, she couldn't see it. But it was so dark without artificial light she wouldn't be able to see her hand in front of her face. He'd also said they were near a small island in the South Atlantic. Jockey told her it was uninhabited by anyone except the souls of those lost at sea.

Yeah, like she'd believed that.

But when bedtime came, she'd seduced her captain into joining her rather than going up to their cabin alone, just in case. After they'd made love, he chastised her for getting cutesy with him in front of the crew and when she'd confessed why she hadn't wanted to go to bed alone, he'd delighted in teasing her about being afraid of pirate ghosts.

Diving was dangerous. The wreck they were surveying was caught on an underwater ridge by a series of shifting sandbars that could make the situation precarious.

Sassi wasn't a diver and knew nothing about salvage operations, but apparently radar gave them an idea of what they were up against. Swain and Tune were the most experienced divers in the group with Hector not far behind and, it turned out, Foist was capable too. Jockey knew how to dive as well, but he provided more back up than anything else. He didn't do the heavy work.

She'd expected a scuba setup like she'd seen on TV. Instead, she was told they were using a surface-supplied method and that was when she phased out. It got complicated fast. These guys were no Neanderthals after all; they were smart and skilled.

On the first day of the dive, the men had been locked in the wheelhouse for hours talking and planning. She'd gotten enough baking done to last two weeks and had to tell herself to slow down or she'd use up all their supplies before the return trip.

Sassi had been practicing taking more time doing things that she usually did fast when she heard the whooping and hollering coming from the passageway. The exuberant sound was startling enough that she went to find out what was going on. The whole crew was out there, talking over each other, barreling toward her, she'd never seen them so high-spirited.

Carried in the wave of male bodies back into the mess, Sassi got lost in the swirl of the crew moving around her making her head spin. A heavy arm grabbed her shoulders and she was yanked against a hard, bare chest.

Swain.

She recognized his scent and the texture of his skin rather than his face, because he pulled her in so tight that her nose pressed into him. He'd been in the water, but must have stripped off his dive suit when he got back on the ship because he was wearing only a pair of dry board shorts now. The rumble of his voice vibrated through her, making it easier for her to distinguish his voice through the maelstrom of other excited chatter.

The cargo they were surveying was more intact than they'd thought it would be. Big haul. Big payout. Half a million dollars split eight ways. Wait. She made an effort to push herself away from her lover's chest.

"Someone translate this for me," she said, glancing up at Swain before turning around to seek out the others.

Swain's arm stayed around her. He pinned her shoulder blades to his torso, keeping her close. He kissed the top of her head, nuzzled her hair, and settled a fondling hand over her breast. Apparently, hitting the motherlode made him tactile.

Jockey stepped through Tune and Hector who were also shirtless and wearing the same kind of Swain-embroidered board shorts as the captain. "We got our first good look," the first-mate said. "We have to map the site and catalogue what's down there, but it's looking good. Our percentage could be worth a payout of half a million dollars which we split eight ways."

"Eight," she said. The captain, first-mate,

engineer, Tune, Hector, Swing, Fidget… and her. "You mean the crew. But that doesn't include me… does it?"

"You're crew, aren't you?" Jockey asked, chucking her chin. "We get done here and the cap'n does the deal for us to come back and lift it all and you'll be sixty grand richer by Christmas."

"I think we can raise the wreck," Tune said. "If they want it, we can do it. Get the fleet down here, turn it into a full op—"

"He hasn't mentioned that," Swain said. "But we'll do feasibility while we're here, a sign of goodwill. It'll take an extra couple of days."

"And could delay our bonus a couple of months," Hector said, but his concern bled to a smile. "But it'll be worth it for the big bucks."

The volume level rose again, but Sassi was just stunned. The bonus wasn't imminent. She wouldn't get a bonus unless she completed the job, which meant sticking with the crew until the whole job was completed not just this initial survey phase.

Maybe she would get something for being around for the first month, but it would be a fraction of what the others got because she'd only been present for the first leg of the voyage. Except, any payout would be useless to her. The guys were talking about this taking months… way beyond her Dario deadline.

For the first time, she felt seasick and had to slap a hand over her mouth. A part of her had assumed that she'd be okay once they returned home and she got paid for her work and received her bonus.

Sassi had believed she'd be able to toss Dario's money in his lap and then spit in his face. Marriage? Ha, take that, you sleazy fucker.

But that was just another of her silly fantasies. Damn her for letting her mind lull her into a false sense of security.

Her stomach revolted and she wretched. Forcing Swain's arms away from her body, Sassi ran as fast as she could out onto the deck and sucked in a long lungful of fresh sea air. Trying to tell herself that she was safe on Eros, that nothing could hurt her, and that Dario wasn't here to put his hands on her, Sassi started to calm down.

She was okay. She was safe.

But for how long?

When she returned home and stepped off Eros, she'd have about sixteen thousand dollars, maybe a fraction more if they were a few days over and Swain was generous. But they owed Dario thirty thousand. She'd have less than two weeks to come up with fourteen thousand dollars… it just wasn't possible.

That left her with a dilemma.

Did she admit to Dario that she had the sixteen thousand and beg for more time, or did she hoard the sixteen thousand as escape money in case she got the chance to make a run for it? Life on the run… she couldn't do that unless her brother and Karen were safe… unless Eros was safe.

Oh no.

Stuart had dumped Karen to save her from Dario who could use the temp agent to torture her brother. It had been easy for Sassi to debate the virtue of cutting those ties with her brother when she didn't have ties of her own. She didn't have close friends or a man to care about… not back then.

While her brother had been smart to isolate himself, somehow Sassi had accidently done the complete opposite. She'd forged friendships and started a relationship.

A doomed relationship.

Ironic that she should reach this disgusting truth on her thirteenth day at sea.

She'd have to marry Dario Correa.

Acid churned in her stomach, compelling her to run the width of the deck to heave over the starboard side. She could travel seas and oceans for days without losing her lunch, but the thought of giving herself to Dario made her puke.

When her stomach was empty, she folded her forearms on the edge of the ship and rested her forehead against them, trying to breathe through the nausea.

"It's a lot of money."

The sound of Swain's voice beside her made her head roll on her arms. She couldn't quite bring herself to lift her temple from the back of her wrist. "It is," she said, licking her dry lips. "I'm happy for you." The nausea wasn't helped by standing this close to the man she could never have. "Excuse me."

Turning away from him, she left the deck, intending to go to her cabin. Except, her cabin was the captain's cabin, and that didn't feel right. Sassi chose to go into her original cabin instead.

Washing out her mouth and gargling some mouthwash, she brushed her teeth with a finger, then splashed water on her face. Breathing out, she held her cold damp hand on the back of her neck and looked at her reflection.

Mrs. Correa.

Mrs. Sassi Correa.

She had to stop thinking about this; it was making her feel sick again.

"You're happy for me? What does that mean?"

The sound of his voice again made her sag. "Captain, can I have just a minute, please?"

But Swain wasn't wielding contrition or sympathy. "No, you can tell me what you meant and what you're doing in here instead of upstairs where you belong."

In his cabin, that's what he meant. He wanted her

to explain her statement and why she'd come to her old cabin instead of going to the bedroom they'd shared since their first time together. Sassi didn't know how to deal with Swain's anger when her own emotions were so screwed up.

Suddenly, she felt exhausted. All of her energy seemed to just drain away.

But Swain was blocking her route out of the head and even when she tried to go around him, he didn't take the hint and stayed in her way.

"Can I get by?" she asked, not impressed by his attitude or swayed by his scowl.

"No," he said. "Crew don't walk away from the captain when he's talking to them. Tell me what you meant."

Exhaling, she had to accept that he was right, she was subordinate to him whether she liked it or not. "I meant what I said. I'm happy for you and the guys. You deserve the windfall. You work hard and this is a great find for you."

"But not for you."

They weren't supposed to be talking about this. Sassi didn't know what to say to him because anything she did say would lead to more questions and when he was glaring like he was, he wasn't easy to deal with… not that he ever really was.

"You said it yourself a couple of nights ago, you take crew members on when they're needed. You needed me for this trip. You won't need me on the next one."

He inhaled irritation. "You started this journey with us, you get to finish it," he said like it should be obvious. "I'll offer Raise to one of our other captains if he's out of jail."

Captains of the other ships in his fleet built their own crews, but often did so on Swain's recommendations. Jockey had told her about the fleet and the respect Swain had among all of his people. A post on Eros was the most coveted. Because Swain was so loyal, he tended to use the same people all the time, so it wasn't an easy ticket to get. Jockey liked to talk about Swain's work, about his success. He was like a proud father when he got started on talking about their captain.

Most of the time she was proud of him too. But, in that minute, she couldn't locate that positivity and just felt annoyed. Why was it okay for him to have attitude and be snippy, but the rest of them had to be patient with him?

Rank.

Yeah, that was the answer. The captain was their superior, so they had to be submissive, didn't mean she always liked it.

Everyone had problems. She was in the shit and caught up in her own, but this Raise guy shouldn't be punished because her family was so screwed up. "That's not fair, he's your cook. I was always meant to be temporary. This is Raise's post, not mine."

She tried to get past Swain again, but he got hold of her. "You started this, you get to finish it. I choose my crew."

Wrenching free of his grip, she stepped back. The space was so small it felt like a tomb. But she'd rather die here than in Dario's bed. Every time the bastard's name came into her mind, her anger ratcheted up a notch.

"And why would you choose me over him?" she snapped. "I thought you valued loyalty, how many years was Raise with you?"

"Half a dozen," he said. "But the fucker screwed it up for himself when he broke the law. I don't employ criminals I can't trust!"

If he was going to raise his voice, so was she. "You're a hypocrite!"

"Oh, now you've got a fucking problem with my past? Toss that in my face, Waif, nice."

"No," she said, lunging forward to grab his forearm as he tried to turn away from her. "No, I don't give a damn about what you did when you were a kid. But don't pretend that you're firing Raise because he made a mistake. You're doing it because he doesn't suck your dick!"

Bristling, he widened his stance, taking up more of the space in the cabin until he filled the doorway of the head entirely. "How do you know he doesn't?"

"Oh, haha," she said, "yeah, you get snide. You know what I'm saying. You're making this personal."

"Personal," he said and swayed forward like he was considering stepping into the head, but there wouldn't be space for them to argue in there. "You're a better fucking cook than he is."

She didn't believe him. "And that's all it is? You're making a business decision?"

"Yeah," he said. "Yeah, that's it."

"I don't believe you."

"I don't give a fuck what you believe. You're crew. Subordinate."

"Unimportant?" she asked. His brows bobbed almost in a satisfied nod that dared her to contradict him, so she did. "Then why the hell did you call me precious cargo, huh? If this is all business, and you're really asking me to come on the next job for professional reasons, why didn't you offer me it when Clive was trying to poach me? You're full of shit. You flip-flop—"

"Me? You announced fucking terms before we screwed! Who the fuck does that?" Grabbing hold of her, he finally came inside, but only to spin her toward the small mirror above the sink she'd been staring into a minute ago. "Look at yourself."

With one strong arm around her torso, he

clamped both her arms to her sides and grabbed her chin hard to angle her head, forcing her to face her reflection.

"Let me go," she said, trying to struggle, but he was too strong for her to resist.

"I want you to look at that stunning fucking face and tell me why the fuck you always look so sad… I see you laughing, in the mess you have joy about you. When we're naked together, you're loose and happy… But when I turn any corner and find you alone, you're fucking mourning… What is it that's hurting you? Whatever the fuck it is—"

"I told you, you don't know me," she said, closing her eyes because she couldn't bear to look.

Swain shook her head, squeezing her chin tighter. "Look at us! Don't hide! Face what's fucking happening here!"

But that was the problem, what was happening here had the potential to threaten both their lives. "I can't! You don't get it! You don't know me!"

"You think I don't fucking know you? You think I don't know the woman who sings in the shower and dances in the galley? I don't know the woman who folds her underwear, but leaves socks all over the cabin floor? I don't know the woman who sleeps on her back, tucked against me, using my bicep as a pillow? The woman who mutters my name in little gaspy whimpers all night long? I don't know her?"

"No," she said, frustrated by the tears that heated her eyes. Sassi wanted him to know her. She wanted this to be as simple as he was implying it was. "You don't… I told you not to ask questions and you're pushing me—"

"'Cause the wellbeing of my crew is—"

"Stop!" she said and elbowed him hard, pushing and shoving at his arm until he finally let her go. Spinning around, a furious tear skidded down her cheek. "I don't want to only be your shipmate!" He tried to touch her face, but she shoved his arm down, angry that he was making her vulnerable. "But I can't ever be anything else!"

"Why?"

"Because I belong to another man!"

The words hit him hard.

The frown on his face became an intense scowl that made his eyes darken like black holes so fast they seemed to suck the air from the room. "This is about what happened in Miami."

She'd said too much, more than she should have. "No," she said and tried to push past him, but she had no chance of getting out when he blocked her way. "Please, Swain, just let me get out of here."

"What's his name?" She didn't answer. "Do you love him?" Again, she said nothing, just kept her head bowed. Seizing her upper arms, he shook her hard. "Tell me!"

"No! Look, I told you that I was yours for the duration of this trip, nothing has changed. I'll share your bed. I'll give you my body—"

"A body that belongs to him," he said and thrust her against the sink. "So this was what? A way to pass the time because you were bored? You have a lover's tiff so you run off to sea to punish the guy? Fuck… are you married?"

Panicked and scared and tired, Sassi just wanted to undo the last ten minutes. "No," she said, her heart pounding in her chest. "No, I… I'm not even with him… I never have been. I said that wrong, Swain, I'm sorry… I don't belong to him, I… I belong to you."

Though some of the tension left his shoulders, his expression stayed as severe. "For how long, Waif?"

Thirty days had been the length of her original contract, but they were already two days behind schedule. On top of that, if they were going to extend the survey time then they might stay here longer than had been the original plan.

In so many ways, it didn't matter anymore if they were late. What difference would a couple of days make when she knew she could never make up the extra fourteen grand anyway?

But instead of being sad, admitting the truth to herself gave her a new optimism. These were her last days of freedom. Eros was going to be the last home she ever knew. It would be the last place where she'd be able to make her own choices.

She could spend her final days of liberty embracing the chance she had to experience fun, being happy and free, or she could be depressed and forlorn. Sassi knew which she'd prefer. There would be plenty of time to be miserable when she was married to Dario.

It took a few moments of silence, staring up into Swain's eyes, to make him relax enough that she could slide her hands up his chest.

Boosting to her tiptoes, she threaded her fingers together at the back of his neck. "Did you know that swain means lover?"

He grumbled, "It's my fucking name, yeah, I know what it means."

"I guess that's why you're so good in bed," she said, touching her top lip with the tip of her tongue.

"The babygirl thing doesn't work," he mumbled, but his hands called him a liar when they cupped her ass to squeeze her close.

"I know," she said because it was best to agree with him and let him think he was right. "I don't want to argue with you, lover. We agreed, no questions. For the next two weeks, I'm yours… all yours… do you want me to be yours?"

Picking her up to sit her on the narrow sink, he

pinned her to the wall when he moved forward to bear down on her. "Don't ever tell me you belong to another guy, not ever," he said. She shook her head. His palm moved over her cheek until his fingertips got tangled in her hair. "And don't think about him when you're with me. That's an order, Waif, I don't want him in your head."

"You're the only man I want, Swain," she said. "I promise you that."

He breathed out, giving up the fight though it was obvious she infuriated him. "I'm fucking dancing on the head of a pin for you, Waif."

"I'm sorry, Captain. Want to take me upstairs and show me how pirates keep their wenches in line?"

"I want you to be happy," he said and when she twisted her lips to a wry smile, he drove a hand into her piled hair. "This is gonna be another one of those fantasies you always talk about, isn't it?"

Nodding, she bit her lip. "Show me how good you are with your knots."

"Oh that one," he said, picking her up from the sink. "That's one I've been looking forward to."

Carrying her out of the cabin, he didn't put her down or even hide that she was in his arms. There was no one around in the passageway, but any of the others could walk out of the mess at any second and catch the captain carrying the cook to his bedroom.

Usually Swain was reserved about their relationship in front of the crew. He didn't object when she touched him and he was different in the way he spoke to her compared to the other members of the crew, but that could be because of her gender rather than their relationship. Though she did get the impression there were times he was picturing her naked when he was dishing out orders.

"Some of your knots are pretty secure," she said.

His mouth slanted giving his dark eyes a sinister gleam. "You know some that are impossible to get out of, don't you? I think we should set some terms for—"

"Too late," he said, bounding up the stairs to their cabin. "It's time for me to play out a fantasy of my own."

He'd accommodated so many of hers that Sassi couldn't refuse. If he wanted her tied down and helpless, she'd submit. If he wanted her gagged and blindfolded at his mercy, she'd consent. Swain was the last lover she'd ever choose for herself. Memories of their intimacy were all that was going to get her through the nights she'd be trapped in Dario's bed.

TWENTY-ONE

YAWNING, SASSI TURNED onto her back and smiled at the circle of sunlight that was projecting onto her chest from the porthole behind the desk that stood parallel to the length of the captain's bed, about eight feet away.

"Captain," she whimpered. Her eyes closed again, but she pouted in the direction of the desk where she knew he was seated at the computer, facing into the room. "I feel neglected."

"We had sex twenty minutes ago," he said, his voice betraying that he was distracted.

The memory made her smile and she let the sheet fall from her breasts when she stretched out flat. "Yeah, but I haven't fallen asleep with you for the last three days."

The guys had been diving the wreck several times a day for the last eleven days making this her twenty-fourth day at sea. She should be freaking out that they were over-schedule, but she couldn't bring herself to feel any urgency about returning to land when life was so perfect out here.

"I have to do this analysis and write my reports," he muttered. "You know what a goldmine this is. We want to get everything right."

They'd stayed the extra time to do a preliminary feasibility study for raising the wreck. It wasn't a huge vessel, and the crew was optimistic about getting it off the ridge it was lodged on, though the sandbanks were a variable Swain didn't like. He'd voiced his desire for caution to the crew, but not as vehemently as he had with her when they talked in the wee hours, wrapped in each other in his bed.

Swain talked like she was going to get her bonus, like she was going to join them on the next leg of the job, but his expressions and body language told her he knew it wasn't a reality. Addressing their relationship was pointless when there was no future. This whole trip was a fantasy, but for the time being they were both pretending it was part of their larger reality.

"Won't you have time to write them up when we're back home? What kind of sailor ignores having a naked woman in his bed?" Probably the kind who was getting used to the picture. "I should make you work harder for it." But knew she wouldn't and got no response. Cracking open one eye, she saw him smirking at the pictures he scrutinized. He might not be talking, but he definitely heard her. "Do you need help? I can string sentences together if you need someone to do the boring stuff."

She couldn't really be bothered moving, but knew that he'd prefer to be diving or at least on the quarterdeck monitoring what was going on. He didn't like to be cooped up inside with only their trio of portholes on the wall behind him giving them their link to the outside.

"No, I need to keep my head in this," he said,

and glanced up at her. "And you're naked… that's helping."

"Shame you put your cock away. Our relationship is completely lopsided," she said, hiding her smile when she thought about his surprise intimate inspection that had brought them to bed earlier.

Strange coincidence how she was the only crewmember expected to strip naked for their esteemed captain and the only one with breasts.

"You make a better picture," he said, though she'd disagree. His body was ripped and she was treated to it more frequently now the crew was regularly stripping off to go into the water.

Moving onto her side, she tucked his pillow beneath her cheek. He shuffled some papers and typed something. "Dinner is cooking, it will be ready on time. Can I go to sleep, Captain?"

"Looks like you're already halfway there."

"I'll jump-to if you need me to," she said on a yawn. "You want a cookie?"

He smirked again; she just caught sight of it on another sleepy blink. "Go to sleep, Waif. I'll wake you if I need you."

Rolling to her back, she stretched again and let herself sink into the mattress. "You're a good, kind, generous captain," she said on a sigh, tucking the sheet around her.

"You would say that; you're the only one who gets oral from me."

And he'd treated her twice already that day. Sassi had only been teasing when she said she felt neglected. She'd never had a man so attuned to her sexual needs. They might not be able to discuss the emotional stuff and they might never have a future, but the present was pretty damn good.

TWENTY-TWO

SWAIN HAD NEVER been on a trip like this one.

Being with Sassi was unlike any other experience because she wasn't like the other women he'd been with, or any other woman he'd met.

She'd been asleep in his bed for almost an hour. It didn't matter how many times he stole glances at her, or how many times he just outright stared at her slumbering figure, he still couldn't quite convince himself that she was really there.

The cabin door clanged. Scanning Sassi, he made sure she was covered with the sheet. At one end, she had a leg curled around the cover and at the other it teetered just on the apex of her breasts, but nothing intimate was in view.

"Yeah," he called out from his place behind the desk, keeping one eye on his woman to make sure she didn't wake up.

The door opened and Hector came in with Foist and Jockey. The diver strode across the room with his arm extended to present a stack of pages, but he slowed to a stop when he spotted the woman in the bed. Hector registered her there, as did Foist and Jockey, but when Swain snapped his fingers, the men's attention came around to him.

"We got the last of today's reports," Hector said, finishing his journey to the desk to hand the sheets over though he kept glancing toward the bed.

Swain didn't like any guy looking, but he noticed Foist openly admiring the woman in his sheets, making his anger hotter.

"You two got some kind of problem? You're worse than fucking horny teenagers. Eyes front, you bastards."

Foist wasn't shy about sauntering to Hector's side, smirking all the way. "This from the guy who got laid a half hour ago… You're looking at a pack of rats who've gone without for almost a month. Your lady looked mighty fine the first day we saw her… Out here she's like the last woman on earth and you've got access to her. Any damn time you want pussy, it's laid out right there for you, ready to take your cock on command."

Swain didn't have a problem with explicit language, and understood what his engineer was saying. Turned out he'd been right on the first day, having a woman around could cause problems in the crew. He'd just never expected that his crew would have animosity toward him. Though, he'd never expected to be the one to have trouble keeping his hands off their only wench.

Still as Foist and Hector drooled, Swain sensed not only an interest, but a respect too. She had an amazing figure, but he didn't doubt that his crew had come to care for her, meaning he trusted all of them to keep their hands off.

Foist wasn't much of a joker, and he only fought when he was provoked. Swain doubted there was malice in what his engineer was saying. It was just a friendly explanation and maybe an implied request that they be allowed to enjoy their brief chance to be this close to a naked female form, any naked female form, even one they couldn't have.

Jockey laughed and came between the two men to slap a hand on their shoulders. "All the boys wanna swing for you, cap'n… they're jealous dogs."

As mad as he was that any guy might think of Sassi in a carnal way, he couldn't blame them. He thought of her that way plenty and like Foist said, Swain could take advantage of her any time he liked.

Smugness made him lock his fingers at the back of his head and lean back in his chair. "Swing all you like, snipe," he said to the engineer. "You could knock me out cold and toss me in the drink, Sass still wouldn't touch you dogs with a barge pole. She's got class… and taste."

The men inhaled and ooh'd at the insult, but Jockey kept laughing. Swain didn't mind teasing like this. It hadn't been easy to get used to sharing Sassi with the crew, but it got easier as it became more obvious to his men that their relationship wasn't just a casual distraction for either of them.

Sassi was his and they knew it. Didn't matter how much they flirted with her or how many cookies she baked them, Swain was the first man she looked for in every room, and she was disappointed when he had to leave her.

Her strength inspired him. There wasn't a task she wouldn't think about tackling if he put it to her. He often found her helping Fidget with his duties. Swing had been doing a lot of grunt work on deck while he and the others were diving because that freed up Jockey to take anchor watch. No doubt that his lady pulled her weight, just like any other member of the crew. Not only didn't she want special dispensation, she'd be offended if he suggested it.

"Don't see any evidence of that around here," Foist jeered.

Sassi muttered and turned a fraction making the sheet shift further up her thigh. Swain was transfixed and didn't realize his men were too until Hector sighed.

"She is beautiful, cap'n."

"Don't got to tell me that, Hect," he said. "Now you rats clear out afore she wakes up and gives me new orders."

Sassi had never implied in any way that she had control or influence over him, not to him or to the crew. But, shit, he'd drain the ocean and raise Atlantis for her if she asked him to.

It had taken him time to get used to being with a woman in front of his crew, and he appreciated Sassi being patient while he adjusted. While they weren't overt in their intimacy most of the time, he'd gotten used to touching her or being touched in a way he'd never connect with another crewmate. Sassi was becoming his new normal; he wasn't sure he'd be able to go back to the old one.

Foist and Hector did as they were told and left the room, but his first-mate stayed put, waiting until the others were out the door before turning his attention to the bed.

"I don't know how you did it, boy, but you did good," Jockey said.

Often when he was working, Jockey would spend time in the mess, eating cake and talking with Sassi. More than once the old man had passed on cards to hang out on deck with her. It meant something to him that they got along. Jockey was his family, and his approval still held weight.

One thing Swain hadn't done was tell Jockey about Sassi's trouble or her terms for their intimacy. It was possible she'd told the first-mate herself, but Swain had never wanted to ask.

"She's something," he murmured.

Jockey twisted to face him. "I'll jump ship when we dock."

That snapped Swain's attention away from the beauty in his bed. "What?" he asked, scowling at the crazy suggestion. "No. What the fuck you talking about?"

"You and Sassi will want the place to yourselves. You don't want my scurvy—"

"She's not moving in," Swain said, figuring out what Jockey was aiming at. "When we get back to port it'll be just you, me, and Eros again."

"Well, now," Jockey said and he didn't look happy. "I didn't figure you for the sort."

"What sort?" he asked, leaping onto the defensive 'cause it wasn't right that the old man should judge without knowing the facts. "She ain't said nothing about berthing here on a permanent basis."

In fact, she'd made sure he knew the opposite was true.

"What kinda gent are you? You know she told Gumdrop that she had no place else to go," Jockey said. "She said it right in front of Swing. He heard it with his own ears. Said she'd be sleeping on the beach if you hadn't taken her in... now you're gonna toss her overboard?"

Every time Swain tried to bring up her problems, she shut him down, and usually got damn angry that he'd tried, so they'd end up arguing. He didn't like feeling useless and wasn't used to being out of control. But while Sassi had access to all his switches and levers, she'd managed to hold onto her own. She could control him, but he couldn't do the same with her.

"I'll keep a berth open for her," Swain said, watching her sleep again.

Out there in the world she'd be vulnerable. Her father was dead. Her brother had cut out on her. Yet, she believed she could stand up to the world. Nothing fazed his Sassi, she just pulled herself up by her bootstraps and trudged on.

"That's not what lassies want to hear," Jockey said, sitting himself on the corner of the desk. "Women are a brutal squall, unpredictable and fierce, but you never let 'em control you. Keep the wheel, son, ride the waves, maintain your headings."

Shaking his head slowly, Swain's gaze drifted to her peaceful face. "She's hiding something from me, Jock."

"Something like what?"

"She's in trouble."

Jockey slid off the desk. "Then you gotta start bailing for her. If she's taking on water, you keep her afloat, whatever it takes."

Balling his fist on the desk, Swain clenched his jaw. "Why fucking bail if I can't mend the leak? She says one thing, but her body tells me something else… I don't have a fucking clue what she wants, Jock."

"Step outta the wheelhouse, Swain, just like I taught you when you were a nipper. Get the spray on your face and feel the wind. Trust your senses, not the instruments."

"I don't know what that means," he said, knowing damn well how to sail a ship even if he couldn't navigate his relationship with this woman.

"You gotta feel her emotions, ride 'em like you would the waves in a storm. If you know you can make it, keep your eye on the crest. You hesitate, you founder… Do you want to keep her?"

Sassi was complicated, he often thought she was too complicated. He'd been conned into believing their relationship would be simple because out here it was, but it wouldn't be like that back home.

"I can't keep her against her will," he said and forced himself to look away from her. "There's another guy."

It made him feel sick to think he'd be delivering her to the arms of another man, to another man's bed. Jockey sucked in a long breath and sighed it out. "Now it makes sense…" Swain looked up hoping for some clarity. "We could've finished the survey yesterday, but you're still saying two more days. You're trying to keep us out here… To keep her out here because as long as she's here, she's yours."

"She is mine," he said. A surge of anger made him growl and shove a hand through his hair. "I don't make operational decisions based on a piece of ass."

Shooting to his feet, Swain was sick of mooning after the woman who'd made it clear she ranked him lower than some guy who'd apparently never touched her. According to her words anyway, he didn't know how much he could trust those. How could she say she belonged to another guy if she'd never been intimate with him?

"If that's all she is, order the return," Jockey said. "We pack up today, get underway by sunrise."

Back home. Back to reality. Glancing at the sleeping woman again, Swain wavered for only a second before giving his first-mate the nod. Swain couldn't keep them at sea forever; he'd have to face the truth eventually.

Until Sassi stepped off Eros, she was his. It was the only thing he'd been assured of in their relationship. Fuck knew what would happen after that or how he'd feel watching her go. But he was done putting his life, and the lives of his crew, on hold for a woman whose only plan was to abandon ship as soon as she possibly could.

TWENTY-THREE

JOCKEY TOLD SASSI that they were making good time. Without the delay of the pan-pan or the night in Miami, they should knock at least three days off the time of their return trip. Though they'd be stopping somewhere to refuel. But Jockey wasn't worried about that taking too much time apparently.

They were about four days into their voyage home, on her twenty-eighth day at sea.

Sassi missed being at anchor already, being still meant there was no imminent danger and… No, that wasn't why she missed it. Sassi missed it because it had been a perfect existence for a while.

Lazy afternoons in the galley practicing her techniques, swimming, sunbathing, scrubbing the deck with Fidget and touching up paint on the bulkheads. And regular afternoon delight, of course.

She got to spend time enjoying her man almost every day; sometimes just a few minutes, sometimes longer. Even if he was working, he'd talked to her, listen to her, just exist with her, and he didn't mind her presence loitering around.

It didn't matter if they were interacting or if he was busy with tasks or crew, Swain would let her read on the quarterdeck while they were diving or practice her knots in the wheelhouse when he was on watch or making plans with the others.

Since they'd been on their return trip, he'd had moments of being distant. She didn't like it when he detached himself. Sassi recognized that the grumpy captain she'd first met was joining her more frequently. While she didn't like to see him in a bad mood, she'd identified the cause: their relationship. It would be over in a matter of days.

Sassi didn't like to think about being without Swain since he'd been such a massive part of her life every single day for weeks. There wasn't going to be a period of adjustment or a gradual weaning off. She was going to have to go cold turkey.

Sitting in the mess feeling the ship rise and fall in the waves that were also pushing them left to right, she tried her best to move with the motion, tensing her core and relaxing into the rhythm. But it was difficult for her to stay balanced even at the calmest of times.

The ocean had a sense of humor, at least that's what Swain had told her once when she'd stumbled on deck after an unexpected wave made the ship sway. In this storm, the lurching made her cling to the bench beneath her thighs and hold her breath.

Swain.

Yes, if she thought about him, about being in his arms, his mouth, his body, she could distract herself from the sound of the wind battering the bulkheads and whistling through the portholes, doors, and hatches that were all supposed to be sealed.

Once in a while there would be a thud, a bang that echoed down the passageways and sent a chill zapping through her. Up on the wave and down, up and down, listing left, then further right.

"You okay, Miss Sassi?" Swing asked.

He and Fidget had been ordered to stay in the mess with her while the other men battled the storm raging in the night around them. "It's like a rollercoaster," she said and smiled.

That's what she convinced herself it was and with Swain at the helm she knew there was nothing to worry about. She was precious cargo, that's what he'd said, and he protected precious cargo. She'd be fine. Just fine.

When they'd known the storm was coming, Swain had briefed her to tie everything down, like, literally. He wanted all the equipment in the galley stowed behind locks. Sassi didn't want anything to break or to have a mess to clear up, but she'd gleaned a better understanding of Swain's strict orders when Jockey explained how something as simple as Tupperware could become a weapon, a dangerous hazard that could kill someone if it came flying off a shelf in the midst of a storm.

Sassi didn't want to be responsible for killing anyone, so she'd checked and re-checked everything to make sure nothing in the galley, or in their cabin, could become a threat. That meant tidying up all of Swain's papers from the desk. The computer could be packed away and the printer was fastened to the file cabinet and the wall, so their room was safe. It had also never been so tidy.

"The cap'n is good in storms," Fidget said, his voice was quiet, but not as unsure as it had been when she'd first come aboard. "He says he just feels how the ocean moves."

Initially the apprentice hadn't wanted to talk to her directly at all. He'd talk to Swing and speak to the others when spoken to, but it had taken time for him to come out of his shell with her.

In addition to keeping herself busy, that was another reason she'd tried to spend time with him while the other crewmembers were diving. She didn't want him spending too much time alone and because she'd managed to bond or find something in common with the other crew members, she didn't want him to be left out.

Swing nudged his buddy and snorted a laugh. "Don't gotta tell Sass that, bet she lets the captain steer her."

It was sort of impressive that Swing could still make sex jokes when the rain had just started pounding the portholes like a hail of biblical locusts. It felt like they were in an abyss at the start of the apocalypse.

Trying another smile, her stomach bounced from her guts to her throat on the next hump. Shit. Closing her eyes, she let her head bump on the wall and thought of her man at the wheel. She believed in him, she did, and wanted to send as much positive energy his way as she could.

A smile managed to quirk her lips. Her mother would be proud.

Sassi had never been one for new age ideas or alternative medicine, not that she was against it, she'd just never given it much thought. Her grandmother had been strict in her ideas of what a woman should be and airy-fairy was against all those rules. Agnes Robins had believed in appearances above all else and no matter how a family may be crumbling on the outside, it should never be obvious to outsiders.

In that respect, Agnes would be proud of how her son had handled his debts and the shame he'd brought on them all. At least no one respectable had known about it. Sassi couldn't be as noble. There she was in the midst of a storm that could tip her home on its head and toss them all in the drink and there still wasn't any other place she'd rather be.

"We do lifeboat checks all the time, Miss Sassi," Fidget said.

It was so nice that he was trying to comfort her, but she was actually doing okay and didn't feel sick, just a little off-balance. Swain was good at doing that to her. She figured Fidget's reassurance was more for his own benefit than hers. If he needed to say these things out loud to help alleviate his fears, then she wasn't going to ask to stop.

"Thank you, Fidget," she said, leaning over the table to take his hand. "Would you like to come sit by me?"

Again, she didn't need the comfort, but on this side of the table, there was something to lean on. Fidget and Swing's side only had a narrow bench. Fidget wasn't usually allowed to sit on this side, but she slid up and patted the bench beside her.

Fidget wasted no time in skipping over to her side and she took his hand on the seat between them, giving him an anchor of his own.

"We've got great lifeboats, the best," Swing said. "You seen inside 'em?" She shook her head. "Cap'n is always telling us to check stocks, to rotate, make sure they're seaworthy and all. So even if we founder, you don't have to worry, there's plenty of space for seven in the raft. Bet we could all lie down flat. You for sure, you're a skinny thing... that why the cap'n calls you waif?"

"I thought he called her wife," Fidget said.

He'd probably misheard waif, though Swain had called her his wife more than a few times. The boys were debating her pet name, but she was frowning, stuck on the number Swing had said.

"Eight," she said aloud, interrupting them. "You said the lifeboat was big enough for seven. You meant eight."

Swing shook his head. "Only seven go aboard," he said. "Captain stays with Eros."

The captain went down with the ship. Was that what he was saying? How had that idea not occurred to her? She was with a man who was actually suicidal!

She stood up, the ship moved and she sat back down. Sassi couldn't go to the wheelhouse and ask about the evacuation plan now, and she couldn't beg Swain to make her promises that he would never do something so crazy.

Her grip on the bench beneath her got tighter.

In a few days, she'd walk away from Swain and never see him again. But did that mean she wanted to read his obituary in a newspaper next week? No, it didn't.

After the shock wore off, she stopped feeling distressed and started to get angry. Sassi hadn't wanted to fall in love with Swain because she knew marrying Dario was a real possibility. But now she knew that even if she wasn't betrothed to that monster, she still had to distance herself from Swain who had chosen this crazy and dangerous career for himself.

While the sea was calm and the sun was shining it was easy to think of this ship as a private paradise. Tonight, she'd discovered it was anything but.

TWENTY-FOUR

AFTER GRABBING A couple of hour's kip, Swain went for a shower and then stuck his head through the hatch that led from his cabin to the wheelhouse. He got a quick report, weather and heading fine, speed, no issues, no delays.

Great.

He decided to get some grub before going upstairs to relieve Hector and Jockey. It was early for lunch, but not much, and he'd still been in the wheelhouse while the others had breakfast. He hadn't eaten a thing since last night. Sassi should be able to throw something together. She always had something on the go and she'd understand why he had to be on the bridge at sunrise as the storm cleared.

He'd slept with the woman every night for weeks. Waking up without her felt odd and gave him new appreciation for her comment about him neglecting her. He wouldn't tonight. He'd figure out the schedule and make sure they got an early night. He hadn't even had a chance to ask her how she'd handled the rougher waters.

Swain had never hurried to his mess before. He'd always been take it or leave it about food, never that bothered. But it wasn't the food that was kicking up his speed. When he ducked in the door and made eye contact with the woman shaking her booty in time with the song she was murmuring to herself, he was surprised to see her gaze cool and her body stiffen before she drew her eyes away from him.

Hmm…

Instead of saying anything, he went over to her and attempted to slide a hand around her waist. But she picked up his wrist and dropped his hand before moving away.

She loved it when he held her and kissed her neck. Wasn't she freaked by the weather? With his tongue in the corner of his lips, he considered what might be eating her. He'd done good work last night, they were all alive, weren't they? Okay, so it was hardly navigating a hurricane, but it was rougher than she'd ever experienced before. Shouldn't she be grateful?

"Okay," he groaned and scrubbed his hands over his face. "Is it the beard?"

He hadn't shaved since they'd weighed anchor. Not deliberately, he'd just been keeping himself busy trying not to think about what would happen when they landed.

"Nope," she said. "I guess you're here for chow. Sit down."

Was that an order? He'd guess from the glower on her profile that it was. Seemed he didn't move fast enough for her because she gave him a push with the side of her body to get him out the way so she could reach the fridge.

Without going too far, he crouched to murmur in her ear as she transferred sauce from Tupperware to a pot on the stove. "Guess no one around here told you

I'm the captain."

Though he noticed she was wearing his hoodie under her apron again and it proudly declared that she held that rank. Seeing her in her own clothes that bore his name was a turn on; her uniform declared her to be his and he loved that. He'd never looked at his uniform as a mark of possession before he'd seen it on her body.

But seeing her in *his* clothes took his arousal up another notch, then she'd started wearing his uniform, apparel that bore his name and his rank, and that triggered every primal instinct in his animal brain.

He'd never told her that. She knew too many ways to turn him on already; he didn't need to be giving her more ways to fuck with his restraint.

"I know exactly who you are, sir," she said, stomping over to the cabinet to pull out something else.

"Sir? Hmm, okay," he muttered to himself and was forced to catch the tub she thrust at his chest.

"Go, sit, eat a donut," she snapped and turned away from him.

He grabbed her wrist and pulled her back. "What is going on? What's changed since the kiss I got on the way to the wheelhouse last night?"

And boy was it a kiss. He'd told her to sit in the mess and not to move and she'd launched herself on him, telling him to be careful like he was going to war rather than the wheel he could manipulate blindfolded.

The boys had given him some grief about it, but he was getting used to their teasing and as long as he had the only girl on board, he'd take it. Swain figured he could cut them some slack. Like Foist had said, they were all horny mutts who hadn't touched a woman for weeks. Swain had been spoiled by his every single day.

And it wasn't until he'd had Sassi that he realized how much he needed the touch of a woman while he was on the water. Though that might have been more to do with the woman herself, because he couldn't see himself ever bringing another one along.

Well, he'd employ other women, but he'd leave them to the other guys. He sure couldn't go through this experience again. He loved being with Sassi, no other woman would match up to the standard she had set.

He loved Sassi.

It wasn't just being with her physically or talking to her that he loved. He was in love with the frustrating woman. That truth had hit him at the most inconvenient moment last night when they'd been riding a high crest, listing, with near zero visibility.

A shot of adrenaline for a second had seemed to be anxiety and it actually knocked him from his focus. Swain didn't get anxious when he was in the wheelhouse. Weather didn't scare him. He'd always figured when it was time for him to join the Locker, he would. He'd fight it every step of the way, but one day he wouldn't be the victor.

Then he'd thought of her.

Sassi.

She wasn't meant for the Locker like him and the others, not now, not yet. His woman was nothing but potential and he wouldn't be responsible for cutting that short. Her life was in his hands and he couldn't let her down.

Love was the only explanation for the strength of his reaction to that realization.

And on this new day after that epiphany, she was pissed at him… fucking great.

Sassi was giving him the silent treatment as she put some rice out on a plate and poured him a coffee. "Waif," he said and she ignored him. "Psyche?" What the hell else could he do to get her to talk to him? He wasn't fucking used to this. "You know, Sass, most people respond when the captain talks to them. You can't ignore the captain."

"I'm not ignoring the captain," she said, putting the sauce on his rice and handing him the plate. "I'm ignoring my lover."

At least he was making progress in figuring out what bug was up her ass, incremental though it was. "Okay," he said, his stomach rumbling at the scent of the food she'd given him. "The captain's ordering you to talk to your lover… what the fuck is going on?"

"That's unfair," she said, snatching the donuts to put them away; apparently, he'd missed his chance with those. "My captain shouldn't meddle in my private affairs."

Shit, this was complicated. This was why he should never have had relations with a subordinate. Had he really just been thinking that her being aboard was a good thing?

Giving him his coffee, Sassi was happy to turn her back and return to preparing lunch for the rest of the crew. They were getting something else that was cooking in a massive pot at the back of the stove; it smelled good.

But him, the man in command, he was getting leftovers. Opening his mouth, he figured he should charm her, except he had no idea what the fuck to say to charm a woman. He didn't coddle, he commanded, said what had to be said, told the truth. He didn't pander.

"Your captain wants to know why his crewman is upset."

"I'm not upset, I'm angry," she said. "Are you going to eat your food? Supplies are low, I don't want anything going to waste and since I've already heated it up, I won't do it again."

There wasn't an ounce of shame in her. No one talked to the captain like this. It was blatant insubordination.

Tossing the plate and the coffee on the counter,

he marched over to crowd in beside her. "You're sailing damn close to the wind, Waif. Shape up or ship out, hear?"

Throwing her spoon in the pot, she spun to face him, thrusting her fists to her hips. "Oh, don't you worry, Captain, I'm counting the damn minutes. This is my twenty-ninth day at sea with you. We were supposed to be home tomorrow."

"That what you're pissed about?"

"I don't give a damn about that. I give a damn about…"

She tried to stop herself, but he wouldn't let her off that easy. "You give a damn about what? If you don't clue me in, I can't fix it."

But she carried on seething. "That's just it, Captain," she said, her jaw tight. "You can't fix everything."

"On this fucking ship I can," he said. "Try me."

At first, she said nothing, and he thought this might go on all day, then she inhaled. "When we met, I thought you were an idiot."

He snorted. "Thanks."

"I was scared of you. Not scared… wary… Not enough that I'd run and hide, but I was always ready to fight you."

Sassi was never scared, she never showed it. She'd sassed him, stood up to the punk in Miami, and never shrunk even when the crew was getting rowdy. Sassi Robins was made of iron, and had a stronger will than any man or woman he'd ever met.

"I noticed," he said, noting the way her fists were bunched tight. "You're still ready."

Tension rattled through her. "If I thought punching you would make me feel better, I'd do it."

"I'd let you."

"I know."

And that quick-fire exchange was enough to take the wind from her sails. She exhaled like she'd been holding her breath underwater for three minutes, and he saw her snit seep out of her.

"Swing told me the captain goes down with the ship," she said. Her anger had been replaced by pain. "Would you really do that? Would you really have left me last night?"

Damnit, now he couldn't be mad at her either. She had been worried about him. It wasn't anger, it was protection. She'd been protecting herself because whatever the idiot Swing had said to her had made her fear losing him.

"Sweetheart," he said, stroking his hands up her arms to cup her face. "Last night wasn't that bad. We were never at risk of going down."

"I wasn't afraid," she said, edging nearer. "Not until he made that comment and it made me think, one day… you might…"

"He shouldn't have said anything to upset you. He'll get a dressing down, don't worry, Waif."

But she shook her head. "No, it's not his fault. He didn't mean to get in my head. But I just got this vision of…"

Her gaze dropped. Swain put a finger under her chin to bring it back up. "Saying goodbye." Her simple smile was agreement, not happiness. "This vessel and everyone on it are my responsibility."

"I know, but just promise me you'll never—"

"I can't promise you that, Waif, because chances are if I order everyone to abandon ship, I will be staying behind." She opened her mouth to object. "That doesn't mean I'll die… but I'm willing to."

"You're willing to die for Eros," she murmured.

Swain hated the thread of hurt in her voice, like she believed it was a done deal, like he was telling her he was going to walk out there and jump overboard.

"Yes," he said. "As I would for Foist or Tune or Fidget."

"And Jockey?"

"And you," he said, brushing the pad of his thumb over her cheek. "You don't accept command of a vessel unless you're willing to do whatever it takes to keep everyone safe."

"I respect that so much," she whispered. "But it scares me too."

On any other day, with any other woman, he'd either make a joke to shrug her off or propose to keep her. But, if his calculations were right, in less than four days this magnificent, enigmatic woman would slip through his fingers.

She might be reacting like his woman now, but their time was trickling away and it made him see what she'd meant after Miami about time.

Distance meant nothing, because they were on a bungee rope, set to boomerang right on back to where they'd started. Time was their enemy, space their ally, but even that was working against them now.

When they docked and she departed, it would be like she was never here. He'd had zero impact on her life. Sassi would drift away like salt washed from the hull and the only record they'd have of their time together would be their fading memories.

TWENTY-FIVE

SASSI HAD MOVED her backpack from the captain's cabin down to her original cabin while the rest of the crew was securing their lines.

The galley was spotless. She hadn't needed to feed anyone since breakfast though it was mid-afternoon now. In deference to their proximity to shore, the crew had chosen to forego lunch. Both to give her an opportunity to clean up and because they were eager to get back to the mainland. No one wanted to delay, even for food, so they forged on full-steam ahead.

The captain didn't give her any indication that he was reluctant to return home either. This had been a tough trip for him and he had preparations to make before he could turn around and go right back to where they'd come from.

Swain would soon be meeting with the client to present his findings and negotiate the next step of the job. They might have a short turn around, so the crew was desperate to make the most of their time on land while they had it.

For her though, it was over. Thirty-three days on the water. It wasn't bad for her first nautical billet, especially given that she hadn't missed the shore, not once.

There was so much more noise on the land than she remembered. There were so many sailors going about their lives, loading and unloading cargo, preparing for departure, and returning home. The seagulls were wailing and noise from engines and machinery razed the air too.

Sassi hadn't even left the ship yet and she already wanted to be back on the ocean.

"Where's the rest of your dunnage?" Swain's voice asked from behind her and she turned to see him leaning against the doorframe, his hands in his pockets.

Foist passed in the passageway behind him, slapping the captain's shoulder and then holding a hand up to her in a wave. "See ya on the roundtrip, Shortcake."

Smiling at the man who didn't miss a step in his rush to get to shore, she felt a pang of sorrow. "He's in a hurry."

"Tune and Hector already split. Swing took Fidget into town, he says for ice-cream, but that's their code for hitting a bar."

"I guess the guys have got some time to make up," she said. "They've had a lot of lonely nights."

Pushing his shoulder off the door, he stepped into the cabin. "Yeah, they have. We were lucky to have each other taking the edge off."

It might have been hope she heard in his tone, but she didn't know what he wanted. If it was reassurance that this had been more than a casual affair, she couldn't give it to him.

"I guess we were," she said.

Swain came to a stop in front of her, his hands still in his pockets. "I think this is the first time I've made landfall clean-shaven."

Laughing, she brushed a hand over his stubble. "And only you would call this clean-shaven."

Taking her hand, he turned his head and kissed her palm, closing his eyes as he did. "You don't have to rush off. There's a grill down the dock, The Port Hole, does great steak and…" Sassi withdrew her hand from his. "Or not."

"It's sweet of you to offer," she said. "But you don't have to worry. We both knew what this was. I'm not expecting you to call."

Bobbing his head, he slid his hand back into his pocket. "Good, 'cause signal in the South Atlantic sucks and you don't get a discount on overseas charges based on how far over the sea you are."

The man who'd been ready to give Sassi her marching orders before she'd ever set foot on his vessel was standing in front of her now making her laugh, it was a remarkable evolution.

Last night they'd gone to bed early and he'd made love to her, really made love to her before holding her for hours like he didn't want to dare close his eyes. Sassi hadn't wanted the night to end either. But, at some point, they must have drifted off. She'd woken up to his rough hands demanding more from her and then this morning she got another dose of his gentler touch.

Breakfast had been a rush, then her captain had to be on watch in the wheelhouse. The day had been a frenzy of activity. There had been no time to talk. Except there was really nothing to say. Maybe that was why they'd both avoided the subject of today.

They'd known it was coming and now it was here. There was nothing either of them could do to change the circumstances they were in.

"Well…" he said and slid a folded piece of paper from his pocket to hand it over to her. "Made it out to cash like you asked."

Opening it, she read the check was for eighteen thousand and she narrowed her eyes on his. "If you're paying me for the sex, I'm insulted," she said, playing it straight before letting her sass curl her lips. "Thank you."

Pulling him down, she touched a kiss to his jaw. "You said you were leaving all that equipment in the kitchen. Figured I should round up."

The cookware and utensils were hardly worth the extra he'd put on her check, but she wasn't going to make a big deal of it when she knew everyone was being paid for a full five weeks even though they were a few days shy. Swain was a generous captain, more generous than she ever could've begun to imagine when they'd first met.

She couldn't bear to take her lips from his jaw. When his mouth began to drift, she knew he was going to kiss her. Sassi closed her eyes and accepted his mouth. Relishing the feel of those bold hands sinking into her hair to cradle the back of her head, she wanted him to never let go.

Sassi wasn't ready to open her eyes when he drew back. "I've had an amazing time, Captain," she whispered. "Thank you for taking me on your adventure."

"We're here, okay?" he replied, his cheek caressing hers. "Could be for two weeks, could be for six months. There's always a berth for you on Eros and I'll put out word with the fleet… If you ever need a bolt-hole or a billet, look for the Swain name. Anywhere it is, you're welcome."

"Don't make me cry," she muttered, giving him a light push to part them as she dropped onto her heels again.

But he kept cupping her face. "I'm proud of you, Waif. You stuck it and you didn't complain… and you didn't get sick."

"I wanted my ten grand," she said and his flat smile broadened a little.

Putting off the inevitable only hurt both of them. Picking up her backpack, she started to pull it on. He grabbed the top to take its weight. "Let me help you with—"

"No, I've got it," she said, and pulled the weight onto her shoulders then tightened the straps.

The suitcases she'd brought were useless to her. They'd held kitchen equipment and food, none of which she had anymore. Without a fixed address, there was no point in her carting empty luggage anywhere.

Grabbing the hobo bag she'd barely looked at for weeks, she slung it over her head across her body, and then took a deep breath. "Got it?" her captain asked.

Snared in his gaze, Sassi was reminded of the night they'd sat opposite each other in Miami. Wishing she could reverse time and go through their whole journey again, she was left with nothing but a painful longing in her heart.

"Fair winds and following seas," she said.

He licked his lips to hide his amusement. "Jockey gave you that one?"

Laughing, she nodded. "I was worried that I wouldn't know what to say… But I like it… I'm jealous you get to go back out there while I have to be a landlubber again."

"You've been a pirate's wench," he said, touching her nose. "Don't be surprised if it feels like the sea calls to you now. If it does, don't fight it. The ocean grounds you; it helped you through this. If you need a friend, the waves will comfort you. Listen to them."

Sassi did feel an affinity with the water that had surrounded them for so long. The time she'd spent on deck, especially in the evening, had been the time she'd really bonded with Eros and her position onboard.

Opening her hand against the wall of the head that abutted the foot of the berth, Sassi bit her lip to restrain her emotion before she spoke. "Thank you, Eros," she said to the ship, smoothing her hand down the cool wall. "Look after her, Captain, like she looked after me."

"She'll miss you," he said.

They weren't talking about only the ship anymore, not from the way he looked through her. "I'll miss her too."

"Be good, Waif."

"Stay out of trouble, Pirate," she said.

Swain backed out to let her move past him into the passageway.

Going out onto the deck, Sassi found Jockey unlashing the gangplank. "Expecting guests?" she asked, startling him from the task.

"Thought you'd like it, lass," he said. "You didn't say goodbye to the crew?"

Because all of them thought that she was coming back for the next leg of the job and she didn't want to explain why she wasn't. Sassi couldn't tell Swain the whole truth and she trusted him more than any other person on the planet. There was no way she could explain it to the crew. It would raise too many questions that she wouldn't be able to answer. Why wouldn't someone want to go on a trip that could earn them so much money? Especially when that person had relished her role and been devoted to her captain.

How did she explain to her crew that she couldn't go because her fiancé wouldn't let her? Not that Sassi would ever ask. She wouldn't mention the name Eros in front of Dario for fear of making the crew she'd come to love vulnerable.

"Those boys have their fun to get to," she said.

"No need for me to hold them back."

"Don't be a stranger. They'll miss you," Jockey said, surprised when she hugged him.

"Take care of him, Jock," she whispered and kissed his cheek before meeting his eye and accepting his nod.

Widening her smile, she moved toward the gangway, taking one last look over the ship. Damn, she was going to miss this place and these men, but it was time for life to catch up with her.

Jumping off the ship to land on the dock, she was so proud of herself for taking the leap. But ending up in the water would be the least of her troubles. It might actually be a reprieve.

Turning around, she saluted at Jockey just as Swain stepped out of the passageway behind his first-mate. With one last look at her captain, she came about and strode away.

TWENTY-SIX

"IF YOU'RE THINKING about going after her, now's the time," Jockey said.

Swain didn't know what to think or what to do. Sassi had been around every day for weeks. There was still a part of him that expected he'd find her in the galley at breakfast time, like maybe this wasn't really real.

Jockey could be right, and he considered heading after her.

Watching her progress up the dock, Swain thought about what she might do if he ran after her and told her to stay. But before he could decide if he had the balls to do it, Sassi stopped walking. Concern, and hope, made him step forward. Was she going to come back? Had she realized that leaving Eros was a mistake?

No. Apparently not. She let out a loud shriek that was a gasp of elated surprise. It carried through the salty air, stopping several sailors in their tracks. Sassi started moving forward, away from Eros again, fast, faster than before. She ran down the dock, unclipping her backpack as she went, throwing it off her back onto the ground just before she leaped into the arms of a dark-haired guy who was standing there with his arms open.

They were too far away for Swain to pick out too many details, but he thought about what she'd said to him in the head during one of their arguments. She belonged to another man, and although he'd never expected to lay eyes on the bastard or to see them together, Swain guessed that he just had.

Lucky fuck was standing there all cocky while his gorgeous wench launched herself on him and coiled herself around him to hold on so tight. She was still holding on even now and all Swain could do was watch.

"Guess you missed your chance," Jockey said, slapping his back. "We'll go to The Port Hole tonight. You like it over there. Few burgers, few beers… We'll get the bourbon, the good stuff, celebrate our good fortune."

Celebrate the job they hadn't actually secured yet, that was what his first-mate was suggesting. But the job wasn't why Jockey was making the offer.

Watching Sassi slither down the guy who kept an arm around her as he went to retrieve her backpack, Swain gave the stranger points for carrying the luggage while Sassi grabbed his hand and started to talk, her gestures were so animated Swain would guess she was going at a thousand miles an hour.

His Sassi was his Sassi no more. His waif was no longer a stray, she'd found her home. It angered Swain to know he hadn't been the man to give it to her.

TWENTY-SEVEN

"BUT, STUART…" Sassi said, striding up the dock, clinging to her brother's hand with both of hers. "What are you doing here? How did you even know I'd be here? How did you—"

"Karen told me," he said. "I called the docks, they told me when you were due in. A boat, Sass? Seriously? You've been on a boat for a month? What the fuck do you know about boats?"

More than she had when she started; more than she could ever have imagined. "Eros is a ship," she said, "and I knew nothing about them when I boarded, but… I had a good crew."

Stuart had her backpack on one shoulder and he pulled his hand away from hers to put his arm around her again. "Did he pay you?"

Stuart had no idea that he was insulting her former lover… former as of a few minutes ago. "He? The captain? Yes, he paid me."

"And how close are we?"

"Close," she said. "When did you get back?

Where are you staying? Have you seen Dario?"

"How close?"

Sassi wasn't surprised that Stuart had charmed his way through the dockside gate. Either he'd found someone to flirt with or he'd given some story about belonging to one of the ships. No doubt he had drinking buddies down there or maybe some of his former weed clients were around.

They went through the gate and he led her to the street where Sassi was shocked to find Karen waiting for them in a car. Stuart put her in the back, tossed her bag in the trunk and then got into the driving seat.

Karen twisted to look at her over the shoulder of the front passenger seat. "You look amazing, you're tan like you've been on vacation for a month. Did you do any work?"

"I don't care what she did as long as she got paid," Stuart said and signaled to merge into traffic. "We're going to cash your check and then we're going back to Karen's to figure this out once and for all."

The worst part about her panic and the drama she'd feared would be waiting for her at home, was the idea of dealing with it alone. She hadn't suspected for a second that Stuart would come swooping back in to play the hero, but there he was.

Her brother wasn't the coward Karen had said he was and if this couple were together now, Sassi hoped that meant they were all the way together again. Her brother had his head screwed on better when Karen was around.

They were a family. Maybe she wouldn't have to marry Dario after all. Maybe they could actually figure this out.

TWENTY-EIGHT

KAREN'S APARTMENT WAS a studio; it was small, but it would work as a crash pad.

One way or another, this was all going to play out in less than two weeks. There were nine days until her deadline was up. Dario would get his money and they could all move on or she'd have to marry him to save their skins.

Karen made coffee and listened to Sassi's tales from the high seas. Stuart paced, stealing glances at the cash on the coffee table that they'd gotten from the bank before coming back to Karen's place.

"I've been doing nothing but talk since we got back," Sassi said. "What about you two? Are you back together?"

Stuart stopped pacing to lock eyes on Karen. Sassi recognized the exchange of reticent lovers. Maybe her brother hadn't come back for her or maybe the couple thought she'd judge them for being intimate with all this trouble going on.

But every person who knew what was going on

with Dario was in this room. If Stuart needed support or wanted to talk, Karen was the only one who understood their predicament, which would've given her brother the perfect excuse to knock on Karen's door.

"I couldn't leave without explaining," Stuart said, still locked on Karen. "I got back into town last week. I felt like shit for the way things ended."

That meant he'd been in the wind for almost a month. "Did you pull together any funds?"

"I have an idea," Stuart said, rushing over to sit on the coffee table between where she and Karen were on the couch.

"An idea?" Sassi asked, her sixth sense twitching. Stuart hadn't answered her question and he was too happy for a guy whose sister might be walking down the aisle to the head of a vile money lending gang in a couple of weeks. "What kind of idea?"

"A way we can turn your eighteen grand into twice as much."

Sometimes it was like their father was right there with them. "No," she said, quelling an urge to throw her body over the money to protect it. "We are not gambling on any crazy scheme. Did you forget how we got into this?"

"We got into this 'cause of Dad's gambling. This isn't a gamble. It's a business transaction… this boat you were on—"

"Ship."

"Right, ship," Stuart said. "The guy in charge, did you get friendly with him? What can you tell me about him? Like, is he a smart guy?"

"The captain? Yes, he's smart," she said, confused about what her brother was getting at. Karen had her knees tight together and her hands clasped around her mug in a posture that was suddenly anything but comfortable. "Why do you care about Swain?"

Stuart took her coffee away from her to set it aside. "I need you to introduce me to him."

"Ha!" Sassi laughed and pulled her hands away from her brother. "Not a snowball's chance, Stu. No way in hell. Why would I do that?"

Stuart was all confident innocence, but she didn't buy it for a second. Sassi knew her kin too well to believe he was anything close to naïve. "You said he's a business man, I have a business proposition for him."

Dubious, she eyed her sibling. "What kind of proposition?" Stuart didn't say anything, he looked to Karen as if he was appealing for help. But the temp agency account manager said nothing. "Look, you can already tell I'm against this idea. There's no way you'll change my mind by not cluing me in. Either you tell me everything or you don't get near Swain."

Her brother wasn't going to get near Swain anyway. She'd told her captain that once they docked their association was over. Going down there with Stuart would just look like game playing and she wasn't interested in making her captain's life more difficult.

Besides, Swain and his crew had another job on the horizon and it was going to make them a lot more money than the few measly bucks she and Stuart would be able to offer them with any hare-brained scheme, whatever it was.

"He's got a boat, a ship, and I know a guy. Well, they're a team actually, and they use one of the islands as a kind of conduit for merchandise. Thing is, they've had some logistical problems, and I know they'd be damn interested in connecting with someone who could offer logistical support. It's complicated, but—"

"No, it's not," Sassi said, so angry that she wanted to hit her brother hard. "You're talking about drugs. You want me to ask my former boss, who runs a totally legit, above-board company to ferry drugs for you on his ship. I can't fucking believe you, Stu!"

But her brother wasn't contrite. "It'll be lucrative for him, it makes sense. Trust me, this will work. I'm sure this Swain guy will be going out there anyway, and it's just a quick stop, he doesn't even have to be involved. He can let the guys load and unload, all he has to do is show up."

Trust Stuart to find some way of justifying doing something completely wrong like it was benign and she was overreacting. "That might work as a reason for you, Stu, but it won't for Swain. He knows everything that goes on with his ship and he'd never take on cargo without checking it himself."

"This is a one-off—"

"This is a nothing because it's not going to happen," she said. "He could lose everything!"

Stuart flew to his feet. "And what the fuck are we doing this for? Fun? We're fucking desperate, don't you get that? Desperate! I'm not fucking happy at the idea I might have to send my fucking baby sister down the aisle to that fucker, but you're not the one who'll have to watch him torture your fucking girlfriend! The only fucking person you've ever loved! You're not the one worried about having your fingernails pulled out with pliers."

He was furious, but his strong reaction was rooted in fear. Reaching up, Sassi took his hand. "I know, Stu, but I'm never going to let that happen. If I have to marry him to keep you and Karen safe, I will. I'm sorry if you think I don't understand. I do. I really do. But it's useless, Swain won't do it. He's too good a man."

And he had a past that could create problems for him if they were caught. With one felony on his sheet, even a juvenile one, his punishment could be harsher than everybody else's. Sassi didn't know how it worked. He'd probably lose his license, which would mean losing the company. No, she'd never let him take that risk. Her marrying Dario was a better option than asking her captain to lose everything that he'd spent his life building.

"We can do this," she said, sensing her brother's frustration. "We're only a few thousand dollars short."

"I have five grand."

Optimism made her pull him onto the coffee table again. "There you go! We're seven grand short. That's nothing! I can try to pull in some clients, we'll get jobs, ask for advances, maybe we can sell something, like Karen's car that's got to be worth a thousand or two, we'd pay you back. If we get close, we can ask Dario for more time and…" Stuart made eye contact with Karen who seemed paler than she had before. "What?"

"We need more than thirty grand," Stuart said, taking his hand out of hers.

The tension between the couple was scaring her. "I don't understand."

"Dad owed more than thirty grand. He owed a heap more to a bunch of people, little amounts all over. Couple of grand here, few hundred there, he owes one guy ten K."

Sassi had suspected that there would be more lenders. But as far as she was concerned, they'd deal with them one at a time. Asking for trouble would get them nowhere. "How the hell do you know that?"

Karen got up and went to retrieve something from the windowsill. When she brought it back, she handed it over to Sassi who unfolded the paper to read it. "Stu didn't come back for me… One of the things I brought from his apartment was the bag with your dad's hospital stuff in it."

Scanning the scrap of paper, Sassi read names and numbers, scrawled in different colored inks, at different angles, some upside down, some slanted, but there was no mistaking what it was.

"Dad kept a ledger."

"Such as it is," Karen said, sitting on the couch again. "I was just organizing things. I didn't even realize it was your dad's stuff when I opened the bag, but... When I figured out what it was, I emailed Stu... about a week after you left."

"I was in Texas," Stuart said. "I didn't even go into the coffee place to check my email, but when I saw they had computers I thought it couldn't hurt..."

"I'd scanned in the page at work," Karen said. "I emailed it to him and to you... I didn't know if you had access on the ship."

Shaking her head slowly, Sassi turned the piece of paper, picking out names she recognized and others she didn't. "I haven't checked it at all."

"I could've kept running," Stuart said. "But this was different. This wasn't just Dario... Everyone will be coming for us Sass... we won't be able to walk down the street without looking over our shoulders, you know? I don't know how we'll fix it or if we'll all end up on the run. But I know that if I run again, I'm taking both of you with me."

Sassi couldn't imagine a life on the run. Never being able to relax or come back home. They'd have to take on false identities, to keep moving, they'd never be able to stay still.

"What about mom?" she asked, thinking of the woman who had a habit of keeping her wheels turning.

"Fuck knows where she is," Stuart said. "We can't rely on her. Wasn't she in Italy the last time you spoke to her?"

Yes, she had been, but that was two years ago, maybe more. "She could be in danger too... we have to find a way to warn her." When Sassi forced herself to stop reading the names, she started to take in the numbers. "There's a hundred grand of debt on here… at least." Without including the thirty they still owed Dario. "Fuck, Stu…"

And there would be more. "Dario has to know about it," Stuart said. "He has to be holding those guys back. I think it's his ace card. Even if we show up with the thirty K, he'll drop this on us."

"And offer to take care of it," Sassi said, playing it through as Stuart had. "So I'll have to marry him either way."

"How many of these guys will give us extensions?" Stuart asked. "I know you don't know a lot of the guys in dad's circles, but I do, and Sass… some of them are just plain fucking evil."

"What was he thinking," she exhaled, dizzied by the letters and numbers on this dog-eared sheet.

Karen shimmied down the couch to offer a comforting hand. "He was an addict. I'm sure he didn't mean for this to happen or for you guys to be left with his debt."

Pulling her hand away, Sassi thrust up to her feet and scrunched the paper. "He had the balls to say my attitude would kill him? He's ruined everything! All of our lives!"

"Yeah," Stuart said, matching her stance. "And if he was here, I'd put my fist through him a few times. I wish we could just tell these guys it wasn't our problem, I wish we could. But they want their money, Sass, and we're the only link to him they have left."

So that was it. The situation was hopeless. Their last shred of help was gone. "Then why are we putting it off?" she asked, letting go of the ledger. "If Dario is our only way out, why don't we just go to him, get it over with. What's going to change in the next nine days?"

"I don't know," he said. "But I'm not giving up. We're going to keep thinking and working until the very last second. You're not going to give yourself to him willingly; you're going to fight it. Use that attitude that pisses the rest of us off. You don't lose hope!"

"What hope is there?" she asked, bending to scoop up the paper that had landed on the couch. "Look at his legacy! This is what we have left of our father and I'm the only one who can keep all of us alive."

"No, you're not," Stuart said, his anger and fear becoming a deeper annoyance. "Your friends on the boat can…" But she was shaking her head. "Shake your head now, but I'm not giving up and I won't let you give up either." Reaching to the back of the couch, he swiped up his jacket. "I need some air."

She and Karen watched Stuart stalk out and slam the door. "He really doesn't want you marrying Dario," Karen said.

"I'm not wild about the idea myself, Karen," she said. "But if it has to be done to keep you two safe. I'll do it…" Worried about her brother and what he might do, her attention moved around to the door again. Karen must have read her mind. "I'll go check if he's okay."

They shared a smile as Karen went to the door and out after Stuart who could be impulsive and reckless. He wasn't a bad guy; he just tended to act on emotion and had always been happy to take the easy way in life rather than pick an ideal or a goal and stick with it.

Out the window, Sassi just managed to see a slither of the ocean between the buildings and the horizon. It felt odd that the ground was static beneath her feet. She'd been so used to the movement of the ocean keeping her on her toes that it made her a bit light-headed to be completely still.

And alone. She hadn't been alone for a month. Even in a room without others, she knew there was the possibility of a person walking in at any time, and everyone was only ever a shout or intercom call away.

Not anymore.

Sassi didn't have time to pine for the life she'd just lost or the relationships she'd abandoned. Going to her backpack, she opened the top, ready to unpack and move on. The item folded then squashed on the top made her pause.

She hadn't packed it, she knew for sure because she hadn't packed any of her uniform apparel. In the end, she'd figured if she asked to keep anything her captain would know that she didn't really want to go.

But it turned out that she hadn't needed to ask.

Scooping up the huge black hoodie from the top of the pack, Sassi bit her lip in response to the heat that blurred her eyes. The act of pulling it on over her head made the first tears escape her eyes. Sassi took the cuff to her nose to breathe him in, and gave into her longing.

Turning to the window, she fixated on the distant slither of blue ocean beneath the horizon. "Pirate," she whispered.

Sinking her hands into her pocket, she touched something rough and when she pulled it out she found her knot. The knot he'd tied for her. She'd meant to leave it for him, but he must have found it beneath his pillow and put it in her backpack with his hoodie before she'd moved it from his cabin to hers.

Her captain. Her Swain… He'd been one step ahead. After existing with him for a month, she shouldn't be surprised that he'd anticipated her needs before she knew she had them. But the thing she needed more than anything else was him.

Except, having him there to support her was one fantasy neither of them would ever be able to fulfill.

TWENTY-NINE

SASSI HAD BEEN staying at Karen's for three days. Stuart was still going on about her talking to Swain about his illegal plan. Sticking to her guns, Sassi didn't doubt for a second that she was doing the right thing by refusing.

Karen was at work and Stuart was out trying to find some while Sassi stayed in the apartment to bake. She'd gone around the coffeehouses and restaurants in the area trying her best to regain some ground with her business. So far, she'd only managed to secure a one-off deal with a coffeehouse who'd ordered some items as a test of her skills. No problem, she didn't mind being tested, as long as she was being paid.

A knock on the apartment door made her rush for the sink to wash her hands. She had just grabbed the towel when the knock came again. Sassi didn't know any of Karen's friends, but she'd guess that they should know she was at work.

Opening the door, Sassi was ready to be polite in dismissing whoever was there. When she saw her captain on the threshold, as surprised as she was, she almost closed the door right in his face.

"Waif," he said. No words came out of her. What was he doing here? What would happen if Stuart came back to find him here? Her brother would open his big stupid mouth, that's what would happen and he'd offend her captain. "This makes my life easier. I was looking for Karen, but…"

"She's at work," she said. "I can give you the address."

If she could get rid of him quickly, there would be no chance of him and Stuart running into each other.

On her backward step, intending to look for a pen, Swain grabbed her wrist. "I was looking for her because I was looking for you." Dropping her gaze, she looked at his long fingers curled around her pale, sensitive flesh. "She was the only way I knew how to get in touch with you. I didn't expect to find you in her apartment."

Flattered, but trying to keep herself on guard, Sassi dragged her attention up and cleared her throat. "You were looking for me?" But her burgeoning internal glow only lasted a moment before her thinking switched back on. "Looking for me? Why were you looking for me?" Pulling her hand free of his grip, she edged back. "You shouldn't be looking for me. We agreed that—"

"I told the crew you were jumping ship and they didn't take it well," he said. "Guess they like your chow. So if I don't want a mutiny, I have to hire the cook they want… I need you on my crew."

That made her blink for a score of seconds. She couldn't believe it. "A job? You came to offer me a job?" she asked and frowned. "I told you once we got home that was it. We'd be over."

"This isn't about us," he said, propping a hand on the doorframe to lean in. "From here on out, there is no us. You have my word. I'll be your captain. Nothing else."

It would be so rude to laugh in his face, but if she was more relaxed, she might have done exactly that. "Nothing else?"

"I'm happy to talk to him, if you need me to."

That brought her up short. Her head tilted. "Him?"

"The guy waiting ashore for you."

Stuart? Oh, God, no! The men could never meet, not ever, because if they did, Stuart would start spouting his dumb plan. After that, Swain would probably hit him and hate her.

"Talk to…? No! Absolutely not. No way. Not ever. You're not talking to him. You're not allowed to talk to him… not ever."

"Did you tell him about us?"

Her mind was beginning to race. "No, I didn't," she said and tried to pull his arm down from the doorframe. "You have to go, Swain." His arm was so strong, so thick and sure that she couldn't budge it. Sassi could use some of that strength right now. She could use those arms, their comfort and security. And his mouth, and his berth, and his… Damn, these weren't the thoughts she was meant to be indulging in. "Please, Captain, you have to get out of here. He could come back any minute."

Stuart might stroll back if he had lined himself up some future work or if he got bored looking. It was as likely that he'd find himself in a bar somewhere or drawn into some con with his old buddies. With Stuart it was just never possible to tell.

"I'm not doing anything wrong," Swain said, his scowl either rooted in anger or offence, maybe both. "I'm offering you a job, Sassi. You said you didn't want to be stuck on land. I'm offering you the ocean, Waif. If you want it, it's yours." Her fingers slid away from his arm because the sincerity in his eyes made her heart open to bleed for what they could never have. "If you explain the payoff to him, he'll understand why it could benefit you both."

If she went back out on the water with him, her decision wouldn't have anything to do with money. "And what's the benefit for you, Captain?" she asked. "Why me?"

"The crew want you."

She could believe the guys being annoyed that she hadn't told them she wasn't sticking with them and she could understand them being disappointed at missing out on her baked treats. But Swain would've dealt with those concerns. He wouldn't be here unless he wanted to be, unless it was important to him too.

Her body loosened and she gave up her panic. "Swain," she whispered and took his hand from his side to pull him forward.

He came inside and she pushed the door to close it behind him. Without pausing, Sassi backed herself to the wall, pulling him with her. Already she felt better, just being there between him and the wall.

Resting a hand far above her head, he leaned in. "Waif?" he asked, his thumb brushing her jaw. "What's wrong?"

"Right now? In this exact minute?" she asked, sliding her hands up his torso to the back of his neck. "Absolutely nothing."

Pulling his mouth down to hers, she gave in to her fantasy. Her captain kept her safe. He cared for her and protected her. As long as his lips were pressed into hers, Sassi could be sure that nothing would hurt her.

The need of her body made her arch into him and while his hands didn't touch her, she rubbed herself against him. But she wanted more, craved more.

Instinct made her reach for the straps of her

dress. Sliding them from her shoulders, it took a second for the fabric to hit the floor and about the same for her to unclasp her strapless bra to let it join the material at her feet.

Swain kept on kissing her, giving her mouth all the attention it needed. When his lips skimmed over her jaw to her neck, she breathed out his name. This was them on dry land, after only being alone for a few seconds. How could he ever think that they could be professional at sea when they'd be alone out there for weeks at a time?

Guiding his hand to her breast, she wanted him to take control. "Psyche," he murmured and pulled back. "You can't."

"I can," she breathed, pulling open the buttons of his jeans. "Please, Captain."

Resting his forehead on hers, Swain cupped her face. "You said he could come back any minute."

Stretching to the side, she turned the lock on the front door, and slid on the chain. "We'll have some notice."

Pulling back, Swain landed a glare on her. His quick judgment and abrupt anger made her blink. "Have you fucked him today?"

Shock made her mouth open. "What?" she asked. Threads of clarity bound in a solid rope that made her shove at him. Swain didn't know that the man on the docks was her brother. He assumed Sassi was sleeping with him. "You bastard, you think I'm a slut? No! There's been no man since you! I'm not a whore! I'm not a cheater either! How the hell could you think that of me, Swain?" Pushing him again, she moved away from the wall and shoved him toward the door. "Get out of here! Bastard! Get out and don't dare come back!"

His hand landed on her collarbone beneath her throat, and he thrust her back against the wall, pinning her in place while he explored her eyes.

"No one since me?" She shook her head and didn't care how pissed he was. She would match and raise him. His gaze travelled down her almost nude body. "Panties aren't allowed during naked inspection."

His growled words came only a second before he seized the delicate lace at her hip and tore it from her body. Shit. Her captain knew how she loved his rough, overbearing behavior. Even when she wasn't happy with him, he could arouse her. Sassi had barely had a pair of panties left by the time they returned from sea.

Running his calloused hand over her body, her breasts and her abdomen, he let the heel come to a stop just above her clit. With his fierce, narrow eyes on hers, he curled his middle finger to slide it into her slow.

Sassi exhaled. Her eyes closed. "Swain…" Oh, he felt good, and as always, knew just how to torment her with his gradual pace. With his skillful fingers, he teased her to climax, watching her every second, and leaving her boneless against the wall. Struggling to lift her arms, she managed to fumble for him to pull him down to her level for another kiss. "I could never be at sea with my captain and not submit to him."

Her arm sagged to let her hand slide down his body. She'd just touched the cotton of his underwear when he withdrew.

Grabbing her wrists, he forced them to the wall by her face. "We have to keep our hands off each other. I gave you my word I wouldn't touch you."

Naked, panting and still quaking from the aftershocks of orgasm, Sassi couldn't be asked to even consider being professional with this man she was addicted to. "You're my captain," she said, clinging on to the security that gave her.

"No," he said and let his hands fall away from her wrists. "Fuck, you're right, Waif… How the fuck can

I keep my distance from you? I've had you in my bed too often to leave you alone on board. I thought I could do it. I thought since you had another guy that it… that we would be able to restrain ourselves."

The sexual pull between them was too great to ignore. The spark of attraction had been there from the first minute they'd met in the dark on that dock, even if neither of them had realized it at first.

But now they knew it was there, and what it was like to enjoy each other, it would be impossible to resist temptation.

"I'm not good at restraining myself," she said and tried to reach for him again.

But he walked away from her hand and went to the door to unlock it. "I'm sorry I came here, Sass. I shouldn't have interrupted your life," he said, frustration and anger bleeding from him. "We should've left it alone." Opening the door, he stepped into the hallway, then glanced back at her. "Move on. It ended the day we docked, just like you said. This never happened."

She was going to object, but he didn't give her the chance because he turned and marched off down the corridor.

Her captain had just fulfilled a fantasy she'd never let herself have. Thinking that he might come back for her was dangerous because hope could make her hesitate.

Closing the apartment door, she knew it was unhelpful to wish that he'd stayed with her. Just like Karen kept Stuart's thoughts straight, Swain cleared her mind. Sassi wanted to chase after him, to put her hand in his and ask him to take her out to the ocean and to keep her there safe forever.

But that was a fantasy. Reality was her future with Dario. She'd never feel the touch of her captain again.

THIRTY

THE NEXT DAY, after her brother and Karen were out, Sassi donned Swain's hoodie and made the trip to the coffeehouse to drop off her baked goods and pick up her check.

It was only a couple of hundred dollars profit, but it was progress.

Though Sassi was going on old information. She'd been so set on hitting the thirty grand target that she kept trying to ignore the huge debt they'd have to cover beyond that.

Striding down the sidewalk, Sassi decided to start calling around the businesses she'd contacted over the last few days in hopes that someone wanted to put in an order. Doing something was better than doing nothing and Stuart wouldn't let her get in touch with Dario.

As it turned out, she wasn't the only one growing impatient. A car pulled up to the curb ten feet in front of her. Sassi didn't think much about the vehicle until all four doors opened at once and four men stepped out.

She slowed when she recognized the men from

the warehouse where Dario had set the deadline. For a second, she thought about running, but what would be the point? Dario wouldn't take that well and she didn't want him paranoid or jumping the gun.

Sassi stopped and tucked her hands into the front pocket of her hoodie, curling her fingers around her lover's knot for solace as she steeled herself.

"Hey, boys, what a coincidence," she said as the men got to her.

The lead guy grabbed her arm. "Boss wants to see you."

"Course he does, I'm an easy woman to miss," she said, letting herself be tugged along and stuffed into the car.

***

THERE WERE FIVE days left until the deadline. Sassi couldn't figure out what this was about. But didn't like that she recognized the warehouse she was driven to. The industrial area wasn't as busy as it used to be, so this place was good for quiet meetings. Before their initial meeting, Sassi hadn't been suspicious of the location because it wasn't too far from town. But now it seemed more sinister. She wondered how a meeting would play out if Dario didn't get what he wanted.

The men stopped the car right by the metal side door. The guys got out the front to open the back doors and the men flanking her in the back got out too. One of them kept hold of her arm like they were worried she might run off, but Sassi didn't know where they were worried about her going.

Worst came to worst, there was a channel of water that led to the ocean nearby, but there were no vessels around here. Making a run for civilization would probably get her shot even though it was less than a quarter mile to the street.

"You don't have to pull," she said to the men who were tugging an arm each.

But they didn't stop yanking at her. Ignoring her, they took her inside to the empty concrete office space with its once-half-glazed wall and there she found Dario and three other men.

"Mi amor," Dario said and opened his arms. His men hurried her forward, boosting her body toward Dario so she fell into him. Dario took the opportunity to wrap his arms around her and nuzzle her hair. "You smell like the ocean."

No, she didn't. Everything around town smelled a bit like the sea because they were so close to it. But Sassi had lived on the ocean, out there surrounded by the deep blue, and the potent scent was intoxicating in its purity.

Swain, he smelled like the ocean. Her captain had it running through his veins. Sassi hadn't spent her life as immersed in it as he had.

As soon as she could wriggle out of Dario's arms, she did. "What's going on?" she asked. "I still have five days. Why drag me here now?"

"I missed you."

Yeah, right, like she believed that. "You could've waited five days," she said, sneering at him. "You're a busy guy, right? In fact, don't you have some bar downtown where you do all your business?"

She didn't think that he owned it, though he probably swanned around the place like he did. Stuart had said something once about Dario having a financial stake in it, but she didn't know how much of one.

"It's a place you'll get to know well when we're married," he said, picking up her hand to kiss the back of it.

Sassi was struggling not to pull away, not to grab

her hand back or slap him across the face. She didn't want to be near this man and definitely didn't want his lips on her. But there were seven other men in the room, she'd be an idiot to provoke them now.

A brief notion of how this would play if her crew was here made her smile. These eight guys wouldn't stand a chance if Swain and his men stood up to them. But her feelings of triumph were short-lived and ended in a shudder when she actually pictured the reality of that moment. Sassi didn't ever want her captain in Dario's presence. Her crew was about honor and Dario's men would fight dirty.

Her crew was never far from her mind. But she forced herself to stop thinking about them to focus on her current predicament. Readjusting her thoughts, she considered what she was supposed to know, and more importantly, what she wasn't supposed to know, before she responded.

"I have five days left," she said.

Dario had never mentioned her father's other debts. Stuart was sure that Dario was close enough to the money-lending community that he would know about the other creditors waiting in the wings. But if this was a game, she couldn't let him know that she knew his strategy.

"I know," Dario said, putting an arm around her to turn her around and walk her toward the internal wall. It still had its rusty metal frame, but the panes of glass that used to hang in them were long gone from neglect and vandalism. "I'm just checking to make sure we're all on course."

Dario always had a smug edge to his voice, but it really irked her that he was playing her. He wanted her to fail. He knew she would. Hiding from her that her father had other creditors meant that he could slap her down later when she didn't expect it.

If Sassi hadn't known the truth, her fantasy would've played out. She'd have paid him his money and spat in his face. Dario was probably betting on that. He wanted her to be cocky so he could lord his superiority over her after he cut her knees out from under her. Men like him were scum; the type who wanted to humiliate women rather than empower them.

"We're on course."

"Good. Good," Dario said, turning her around to press her back into the door frame, though the actual door was missing from that spot too. He put a hand above her head and leaned down, penning her in. "How much did you make today?"

Was he keeping track? He couldn't have had her brought here just to collect the few measly bucks she had.

"Not much," she said. "I don't carry my savings around with me."

"Our savings," he said. "You know when we're married, I'll take care of you. You won't have to worry about money and bills. They'll be my responsibility. All you'll have to worry about is being the perfect wife... You do know what I'll expect from you, don't you?"

Swallowing, she was reminded of the only time she'd been ill on Eros. "There's five days left on the clock," she said, unwilling to talk about what might be inevitable. "If I don't get your money together, we can talk about marriage as much as you want. But I still plan to make it."

The slow smile that widened his lips was so satisfied. She knew he was thinking about the bomb he planned to drop, though she didn't expect him to drop it now. "I'm sorry, Sexy Sassi," he said, touching her temple to run his fingertips through her hair, making her tense. "But that's not going to happen."

"You don't know that."

"I do," he said then laughed. "The next time I

use those words it will be the happiest day of our lives…
All the years I've wanted you… all the years I've wanted
this body to be mine… I can't believe it's finally going to
happen."

Although she was wearing Swain's thick hoodie,
she was disgusted by Dario's hand when it fell over her
breast. She swatted it away. "It isn't," she said, disgust
contorting her expression. "It won't happen. I'm going
to get you your money."

"You can't possibly get everyone their money
though, can you?" he said, raising a brow. "You see, mi
amor, I'm not the only man your father took money
from… He owes thousands to others all across the
city… To men who won't be as understanding as I have
been."

She only had a second to decide how to respond
and she chose to go with ignorance because if she told
the truth, that she knew about the others, he'd probably
wonder why she hadn't come around to his way of
thinking already.

"You don't know what you're talking about," she
said.

Insulting him might not have been the right way
to go. Dario grabbed her throat and squeezed. "I know
everything. You are going to belong to me. I always get
what I want. I've held back every man who wants to tear
out your guts and bleed you for every cent… If it wasn't
for me, you'd be ruined already. Your brother would be
dead. You'd be chained to some gangbanger's wall, and
you'd never be free. I am your only hope, Sexy Sassi."

Tugging on his wrist to try pulling it from her
throat, she fought to drag in a breath. He wasn't trying
to kill her; he hadn't cut off her airway completely. This
was about control and she despised him for his hold over
her, not this physical one, but the chokehold was
symbolic of the position she and her family were in.

His men weren't going to help her and she had no chance of getting him to let go if he didn't want to. Thrusting her knee up, she got him in the groin. Hissing in pain, Dario let go to double over and she saw her chance to run.

Darting forward, Sassi got past him, but was blocked by his men who closed in around her. Two came up behind her to grab her and force her around. Dario was still bent over and breathing through the pain that was obvious on his face. Damn, it felt good to have done some damage.

"You won't ever…" Dario's voice didn't manage to get strong enough to sound threatening. "Bring her."

The men wrestled her forward despite her struggling. Dario managed to stand straight again, though there was still an edge of discomfort in the curl of his lip. "You might have me in five days," she spat, fighting the men who wouldn't let her go. "But I don't belong to you yet."

"Yet," Dario said, twisting to smack the back of his hand hard across her face.

The pain was intense enough to make her eyes blur, but she couldn't deny she sort of deserved the hit. If she was willing to lash out, she had to be willing to take the hits in return. And she'd rather be beaten by him than kissed or caressed.

"You won't get me until I've exhausted every other option," she declared. "Until then, you keep your fucking hands to yourself."

Dario might have ideas of beating the sass out of her, but she wouldn't make it easy for him. No fucking way. She was going to hold onto her attitude until he ripped it from her soul.

With pain in his tone, Dario began to laugh. The slow exhale got stronger, making her uneasy. "You stupid little girl, this isn't high school anymore. You don't get to screw around with me. You don't get to play games. You're going to marry me and you'll be the perfect wife. The perfect submissive wife who will defer to me in everything. You will worship me and never make a decision without my input."

Sassi thought she was bad for indulging in her fantasies; this guy was downright deluded if he believed that could ever be reality. She didn't mean to laugh, or maybe she did. It wasn't a sinister or satisfied laugh like his. No, hers was just filled with ridicule and humor.

"Who the hell do you think I am?" she asked. "You sure you want to marry a woman you clearly don't know?"

Dario looked like he was ready to explode. But if he wanted to hit her again, she'd take it. Sassi had a feeling their marriage was going to be nothing but arguments like this and physical violence. But she was keeping score. For every hit he gave her, she planned to give him one back, even if she had to bide her time.

Nodding at one of his men, Dario sucked an inhale through his nose like he was trying to get himself together. "I'm glad you can laugh, mi amor," he said. "Because I'm looking forward to reminding you of just how powerful I am."

Powerful? Who did he think he was? The President? She didn't care about a man who had power, at least not one who bragged about it.

The guy he'd nodded at took a buddy and went deeper into the warehouse. They disappeared into a back room and she was left to wonder what was going on… but not for long.

Less than thirty seconds later they came back out, dragging a man between them; a gagged young man who she recognized.

Gasping, Sassi tried to rush forward, but the men around her grabbed hold of her. "Fidget!" she called out.

At the sound of her voice, the youngster's attention flew to her. But his hands were tied and the material over his mouth prevented him from responding. Dario's men pulled Fidget through the warehouse and into the office. It broke her heart that he fought harder when he saw her. "It's okay, honey, calm down… We're going to be okay." Turning her fury to Dario, she growled at him. "You bastard! He did nothing to you! What are you doing with him?"

"Proving a point," Dario said, moving in at her side to spit his words in her ear. "I know about your captain."

Dread tingled against the back of her neck, tickling her spine until it lodged as a sickness in her gut. "You know nothing."

But if he had Fidget, she couldn't be sure the apprentice hadn't mentioned Swain. If Pello had reported back, and he probably had, Dario might have known about Swain for a month. He'd have had weeks to gather information and figure out where she was and who she was with.

As for their intimacy, Pello couldn't have told Dario anything because she and Swain hadn't been a thing when they saw him in Miami. But she wouldn't put it past Pello to have lied and he did accuse her and the captain of being cozy together.

Fidget knew she and Swain had been together and she wouldn't blame him for telling the truth, especially while he was scared.

"I told you I would hurt anyone you cared about. Marry me and I'll take care of you. I'll take care of your father's debt and your freeloading brother… If you disobey me again, I have more victims to nail to the wall. Thank you, mi amor. Your brother, his woman, and your crew will suffer if you don't do everything you're told."

He'd taken Fidget as a warning, proof that he

could get to those she cared about even before she was aware he knew about them.

Swain would find out what had happened here. If not from her, then from Fidget. Their captain wouldn't take kindly to his crew member being intimidated.

"Hurting him was a big mistake," she said. "You've welcomed another enemy into your life."

"I haven't hurt this infant. He's hardly worth my men's time. We didn't touch him. We took him to prove to you that I am everywhere."

Hope surged through her. "Then let him go," she said. "You don't have any use for him. Just let him go."

"We may," he said and smiled at her, admiring her figure. "I like this side of you, this fear…"

Manipulating him was the only way to get what she wanted. Fighting with him could cause Fidget harm. "Dario," she said, softening her voice and her demeanor. "Please… I'll be grateful."

Interest made him examine her closer. When she tried to move toward him, he waved at his men to release her. "Grateful? Show me how grateful?"

Sassi didn't want to touch him, but for Fidget, for his safety, she would. Clasping Dario's face, she drew him down and kissed him softly. He grabbed her into his embrace and deepened the kiss. Responding to the least of her ability while trying not to anger him, she strained to see Fidget to check if he was okay.

But when she caught sight of Fidget, he looked so hurt. She knew why, he was thinking of Swain. In his eyes, she was their captain's wife. Sassi had formed a friendship with Fidget, they had respect, and the crew was supposed to be loyal. Now he probably assumed she was a slut who'd used and discarded their captain.

Dario groaned, his tone filled with pleasure. He tugged her closer. Sassi had to conceal her wretch when his erection nudged into her stomach.

"Keeping him is a waste of my time. He's worthless to me," Dario said.

So it didn't matter if she influenced choices, he would claim credit for the results. She didn't care so long as he let Fidget go free.

"Let me take him home," she said, hoping she'd be given a chance to leave too. Dario peered at her with suspicion. "You think I have no way to get the money to cover all my dad's debts, you're probably right. I promise you, Dario, I will marry you. I will come quietly."

This time his happiness was arrogance. "You are a fast learner, mi amor."

"Let me take the boy home, please…"

"Then you will come back to me?"

She nodded. "There are five days until the deadline," she said. "Let me use that time to tie up my loose ends. You know I'm in town. You know where I am. Where else can I go? You've proved your point… You're everywhere."

Flirtation worked with him. Seduction manipulated him. Sassi saw that stroking his ego got results. He kissed her again and she let him. Anything to ensure Fidget's safety. When Dario's lips left hers and he loosened his hold, he snapped his fingers at the men and ordered them to take Fidget back to where they'd found him.

"You have five days, mi amor," Dario said.

Fidget was pulled out of the warehouse first and she was crowded out next. Both of them were bundled into the back of the car with one of Dario's stooges.

In the center position in the backseat, Sassi reached over Fidget to put his seatbelt on and helped him take the gag from his mouth.

"Miss Sassi," he said quickly.

She put her fingers to his lips. "Shh, honey. It's okay. Not here. Not now," she said and linked her fingers in between his. "Are you hurt?" He shook his head. "Good. Good… Just sit tight. We'll be safe soon, okay? Just stay with me."

Taking comfort from her connection to him, she hoped that she was giving him some. Shame and embarrassment warred in her too. Sassi didn't want Fidget or the crew to think she was a whore who'd made a fool of their captain.

The captain. Shit. How was she going to explain this to him? He'd be so mad that Fidget had been endangered and he should be. She was mad too, and it was no one's fault but hers.

She wasn't supposed to fall in love and she had, with every member of the Eros crew.

The car took them to the docks and they were let out without incident. Sassi kept Fidget's hand to guide him through the security gate.

"Where are we going?" he asked but went with her.

"You need to be somewhere safe," she said. "Where's Swing?"

"He met a girl. They've been together a lot."

So Fidget had been alone and vulnerable. Jockey was right that Fidget needed Swing with him. If the friends had been together, Fidget would never have been taken. But it wasn't Swing's fault, it was hers.

"Come on, honey," she said, pulling him along to move them faster.

"Cap'n will be mad," Fidget said when they got near Eros.

That was an understatement and she wished she could avoid that wrath. But she wasn't leaving Fidget alone; she had to make sure someone was looking out for him.

"I know," she said. "But not with you. The captain's going to look after you. He'll make sure you're safe."

"Miss Sassi," he asked, stopping when they were just a few feet from Eros' bow. "Who were those people?"

"Don't worry about that," she said, urging him on. "You won't have to worry about them again. Go aboard."

"Swing and me was staying in a boarding house in town," Fidget said, looking past her.

"Now you're staying aboard Eros," she said and gave him a nudge. "Go on."

Fidget went aboard. "But the captain…"

"I'll talk to the captain," she said, sealing her lips before she took the leap onto the deck. Shit. She wasn't supposed to be back here. She should feel guilt and trepidation being aboard. Instead, a feeling of warmth cascaded through her as she took Fidget into the passageway and along to the empty mess. "Wait here."

Leaving Fidget in the mess, she went through the ship looking for Swain, or for anyone. She didn't go into his cabin, but she knocked on the door and cracked it open an inch to call for him. He didn't reply. No one was there.

Okay. She couldn't leave Fidget alone. Sassi had to make sure someone was going to look out for him.

Going to the mess, she smiled at the boy who was seating himself on a settee in the rec area. "No one's here… We'll wait," she said and smiled. "Are you hungry?"

THIRTY-ONE

WHILE FIDGET WAS eating in front of the TV and the cookies were baking in the galley, Sassi told the apprentice that she was going to make a call.

They'd passed a phone on the dock and she needed to warn Stuart about what had happened. Running from the ship, she leaped onto the dock, and hurried to the phone. While dialing to reverse the charges, she turned to keep an eye on Eros.

Fidget wouldn't leave because she'd told him not to and he'd always followed her orders. It was amazing that he wasn't madder at her. Being on Eros, in the mess, seemed to relax him, giving her a break from answering questions.

"Who the fuck is this?" Stuart's voice bellowed down the phone line.

"It's me," she said. "Listen to me, Stuart, it's over, okay?"

"Over?" he asked. "Sassi? What the hell are you talking about?"

"Dario sent his guys for me and—"

"The bastard, I'll fucking kill him! We have five days!"

"I can't explain everything," she said because her brother wouldn't understand how she felt about Fidget or about her crew. "Dario told me about dad's other debts, he promised to take care of them and I… I said I would marry him. It's over, Stuart. We did our best, but… it's over."

"No," he said. "I won't let you give up! I won't give up!"

"You can be happy with Karen now," she said, and took a careful breath. Sassi had to sound sure and determined. Her brother had to believe she was making this choice consciously and not because she'd been left with no other options. "Be happy with her, okay? I'll take care of everything else."

While he was still arguing with her, she returned the phone to the hook and leaned against the pole it was on. But she couldn't loiter. Fidget, she had to make sure he was going to be okay. She had to look after him until she could entrust his care to someone else.

Steeling herself, she gathered all her courage and marched back to Eros. Fidget would respond to her strength. Going aboard, she finished making the cookies and feeding Fidget. When he was done eating, she suggested he go for a nap in his berth and he did.

Sassi was wiping down the counters in the galley when footsteps made her turn.

"When we said come visit, we didn't mean you had to work for it," Jockey said and a grin split his face. "You staying, lass?"

Pulling a coffee cup from the cabinet, she filled it, then grabbed a couple of cookies from the cooling rack to take them over to him. "Fidget's asleep in his berth."

Jockey's joy morphed to concern. "The boy in

trouble?"

"No," she said. "He… he was… But I told him he'd be safe here… Can he stay here? Just for a week."

Jockey took the cookies and the coffee to put them on the table. "You gotta explain this to me slow. The cap'n will—"

"I don't need to see the captain," she said, sidestepping, trying to get around the first-mate. "Fidget just needs someone to look out for him. Swing has a girl, he's busy, and Fidget's vulnerable on his own."

The first-mate's frown betrayed his wary confusion. "Vulnerable? Lass, what's going on, girl?"

Sassi told herself to stay strong, just for a while longer. "Look after him. Stay with him. Don't ever leave him on his own. Everything will be fine in a week," she said and managed to sneak past Jockey to hurry down the passageway onto the deck.

Leaping off Eros, she was determined to put some distance between her and the ship. Except to her horror, there was Stuart stomping down the dock toward her.

"Stuart," she said, stopping and backing away a few steps. "What the hell are you doing here? How did you find me?"

"Google," he said. "Your phone number came up on Karen's phone."

Shit. Why hadn't she thought about hiding the number? Because she'd been too busy thinking about reversing the charges and hadn't considered that he might reverse search the number.

"You shouldn't have come here," she said.

"What the hell are you doing here? You tell me it's over and you're marrying Dario, but you're here… What's going on?"

Sassi wished that more people were like Fidget. He was used to being subordinate on the ship and had respect for those he considered more in the know. If Swain needed him to be aware of something, he clued him in. But Fidget didn't always know everything that was going on. He was used to that, so he didn't push.

Stuart wasn't so easy to deal with.

"Nothing," she said.

"If you won't tell me, I'll get answers from these bastards," Stuart said, marching past her to head for Eros.

"You can't," she said, running after him to put herself between him and the ship's gangway. "You can't get on the ship."

"I fucking can," Stuart said, though seemed to be assessing just how he might go about it. "Get out of my way."

"You can't get on a ship without the captain's permission."

"You were on it," he said. "I saw you, two fucking minutes ago."

"I have permission… I had permission…"

Maybe that had been revoked, she wasn't sure. But she could be confident that even if Swain had been aboard and hadn't expected her, he wouldn't have called the cops on her. He might call them on Stuart because Swain was particular about trespassers.

"You can't fucking stop me. I'm getting on this fucking barge and I'm gonna talk to the guy in charge. He needs to stay the fuck out of our business if he's not gonna help us!"

"He's not on board," she said, keeping her hands out in front of her to block her brother. "The man in charge, the captain, he's not onboard. You're wasting your time. Let's just get out of here."

Stuart peered at her. "You called me from here like an hour ago. You telling me you were sitting here alone staring at the wall there?"

"It's called a bulkhead and no, there are people on board, two of them actually, but not the captain. He's not here."

Thank God, she thought to herself.

"Then I'll wait," he said and tried to swerve around her.

Sassi put herself in his way. "No. No! You are not boarding this ship! Not a chance! No! I won't let you!"

"Move!"

"No!" Sassi said, adamant about keeping her brother away from the Eros crew who were in enough danger because of her. She didn't need them taking more grief. "Get away! You are not allowed onboard this vessel!"

"You heard the lady."

Swain's booming voice might have startled Stuart into turning around, but Sassi let her head fall into her hands. Wishing the sea would sweep her away, she considered edging backwards and stepping into it. Except knowing her luck, she'd fail to fall in the water given how close the hull was to the dock.

When she did look up, Swain was ten feet away, pacing toward them, a fierce look of anger and possession on his face.

Great.

This wasn't going to go well.

"Who the hell are you?" Stuart demanded.

Swain was bigger than her brother and definitely looked meaner, but that wouldn't discourage her sibling from being an ass.

"He's the captain," she murmured from behind Stuart.

Swain was balling his fist like he might be planning to knock Stuart out and ask questions later.

"Then you're the fucker I'm looking for."

Stuart was angling for a beating and if he insulted Swain one more time, she'd give him it herself. Swerving around Stuart, Sassi put her body in front of her sibling and opened her arms.

With her back to her brother, she appealed to her captain. "If I asked you to step aboard and pretend you never saw us, I'd be kidding myself, right?" she asked Swain who scowled at her. "That's what I thought."

"Start talking, Waif or I'm gonna make assumptions no one's gonna like," the captain said, fixating his dislike on Stuart.

"It's nothing."

"Nothing. Nothing," Stuart said, trying to push down her arms. "Always fucking nothing with you. Something this fucker said changed your mind today. Something. It had to be him."

"This is the first I'm seeing him today," she said over her shoulder, fighting to keep her place as her brother fought to move her. "He said nothing."

"Then what the fuck are you doing here?" Stuart demanded.

"That's a good question," Swain said. "And one I'll get answered as soon as you take your hands off her and get the fuck out of here."

"I can touch her any way I want to, you bastard," Stuart spat. "She's about to do something crazy and stupid. I'm allowed to be pissed."

"Crazy and stupid like running off to sea?" Swain asked her brother, but he was looking at her. Her captain assumed that she was there to take him up on yesterday's job offer. They'd agreed it was over. Did he think she was going with him like… with him? "Do you need me to cast off, Waif? I'm sure Jock's onboard."

"He is," she said. "And Fidget too."

"Then we got all the crew we need to ditch this asshole."

"Who you calling an asshole, asshole?" Stuart said.

Rage flipped her around to smack his chest. "You insult him one more time, Stuart, and I'll toss you in the drink myself! Around here we respect our captain and if you think I can't build myself an army to take you down you can kiss my ass. Do not swear at him again, hear?"

Sassi might be taking on one too many of her former lover's mannerisms. But, as she considered this, her captain's hand curled over her shoulder to grip her tight, giving her the support she needed. Lifting her shoulder and dropping her cheek to press it on his knuckles, she relished the feel of his long, capable digits.

"He's your brother," Swain said.

Turning to her captain, she felt relief at the acceptance of his fingers when he brushed the back of them down her cheek. "You thought he was my lover."

"You said there was another man."

"It's not him."

They stared at each other for a second until Stuart's exclamation of hysterical disbelief startled her into facing him again.

"You fucked your boss?" Stuart asked her. "That was smart, Sass, real smart. Where the fuck were you for the conversation we had about us distancing ourselves from people?"

Sassi had planned to never reveal her affair with Swain to her brother.

Now they were there, she wasn't going to deny it. "It wasn't like that," she said. Swain's hand rested on her shoulder again. "He's my captain."

Stuart's brows rose. "So he fucks all the women on his staff? Nice work if you can get it."

"Crew and no," she said, pissed he was being glib. "I'm the only woman on his crew."

"And fucking him came as a bonus?" he said and lifted his eyes over her. "You're a real fucker."

"Yeah, much better I should wait 'til she needs me most then cut and run," Swain said. "You're a real hero." He sighed, like he had better things to be doing than this and he did. "You need me to hit him, Waif, or you just wanna keep arguing with him?"

"I don't need you to hit him," she said, sad when his hand left her and went aboard Eros.

"Oh, now who's the champ?" Stuart said, turning to the ship. "You fuck my sister for God knows how long, have your fucking fun and when things get desperate and she's about to lose fucking everything, you just sail away on your fucking boat and forget about her. You are an asshole and I don't care what she says. You're no better than him."

Smacking Stuart's arm, something burst in her chest. "What the fuck did I say to you? He's not an asshole. And he's a million times the man that Dario is! He doesn't know anything about what's going on. I didn't tell him anything and keeping quiet almost cost a dear friend of mine his life! As if that wasn't enough, I've been choked and slapped and taken about as much as I can today! So everyone has to stop fucking fighting and just accept that I have made a decision to end this. Today!"

"Waif," Swain's voice was cool and calm behind her, but his composed reserve only increased her dread.

Oh no, this was it. She'd said too much. Her captain wasn't going to let her away with excuses anymore.

"Yes, Captain," she said in an almost Pavlovian response to his stern tone.

"Come aboard."

Turning, Sassi accepted her captain's hand for balance and stepped onto the ship, going behind him when he guided her there.

"You're not crew, Robins," Swain said to Stuart. "But I'll only get what I want from her if you're around. I'll invite you aboard as a guest. If you outstay your welcome there won't be any damn warning, I'll just toss you over."

"Whatever," Stuart said and inched forward.

Sassi rushed into the gangway and blocked him again. "You say 'yes, Captain' and show him respect or I'll have Jockey out here so fast your head will spin."

"What the fuck is—"

"I won't let you aboard unless you promise to respect my captain, Stuart. I won't do it."

Stuart thought she was nuts, that much was obvious, but he grumbled an exhale. "Fine," he said. "Yes, Captain. Satisfied?"

No, because if he refused, she'd have a valid reason to bolt without giving Swain any answers. Stuart came aboard, wobbling and taking a minute to get his balance even though Eros was barely moving. Swain didn't wait for Stuart, he marched on, heading down the passageway.

"I made cookies," she said, pushing Stuart, and hoping Swain would react to her statement, he didn't.

Her captain went into the mess where they found Jockey at the dinner table, coffee and cookie in hand. "Lass, you've got some explaining to do," he said and glared at Stuart. "Who's the landlubber?"

"He's my brother," she said, going into the galley to pour coffee for Swain and for Stuart, who was still looking around the place like they'd just teleported him to a new planet.

"The lass tell you we got Fidget berthing a week?" Jockey said to Swain. "Boy got himself in some trouble I guess."

"The lass," Swain stated, taking his place at the

head of the table. "Has got a serious amount of talking to do."

Trepidation made her avoid looking at him when she took the coffees over to the table. "Would anyone like a sandwich? Pasta? I can make a pot roast, there's—"

"Dock it, Waif," Swain said, nodding to the seat at his side where she'd always sat since they first slept together. "Robins, put your ass on the bench too… We're gonna get the whole story out. It's about fucking time I knew what the fuck was going on. No terms, no time limits, the truth, Waif… All of it."

"Swain," she said, swooping onto the bench to grab up his hand. "I'm sorry, cap'n."

Hooking a finger under her chin, he raised it up to examine her neck and from the tick in his jaw, she'd guess there were bruises around her throat.

"I'll take him down, Waif. But you've gotta tell me everything. Every detail."

THIRTY-TWO

WITH HER HEART pounding in her chest, Sassi tried her best to fill her captain in. Where she struggled, Stuart leaped in to pad out the details until he'd taken over telling the story completely. Jockey asked questions, Swain brooded, and eventually everything came out. She and Stuart confessed everything from their father's debt to Dario's demands where their trouble had started.

She told him about Karen and how she'd gotten the job with him, and how the siblings had decided it best to keep distance from those who could be used against them. They talked about Stuart breaking up with Karen and Sassi learned some new details about what Stuart had been up to while she was at sea.

The story culminated in that day with her dropping off the baked goods, Dario's men, and what had happened with Fidget.

Swain wasn't an easy man to read. It was obvious he was tense and angry, but she didn't know what he was thinking, other than how he probably wished he'd never met her.

"I brought Fidget here because I need him to be safe," she said. "This will be over when I go to Dario. I won't leave him once I get there. But I had to make sure Fidget was being looked after." Turning to Stuart who was on the same bench as her she stretched her arm toward him. "You can keep the money in the apartment. I just need a couple of thousand, something I can keep as back up in case there's an emergency or I see a real chance to get away."

"A real chance?" Stuart asked. "Now is your real chance. We'll buy you a fucking ticket to Europe and you go to ground."

"Then what?" she asked. "I don't know anything about changing identities or how to live on the run… or about life in Europe. I wouldn't even know how to get an apartment or a job."

Stuart thought about it for a second. "You mentioned mom before," Stuart said. "Do you have any way to get in touch with her? She manages to do a damn good job of hiding."

Their mother wasn't hiding from anyone, they just never tried to look for her. She just wasn't in their lives, and they didn't expect her to be. "I can't go to mom," Sassi said. "That would put her in as much danger as you are. Besides, if I run, where does that leave you and Karen? If I'm not here, he'll want his money."

"I know some people," Stuart said. "I have contacts. I'll talk him into hiring me, I'll work off the debt."

That was a ridiculous idea because with someone like Dario he'd always find a way to keep Stuart on the hook. It would take years, her brother would never be free.

"How long will that take?" she asked. "And what about Karen? Is she supposed to wait for you? Her family already hate you, working for a known criminal is not going to raise their opinion of you."

"They don't hate me," he grumbled, but both siblings knew they did.

"The point is, how can you ever be happy with the woman you love if you're working for Dario? Karen would always be in danger, always. He'd give you the worst jobs, and any time you fucked up, any time Dario was in a bad mood, he'd take it out on her…" Sliding further toward her brother, she fumbled for his hand. "And what about us? We could never see each other again, do you get that? I'd be on the run for the rest of my life and if you were linked to Dario, I would never be able to see you again. He'd always be around, lurking."

Pulling her to him, Stuart squeezed her hands in both of his. "You are my baby sister, I swore to dad I'd take care of you… How the fuck can I promise that then let you marry a guy whose only mission will be to crush you?"

Raising her chin, she tried her best to project nothing but defiant confidence. "Do you think I'd let him? When he told me I'd have to be a dutiful wife who deferred to him and didn't have opinions, I laughed in his face. I don't care what he does to me, I'll give it right back. Why do you think I got choked? I insulted him and he couldn't take it. He slapped me 'cause I kneed him in the balls for getting too close. Don't you worry about me, brother. I know how to handle myself around strong men… Just ask the guy sitting behind me. They don't come much stronger than him and I never showed him an ounce of fear."

"If you let me ask him about—"

"No," she said. "What happened today scared me. Not what happened to me, but when they brought out Fidget, I… I've never felt shame like that, terror… Dario made his point. I can take whatever he wants to hit me with, but I can't let him hurt the people I love. I won't let you risk your life and I won't risk this crew's lives or livelihood."

"You love this crew?" Stuart asked her.

"I do," she said without having to even consider her answer for a beat.

"And him?" Stuart asked, examining her as he nodded past her at Swain. "Do you love him?"

Sassi had never let herself think about her feelings for Swain because he'd never been an option and never would be.

"I'm getting married in five days, Stu. Nothing else matters."

"It matters," Jockey said from his seat opposite them, though he didn't stay in it long.

Agitation made him leave the table and she didn't like to see the usually collected man so fraught.

The first-mate didn't often scowl, but he was angry now, and it was her fault.

"She's right," Swain said, the first thing he'd said for a while. "We have to worry about everyone's safety first and foremost."

Yes. This was where his sense of responsibility as captain would work in her favor.

"Thank you," she said, twisting to see Swain's tense frown was fixated in the middle distance. "Will you please look after Fidget? What am I saying? Of course you will. Thank you."

"Fidget isn't the only one we have to look after," Swain said. "He's safe for now and he'll stay where he is." Swain left his seat to go to a lock box on the wall that she'd noticed before but had never been curious about. There were plenty of things on ship she was clueless about. "Robins, you'll be coming with me."

"Where?" Stuart asked, but didn't hesitate to leap to his feet.

Sassi gasped when she saw Swain pull a gun from

the box. He checked the clip. "Rounding up our people. We'll get the crew and your girl back here. Eros is easy to secure and with my men aboard we'll be able to tackle any threat. We'll get her supplied and fueled so if we have to cast off and regroup offshore we can."

"Right," Stuart said like he had a clue what any of that meant, but he had no idea what getting underway would involve.

Swain went to Jockey to slap the weapon into the first-mate's hand. The men shared a charged moment like initial orders were being given telepathically, though Swain did follow up with actual orders.

"If you have to, take her out…" Swain knew how to sell sinister, but Sassi was flabbergasted that he might be suggesting Jockey hurt her. Her captain was mad, but that mad? He must have seen her shock because he growled at her. "Eros from shore. If I thought you needed to be shot, I'd do it myself, wench."

And probably enjoy it too, he sure was mad enough right now.

"Wait," she said, scrambling from the bench. "What are you talking about rounding up people? You don't have to bring the crew here. Everyone will be safe as soon as I go to Dario. If I need to do that now, this minute, to keep you all safe, then I will. I don't want you to worry, Captain, I won't let you down. I won't back out. I will do what's best for the crew and for my family. I will marry Dario Correa. After that, he'll leave you all alone. I promise, Captain, I will marry him."

"No, Waif, you won't," he said, dismissing her without even looking at her. Grabbing his arm, she was determined to have his attention, but he yanked his arm away from her to turn and glare. "I will make this ship a fortress. We're preparing for a siege. I don't care how long we have to stay here, you are not to leave this vessel without my permission."

Stuttering and blinking, she couldn't remember ever seeing him so vehement. "You won't give me permission," she managed to murmur, knowing her captain. "It won't matter how much I beg, you won't grant me permission."

It wasn't even determination in his stature, it was arrogant entitlement. Swain was so used to giving the orders and having everyone follow them that he didn't even see her claim for the accusation it was.

"That's right, I won't," he said. "So if there's anything you need, you better give your brother instructions because Eros is going to be your home for as long as it takes."

Finding her strength, Sassi asserted herself. "No, you can't do this, you can't," she said, starching her shoulders. "No, I won't let any of you take over. I won't let you take risks when it's in my power to save your lives. I'm leaving… I'm going to marry him and no one can stop me."

Spinning around, she didn't get a single step before Swain snatched her wrist and bent down to toss her over his shoulder. They'd been in this position before and although she kicked and screamed as she had the last time, it didn't slow him down.

Swain strode through his ship, down the passageway and up the stairs into his cabin. Dumping her on her feet, he went back to the door to lock it tight before turning on her, his chest heaving with fury.

"I don't even know where to start, Waif. I don't even know where to fucking start!"

"Don't shout at me!" she said, not really thinking about the fact that she was shouting at him.

"You should've told me! From the very beginning, you should've been honest about everything!"

"And what would you have done?" she asked. "This was my mess and I'm the only one who can fix it."

His eyes narrowed. "You think because that mangy, scum-sucking asshole gave you an out from the debt, you should take it? Don't you see he's set this up? He's been biding his time! Playing with you! Why would you want to marry a guy who—"

"I don't *want* to marry him. Holy fuck, Swain! You think I *want* to marry the asshole? I thought all I needed to do was raise thirty grand and I was sure we'd make it. One way or another, I had to believe we would… I had no idea how much else my dad owed and now that I do…" She took a deep breath. "It's hopeless, Swain. Hopeless. You would do the same thing if you were me."

He shook his head in a shallow, disbelieving arc. "Give up? Not fucking likely."

"If the only way to save your crew was to give yourself to someone, you'd do it. You'd sacrifice yourself for their wellbeing."

"Jesus fucking Christ," he said, storming over to grab her shoulders. "You are my fucking crew! Why the fuck do you think I'd let you do this?"

"You have no choice," she said, hating how the ferocity of his gaze sped her heart. "This isn't even a choice. It's math. One person versus a bunch of others. I never for a second thought he'd come for the Eros crew, never for a second! Now that he has, it's game over. I won't risk your lives."

His hands fell to his sides when he straightened. "Coming after my people was a huge mistake," Swain growled. "It won't end here. He made a new enemy when he touched Fidget."

"I told him that," she said, trying to touch him, but he backed away. It hurt so much to see the disgust on his face whenever she tried to make contact with him. "I'm sorry, Captain. I can't say it enough… But that's why you have to let me go. You have to let me be with him. It will ensure your safety and the safety of the crew. It just makes good sense."

As a captain he understood there were times when something had to be sacrificed for the greater good. Usually that would be equipment or cargo. He'd said it himself when they discussed the captain going down with the ship. Swain had to be willing to make the ultimate sacrifice to save the people under his care.

Sassi might not have chosen this course, but her brother and Karen, the Eros crew, Jockey, Fidget, Swain, all of them were in danger. If so much as one of them were hurt, it would irrevocably change them all. Sassi couldn't let it happen.

"Take care of the crew," she murmured and tried to step past him.

Before she could get past, he grabbed her arms and rushed her back against the ladder between the head and the closet. "I will tie you to the fucking bulkhead before I'll let you go to him," he growled, bowing lower to get in her face. "I'll cast off and keep you stranded in the middle of the ocean for the rest of time before I'll let you live your life at his mercy… You are my crew. You are my responsibility."

"Not anymore," she said, angry tears seeping from her eyes. "I wish…"

"What do you wish?"

She shook her head. "There's one fantasy I can't share, even with you, Captain… You have to let me marry him."

"Do you love him?"

Sassi tried to shrug him off, but he held on. "Don't be stupid," she said. She'd taken that question from him during another argument before he knew what was going on. Now he was aware of the situation, she was insulted. "I can't stand the guy. I despise him. He makes me sick. That one time I puked over the side was because I got a vision of being intimate with him. The idea of sleeping with him, of his hands on me, makes me want to take a blade to my wrists."

"Then why the fuck would you—"

"Because if it's that or you being in pain, I'll take it," she said, trying to push away, but he thrust her to the wall again, boosting her fury. "I would do anything, anything! To make sure you were free to live your life happy! You mean more to me than everything and everyone else on this planet combined!" She bit her own lip, angry at her careless stupidity. "When Dario figures that out he'll come for you."

Gritting his teeth, Swain dipped lower to lock his eyes on hers. Only his lips moved while his teeth stayed clenched. "Let him," he hissed. "Let that bastard come for me."

"No," she said, hating the tears on her face and the rage in her captain's eyes. But there was little she didn't hate about their current predicament. "I won't let him hurt you. You're the one I… If he touches you, I'll die, Swain… I wouldn't be able to handle it."

"And you're asking me to let him touch you? The woman I've adored for weeks? No. It ends now. It's over for you. You get your ass downstairs, you cook for a full complement and you wait."

This was too much. She couldn't understand how he could give her such a benign order and expect her just to forget what was going on.

"Cook?" she asked. "Wait. Swain, I—"

"Follow orders, Cook." Pushing away, he put some distance between them. "You're crew and Eros is your home. You do not leave this ship without my permission," he said, using his stern captain voice.

Damnit, she'd told Stuart not to disrespect the captain and that would include not disobeying him. So although she was cursing inside, Sassi straightened up and took a breath, resenting every second of his attitude probably because it turned her on as much as it infuriated her.

"Yes, Captain."

"Very good," he said, and spun to storm out the room, leaving her alone in the space that had once been their intimate haven.

Sassi didn't know exactly where he was going or what he was going to do. If he was taking Stuart, the men would have a chance to learn more from each other. She just hoped Stuart wouldn't open his mouth about his plan or if he did that Swain would be patient.

THIRTY-THREE

IT DIDN'T MATTER how she tried to busy herself with cleaning in the galley or preparing food for the men on their return, Sassi couldn't stop worrying. Her fears about what they were facing weren't helped by the man making a bad show of reading his newspaper at the mess table.

Jockey had started by staring without making even an attempt to pretend he was reading. He'd moved on to forcing himself to flick some pages. But it had been a good ten minutes since she'd heard the paper move.

Sassi hadn't been able to look at the first-mate. She just stole glances from the corner of her eye, relying on peripheral vision. Even without eye contact, she could feel his disapproval burning into her.

Her paranoia reached critical mass, she couldn't take it anymore. Coiling the towel in her damp hands, she groaned and let her head drop. "You don't have to keep glaring at me. It's not possible for you to hate me more than I hate myself for what happened to Fidget," she said, keeping her back to him because she just couldn't bear to face his disappointment. "I'm sorry, Jockey, truly I am. I'll live with the guilt of this for the rest of my life."

The click and fizz of a soda can opening came before he spoke. "Good," Jockey said. "Might stop you making the same mistake again."

Sassi never would. If she hadn't been selfish, this would never have happened. If she'd just agreed to marry Dario from the get-go, no one would've had to run or hide or fear for their life.

"I know you hate me. I deserve it. After what they did to Fidget, you should hate me. You all should."

"Lass, you got your head all screwed up. No one hates you and we ain't mad at you for them taking Fidget. You brought him back, didn't you?"

She didn't get it. Although he seemed to be speaking in support of her, he didn't sound happy. When she finally peeked at him, she could see his anger. Jockey was usually so tolerant and easy to get along with; it was tough to accept what she'd done to their friendship.

"I don't understand."

Drawing in a breath, his chest expanded, and he looked at his can as he spoke. "Taking that boy was out of order and the cap'n will deal with that, don't you worry. But no one blames you for what those bastards did."

"Swain is so mad and you're—"

"You didn't warn us," he said, his eyes rising from the drink. "He takes his responsibility to us serious. It's his integrity at stake. He looks after us and we help him by looking out for each other. We always look out for each other. Now that don't mean we expect each other to always behave and make smart choices, no missy. But, if we're in trouble, if we screw up, the first person we trust, the man we go to… is our captain. Doesn't matter if that trouble never chases us, never finds us, we burden him to protect the crew."

Taking a step toward Jockey, the sound of his disappointment made her sick. She hadn't even felt so wretched when her father was unhappy with her. "That's just it, I didn't want to burden him. This was my family's screw up. I was protecting the crew by keeping them and my captain away from it."

"By keeping us in the dark? You don't see the hurricane and turn your back pretending it won't hit. You don't wait for the swell to push you into the rocks… If you were out there watching the horizon and you saw a speck that you knew was a waterspout, what would you do?"

Shame hollowed her out. "I'd tell my captain."

According to her captain, waterspouts were the tornadoes of the sea. "Could be gone by the time we get there, could go in a whole other direction and miss us. So why would you tell the captain? Why bother him with it? Why?"

Sassi sighed, beginning to see his point. "Because it could hurt us and if he knows… he can change course or prepare for it to hit."

"That's right," Jockey said, sinking back to finish off the soda. Crushing it in one fist, he wiped his mouth with the back of the other. "Whether it hits or not, cap'n should know everything that relates to his vessel. Everything. Sometimes he can't be everywhere all at once. He relies on his crew to be his eyes and ears. Us. He trusts us to help him be a better captain."

Desperate to make amends, Sassi surged a few steps toward the table. "He couldn't be a better captain, Jockey. He's an incredible captain. I trust him with my life."

Spreading a hand on the table, he smoothed it out. "See now that's how you hurt him, how you've hurt me and Fidget and the boys, because we trusted you with our lives too."

Fear and sorrow burned her throat as tears heated her eyes. "I would never hurt any of you!"

"You saw the storm, lass, and you turned your back without sounding the horn."

Sassi wanted to argue, to apologize and explain how she'd meant to protect them. But he didn't understand. She wasn't sure that she did anymore either. "I guess I didn't think it would come this way," she muttered.

It wasn't nice to feel two inches tall. Sassi had thought she couldn't feel any worse after seeing that Dario had taken Fidget, but she was learning that was just the start of her downward spiral.

"Threatened to hurt everyone you loved, that what you said? This Dario. He said you marry him or he makes anyone you love suffer, was that the deal?"

"Yes," Sassi mumbled.

"And you didn't think the cap'n was at risk?" he asked, his curiosity making her gaze float up. "You didn't think about Eros and the crew? You weren't worried for us at all?" His next sigh was so crestfallen that her mouth parched. "Well, lass, you fooled this old fool, 'cause I'd have staked my rations you felt something for us after a month out on the blue with us. Guess not all crew's made equal."

"Please don't say that," she whispered, her voice cracking half way through the sentence. "I feel for you all. I... I thought walking away would protect you. I thought if I gave you up. If I sacrificed what I wanted, that I could keep you all safe."

Jockey peered into her, ignoring the tears that were staining her cheeks. Dealing with a despondent and judgmental Jockey was, in a lot of ways, harder than dealing with the angry, vengeful Swain.

"What is it you want, lass? What did you

sacrifice?"

It probably seemed to him that she hadn't sacrificed anything. Dario might have given her bruises, but so far, she was the only one he hadn't threatened to hurt more seriously. From Jockey's point of view, she'd got herself a job at sea, had some adventures with her pirate captain and strolled off back to shore eighteen grand richer.

"Nothing," she said, figuring that his point of view was pretty accurate. "I didn't sacrifice anything."

Exhausted and fearing that her legs wouldn't hold her up much longer, she sank down onto the backless bench opposite him.

"The cap'n?"

"What about him?" she asked, resting her hands, that were still coiled in the towel, on the table.

"He told you he'd be keeping a berth open for you, but you didn't want it."

A berth on the next leg of the job or on another ship in his fleet? "None of this is his fault. None of it. He couldn't be a better man. I made it clear to him that I wasn't looking for a permanent contract."

Jockey was smart enough to read between the lines and decipher they weren't just talking professionally. "He not good enough for you? If you'd trusted him from the start, this would all have been taken care of by now."

"We were strangers at the start. You saw how we butted heads. I did trust him. But I guess I'm hardheaded and stubborn. I believed I could take care of it myself. I didn't want to lean on him. I didn't want to be weak or feeble on this ship of capable men. My dad was dead, my brother had split. I was alone."

Jockey drew in a breath. "And you'd been let down by every man who should've been there to support you," he said, showing some understanding, which gave her hope. "The captain ain't like that. He'll never abandon you."

"I know. But I somehow convinced myself that telling myself I didn't love him was enough. If Dario didn't know about Eros or my infatuation with my captain, you'd all be safe and you'd never have to hear from me again."

"And if the cap'n heard that something had happened to you days after you walked off his deck, you don't think that he'd take that bad? He's responsible for you too, lass."

"I'm not on his crew anymore," she said. "My contract's over."

"That ain't why he's responsible for you. He'd walk away from the ocean for you and that's the biggest sacrifice a sailor can make for his girl."

Yes, it was, Sassi didn't have to be told that. But another truth crept up on her. "I'm not his girl either. I never really was… I let myself believe it, that I was or that I could be… but it was a fantasy. I could never be with a man like him forever."

His brow creased. "'Cause of the sea?'"

Leaping in to alleviate that almost accusation, her shoulders went back. "No," she said. "I'd live my whole life on the waves for him and never miss dry land."

"Then why would you—"

"He deserves better. He deserves more," she said, touched by just how blessed she'd been to belong to her captain, even for a short while. "He doesn't need to be with a woman as screwed up as me. I have no home. My father was an addict. My mother's a flake. My brother is lazy and shifty, and I can't even tie a true lover's knot. Swain is so… skilled and together and—"

"He's a grumpy ass who don't deserve to be idolized."

But the truth was, Jockey valued the captain and

had as much admiration for him as she did, maybe more. "He's not grumpy," she said, her lips curling in a faint smile. "He acts hard sometimes and impatient because it gives the crew confidence to see he's a serious man. They think when he's aloof and distant that he's thinking about the course and the weather. They like to think the orders he's barking are considered and wise. No one wants to give a joker their life and that's what his crew do, they sign over their wellbeing to him every time they come aboard."

"That's what you did and he feels like he's let you down," Jockey said, getting up to come around to her. Sitting with his back to the table, he picked up her hand. "Did you even realize what you were doing when you came to us?" She shook her head. "We've had crewman come and go plenty before. But you were different to him… You are different." Gulping in some air, Sassi hiccupped out a sob, but quickly covered her mouth. Jockey softened further, which didn't help her strained composure. "You're a part of Eros now. You're more valuable to him than the fleet, than the ocean, than any man…"

Jockey needed something from her, some sign that she understood and wouldn't take their loyalty for granted ever again. Fidget came in yawning and stopped when he saw the cook and first-mate holding hands.

Smiling at him, she left Jockey to go touch Fidget's face. "How are you feeling, honey?"

"The cap'n come back yet?"

"The captain knows you're here," she said.

"Is he mad at me?"

"No, honey," she said, pulling him into her arms, because as much as she wanted him to have a hug, she needed one too. Pulling away, she widened her smile. "The crew are coming back to quarters. Will you help me make up the berths? We'll wait 'til the captain's back with the others for chow, okay?"

Fidget glanced at Jockey. "Skipper?"

"The cap'n's wife gives you an order, you follow it, boy," Jockey said, picking up his newspaper. He folded it while he stood up and took it around to the pouch at the back of the bench. "I'm going to the engine room to check our levels… You help the lass with the berths then you help her do full inventory of the stores."

"Yes, sir," Fidget said and followed her into the passageway.

There were four cabins on this floor with the mess. Three on the opposite side and one on the same side as the mess. At the starboard end of the passageway was a stairwell that led to two individual rooms, Jockey's and Foist's.

Sassi and Fidget did full changes in the three rooms first before moving to the cabin with the bunks on the same side as the mess. "I know Tune and Hector usually stay in here," she said because it was the largest of the bunk rooms. "But I think we'll put them in the single rooms on the other side of the passageway. Would that be okay?"

One of those rooms was the room reserved for the cook, her room. "I think so," Fidget said, helping her with the sheets. "Cap'n usually decides."

"I know, honey. But the captain isn't here."

If Swain was bringing Stuart and Karen back, it would make sense for the couple to share a room while the more capable engineers had their own rooms. The other bunk room belonged to Swing and Fidget. Sassi didn't want Fidget to be by himself. Swing was big enough to protect the scrawnier, younger boy if anyone unauthorized came on board.

"Miss Sassi," Fidget said as they put covers on the pillows. "Why did you kiss that guy?"

Slowing, she hadn't expected questions. But Sassi

didn't want to brush the apprentice off when he'd been so understanding. "I wanted him to let us go."

"The cap'n said you weren't coming to sea with us again, is that right?"

Putting the pillow on the lower bunk, she propped an elbow on the Pullman bed. "I don't know, honey," she said. "You know those guys want to hurt us and Captain Swain is going to do everything he can to keep all of us safe. So he wants everyone to stay on Eros until we can figure a way out of this."

Which as far as she was concerned was with her marrying Dario. Not because she wanted to, but because she couldn't think of any other solution.

"That's why everyone's coming back?" he asked and she nodded. "But you is in love with captain, aren't you? You are still Eros?"

If anyone could make her cry it would probably be Fidget and his sweet view of the world. Such an innocent boy, simple, understanding, and so accepting.

"I am Eros," she said, taking his hand. "Just like you."

"You heard him! All hands! Get it tied down! Stow all below! Batten down!"

Foist's voice echoed through the passageway and heavy footsteps thundered through the deck.

Darting out the door, Sassi caught sight of the engineer disappearing into the mess. Going after him, she found him munching a cookie in the galley when she got there. Karen and Stuart were going toward a settee in the far corner of the rec room.

"Foist," she said.

The glare on his face when he whipped around made her nervous. She tensed as he marched toward her, fearing he might be ready to scream at her for putting them all in this position. "You keep shore leave interesting, Shortcake," he said. Hooking an arm around her shoulders, he ducked to line up their faces. "You good?"

"I'm sorry about all this, Foist," she said.

"Shouldn't have fallen in love with me, Shortcake," he said and yanked her forward to press his mouth against her forehead.

Jockey came in, wiping his hands. "Got a duty list for you, snipe. Keep Fidget with you," the first-mate said. Foist pulled off his jacket. "Where's the cap'n?"

"Swag Wagon," Foist said, rolling up his sleeves. There were two duffel bags in the corner by the fridge and she wondered if everyone had packed and how long they planned to stay. "He's putting the word out. Tune and Hector are clearing the deck. Swing's loading supplies."

"Good," Jockey said.

Foist went over and slapped Jockey's shoulder. "Feels good to be home," he said and went out into the passageway with Jockey hot on his heels.

Sassi pushed aside her own feelings of shame to turn to her brother who was talking to Karen in the corner. "Are you guys okay?" she asked, going to join them.

"I'm just..." Karen seemed flustered. "Dario came to you?"

"I told her what happened," Stuart said, putting an arm around Karen. "Your captain isn't very patient. He storms around the place saying nothing making people uncomfortable not answering questions."

So her brother's mood hadn't improved and he hadn't found any gratitude for Swain either. "He's taken you in," she said. "He's offering to protect all of us. Maybe you should be more understanding, Stuart."

"We can't just sit around in here," Stuart said. "We have to be doing something."

Karen lowered her voice. "You had an affair with

Carson?"

"No!" Sassi paused. "Wait, who?" she asked, confused for a second before she laughed. "The captain… Yes… Shit, I've never used his first name in my life."

"What did you call him in bed?" Karen asked.

A smirk formed on her lips as her brows rose and her eyes slipped to the side. "Not Carson anyway."

Stuart drew her back. "We don't want to talk about that. We want to talk about what happens next. We need a plan, we're running out of time."

"Next we wait for the captain's orders and then we'll eat," Sassi said. "It's late, there might be cards, but I doubt it. He'll probably order everyone to bed… Let me show you guys where you'll sleep. It's modest, but it has everything you'll need."

She showed them to their cabin, which had a larger head than she'd had in her original cabin. But it was obvious that the couple were surprised. "No double bed," Stuart said.

"Stuart," Karen chastised him. "Sassi's right, we have to be grateful. It's nuts, but I feel better here than I did at the apartment… These guys are big and scary. I don't know if I'll ever say a single word to any of them. But while we're here, Dario isn't going to hurt us… This captain doesn't have to help us. He could tell us to go to hell. But he's helping us, Stuart… What's the worst that can happen by going with this? This morning we were three, this afternoon, we're… more…"

"Ten," Sassi said. "There are eight of us on the crew, Captain Swain, Jockey, Foist, Tune, Hector, Swing, Fidget, and me… and you two make ten."

"There. We're ten," Karen said. "I called work and took some time off. Your captain said we would be here as long as we needed to be… Do you know how long that is?" Sassi shook her head. "Did you, uh…"

Karen was nervous, but Sassi couldn't tell if the anxiety was caused by Stuart being there or what she wanted to say.

"What?" Sassi asked. "Did I what?"

"Captain Swain…" Trying not to prickle, Sassi anticipated what her pseudo-sister-in-law might say. "Did you talk or was it just… physical? I mean, do you think he cares about you?"

"He cares about everyone on his crew," she said.

"Will he talk to you?" Karen asked. "Tell you what he's thinking? We're not leaping into the fire, are we?"

Picking up her hands, Sassi wanted to reassure Karen because Eros could be intimidating on its own without adding the bolshie crew to the mix. "I'll talk to him, I will. I just… I haven't had time yet. But I promise you, you're safe here. No one will hurt you… Eros is a haven, a sanctuary. She and the captain kept me alive for over a month… She's the closest thing I've known to a home in my whole adult life." To relax Karen, Sassi pulled her closer, resting her hands on her upper arms. "If he's in a good mood, I'll ask Swain to take you out on the water one day… There's nothing like it, Kar… You'll fall in love, and feel at peace like you never have before." Their blank expressions amused her, but just talking about being on the waves made her feel better. "I'll let you guys settle in. Come back to the mess when you're ready."

Leaving them alone, Sassi paused in the passageway to look toward the deck. She wanted to go outside and breathe in the air, but there was work to be done. Fidget had his own orders, and someone had to log the stores.

Reassuring herself that she'd get to go out soon enough, she instead went down to investigate the cargo holds to figure out what they had and what she'd need to feed ten people for the next… however long.

Close to an hour later, Sassi finally got her chance to go outside.

It was dark, just the way she liked it. She kind of resented the dock at the starboard side, but there was nothing she could do about that. Going to her usual spot, she bent over to lean on the handrail and closed her eyes to breathe in the salt air. Trying her hardest to imagine they were on the ocean, she couldn't manage to block out the sounds from the dock and the nearby city. There was nothing she wanted more than to be far from any kind of civilization.

She thought there was nothing more she wanted, until someone came up behind her and leaned over her, opening his arms wide to rest his hands on the handrail at either side of her so he could talk into her hair at the top of her head.

"Your captain told you to stay inside."

"My captain told me to stay onboard," she said, moving her hips to rub her ass on his groin. "I didn't disobey."

"It's dangerous out here," he said, taking her arm to pull her away from the handrail.

"Swain," she said, pulling back to stall him.

The longer she stood there saying nothing, the more tense and impatient he became. "What is it, Waif? I've got a crew to inspect."

"I kissed him," she said. Since Fidget had brought it up, she'd been preoccupied with telling the truth. "I kissed Dario."

His lips thinned. "When?"

"Today," she admitted. "He's tried to kiss me before and I've always fought him. But, today I… I kissed him and then, I let him kiss me." The shift of his jaw made sorrow and shame well up inside her. "I was so afraid he wouldn't let Fidget go. I said if he let Fidget go that I would be grateful and he asked me to prove it… so I kissed him… As Fidget was going out Dario kissed me again and I… I let him because… I thought if I fought him he'd hurt Fidget and—"

"I get it," he said, sliding his fingers under her jaw. "Did you feel something? Is that why you want to marry him?"

"Swain," she said, letting her hands creep onto his waist. "I know we're not… We weren't… We didn't make promises to each other, but…"

Frustrated that she could find the words to say what she wanted to, Sassi felt tension begin to move through her.

"Waif?"

She huffed. "I hate myself for putting you in this position. I never wanted you to be hurt, but…" She inhaled through her nose. "Shit, Captain, I feel so much safer and calmer here. I can't thank you enough for letting me, Stuart, and Karen be here."

"They're guests," he said, his thumb moving over her cheek. "You're crew. Hostess, remember? You have a job and I expect you to look after all of us." Hostess like she had been with Gumdrop and Clive. His expression changed like he'd just thought of something. "You'd have made more money on the Dreamboat… You didn't know about the other debt then, you could've hit your target if you jumped ship… Was sex with me that good?"

Her head fell back and her eyes found his. "Yes. But I didn't stay for the sex," she said, edging in. "I stayed for my captain."

Curling a hand around the back of his neck, she tried to draw him down, but he resisted. "No, Waif."

No? Her smile vanished. He didn't want to kiss her. The captain she worshiped didn't want to kiss her. She'd thought walking away from him was painful. She'd breathed through the agony of confessing her family's shame to him.

But this…

Learning he'd come to his senses and didn't want her anymore, it was torture more excruciating than she'd ever imagined. But she couldn't let him see that. She had to accept it. Swain had every right to hate her. Every right in the world.

"I understand," she said. Why should he want to get intimate with her when she was intending to marry another man anyway? "I made up cabins for everyone. I put Stuart and Karen in Tune and Hector's room and moved them into the single cabins. I know there's accommodation on the lower deck, and I know I didn't have your authorization, but I thought if you were securing everyone at night—"

"You did the right thing," he said. "Did you cook?"

They might not be a thing, but she'd have to find a way to be his friend, so she smiled. "Why? Do you want a cookie, Captain?"

He groaned and hooked an arm around her to guide her starboard toward the passageway. "You made dessert?"

"I did," she said, putting an arm around his waist. "But I did use the last of the chocolate chips."

"We'll need to do inventory—"

"I already did," she said. "I filled out an order sheet and gave it to Jockey."

"Good girl," he said and squashed a kiss to the side of her head before pushing her into the mess which was overflowing with people.

It was odd for everyone to be here all at the same time. Usually the crew was split onto different eating schedules with at least two of them in the wheelhouse while the others ate. But they weren't at sea, so no one had to be in the wheelhouse and there were two new people here too.

The men were drinking beer, which was another unusual sight. But, again, they weren't at sea, so she guessed drinking was allowed.

"Chow time!" Swain hollered.

Everyone started to move around the table. Everyone except Karen who was hanging on the periphery, probably unsure what to do.

Knowing how intimidating the crew could be, Sassi went to Karen and took her hand to guide her over to the table. "Not everyone has set seats," she said in her ear because the men were making too much noise to be heard. "The captain has to sit at the head of the table. There's space for four on one side and four on the other." It had been set that Sassi had to sit at the captain's left, but with her being betrothed to another and Swain refusing her kiss, she guessed that was over. "Come sit here." Taking Karen to the end of the table where Jockey was, Sassi put a hand on the first-mate's shoulder. "Can Karen sit between you and Stuart?"

Jockey got out to let Karen slide onto the bench between her boyfriend and the first-mate. Foist was next to Swain on the other side of Stuart. Captain and engineer were already deep in some kind of discussion; she'd guess about the engines since Foist had spent the evening in the bowels of the ship.

Tune, Hector, Swing, and Fidget were on the backless side of the bench, and it was clear they were trying to cheer Fidget up. The kid seemed okay, but she was glad he'd get special treatment for a while. Sassi felt bad for Karen who looked overwhelmed, even Stuart was quiet.

Serving family style, Sassi handed out the warm plates first then began to take dishes of food over. The crew wasn't shy about diving in. On autopilot, she did what she'd always done after the feast was laid out, and took Swain's plate to fill it for him as he carried on his conversation with Foist, who was already eating.

Because there was no more space at the table, she planned to eat in the galley, as she'd done plenty of times before Swain changed the rules. After giving her captain his plate, she retrieved her own from the galley and went to the table to fill it, listening in to conversation and commenting as she scooped food onto her plate.

She had to go to the top of the table to reach the last dish and to her surprise, the minute she put the spoon back in the green beans, a thick arm circled her waist and she was pulled onto the bench at the top of the table.

It took her a minute to realize she was sitting next to Swain, and when she did, she looked up at her captain who did a double take when he noticed her attention was on him.

"What's the rule when I eat?" he asked, his volume low.

"I eat with you."

"Beside me," he said and went back to his conversation with Foist.

It was a tight squeeze up there at the top of the table. The bench was wide, but Swain was a big guy. The heat of his thigh pressed into hers and she kept her elbows tucked in because she didn't want to battle him for space when he was giving up some of his sacred position to her.

Stuart was peering at her and her captain, Karen was gawping, but the crew didn't seem to care. Swain was saying something to his engineer about lubrication, while Swing was regaling the guys on his side of the bench with tales of the girl he'd spent the night with.

There was terror coming and Sassi would have to leave the bosom of this group soon, but for the moment, things were just about perfect.

THIRTY-FOUR

THE CAPTAIN ORDERED everyone to bed not long after dinner. Sassi guessed it had something to do with the alcohol the men had brought with them. She was grateful that Karen wouldn't have to experience the crew being drunk on her first night aboard.

Sassi had spent some time with Karen in her cabin, reassuring her about her safety while Stuart was in the head. When her brother emerged, she said goodnight to them both and stepped into the passageway just as Swain jumped down the last of the starboard stairs from the direction of Foist or Jockey's cabin.

"Everyone settled?" he asked when she pulled Karen and Stuart's cabin door closed.

"Yes," she said. "Thanks again for letting them stay."

"Plenty of room," he said, checking the door to the outer deck was locked tight.

They started down the passageway side-by-side. "The crew have been great. Really understanding."

"That's what loyalty is," he said.

Just when they got to the mess door and she was about to say goodnight, he closed his hand around the back of her neck and guided her past the door. "Where are we going?"

"You think I'm going to let you sleep in the mess?" he asked, stopping her a few feet away so he could reach inside to kill the lights and secure the door. "I saw you take a pillow from the locker earlier."

"Where am I going to sleep?"

It was obvious where they were going when he returned to her and put his hands on her shoulders to push her to the opposite end of the passageway.

"Where you always sleep on Eros," he said and took her up the stairs into his cabin. "If there's a chance of assault, only our strongest members are allowed to sleep in cabins alone."

Diplomatic of him not to call her weak. Her amusement died when he pulled off his tee-shirt and sat on the edge of the bed to remove his boots.

"Dario's never threatened to hurt me," she said. "In fact, I'm probably the safest person on board. I could sleep on deck and know he'd never send his men to hurt me… not seriously."

Sitting up, he straightened his arms behind him to lean back, his weight on his hands. "You said you didn't want him to hurt me."

"Right," she said, hoping that Swain wasn't implying she had the power to help him if Dario's men swooped in and there was a physical confrontation.

"What is it Dario wants with you?" he asked. "What's the first thing a man does with his wife when they're alone?"

"On the wedding night?" she asked, going over to sit beside him, thigh-to-thigh though there was plenty of space on the bed for her to sit further from him. Blinking her eyes up to his, she moistened her lips. "Sex."

"Shit, Waif, that sultry fucking tone of yours does a guy in, you know that? I don't blame this guy for wanting you so much."

That was a mood killer. Sassi was about to stand, but her captain bowed to block her, capturing her lips with his to stop her from leaving the bed. Not only that, but he used the force of his kiss to lay her down on the bed she'd thought she'd never be in again.

Swain kissed her for another minute before his hand snaked up beneath her hoodie to seek her breast. "You wouldn't kiss me on deck," she said when he gathered up the fabric and lifted her torso to take her top and hoodie off at the same time. "Were you mad at me?"

"Oh yeah," he said, standing up to pull off her jeans and panties. "I'm mad as hell, Waif."

He picked her up beneath her arms and dragged her to the top of the bed. Unhooking her bra, he tossed it away before he opened her legs and settled himself between them.

"I didn't want to hurt you," she said, skimming her hands up and down his back as he kissed her face and neck. "I thought I'd draw a line under us and then go off to deal with Dario and you'd never have to know anything about my father's debt, or Dario's demand."

Swain stopped kissing her to glare at her instead. "I told you never to think of him when you're with me," he said. "He is the one you were talking about in your cabin downstairs, isn't he?" She nodded. Stroking her waist, he made her shiver, then took her breast in his hand to massage her, ratcheting up her need. "You never belonged to him, Psyche. You never wanted to be his."

"No, Captain, I didn't," she said, her belly swirling with heat that seeped into the blood rushing through her. Her whole being was begging to be filled with the endorphins of pleasure his body promised hers.

"That means you're still mine," he said, taking

her hand, he pressed it flat to his pec. "Unless you tell me otherwise."

"I'll never tell you otherwise. I'll always be yours," she murmured. He didn't need to trick her into submitting or to manipulate her by reminding her how much she loved his body. Sassi wanted to be his, she'd always wanted to be. "Even after I sign my name next to his, I'll be yours."

"Psyche," he said, shifting to rest his forearms in close by her ears to finger the hair on the top of her head. "You're going to be free. I'm going to make it my life's mission to make sure you are never made to do anything against your will. I won't let anyone crush that spirit of yours and I sure won't let any man put his hands on you."

In anger? Is that what he meant or more? Even this close his eyes still looked as black as the night, and she could understand how someone could get the wrong impression of this man who appeared so intense. Sassi couldn't feel anything except gratitude and confidence when she looked at him.

"You're an incredible man, Captain Swain."

One side of his mouth lifted for a brief second. "We're not gonna have sex."

Disappointment smacked her hard. He'd kissed her, stripped her naked, and laid her down in his sheets. She hadn't thought about how much she wanted to feel him inside her or how she might make that happen. With the insistence of his cock hard against her, she had assumed that she was about to get laid.

"Okay," she said. "Good. Phew."

Rolling off her, Swain lifted his hips to take off his pants. He adjusted the erection in his underwear and kicked the blanket down.

"Shift, Waif, it's hot tonight."

He reached over his head to switch off the light.

"Not hot enough," she muttered. They lay

together, side by side, in the dark. The sound of the water lapping on the hull helped her to relax and she already knew this was going to be the best night's sleep she'd had since the last time she'd been in this bed. "Give me your arm."

Sassi sat up and he extended his arm toward the spot she'd vacated. She scooted over to tug it under her head so she could lay back down, putting her head on his upper arm. He coughed once, and bent his elbow, bringing his hand over her breast to fondle her.

"Your tits feel good, Waif. I've missed those."

If he wanted her to seduce him or force him into sex, he'd be left wanting. Sassi was too stubborn, even though being intimate with him sounded like heaven. If her captain wanted it, he could have it, but she wasn't going to beg.

Turning her head up, she couldn't see him, but had to ask, "Stuart didn't say anything stupid to you, did he?"

"About us?"

"No," she said, "about—"

"Drug smuggling." Groaning, she tried to sit up, ready to apologize every way she knew how. But Swain strengthened his arm and held her down. "Your stories prepped me to deal with your brother, Waif. Don't worry about his big ideas."

Snuggling closer, she was so pleased he wasn't offended by her brother's idiocy. "Least he didn't hit you with a chair."

"I wish he'd tried," he mumbled.

So he could defend himself? Maybe her captain wanted to knock her brother out. Stuart could be persistent. If he brought up the drug thing, Swain would've smacked him down. But if Stuart had kept twittering on about it, Swain's patience would've been tested.

Her twittering on about it might not be the best idea either, so she changed the subject. "Do you want pancakes for breakfast or donuts?"

"Both," he said. "Are you doing bacon?"

"If you want," she said. "You're the captain, you get anything you want for breakfast."

His humid breath cascaded through her hair. "Do I get breakfast in bed?"

Although her body's need for him grew, she tried to play it cool.

"Pussy bar's open any time you want to chow down."

Squeezing her breast once, he let his fingers gather around her nipple to brush and tease it to an aching point. "Don't doubt that, Psyche. If I wanted it, I could have it."

Laying a hand over the erection still pulsing in his boxers, she tightened her grip around him. "Oh, you want it, Captain, don't even kid yourself."

Picking his hand from her breast, she climbed onto his body and covered his chest in kisses. "I don't want your gratitude, Sassi," he said, his voice cold when he pushed her off him and over to the corner of the bed.

Swain turned his back on her to lie on his side. That was when she figured out his reasoning for the sex embargo. She could reassure him, argue and tell him that she wanted him and no one else. But it wouldn't be fair to play games with him when Dario was her future.

Licking her lips, she shuffled over to him and stroked a hand down his arm then kissed his shoulder. "I am grateful," she whispered. "But I'm in your bed because I want to be, no other reason. I've never been happy anywhere else like I am here with you."

Kissing him again, she was happy that he tucked her arm under his and pulled her chest against his back. "Goodnight, Waif. Go to sleep."

Sighing, she consoled herself with being this close to her captain. "Goodnight," she responded and closed her eyes.

Tomorrow she'd have to deal with Stuart and to convince them all that it was time to let her go to Dario. The sooner she could go to him, the sooner her friends would be safe. But, tonight, she was in her safe place, and this was the closest she'd ever get to happy ever again.

THIRTY-FIVE

BREAKFAST WAS HER specialty. Sassi had left her captain asleep in bed and gone to the mess to prepare for the stampede of crew and family that needed fed.

When they were on the water, Swain was awake before her. That day, she'd been the first up, ready to do whatever was necessary to help everyone out. Jockey confirmed he'd put in her order for supplies and let her know they should be arriving later that day. Swain had been around to overhear the conversation and told her not to accept the order without one of the crew with her.

He wasn't worried about her capability, he was worried about her being alone and vulnerable. But there was no time to dwell on his concern. The crew went to work on the captain's orders. Sassi gave Karen a tour of the ship, and Stuart stayed in bed until after lunchtime.

That was roughly about when Swain lost his patience and marched into her brother's cabin, hauled him out, and gave him a list of duties to complete. If there was one thing her captain couldn't abide it was laziness. Stuart sort of started to object, but when the crew closed ranks behind Swain, he'd shut up and jumped to fast.

After everyone had eaten lunch and Stuart was helping Fidget with his jobs, Swain left the ship. She hadn't known he'd gone at first, she was cleaning up in the galley. But she'd asked Jockey where he was and been told their captain was in town.

That must have been three hours ago, and he still wasn't back.

With all the activity on the ship, Sassi craved some peace and solitude. But her captain had an aversion to her going outside. Instead of going on deck, she climbed through their cabin's overhead hatch to sneak into the wheelhouse.

Lying on the long side of the settee, she'd been half asleep for a while. It was probably time for her to think about dinner. But she'd already rolled the meatballs and made the sauce, so it wouldn't take long to get the meal ready and she didn't want to start until the captain was safe aboard.

She had been so lost in her own slumbering thoughts that she didn't hear anyone approaching before he spoke. "What you doing up here all by yourself?"

Relief made her smile, her captain was home. "Fantasizing."

"About what?"

Sassi kept her eyes closed, basking in the moment. "About being on the water," she said, taking a deep breath. "I'm imagining that we're out there on the ocean, just the crew. You and me had wild, incredible sex last night and we're going to do it again tonight... I'm thinking about making dinner, hoping you'll like what I cook and that my dessert pleases you... It's just us out here in the middle of the ocean... nothing around for miles."

"Is that a fantasy or a memory?"

"A fantasy," she said, still in her sleepy state. "Because there's no Dario, no time limit, no worry and pressure. Just me, my captain, and the ocean."

When he didn't speak, she let her eyes flutter open. He was bent down, gazing at her, resting his weight on his forearms that were folded on the side of the booth.

"You paint a pretty picture, Waif."

Climbing onto her knees, she shuffled toward him and curved both hands onto his forearms. "Take me out, Captain," she whispered, trying to kiss him though he resisted. "Let me have the water one last time… Cast off and steal me from reality… right now… please."

"No," he said and had no trouble backing away from her.

Noticing a huge khaki bag on the chart table, she guessed he'd come up here for an operational reason, not a personal one.

"I don't understand what I'm doing here," she murmured, trying not to become petulant, though she felt overwhelming frustration. Swain turned to her. "Sitting on my ass doesn't help anyone and if the end goal is me going to Dario then why the hell am I wasting your time here? Why shouldn't I just go to him now? This minute?"

"You're not going anywhere near him," he snapped. "Never again."

Life wasn't a fantasy. Swain seemed to be building a perimeter around her that no one was allowed to breach. While it might be welcome where Dario was concerned, it wasn't welcome everywhere.

"I'm not allowed anywhere near you," she said, clambering out of the booth and stalking aft to put some space between her and him. "Sometimes you kiss me, sometimes you can't have me far enough away. If it wasn't for the reaction your cock has to me, I'd think you were playing some sick game with me."

When she got to the windows at the back of the wheelhouse, she turned to lean against the rail that ran around the wall of the room, resting her hands on it at her sides.

"We're irrelevant," he said, marching over. Apparently, he wasn't happy with her creating distance. "You said it yourself downstairs in the mess. Our feelings don't matter, keeping everyone safe matters. I won't let myself get distracted."

Sassi didn't have his willpower. She wanted to. She wanted to be stubborn and focused and have his resolve. Instead, she felt like she was falling apart, and the more she crumbled, the more she needed him to pull her together.

Toying with him, she leaned in to pout at him. "Do I distract you, Captain? I'm not sure I do."

"Waif," he exhaled and crouched to get in close.

Picking up her hands, he guided them to his shoulders and scooped his arms around her waist to lift her up and perch her ass on the rail she'd been holding onto a second ago.

The tenderness in this slow kiss gave her more of an answer than she'd expected. It was so deep and probing that moisture seeped between her sealed lashes. Running her fingers into his hair, she held his mouth to hers and coiled her legs around his hips to lock her ankles at his lower back.

This was a public place to be making out, but they were at the end of the dock, so there weren't many people near the aft of the ship. Though any of the crew on the quarterdeck would see that the captain had her pressed to the wheelhouse windows.

"Let me be with you," she said, trying to squeeze her hands between them to unfasten his pants while his mouth worked on her neck. "One last time, please."

Maybe that was what really held her back from defying him and going to Dario to end this on her own. She wanted to be with her captain once more, to make one more memory with him before she had to give herself to Dario.

"Waif," he said, gathering her wrists together against his torso. "When this is over you get to decide what you want."

Her begging lips sought his again and he gave her a hard kiss. "I don't understand. How can you even doubt what I want," she panted. "I want my captain… please."

"When this is over," he said. "If you want him, you can have him… But he needs you to be free. You need to be free. Free of your father, your brother, free of Dario, free of me… You'll be free, Sassi Robins." Brushing the hair from her face, he clasped her cheeks. "I promised you your freedom and when you have it, you can pursue your greatest fantasy, whatever that is."

"Swain," she whispered and pulled him to her for another kiss.

She couldn't understand what he was saying. But he was her captain and he was promising to make her dreams come true. Freedom from all the worries she'd been living with would be a fantasy come true, but freedom from him was a curse. Sassi would take being forcibly parted from Swain as a punishment.

Tightening the circle of her legs, she pushed her pelvis to his, massaging herself on the hard-on desperate to burst from his fly.

"Helluva meeting, cap'n."

Sassi was still dazed by the impact of her captain's kiss; too dazed to register there were others in the wheelhouse with them. Even after Swain took his mouth away from hers, she took a minute to focus. Her captain was twisted away from her. She peeked around him to see Jockey, Foist, Swing, Tune, and Hector there just inside the wheelhouse door, each as amused as each other.

Swain cleared his throat and tried to back away, but her legs were still around him and they wouldn't let him go. Her captain had to use his strength to unlock her ankles, pulling them apart and away from his body to put her on her feet.

Easing her away from the wall, he tried to urge her to keep on walking, but she didn't. "Turn to, Waif," Swain said.

Sassi knew that meant she was supposed to get back to work, but her head was still spinning. "I need… just a second," she said, still holding onto his arm. Blinking a few more times, Sassi cleared her throat and shook her head. That was when she saw just how hilarious the crew thought her muddle was and she glared at them all. "You know, our captain won't mind if I spit in his food, can the rest of you say the same?"

"I'd swallow your spit," Hector said, relaxing her. It was just like him to flirt with her even now. "I don't think there's a man on crew who wouldn't."

The rest of the crew only laughed for a second before they noticed the tense captain at her side.

"He'll get his sense of humor back in a couple of days when I'm back on shore," she said, kissing her captain's arm because he was too busy scowling at his men to offer her his cheek. "Chow will be ready when you boys are."

Swain hadn't moved, but she couldn't ignore his orders any longer. Heading for the hatch, she sat on the floor and climbed down the ladder, pulling the hatch down after her to lock it from the inside.

The male crew members had ship operations to discuss and she had a meal to prepare. Life went on, and it would keep going on even after she and Eros were torn apart.

THIRTY-SIX

STUART ROBINS CAME tripping into the wheelhouse before Swain had a chance to say anything to his crew.

"Yo, cap'n, we're only messing about your girl," Tune said. "We know the wife's hands-off."

Swain didn't doubt that for a second, he trusted his crew with his life and with Sassi. But with another man trying to muscle in on her against even her will, he was particularly sensitive to the subject of her virtue.

"What the fuck is going on?" Robins asked. "What the fuck we doing up here?"

"Taking care of things," Swain said, shaking off as much of his grouchy mood as he could. As long as Sassi was on Eros, sleeping in his berth at night, she was safe. That was what he had to hold onto to keep his sanity. She was his focus and all that mattered. "Close the door, it's time for strategy."

Robins frustrated him. Sometimes he said things that made Swain think he was going to take care of his sister in the way a brother should. Most of the time he just came across as lazy, looking for the easy way out.

The wheelhouse door was closed and the men gathered around the chart-table.

Swain unzipped the side pocket of the duffel bag and pulled out a stack of papers. "Okay," he said, when everyone was in position. "We have a list of creditors who need to be satisfied. This really is as simple as that."

"Simple," Robins scoffed and folded his arms, but tensed when he caught sight of the top sheet Swain was holding. "Where did you get that? That's the piece of paper Karen found in my dad's stuff."

"It's a copy," he said, turning it to show he had both sides of the ledger.

"Where did you get it?"

Was the guy going to give him shit? Why did it seem he wanted to start a fight when there were more important things to be doing? Swain would happily beat the crap out of Robins if it would make the dude feel better, but that would wait until they'd dealt with the threat.

"Your sister's email," he said.

"Her… what the fuck? How the fuck did you get into her email?"

Clenching his teeth, Swain worked his jaw trying his best to hold onto his patience. Sassi. He had to think of Sassi and how annoyed she'd be if he decked her brother.

"With her password," he said.

"How the hell did you get her password?"

Every minute he spent with Stuart Robins made it clearer how Sassi ended up in her predicament. The brother was easily distracted by frivolous details. If the father had been the same, he wouldn't have thought to deal with his debt before passing it onto his children.

It would've been good if Robins could've used some of this outrage on the guy trying to enslave Sassi.

"I walked into the head after breakfast when she

was taking a shower and asked for her fucking password."

"When she was naked?"

Smacking the side of his fist on the back of the booth at their side, Swain lost his patience. "You want to do the big brother thing and threaten my ass for screwing your little sister, go right ahead *after* we've dealt with the fucker trying to drag her down the aisle."

"And don't do it in his own fucking wheelhouse," Jockey said.

"Or while his crew are at his back," Hector followed up, a growl in his tone.

Yeah, Robins wasn't in his comfort zone. But if he was anything like his sister, that wouldn't stop him from charging ahead.

"None of you got a sister?" Robins asked, appealing to them all.

Tune laughed. "Any of our sisters hooked up with a stand-up guy like the captain here, we'd have a fucking parade."

"Can we get back to the goddamn point?" Swain said. The crew was relaxing and even Robins seemed to soften, but he didn't want anyone at ease, he wanted them all on alert. "We're going out tonight, start as a group, split into pairs, whatever it takes. We're putting word out that Henry Robins' debts are being settled."

Huffing, Stuart Robins widened his stance and leaned back. "Easier said than done, Captain." He spat the rank, which made the rest of his crew bristle, but Swain held up a hand to calm them. "If it was that easy, I'd have done it already. You're talking over a hundred grand, and that's without Dario's line. You wouldn't listen to my plan. So where the fuck are we going to get that kind of money? Rob a bank? I guess we've got the manpower for it."

Reaching over to the bag in the center of the

chart table, Swain unzipped it and opened it wide, exposing the bundles of cash to his crew who stood in stunned silence for almost a minute before they started to express their shock and admiration.

"Shit, cap'n," Tune said.

Hector took a block of bills and flicked through it. Swing took two and smacked them together. Swain narrowed his eyes on the gaping Robins, who took a second, but did a double take before making eye contact.

"You're extending a line of credit," Robins said. "Adopting my father's debt."

"I'm paying your father's debt."

Stuart scoffed. "What difference does one creditor make over another?" he asked. "What the fuck is it you want from us? Why are you any better than Dario? Why the fuck should I let you buy my sister?"

"I don't want your sister," Swain said, which wasn't at all true, he did want her, but that wasn't why he was doing this. Still, he corrected himself. "I don't want to buy her."

"She asked you to do this?" Stuart demanded. "Did she?"

"She has no idea I'm doing this," he said, turning his determination to his crew. "And she won't... no one will tell her about this."

"Lie to her?" Stuart said. "Why would we lie to her?"

"I'll tell her when it's done," Swain said.

"Our cap'n's an old-fashioned guy," Jockey said, taking the money from Swing to toss it back into the bag. "A man should take care of this kind of business for his girl."

"She's not his girl," Robins sneered at him.

It pained him that Robins was right, but Swain kept himself rigid and expressionless. He wasn't going to let Robins break his resolve.

"You wouldn't be so sure about that if you arrived two minutes earlier," Hector mumbled.

"No," Robins said and backed away from the table. "Least I know what kind of depraved, sick fuck Dario is... I don't have a fucking clue what you're about... I won't let you extort her like this, you can't have her. Sassi's not for sale."

Robins was right that they didn't know each other and Swain respected that he was being cautious with his sister's safety. But he wasn't going to take no for an answer. Whether he had Robins support or not, he was doing this.

"Your sister is free," Swain said as Robins headed for the door. "I already told her she isn't going to be bound to me, or to you or Dario... All I want is for her to be free to make her own choices. She'll only be free if this debt is gone." Robins stopped. "Fuck, Robins, use your fucking head! Your sister was in here ten minutes ago asking me to cast off and take her away... If all I wanted was her, I'd have taken her away from you already."

Spinning around, he marched back. "You don't get to take her away from me. You can't take her!"

Though Robins was tense, Swain felt calm. "You don't understand my relationship with her. We're private," he said. "Now that everything is out in the open, trust me when I tell you, if I wanted to take her away from you, I could."

"The cap'n don't want to hurt Miss Sassi," Swing said.

"None of us do," Tune chimed in.

"The lass is at home here. She'll always have a place on Eros," Jockey said. "The cap'n wants her to have choices."

"Sassi is part of our family," Hector said. "We take care of family."

"You can be a part of this," Swain said. "Or you can get the fuck off my ship and abandon your sister like you did already."

"If I leave, she's coming with me," Robins asserted.

Tipping his head, Swain held off from laughing. "No… she's not… Don't test me, Robins, or her. You won't like the way it ends."

Considering everyone in the room for a moment, Robins' Adam's apple bobbed and then he started back toward the chart table. "Okay, you said you've got a fucking plan?"

Good. He'd made a smart choice. Swain would let him be involved and would trust him, just like he did with everyone else. But Stuart Robins was already on thin ice. He'd abandoned Sassi once and he'd be a fool to think that Swain wasn't a hundred percent aware of that.

Sassi might be able to forgive her brother, and that made sense. They were blood, the closest relatives that either of them had. But Swain was more particular about who he entrusted her well-being to and that man would never be her brother.

THIRTY-SEVEN

Something was going on.

Sassi didn't know what it was but the guys were cagey at dinner and they ate fast like they were eager to get to something else. Before she'd even thought to stand up to clear the dessert plates from the table, the men had scarpered from the mess.

The water pressure dropped, there was a lot of movement… Yep, they were getting ready to go out.

Fine by her.

She might be stuck on Eros, but she didn't mind the men going out, as long as she knew what was going on.

Stuart and Karen were locked up in their cabin and her captain was in the shower, so Sassi went to get changed in the cabin before returning to the galley to clean up.

She was still by herself twenty minutes later when she heard her captain growling and stomping up behind her.

"What the fuck are you doing?" he demanded.

Spinning around, Sassi was so pleased to see his bare torso that she grinned and hooked her hands on the counter behind to lift her shoulders as she bent her knees.

He was wearing jeans and his boots, but no shirt. The sight of his ripped torso quaked her insides.

"Mmm, you look good, Captain."

"You're wearing my shirt," he said and opened his hand.

Pouting her innocence, she glanced down to the shirt she'd buttoned over her body while he was in the shower. "This? You want this shirt?"

"Yes," he said, his jaw twitching.

"It was lying on our bed," she said, trying her best to maintain her innocence though they both knew it was an act. "Just lying there, Captain, on the bed we share... Captain... the bed we used to make love on. Do you remember what that felt like, Captain...? Sliding yourself into me... using my body for your pleasure... listening to me whimper your name in ecstasy...?"

Touching his nipple with a fingernail, she dragged it downward to his navel loving how hard he clenched his teeth because it was a sign of ragged control.

"Take it off," he growled.

Sassi sighed. "Okay," she said and began to unbutton it.

She got past her breasts and down to her belly before he cursed. "What are you wearing under it?"

Parting the sides further, she exposed her cleavage and the swell of her breasts, stopping just short of revealing her nipples. Letting her hands trail down to the few remaining buttons, she showed him a plunging triangle of bare flesh all the way down to her navel.

"Absolutely nothing, Captain," she said, her sly smile almost becoming a laugh.

His hand shot out to stop her undoing any more

buttons. "Fuck," he said, tightening his grip on her wrist. "Go upstairs and get changed. Now." She shook her head, pulling her lower lip into her mouth with her teeth. "Don't test me, Waif. Get upstairs and change. Now."

"I have work to do here, Captain. I couldn't possibly leave my post while there's all this work to do. Can't you see these dishes that need to be washed? There's so much tidying up to do. There's just not time…"

When she started to turn away, he grabbed her and hauled her back, holding her up on the tips of her toes. "This isn't the time to push me, wench."

Desire and excitement bubbled up through her. She did her best to subdue it to keep playing it cool.

"Is there ever a good time to push you, lover?" she asked, edging her mouth nearer to his. "You want the shirt?" He growled. "Then I want oral."

Surprising him was fun, especially since it lessened his anger.

"What the fuck?"

"Yeah," she said, nudging his arm with her hip. "I think that's a fair exchange, don't you? You get something you want and I get something I want. It is my sworn duty to provide you with something to eat… to nourish you… We can do it right here."

"You want me to eat you in the galley?" he asked. Sassi didn't trust his sneer. "I'll strip you fucking naked and take the damn shirt. I don't give a fuck if the crew see you."

Leaning in, she whispered. "Yes, you do. The rest of the crew don't get to enjoy the captain's girl, remember?"

"Why the fuck are you playing with me? I'll tongue fuck you later. I need the shirt now."

She shook her head. "No deal… maybe if you tell me what's got you guys all in a frenzy, I'll feel more cooperative."

"Frenzy? No one's in a frenzy?"

She exhaled a laugh. "Yeah, right, and I'm a fucking supermodel. There's zero water pressure, which means everyone's in the shower. The guys have been raiding the laundry, and the whole ship stinks like an Old Spice factory… you guys are going for a night on the town, aren't you?" She hit his chest. "How can you think about going out there to party when Dario could be on the hunt?"

"That fucker comes near me and I'll take him down, no problem. It would make my night," he said and his awareness piqued. "But you're not worried about me handling myself in a fight. You're worried about me getting laid."

She couldn't claim the thought hadn't crossed her mind. It was sort of disconcerting that he'd read her so fast.

Fighting to maintain her confidence, she held firm. "You can't get laid if I'm in your bed," she said, folding her arms, plumping her cleavage in the gap between the edges of the shirt. Swain's glimpse of her breasts made him grab for the shirt to pull it tight, overlapping the sides to cover her body. "And, yeah, I'm not so worried about you enjoying another woman when you have a willing one right here… If you want to get laid, let's do it. Right now. Anywhere you want."

"I told you we're not going to have sex."

Sliding her hands down his body, she cupped the bulge in his jeans. "Stay here with me, Captain," she whispered. "Take me upstairs and enjoy me… please, Captain… There's nothing out there you can't get right here where you're safe… Where we're safe. I'll let you do anything you want to me… I'll fulfill any fantasy you've got."

Stroking her face, he dropped his bluster and

bowed to kiss her head. "Let me come home to you sleeping safe in our berth," he said. "That's my fantasy, Waif."

Wrapping her arms around his waist, she squeezed herself close. If he could surrender his mood, so could she. Honesty felt good too. "I feel safer when you're here."

He ran his hand up her back then cupped it around her bundled hair. "Jockey will stay with you, okay? He'll do whatever it takes to keep you safe... Nothing will happen to you here."

"If Dario comes he won't hurt me, he'll hurt Jockey or Karen. If I have to go with him—"

"No," he said, drawing her back to meet her eyes. "You don't go anywhere. If Jockey has to take Eros out to sea, he will... Do you want me to cast off on the way out? Me and the crew can stay on shore and—"

"No," she said, clinging to him. "It's not easy for me to admit that I need you."

"I know," he said, running his hand down her face. "I'll do whatever it takes to make you feel safe... but don't ask me to stay... What I have to do on shore is important... I wouldn't let anything except the most vital business take me away from you now... I feel better with you too because I know I can keep you safe."

They'd never admitted their feelings. They'd never really discussed emotions at all. But it was difficult to ignore how things had developed since he'd found out the truth about Dario.

"If you could tell me—"

He touched his finger to her lips. "Trust me. Waif. No more questions... Go upstairs and get back into uniform."

Hearing that command excited her enough that she gasped. She'd worn Karen's clothes that day, but all her uniform clothes were still in their cabin.

"I can wear your name again?"

Cupping her face, he bent his knees and kissed her. "Waif, you should never have taken it off."

She hadn't really because she'd worn his hoodie every day since she found it in her pack. Except that day, she'd left it in her cabin because she wasn't sure how comfortable Swain was with her wearing it, especially around the crew.

But that day had proved to her how difficult it was for them to deny that there was something between them. And, there, as he kissed her again, she knew trusting him wouldn't be a mistake, but saying goodbye to him might be.

THIRTY-EIGHT

FOR THE NEXT two nights, the men went out. They'd get ready and disembark not long after dinner and wouldn't be back until the wee hours. Jockey and Fidget stayed onboard with her and Karen. They played cards and board games. It often seemed that the two men had been tasked with distracting the women from worrying about their absent men.

Even when the crew was onboard, they had private meetings and talked in whispers. Sassi had asked Swain and her brother to promise that they weren't into anything illegal or planning to confront Dario. After assuring her that they weren't, they both told her not to ask any more questions.

It didn't reassure her that her captain and her brother were singing from the same hymn sheet. It just made their responses seem rehearsed. But she had to admit having them on the same page was better than the alternative.

"I can't keep living like this," she whispered to herself, frustrated by the darkness outside.

Peering out of the porthole above the sink at the head of the galley, Sassi tried to distinguish the identities of the sailor's she could vaguely make out grouped at the top of the dock, but Eros' bow and another ship were hampering her view.

"What's that, lass?" Jockey called from behind her.

The first-mate was at the mess table and although he hadn't said it, she knew he'd been told to stay up as long as she did. Karen and Fidget had been in bed a while. It had to be close to three a.m. But Jockey was still awake, waiting with her, because the rest of the crew wasn't back.

"I shouldn't be here," she said, tossing the towel onto the counter. She'd been filling the cabinets for two days and was washing her hands so much they were starting to dry out. "This is nuts."

Marching down the galley, she had the exit in sight, but Jockey leaped up to get in her way. "Hey, now, lass, you sit yourself down. I don't want to be telling the captain you disobeyed orders and abandoned ship."

"There's only two days left," she said. "If Swain or Stu had fixed this then I wouldn't still be under orders to stay here."

"But you are under orders. We both are. So I can't let you go."

It wasn't fair of her to run off while Jockey was looking after her. She didn't want Swain to blame his first-mate for her leaving or to cause tension between the men. But letting the seconds tick away and allowing this pressure to squash them all was irresponsible and unnecessary.

Her frustration had reached boiling point and unfortunately for the first-mate, he just happened to be in the way of it when it bubbled over.

"You know he won't have sex with me," she

snapped.

Jockey blinked like five times, probably shocked that she was talking about her and Swain's intimacy when she usually kept details to herself.

She and Karen had always been friendly, but they'd never been close, so Sassi couldn't discuss her personal life there either. Truth was, before their dad died, she and Stuart had been lucky to see each other once every month or two. Her brother was always on some get-rich-quick crusade that invariably ended with him poorer while Sassi had been trying to keep her head down to build some sort of stable life for herself. In short, he was happy having adventures and she was unhappy being boring.

It didn't feel right that she should pretend her and Karen were best girlfriends just because they'd been thrust together. Especially since this proximity wouldn't last. When Sassi was with Dario, she would go back to seeing little of Karen and Stuart.

"Well, now, lass, I—"

"I could understand staying here if we were having some kind of passionate affair. If we were making the most of the last days we have together before I have to go and marry another man. But we're not. I sleep next to him every night, naked, and he won't even touch me. Doesn't do wonders for a girl's self-confidence."

Her infuriation was fueling her, but poor Jockey was at a bit of a loss. "You're a pretty girl," he said, struggling to find an appropriate way to respond. "I'm sure the cap'n—"

"What? Has his reasons? I don't care anymore, Jockey. He can go find another woman to terrify every evening and ignore every night. I'm not sitting here like a dutiful wife wondering if he's still breathing and what he's doing... I'll have enough of that with Dario. Not that I'll care if he gets hurt. But Swain, why does no one understand that he's in danger out there? If Dario sees him, he could hurt him. I have the power to stop this… all of this… I shouldn't be here."

Sassi tried to go around Jockey, but there was a thud that stopped them both. Pushing her back into the room, Jockey steadied her then went to grab the gun from the pouch behind the bench. Footsteps came ominously and slowly down the passageway in the direction of the mess.

"Are they back?" she whispered, hurrying in behind Jockey.

Grasping his shoulders, she tucked herself against him.

"Cap'n always sounds the whistle."

And he did. When Swain came back this late he would whistle as he entered the passageway with his posse to let those still awake know their allies had returned and they weren't in danger. Now, they heard a curse and a grumble, but no whistle.

"Shit," Jockey said and stomped away from her to put the weapon back.

The first-mate wasn't worried anymore, but she didn't understand why until a tall guy in maybe his forties staggered into the mess.

"Skipper!" he declared, holding open his arms in greeting, showing a half empty bottle of Jack Daniels in his fist. His grin fell when his gaze raked over her and then his smile became sly. "Jockey, you dog, you got yourself a looker! How you doing, sweetheart? You on the clock or you just take pity on this old salt?"

"You boy keep your mouth shut," Jockey said. "This here's the cap'n's girl."

"No, I'm not," she said.

"Aye, she is," Jockey said, rushing to intercept her before she could walk past this new man. "What you doing staggering on here at this time, Raise? You should know yourself better."

Raise. This guy was Eros' cook. The man who'd had the job for years before she'd come along to save the day after his screw up.

"Got out of the joint today," Raise said, sliding himself onto the bench at the table and taking a swig from his bottle. "Thought I should celebrate before getting back to work… where's the good cap'n at?"

The good captain wasn't onboard, but Sassi guessed Swain would be thrilled to have his old cook back. Now he had no need for her, and her family would just get in the way.

"I'm going to bed," she said, feeling sick.

She'd been determined to go to Dario and end this. But being made redundant exhausted her. With no wind left in her sails, she just wanted to curl up.

"Upstairs?" Jockey asked. "You go sneaking off and the captain will—"

"I know exactly what the captain will do if I leave and I know exactly how my former lover will react," she said. "I'm going downstairs to sleep. If Dario was coming for me, he'd have come by now. I'll leave in the morning. I'll take Karen and my brother with me."

Jockey watched her go. She took the time to nod at Raise, and then went into the passageway and down the hatch to a lower level of accommodation.

It was easy to isolate the accommodation and mess above, which was why they'd been sealed in that section every night.

It didn't matter anymore if it was sealed up without her in it because they had Raise. Eros' true cook was home. She was superfluous. It was definitely time for her to go.

THIRTY-NINE

THE NEXT MORNING, Sassi left Karen in her cabin and took a breath before going into the mess, which was a hive of activity. It was stupid that she felt a surge of jealousy when she saw Raise cooking in her galley.

The whole room reeked of butter and a mist of smoke hung in the air. As soon as Sassi entered, a bunch of the guys tried to talk to her at once, but it was Raise's voice that carried over them all.

"You want breakfast? I've got leftovers," Raise called, still cooking at the stove.

"Uh, no thank you," she said. "We'll be leaving in just a few minutes."

That was enough to shut everyone up. Raise kept cooking, but the rest of the crew stopped, frozen in the midst of whatever they were doing.

Swain wasn't there, Jockey either, but that just made this easier. "Leave?" Foist said, coming to the head of the pack.

"Yes," she said. "Stuart's in the shower. Karen's packing. As soon as they're ready, we'll go."

Sassi hadn't talked to her brother, but Karen would convince him it was a good idea to leave. Spending days on end on a ship all alone was boring for Karen, Sassi got that. She could busy herself with cleaning or maintenance, but Karen and Stuart's relationship wasn't built to withstand close quarters.

"You can't go," Foist said.

As soon as the words came out of the engineer's mouth everyone's attention shifted to behind her. When she peeked over her shoulder, she wasn't surprised to see Swain and Jockey entering the mess.

"How'd you sleep, lass?" Jockey asked.

Foist surged up beside her. "Shortcake says she's leaving!"

Swain's gaze cooled as it zeroed in on her. Sassi held her head high, preparing to have the argument that she'd expected her captain would give her.

"Crew, eat fast," Swain said. "Supplies are landing in less than an hour, be ready to load up."

She thought for a second that maybe she'd got away with it and he was going to let her go without a fight. Then he leaned forward and took her elbow to pull her forward.

"Do we get donuts?" Swing appealed.

"In the top cabinet," Sassi managed to call out over her shoulder before she was yanked out of the mess.

Swain pulled her down the passageway and out onto deck. The feel of the fresh air on her skin made her sigh. It felt so good to be outside again. He dragged her around to her spot and yanked her in front of him.

"I let you get away with your stunt last night," he said.

"My stunt?"

"Sleeping on the lower deck," he said. "I slept on the fucking floor of your cabin all night. You're the only fucking crewman who can get the captain sleeping on the fucking floor!"

There was no gentle build up to this one. If he wanted a fight, Sassi had no trouble giving him one.

"Don't raise your voice," she said. "No one asked you to sleep on any floor. I told you I'm safe. I'm the safest one here. I told Jockey I was leaving last night, but I couldn't go without my brother."

"Is this about Raise? You think because he showed up without an invite that I'm gonna boot you off?"

"No, it's not about Raise."

"So if I fuck you, you'll stay?"

That snapped request took her aback. "If you——"

"I've got Jock asking if full sail's a problem. Don't talk to him about us, Waif. If you've got sex questions, bring 'em to me."

She wished she'd been a fly on the wall for that exchange; she couldn't imagine a more awkward conversation. "Maybe he thought some men might be tempted to act if they were sleeping beside a naked woman."

"You're having a hissy fit 'cause I haven't fucked you?" he asked. "You're gonna endanger yourself and Karen because I haven't stuck my dick in your pussy for a couple of days?"

It had been more than a couple of days. But as infuriating as their lack of intimacy was, it wasn't the reason for her decision. Cursing under his breath, Swain began to unfasten his pants.

"No," she said. "This is nothing to do with sex. I don't see the point of hanging around if——"

Grabbing her shoulder, he spun her around and bent her over the handrail facing aft. "Stop talking," he snarled and tugged up her skirt.

Sassi tried to twist around, but he kept an arm planted on her back. "What are you doing? It's broad daylight!" she said. He grabbed the waistband of her panties and pulled them down her thighs. "Captain, don't you—"

His fingers slid the length of her pussy and began to rub circles around her clit. "You wanna play barter with—"

"No," she said, reaching around to smack his arm away. Sassi spun, but found herself pinned between him and the handrail. Still, she managed to get hold of one side of her panties, but struggled to pull them up. "I have to leave, Swain. We're out of time."

"I told you not to ask questions. I said I'd take care of it. I gave you orders to stay. You don't have my permission to leave the ship."

It wasn't enough and she was exasperated by his cranky attitude. "It's not enough to stamp your feet, Swain. It's not enough to lock me up. We can't ignore this and hope it will go away. You know, I really didn't think you were a head in the sand type of guy," she said, stopping her fight with her panties. "I'm disappointed actually. I always figured you'd be exactly the take action kind of guy who backed up talk with action." She sighed. "If I have two days of freedom left, I'm not spending them in a prison, even if it's yours."

"You think me and the crew have been going out every night 'cause we're addicted to watching strippers?" he asked, easing back enough to give her space to right her clothes, while he fastened his pants. When they were both in order again, he exhaled. "If these were truly your last days of freedom, you and me would be on a yacht somewhere in the Caribbean. I'd keep you there trapped until you called the cops to beg for rescue. I wouldn't be abandoning you on Eros with Jockey every night so I could go hang out with your brother."

That made sense, but didn't give her an explanation. "If you want me to stay, if you want me to have confidence that your plan is better than any I might come up with, then you have to tell me what your plan is. If you tell me you're following one of Stuart's wacky strategies, I'll—"

"There is no strategy or plan," he said.

Quieting, she hadn't expected him to say that and it made her panic. Some part of Sassi had believed her captain was taking care of business. To say there was no plan wasn't confidence inspiring.

So that was it. She was marrying Dario. There was no other option, no other hope. "I better go buy a wedding dress then," she said. "Will you strip at my bachelorette party?"

"You're not marrying him."

Tensing her jaw, she growled her frustration out in a long irritated moan. "You keep saying that but then you tell me there's no plan! What do you think I'll do when he comes here and starts hurting people? If running was your plan, we should've cast off the day we all got here."

"There was a contract between your father and each of the men he owed money to," her captain said, flat calm as a windless sea. "I'm fulfilling those contracts. It's a simple solution and nothing to get yourself riled up about."

His hand moved toward her temple, but she ducked back as the reality of what he was saying sank in. "You're... you're fulfilling my father's contracts? But... but that means you're... you're paying the debt." Probably because he read her shock, his brow began to tense. "How could you do that, Swain? Where did you get that kind of money?"

"I have access to money," he said, sinking his hands into his pockets. "And you'd have known that if you were upfront about what was going on."

Sassi couldn't believe it. She was incredulous. "You… you have money?"

"Sure," he said, raising his shoulders in a loose shrug. "I'm not a millionaire or nothing, so you might have to wait a while for your new stove. But there is money just sitting in the bank and I have an open line of credit. I sink most of my profit back into the fleet. But I have savings. We have to, you never know when there will be a quiet season."

"A quiet…"

"Yeah."

Sassi couldn't believe this. If Swain was paying her debt, she'd owe him forever. Suddenly, the repercussions of what this would mean for their relationship hit her hard. They weren't supposed to have a relationship, and she'd really been ready to marry Dario if she had to. But any distant glimmer of a fantasy she'd had of a future with her captain combusted in that second.

"I didn't want this," she whispered.

"What did—"

Sassi couldn't hear anymore. Marching past him, she rounded the deck and jumped into the passageway, fury and misery warring within her, making hot tears scald her eyes.

She banged on Karen and Stuart's door. "Shake a leg, come on!"

"Waif—"

"No," she said, glancing back at her approaching captain.

Sassi tried to walk away, but men came out of the mess to find out what was going on and she was hemmed in. Damn, she didn't want any of them to see her upset, but there was no escape.

"There's no problem," Swain said to her, holding

out his hands like he was trying to calm a feral cat. "I take care of my crew. That's all this is."

He couldn't really believe that, could he? "No," she snapped, her arm slicing the air. "This is not simple! Don't trivialize this! You… you're…"

But she didn't want to admit it in front of the men. She couldn't bring herself to say the words.

"What's going on, cap'n?" Jockey asked.

The first-mate was behind her with the other crew outside the mess. "She knows I'm covering the debt," Swain said.

Shock made Sassi's jaw slacken. If she'd put the pieces together, she'd have realized that the crew was going out with Swain to pay the money to the less than savory characters her father used to hang with.

Her embarrassment heightened with this discovery that all the men she trusted had been working together behind her back. They all had to be aware of the extent of her humiliation.

"Great," she said. "Bet you all had a nice laugh at my expense. Poor, stupid Sassi with the dad who can't bet on a winner… guess it's something I have in common with my old man."

"Shortcake," Foist said, approaching her.

The pity in the engineer's voice only made her feel worse. "Don't," she said, pulling away from him when he tried to touch her. "I didn't want this… for any of us… I really didn't."

Stuart and Karen's cabin door opened and a blank Karen appeared. "Sassi?"

"Get ready, we're leaving in two."

Turning on her heels, she squeezed through the crew, unable to look any of them in the eye. Sassi ran up to the cabin she'd shared with Swain, but there was nothing for her here. There was no point in taking her uniforms and everything else was replaceable.

She grabbed her knot from the nightstand and was ready to run for her life when the door slammed, trapping her and Swain inside.

"How many times are we going to have this fight?" he barked. "I won't let you leave."

Her fury and disgrace were aflame. "You can't hold me against my will."

"Oh, I can, Waif. Believe me, I can."

"My brother—"

"Will let me because I'm taking care of his problem too. This is a fucking good thing! It gets you both off the hook, why are you acting like this?"

Rage exploded in her. "Because this is it!" she screamed. "This will always be between us now! It will define our relationship! I won't be the girl you spent a month out at sea with, I'll be the girl who decimated your savings! Now every time I look at you all I'll be able to think about is the money and how I'll pay you back!"

He sneered. "I don't want your fucking money. I haven't once considered asking for a cent from you or your brother."

"Then why would you do this? It makes no sense! Why would you give up all that money? Why hand it to lowlifes and write off the debt? I can't understand!"

"Good," he said. "I don't want you to understand. I was hoping you wouldn't."

Now she was even more confused. "Swain! Do you want me to work it off, is that it? But with Raise here, you don't need—"

"No! I don't want you to work it off or pay it back. I want to take care of this and never hear it mentioned again."

"Swain, I don't—"

"This all ends tomorrow," he said.

"Yeah, because midnight tomorrow is the deadline. I have to meet him in the warehouse."

"Yes, you do," he said. "But you won't be going alone and you won't be leaving with him." So there was some sort of plan, for tomorrow at least. "I'd leave you here in safety if I didn't think you deserved to see him get what he's due."

Somehow, Sassi figured he was talking about more than just money. "Captain—"

"I won't be your captain anymore," he said. "When we're done with Dario, you'll be free."

He'd promised her that before and with his regular cook back in the kitchen, she wasn't needed. The saddest part of this was losing her place on the ship… under her captain.

"I'll stay right here," she said, backing up to sit on the bottom corner of the bed. "You want me to stay onboard. I'll stay right here in this cell."

"This is our bedroom," he said. "Not a prison cell and the crew will—"

"I can't face them now," she said, unable to lift her head to even look at him. Sassi had never been so ashamed in her life. "They know everything and with you paying my father's debt after a month of sex… I'm not equal to them anymore, I'm a dockside whore."

"Sassi—"

"I am grateful, Captain—Swain. Shit, I don't even know what to call you." She tipped her head one way and then the other. "One is a rank irrelevant to my position and the other feels too intimate." The air left her lungs. "I really didn't want it to come to this. Thank you for taking care of the debt. Truly, I am grateful."

She didn't blame him for being at a loss because she was too. She still couldn't lift her head. Emptiness was dragging her to its depths.

"Hurting you was never my intention. But I'll take it over watching you walk away with him."

She bobbed her head, letting her gaze wander to

the floor. "I understand…" Laying down on the bed, she curled herself into a tight ball. "I'd like to be alone now… please."

He did hesitate for a minute and she felt ridiculous asking him to leave his own cabin. But what else could she do. She was sassy because confidence drove her through every day and she didn't let herself ever believe anyone was better than her.

But it had just been proved to her that she wasn't as powerful as she believed. Sassi hadn't been able to fix her own life and in fixing it for her, Swain had just guaranteed that they could never have a future.

She was grateful and it was a relief that she didn't have to walk down the aisle to Dario. But her blank mind broke her heart. There were no dreams, no fantasies, and no matter how hard she tried, she couldn't conjure any.

Her captain was no longer her captain. Her lover no longer her friend. She was alone, just like she'd feared being, and she was helpless too.

After he was gone from the room, Sassi turned her face into his pillow and wept. She'd been saved from the life she didn't want, but the price for her freedom was the life she did want.

For the first time, she let herself feel everything she'd tried to conceal, but after it all rushed through her, she came to only one conclusion. Her heart was wounded and the injury was so deep, Sassi knew it would never heal.

FORTY

WALKING ALONG THE passageway toward the mess, Sassi could hear her brother's voice.

"No, no," Stuart said. "I don't agree with this. Sass should be staying right here."

Swain grumbled and she slowed to listen by the door. "She needs closure," Swain said. "If I thought tying her down would gimme an easy life I'd take it. I don't want her hurt or anywhere near this bastard. We've faced every guy your dad owed; this is the only one she's seen. She needs to do this. It's how she'll put all this crap behind her."

"She's locked herself in your fucking bedroom for two days," Stuart said. "Fuck knows what you've done to her, what you've said. If you're forcing her—"

"You don't force Sassi to do anything," Swain said, making her smile. "The girl rows to her own fucking rhythm."

"If he hurts her—"

"I'm gonna be there," Swain said. "If he lays a finger on her, he'll spend the rest of his short life regretting it.”

Rounding to stand in the doorway, Sassi didn’t step inside. “Let’s go,” she said to the two men who were in the galley, ready for action.

Stuart came toward her. “Sassi, I think you should stay here. Let me and the guys—”

“No,” she said. “I want to look Dario in the eye. I need him to know he’ll never have me… that I’m not afraid.”

“You’re not afraid of nothing,” Swain said, marching over, past Stuart and into the passageway with her.

The crew was on deck, Karen was staying with Jockey and Fidget, just like the other nights. Only she, Swain, and Stuart would go inside the warehouse to confront Dario, but the other guys were going to be on standby outside, just in case anything went down.

They’d deliberately chosen to go to the midnight meeting in the isolated warehouse because going to Dario’s bar early would mean taking the battle to his turf and that would give him the advantage. Swain also told her that the men they’d paid were given a little extra to keep their mouths shut, so Dario wouldn’t get forewarning of what was going on.

Under other circumstances, Sassi wouldn’t trust the lowlifes her dad did business with, but she’d bet the Eros crew rocking up to your door would be enough to make any guy think twice. They got some cash and didn’t want to get beaten up, so most of them would keep quiet. And she doubted any of the creditors had any fondness for Dario the bully.

The crew had worked fast as well, which meant word might not have had a chance to travel to the arrogant Dario anyway. He might have heard whispers, but there wouldn’t have been much of an opportunity for him to confirm that Henry Robins’ debt was being bought up.

They left Eros as a stoic group. Menacing in the way they closed around her, the crew blocked her from view of the world. But she recognized the dock beneath her feet and with the water beneath her walkway, she knew her sanctuary was close.

Eros wouldn't be within running distance all night. With every step, it was getting further away and that made her heart rate rise. Karen's car was on the street for them and there were vehicles behind it, ready to transport the crew into their positions.

The crewmen were allowed to go first as they'd have to park further away. As Sassi was in no rush to get to this meeting, she didn't mind dragging her feet.

Stuart got in the front seat and Swain bundled her into the back. She'd been expected to be alone back there, but Swain actually got in after her.

His expression was serious, fixed out the windshield, and Stuart didn't say a word as he drove.

Sassi had no idea how the meeting was going to play out. Despite her faith in Swain's resolve, she had prepared herself for surprises and was willing to go through with the original plan and marry Dario if she needed to.

They hadn't talked since their argument the previous day. Raise had fed the crew and Swain had brought her food, but she hadn't been hungry. Sassi knew her reaction was extreme, and she'd had time to calm down and see that. But she still didn't know what to say to him.

Of course, she was grateful that Swain was bailing them out. But it didn't feel right and she didn't like feeling as though she was taking advantage of him and any feelings he had for her. One thing that had come shining through was her own stupidity and the strength of her feeling for him. Sassi didn't know how this night would play out, but if they did manage to end this mess with Dario, she knew she couldn't let her relationship with Swain finish in this way.

"I've never seen you in a car before, Captain," she said, trying to connect with him before what could be a terrifying climax.

Swain stayed in his stern mode though he glanced at her. "I'm not a fan of wheels."

"I can see that about you," she said, but couldn't blame him for not being in the mood to joke, he wasn't going to lighten up. Sliding across the back seat, she picked up his hand to kiss it, surprising him again. "Whatever happens tonight, Swain, I'm grateful that you tried."

"I won't fail, Waif. I'm not walking out of there without you."

She could believe he was that determined, but she was trying to stay realistic. Getting emotional might lead to mistakes. The most effective way to stay calm was to be in his arms.

Picking one up, she tucked herself beneath it, nestling into his side. Swain kissed her head and held her tight, giving her the most comfort he could offer, given where they were headed.

FORTY-ONE

IT DIDN'T TAKE LONG to get to the warehouse. Although Sassi had been there before, the light from the abandoned office and the cars parked around it confirmed that they were in the right place and that they weren't the first to arrive.

Her brother got out and went to the rear of the car to get a small duffel bag from the trunk while she and Swain got out of the backseat.

With her back to the car, she took a moment to focus herself. "How do we do this?" Sassi asked when Swain and Stuart closed in around her.

"You say nothing," Swain said, as resolute as she'd ever seen him. "We pay him. We leave. You're not going to get aggressive or provoke him because if he touches you Waif, I'll kill him. I'll spend the rest of my life in prison and—"

"I know," she said, reaching up to touch his jaw. "I just want it to be over… And I don't want you to go to prison."

Just the idea of her free, seafaring captain stuck

the rest of his life on land gave her chills. To think he'd be stuck there imprisoned because of her made her sick. "Let's get this over with," Swain said.

Sassi took his arm, but Stuart wasn't ready to move. "I still say we should go in hard, teach this guy not to mess with us," her brother said.

Swain looked determined and angry, but Stuart was amped and she didn't like the idea that his adrenaline might get any of them into trouble. "No," she said.

They could be outnumbered and she didn't want anyone getting hurt. It might feel good to take Dario down, but it wasn't worth the price of their own people getting hurt.

"Not with your sister here," Swain said. "We give the guy his chance to accept defeat."

"He won't take defeat," Stuart said.

Sassi feared her brother could be right. Swain's lack of response was as telling as a shout. Part of him wanted Dario to fight because if he did, her captain would have a reason to take him down.

"Give Sassi the car keys," Swain said, and curved a hand under her jaw to raise her attention to him. "Anytime you want to walk, get out, just go. The guys are around, they'll watch your ass and don't worry about us. That's an order, wench."

She wasn't his crew anymore and he'd absolved himself of being her captain. But Sassi had said a lot of things that with hindsight hadn't been fair. After his revelation, she'd responded with emotion because she was embarrassed and there just hadn't been time to put her feelings together.

"Aye, aye," she said.

The three of them started for the door. One careful, sure step at a time. This was the final meeting. Dario wasn't going to take the news of what Swain and Stuart had been up to well. He didn't want to be paid, but she guessed the bag Stuart was carrying was going to blast Dario's plans to shit.

Stuart went inside first, taking her hand as he went into the warehouse office. When Sassi glimpsed a view around her brother, she saw Dario in the furthest corner, surrounded by six men who were all smoking cigars, laughing and chatting like this was a party and not a showdown.

The men quieted and turned. Their joviality didn't disappear, though they did become more guarded when they spotted Swain.

"What's this, mi amor?" Dario asked, pushing away from the wall to straighten up. "You brought a friend to celebrate?"

"He's not really much of a partier," she said, letting her hand slip away from inside her captain's elbow. Swain moved his body, putting his loose arm in front of hers. She couldn't see his face, but guessed he was making his dislike of Dario and his men apparent. "He's here for moral support."

Dario tutted and began to swagger forward. "Sexy Sassi… I know who this is… this is your capitan." Shit. How did he know that? Did that mean he knew what the Eros men had been up to? Had they walked into a trap? "He has come to say goodbye… or to challenge me?"

The sneer on his face became amusement when he glanced at his men. Dario twisted the cigar between his thumb and forefinger as he approached Swain. The height difference made it impossible for Dario to intimidate with size, but his glower didn't lack confidence.

"Dario," she said and tried to step forward, but Swain tensed his arm and eased her back, while keeping his glare pinned on Dario.

"Did you come to challenge me, hombre?"

A tense moment of held breath passed. Sassi didn't want them to fight. She didn't trust Dario not to be packing a weapon. Swain was confident in his masculinity, so he wouldn't care if someone questioned that. But Sassi could only hope her captain was as secure in their relationship… whatever it was right now. She wished she'd taken the time to be more explicit about her feelings for him, though she wasn't exactly sure what she'd have said even if she'd had the time.

"You've gotta have something before you can be challenged for it," Swain said, his voice deep and gruff.

"And you think I don't have mi amor?" Dario asked, leering at her figure.

Dario tried to reach for her, but Swain's arm moved again, this time urging her deeper behind him. "You don't wanna touch her," Swain said.

"Oh, I do," Dario said, laughing with his men. "And I will before the ink is dry on our marriage certificate. I will forgive my Sassi her final fling. But from now on, she belongs to me. She is yours no more."

"Check your facts," Swain said and nodded at Stuart who flung the bag from his shoulder to the floor ten feet away.

Dario's confidence wavered, not to fear, but to annoyance and he snapped his fingers at one of his men who rushed forward to open the bag. When everyone saw the money inside, all eyes went to Dario whose anger tinged his eyes, but only for a second before he laughed. His men joined in and it was only when Dario paused to suck his cigar that the laughter died down.

"This measly amount will not protect my wife. Her debts, her papi's debts, stretch beyond this."

"No," Swain said. "Every cent has been paid." Dario's expression froze. "Like I said, check your facts. Your money is there Correa. You want to count it, count it. We'll wait."

Dario snapped at his man again and the difference in his stature was obvious. Tense as he paced to the wall, Dario was on edge. Sassi noticed a ring box there on the sill. Had he expected her to put a ring on her finger now? Of course he had, he'd thought he was going to take her tonight.

When the man was done counting, he looked pained to nod at his boss. Dario spun around and stalked to her, but Swain blocked her, putting her behind the wall of his body so she could see nothing else.

"You do this?" Dario demanded. "You go behind a man's back and you steal his woman, you—"

"Actually, you kissed mine," Swain said. "Which is sort of the only reason I need to do this."

Her captain's arm came back and she screamed when the impact of his punch echoed through the space. So much for no violence, he'd just smacked Dario so hard that there were teeth on the floor and a spray of blood beyond them.

Dario wailed and his posse rushed forward. Appearing behind Swain, who was fighting off the men who were running at him, Stuart grabbed her and hauled her toward the door.

"Swain!" she screamed, trying to rush forward, but her brother was pulling her out of the warehouse.

From nowhere, the Eros crew went running past to hurry inside. Although Sassi tried to fight him, Stuart wrestled her into the car and locked the door, trapping her inside. He leaped in the front and sped away. Sassi clambered between the seats and battered his shoulder.

"What are you doing? Get back there! We can't abandon him!" she screamed in her brother's ear.

"That was the plan! That was what he wanted!" Stuart said, frantic and panting. He tried to watch the road and catch glimpses at her too. "You don't think I wanted to take a few swings at that bastard too? But, fuck, Sass, it was the only thing Swain asked. He paid more than a hundred grand of dad's debt and all he wanted was to be left alone with the guy."

Panicking and out of breath from the adrenaline, Sassi spun to try and see what she could out the back, but it was too late, they'd gone too far. There was nothing but darkness filling the window.

Sagging into her seat, she wrapped her arms around herself to try to quell the quaking that wracked her. "If anything happens to him—"

"To him?" Stuart asked and with his adrenaline subsiding, he was beginning to smile. "That crew of yours are one helluva force, 'specially when they band together."

The crew might be there to look out for each other and she didn't doubt their loyalty to each other. But until she knew that everyone got out of there unharmed, she wouldn't rest, and she wouldn't stop shaking.

FORTY-TWO

SASSI HADN'T EXPECTED to be taken back to Karen's apartment or to find Karen there with all of their possessions from Eros. Apparently, as soon as Sassi had left Eros with Swain and Stuart, Jockey and Fidget had moved them all out.

Stuart and Karen were in the living room and had been for the near hour they'd been back in this apartment. Her brother was useless, telling her he didn't know the next part of the plan or why they'd come back here: he was just following orders.

Funny, her brother was following orders.

Sassi understood Karen and Stuart being brought there, but her? Why had she been kicked off the ship? All she could figure was that Swain was worried about cops or about the fight going back to the ship. She'd been tempted to go to Eros and wait there, but Stuart had told her that Swain wanted her here.

Trusting her captain, she waited.

The minute she heard his fist on the outside of the door, she ran to it and pulled it open, grabbing for

Swain before he could even take a breath let alone talk.

"How could you do that?" she wailed, trying to examine him for injuries. There was redness on his jaw and his hair was mussed, but other than that, he looked completely normal. "Were you hurt? What happened?"

"Never mind that," Swain said, stroking her hair.

"We'll give you guys a minute," Karen said, creeping around Sassi and her captain with Stuart in tow.

The couple went out and Sassi pulled Swain deeper into the apartment.

"I can't believe you hit him," she said, trying to guide Swain onto the couch, but he didn't sit. "You're not staying?" She didn't let him answer. "No, you're right. We should get back to the ship... Is everyone else okay? I hope Jockey dressed you down for this. Let me just get ready..."

He caught her arm and she ricocheted back to him. "You're not coming back to Eros."

"I'm not?" she asked, confused about what he meant. "Then where are we going?"

"I'm going back to Eros. You're staying here... Me and the guys are leaving for the salvage next week... We'll be gone for four months."

"Four... four months?"

He nodded, letting his fingers sink into her hair above her ear. "You're safe, Psyche. You're free, just like I promised. You're free of him. You're free of your father, your brother, all ties... You're free of me."

Free of him.

Her hand fell from his arm and she stepped back. Numb and confused and overwhelmed, Sassi was adrift. "You're breaking up with me?"

"You wanted it to be over, didn't you?" he said, showing such serenity that if she could feel anything, she'd probably be insulted. "And, let's face it, we haven't really been together since we got back from sea."

Because they hadn't had sex or talked about them. He'd prioritized the safety of his crew… a safety she'd jeopardized.

"You offered me a job," she said, clinging on to any kind of hope she could. "Right here in this apartment, you came here and offered me a job."

"And you said we couldn't be at sea together and keep our relationship professional… You were right. I might want to think I'm a strong enough man to keep you at arm's length, but these last few days have been torture, Waif. I can't have you under my command for four months and trust myself not to abuse my position."

"Abuse it! Please, abuse it," she said, trying to touch him, but he moved away. "I don't mind submitting to my captain… I love submitting to him."

He was shaking his head. "I'm not your captain anymore, Sassi. I told you, you're free."

She didn't want to be free. She didn't want him to give up on them. "Is this about what I said yesterday? I'm sorry, okay? I wasn't thinking. I was embarrassed and overwhelmed and I… I promise, I won't think of the money when I look at you, okay? I'll… I'll work for free, I'll make it up to you eventually."

Maybe it was the money that had changed things for him. Before he'd spent a fortune fixing her family, he'd wanted her. Since he'd found out the truth, his interest in her had cooled. How could he respect her after bailing her out of her father's mess?

"I don't give a damn about the money, I told you that. I haven't touched you for days because I didn't want to be distracted and I didn't want your gratitude. I didn't want you to feel obligated to me like you did to him. I didn't do this because I wanted to buy you. I won't force you into bed or into marriage. There is no outstanding debt between us. No ultimatum. If you and me are meant to be… it'll happen."

Her pulse was racing again, out of pure terror. Her captain was leaving her. Breaking up with her. Breaking her heart.

"How will it happen if you're running off to sea and leaving me behind?"

"You need time to get over this. Get over losing your father, his betrayal, the debt, Dario… me… I'm not going away forever; it's four months. We'll be restocking in Argentina, but… it's not like I'll get a lot of action in the middle of the ocean."

Was that his way of telling her that he'd be faithful? Sassi couldn't understand how he could tell her it was over and then reassure her he wasn't going to screw around. She couldn't figure out if this meant they were together or not. Except, if they were, she didn't get why she couldn't go back to Eros with him.

If this was pause, it was too much. Sassi didn't want to be without him, not if she had a choice. But it didn't seem like he was giving her one.

"So I'm supposed to wait for you?" she asked, wondering how good she'd be as the patient wife waiting for her sailor to return.

"No," he said, shaking his head. "You're supposed to live your life, to do whatever makes you happy. Get an apartment, build your business, whatever you want to do. And, in four months, I'll dock right where Eros is now…"

They'd have a clean slate.

He was effectively telling her to call him… in four months.

If she pieced her life together and still wanted him to be a part of it, then she could go to him when he was back, ask him out, maybe they'd take it slow… or maybe he'd have changed his mind about her. Sassi had gone from being the captain's wife to being his girl in this port.

Feeling lost and at sea, she couldn't picture any life without her captain and Eros. Every possibility had been erased; there was no fantasy that didn't involve them.

"I've been taking your orders for weeks," she said. "I've been cooking for the crew… I've had a purpose."

"I know," he said, cupping her cheek. "I'm taking that away because I don't want to be a habit you can't break. I don't want to be an obligation."

"What do you want?" she asked. Sensing his retreat before it happened, she grabbed for his belt. "Please, Swain… if this is just your way of letting me down gently, I deserve to know… Do you even want to be with me? Do you feel anything for me? It's not fair to ask me to wait for four months if there's a chance you're going to tell me you were giving me a subtle hint I didn't pick up on… We've never talked about feelings. We've never confronted what we might want from each other."

"If I'm still on your mind in four months, we will."

"Swain," she whined. "Don't do the guy thing. Don't withdraw and give me half answers. You love me or you don't; there's nothing else to talk about. If you love me, we'll figure everything else out. The details aren't important. All that's important is whether or not you love me…" Clarity numbed her again and her fingers drifted away from his belt. "But I guess if after all this you're still not sure… that's all the answer I need."

He stroked her face so gently that she thought he might be about to break her soul. Love, for her, love was easy. It was a given. Sassi had known she loved her captain since Swing had told her about the captain going down with the ship. She'd known she loved him when they had sex on the Dreamboat. Hell, she'd probably known she loved him when he pinned her hands to the wheelhouse wall and told her she had his attention.

While the prospect of Dario's vengeance had loomed over her, Sassi had ignored those feelings. Now that barrier was gone, she couldn't imagine her life without Eros and Captain Carson Swain.

His rough hand felt nice on her skin, but it wasn't an answer.

Or maybe it was.

As he drew his hand from her cheek, Sassi tried her best not to let her lip wobble. Emotion was close to taking over. Her eyes were warming, and she had to find a way of asking her captain to leave before she lost her grip on it.

Just as she was thinking of rushing him out, he broke the silence. "If I don't put space between us now, Waif, I'll be putting a ring on your finger and getting you pregnant before the week is out." Stunned, her tears dried. "Falling in love with you was the stupidest thing I ever did. I had my life laid out. I had my priorities. Everything made sense. Now the only thing in the world that means anything to me is your happiness. That's why I need to know… I need to know you're in as deep as I am. I need your head clear. I need you to decide what you want without pressure because you better have your damn priorities straight before you think about hitching your line to mine. We've got all the time in the world, Waif… We're doing this right."

"I thought you weren't my captain anymore," she murmured. "That means you can't give me orders."

"No," he said. "That's why I'm walking out that door right now and leaving you single." Bending down, he kissed her, but left her wanting more. "It's up to you, Psyche… whatever you want… the world is yours."

Sassi was still trying to think of what to say when he turned and walked away.

Her captain was gone. He'd given her freedom,

told her he loved her, and then abandoned her. Sassi wanted to go after him. She didn't want to be without him, but he was right. So much had gone on that they both could use some space. Just as he didn't want her to feel obligated to him, she didn't want his sense of responsibility to coerce him into misinterpreting his feelings.

But four months apart? Sassi didn't know how she'd survive it.

FORTY-THREE

SASSI HADN'T FIGURED out what she wanted or how she'd go about getting it. Five days had passed since Swain had walked out of Karen's apartment and she hadn't heard a whisper from him since.

Apartment hunting wasn't easy.

Staying away from Eros was harder.

Three adults living in one studio was a ridiculous setup, especially when it was clear two of them wanted to be alone.

Swain hadn't just paid her father's debts, he'd left Sassi with the money she'd earned during her month on Eros and hadn't used a cent of it to pay off Dario. So she had plenty of dough to get herself set up somewhere. The trouble was finding somewhere. Nothing she'd seen measured up to what she wanted.

Sort of by mistake, while looking for apartments to rent, she'd found a section of the website dedicated to houseboats. Surfing through it on Karen's computer, Sassi was wondering if it was a crazy idea when there was a knock on the apartment door.

Karen was back at work and Stuart was God knew where. So she figured maybe her brother had lost his key or one of his silly friends had come over to find out why word on the street was that the Robins' weren't to be messed with.

Sassi was laughing about her brother's newfound street-cred when she opened the apartment door and came up short.

"Jockey," she said, taking a second to get over her surprise before she stepped back to gesture him inside. "Come in, are you okay?"

"Aye, lass," he said and turned to look down the corridor.

She didn't know what he was looking at or why he wasn't coming inside, so she stuck her head out and gasped when she saw all of the Eros crew, minus their captain and Raise.

"Oh my God," she said, her hand leaping to her heart. "What happened? Where is he? Is he hurt?"

"The cap'n don't know we're here, lass," Jockey said. "We need to talk to you."

That didn't help her confusion. "All of you?" she asked, gesturing them in.

There wasn't a lot of space in the studio, but the crew managed to shuffle around in the living room until everyone was inside. Sassi went to retrieve the cookie tins from the kitchen and began to pass them around.

When she got to Jockey, she stopped, dead, and her mouth fell open. The first-mate wasn't waiting for a cookie, he was holding a velvet bag, a little one, just a couple of inches square, and peeking from the top, between the first-mate's forefinger and thumb was a white gold ring. A ring twisted in design to look exactly like her true lover's knot.

"He had it special made," Jockey said. "The jeweler delivered it to Eros today."

Swing appeared over the first-mate's shoulder. "He doesn't know we have it," he said, his mouth full of cookie.

Her shoulders shifted and she cleared her throat. "It's beautiful," Sassi said, forcing herself to look away from it.

Foist grabbed the cookie tin from her and thrust it at Fidget, probably to empty her hands. "Cap'n says you're not coming on the voyage… We ran about all over town doing what shipmates do for each other and he says you're not coming?"

The crew showing up had set her off-kilter, but she couldn't get her mind off that ring, and feared saying something she shouldn't. "I'm not," she said, heading toward the kitchen to put some space between her and the men… and the ring. "Are you staying for coffee?"

"Shortcake," Foist said, passing the couch to join her, cutting her no slack. "What the fuck did—"

"He told me not to," she said, appealing to them to be accepting, though it wasn't easy when she still hadn't gotten over losing her captain. "Please. It's what he wants."

"Is it what you want?" Foist asked.

Looking at each of their faces she read hope and sorrow, disappointment and optimism. Sassi couldn't lie to her crew.

"No, it's not…" That was one obvious conclusion she'd reached not long after Swain had left her. But there was nothing she could do. He'd told her she wasn't welcome aboard, so she had to swallow her defeat. "It's not even close to what I want. But I can't force my way onto his ship."

"You don't have to," Jockey said. "We need a cook."

"You have Raise," she said.

"We'll deal with that," Foist said.

"You pack everything you need, we'll get you aboard," Jockey said.

Swing and Fidget were bristling with excitement. Sassi didn't understand where the confusion was coming from. How could they be excited when Swain had made his wishes clear to her?

"Jockey, he told me not to come," she said. "I can't disobey orders."

Except he'd also told her that he wasn't her captain anymore. If he wasn't her captain, he was her lover… and she'd never shied from standing up to her lover. Who was he to tell her she couldn't decide what she wanted now?

Sassi had never been surer of anything than she was of her love for the captain, the crew, and Eros too. Waiting four months meant wasting time, valuable time they could be spending together. Determination began to take the place of her melancholy.

"Oh, orders… we'll figure this out," Jockey said. "That boy thinks he knows better than anyone. He's always looking out for us. Maybe this is a decision we should take out of his hands."

Because if they tried to talk him around, their captain would circumvent them, and make sure she didn't set foot on Eros. But Sassi wasn't going to let her captain, or her lover get away.

A plan began to formulate. Since he'd dumped her, Sassi had been lost, without direction or ambition. Now, she had both, and was enlivened. Swain had told her to be sure of what she wanted, and Sassi was damn sure she didn't need four months to figure it out.

She licked her lips. "He can't know I'm on board," she said, her gaze dancing over the men. "We have to be at least a day out."

Excitement buzzed and fizzed, filling the room. "Too far to turn around," Tune said and she nodded.

"You love the captain," Fidget said, wearing a broad grin. "I knew you loved the captain."

"Of course I love him, honey," she said. "Now you guys go back to the ship and prepare… I already put my orders in, and my uniforms are there. Let him put all of my things in the cargo hold if he has to, don't raise his suspicion. Just don't let him toss anything that's mine overboard." Sassi didn't think Swain would do that, but just in case. "Can one of you come here the night before we cast off?"

"We'll stow you and your kit aboard," Hector said. "Keep the cap'n busy."

She nodded. "You have to go now. Don't make him suspicious. Work hard for him." They started to go for the door, a hubbub of enthusiasm and anticipation humming around them. "Guys…" They stopped and she smiled. "Thank you."

For a minute there, she'd really been going to let her captain get his way. Sassi hadn't wanted to stay behind, but thought she had no choice. Her crew, once again, had been watching her back.

"Hey, we don't leave a shipmate behind," Foist said.

She waved at Jockey, who was at the front of the group. "Give me the ring."

Sassi made her way through the men who fanned out to make a path for her to get to the first-mate.

Everyone was grinning, and Jockey started to comply, but hesitated. "Maybe we should let the cap'n have a chance to ask you right."

"The captain already married us in the mess, remember," she said, going over to take the ring.

It was a perfect fit. She was amazed at just how beautiful it was.

"Cap'n's going to go nuts," Tune said, as elated as the men around him.

Oh yes, he would.

Her wonderful, grumpy, arrogant captain would be incensed that she'd gone against his orders and snuck on board his vessel. He'd be more pissed when he found out his crew was in cahoots with her and even angrier when he saw she was wearing his ring.

But Captain Swain knew what he was getting into with her. She had never pulled her punches. From the minute they'd met, she'd been headstrong and even when she feared he might be the type to hurt her, she'd held her pepper spray and fought her corner, always ready to defend herself.

Swain would be mad… for a minute… Then he'd realize he had his woman on board, that she was pledging her life and love to him, and that she'd never been more certain of anything.

Facing his wrath would be worth it. Sassi was used to his moods and his outbursts, just as he was used to her attitude and her sass. He'd said he loved her and it was her turn to prove the strength of her feelings for him.

FORTY-FOUR

GATHERING HIS CREW around the chart table, Swain prepared to start his briefing. They'd cast off early that morning and were underway on a course for the salvage site, making good time for the first day.

The crew had been insistent about putting Eros through her paces and forging on full steam ahead. As captain, he liked the attitude. But as a man, he was conscious of how many nautical miles were stretching between himself and his lady.

Except, damn, she wasn't his lady, and he couldn't let himself spend the next four months thinking that she was or that she even might be.

Swain had all the usual faces on his crew and two additional men on his team for this extended trip. Gunther and Anch were good guys who'd worked hard on other vessels in his fleet in the past. He needed all the manpower he could muster on this job. He planned to work hard, to keep his mind and his body as active as possible. Away from thoughts of the wench he'd left on land who'd go about her life without him.

Who could move on without him.

He'd be lying to himself if he claimed not to have concerns that she might have changed her mind by the time this voyage was over. But if she did, he'd have to accept that. He'd set this course. It was on him to ride it out.

But those worries were nothing to the thoughts of how he'd feel if she needed him and he wasn't there. Dario Correa had been a piece of work, and wouldn't roll over and go quietly. If Correa saw another in, found another way to hurt Sassi, then he'd take it, and Swain wouldn't be there for her.

These thoughts were exactly why Swain wanted to stay busy. By all accounts, Gunther and Anch were hard workers. Swain was looking forward to seeing what they could do and how committed they were.

With everyone now settled and oriented, he'd brought them all together to brief the new pair on the site they'd been to before and what the client wanted them to bring back.

Everything was going well. Everyone was engaged and asking questions until Anch suddenly swore.

"Fuck! What I gotta do to get me a piece of that ass?"

Swain thought Anch might be crazy. He looked up from the file he'd put on the tabletop display. The others were all staring through the wheelhouse windows toward the bow.

Swing guffawed louder than the other crewmen's laughter and jeering. "You keep your hard-on to yourself, Anch. That there's the captain's wife."

Shock made Swain pivot to follow their line of vision. Goddamn, motherfuck. Swing wasn't wrong. Sassi was on his fucking forecastle in her damn black Swain Salvage bikini, gazing out over the bow.

"Fuck," he hissed then spun on his first-mate. They'd never had a stowaway before. "How the fuck did she…" Jockey's smirk made him suspicious. "Jock…"

His first-mate shrugged. "That lass got the bit in her teeth. We didn't stand a chance. Said she'd chain herself to the bow and come as a bare-breasted figurehead if we didn't let her ride below decks."

Swain pointed at his engineer. "Come about. We're taking her home."

They were near a full day into their journey, and they'd lose another one taking her back. So much was beginning to make sense, like his crew's desire to build speed and why no one had wanted lunch.

He'd never had a crew refuse chow before. Swain had thought it was some kind of protest that they weren't being treated to Sassi's food, now he realized they'd all been in on the scheme.

Jockey confirmed his suspicions with his next statement, "Well, see, that's a problem 'cause Raise got himself reassigned on the Artemis."

"You're fucking with the roster without my say so?" Swain asked.

This was a day of fucking firsts and his blood was starting to boil.

Jockey opened his arms in a wider shrug. "I got your wife's authorization," his first-mate said.

Swain could tell his oldest friend was loving this. "She is not my fucking wife."

Jockey just outright grinned. "According to her, she's gonna be… and there is nobody here who can do chow like our lass."

"I vote for Shortcake," Foist said and put up his hand. "All in favor."

Every man said aye, even the new guys who'd never tasted her cooking. "Mutiny?" Swain asked, shocked by them all. "We're not a day into the job!"

His crew was snickering and fraying his nerves. "Better go make nice with the new captain," Tune said, laying his hands on the chart table. "You're sharing a berth with her after all."

"Yeah, that one was a deal breaker," Jockey said, waving a finger at Tune.

"How does that work? If she's in charge now, can she order you to eat her pussy?" Hector asked and the men laughed.

Fuck. Swain ran a hand into his hair and turned to look again at the woman now lying on the forecastle soaking up the rays.

"I should toss her ass over," he mumbled to himself.

Jockey came up beside him and hooked a hand onto his shoulder. "She gives the crew something pretty to look at."

"Aye, they can all stop looking," Swain said and twisted to glare at them. "You can all stop looking." Resigning himself to the fact that she was here and not going anywhere, he took a deep breath. "Crew don't get to enjoy the captain's wife."

"Thought she wasn't your wife," Anch said.

He sighed. "She's fucking gonna be."

The men cheered as Swain stomped toward the wheelhouse door. Sassi shouldn't be here, she was supposed to be pursuing her dreams and fixing her life, enjoying her freedom.

Instead, she'd chosen to stowaway on his ship and take over his crew. She'd have some explaining to do, but he'd enjoy disciplining the siren who just couldn't seem to manage to follow orders in the spirit they were given. But, in this minute, he was fucking damn grateful for her defiance.

From the second he'd left her apartment, he'd craved her.

Four months was a long time. Too long. That she'd gone so far as to stowaway inspired him. Sassi didn't want to be parted from him and he couldn't be away from her. She'd followed her heart, just like he told her to, and it had brought her straight to him.

Thank you for reading this tale!
If you can, please take the time to review.

~

Ask your local library for more Scarlett Finn
novels!

~

For all things Scarlett Finn
check out:

www.scarlettfinn.com

CHECK OUT

OUT NOW!

9 781914 517235